Earth's
Emergence
TRANSCENDENCE

Matthew J. Baldwin

ISBN: 978-1-4834-8362-7 (sc)
ISBN: 978-1-4834-8364-1 (hc)
ISBN: 978-1-4834-8363-4 (e)

Library of Congress Control Number: 2018903942

Lulu Publishing Services rev. date: 4/5/2018

Contents

Prologue

Transcendent

Far across the universe, amid distant realms, there exists a galaxy with abundant sentient beings. They are members of an ancient star-faring civilization known as the Olomnri. Their form is humanoid. They have bronze skin that glows with iridescent lines of glittering freckles. Most members of this race are slender, tall, and beautiful, with bright golden eyes, silken glimmering hair, and an aesthetic radiance that seems to resonate as much from their heightened consciousness as from their physical appearances.

They live in a galaxy they call Chronlia. It is a spiral of stars in which hundreds of millions of worlds host trillions of peaceful beings. The Olomnri are a race with lives not limited to decades. Rather, they live for several thousand years before consciously ascending from one life to the next. When one physical life ends, it transcends as a spiritual consciousness to a newborn Olomnri, and by this process the people carry forward their memories, skills, and experiences from previous lives. Living in such a way, the Olomnri have created a society in which there is little fear of disease or violent death.

Before they found this abundance of greatness, though, before this enlightenment was their way of life, constant war was the only mindset. Hostility, domination, greed, and the need to rule over and crucify others drove them all, leading to a war that nearly brought on their own extinction. Conflict seemed inevitable; their world would die because of their madness. But in the last moments, the voice of an innocent child woke them. The last thoughts of a young life caused a sudden moment of clarity for all Olomnri. A great shift took place for their people, a shift that brought an end to the madness that nearly turned their one and only world into a cold and lifeless rock, lost to the emptiness of space.

The shift opened them to discover hidden abilities and inherent talents long hidden behind walls built by their own insanity. Their own suppressive, fearful, and hateful ideologies blocked their true potential all along.

The Olomnri found themselves and broke away from the barbarism and savagery, achieving true harmony. They discovered their ability to transcend consciously from one physical life to the birth of the next, thus helping their civilization's knowledge grow exponentially. They evolved into a civilization of rational intellects, forming a perfectly balanced realm in which life, science, and technology flourished. These advances empowered them to spread their seeds far into the stars and to the edges of their galaxy. They found true enlightenment.

Faster-than-light travel was soon discovered. The Olomnri developed instant communications across limitless distances, terra-forming, and the ability to speak mind to mind through a kind of telepathic communication. The Olomnri multiplied.

Peace and prosperity shaped their culture, and thousands of generations passed with not a whisper of violence. As perfect as their civilization had become, there was still a single law, no one was ever allowed to forget how close they had come to causing their own ending, over a million years ago.

Detailed records of how they lived in hate and fear before the times of prosperity were held in the highest esteem. They were regarded as scripture and were etched into the walls of great structures on every world they built. They erected monuments—great symbols that stood to remind them of the days to which they must never return—on every planet they colonized.

In the dark times, before the shift, Olomnri killed one another for sport, greed, and pride. In peaceful regions, they held death tournaments for the pleasure of the slaughter. Hundreds of combatants entered the fields of sport, and hundreds fell to their opponents' wickedness. Every tournament was broadcast live; these shows served as their most cherished entertainment. Those who went to kill and die would leave, believing their purpose was to prove their skill in dealing death and, thus, to strike fear into all who might consider attacking their own tribes.

Fanatical ideologies upheld by tribal leadership perpetually fueled the people's hate. The strongest, driven by the common, manic desire to kill their enemies, always rose to leadership. After years and years of endless war, they burned and scoured the surface of their world. They scarred it and tore the life from it, leaving it unable to sustain them. Despite it all, the madness only escalated.

The fear and hate that held them in the perpetually destructive cycle offered no relief, it only drove them to more effective ways of killing one another, their fellow Olomnri. By their ways they slowly killed their on planet.

Before what would have been the last salvo, the shift began. When it happened, Lighnia and her family sat at their dinner table for a typical meal. "It is incredible how cunning and courageous the northern tribes are this year," her father enthusiastically commented between mouthfuls. His words made her heart sink. It was the typical topic of conversation, and her mother adamantly picked it up.

"Yet the way they sneak and conspire! They are repulsive. I prefer the middle-landers. They are fierce and courageous; their leader is a master slayer," she argued, making points on who would gain the most glory in the next tournaments.

Lighnia felt sad. She wished for it all to be different and silently thought of what it would be like if her planet were a more peaceful world, "If only, if only knowledge and enlightenment were held up as high as the killing of our own kind." She said softly between a slow scoop of her broth.

Then, without warning, a thunderous crash echoed across the sky over her city.

A nuclear detonation went off overhead, and the shock wave that followed was devastating. Entire blocks of buildings crumbled, and Lighnia's was not spared. Where once a city stood, a ruined landscape of rubble, fire, and smoke took its place.

When she awoke, she found herself trapped in the ruins of her collapsed home. There was no sign of her family or any sounds of the living, and she knew they were lost. Alone and mortally injured, she understood her fate and accepted it with a single tear.

She drifted in and out of consciousness and suffered dreadfully but somehow she found an inner peace. She loved to sing but was physically unable, so she began a melody in her mind, and with it came a sense of calm, and so she embraced it.

Her beautiful voice would have been a comfort in this tomb, but she did not have the strength. She was pinned by a beam that somehow stopped just short of allowing her a quick death. She wished it had been quick and painless because the pain was so great. She could hardly breathe. The pressure on her body only allowing quick short breaths, but somehow, she was still alive.

The only sound she could make was a faint whimper, and even that caused the pain to shoot up from her crushed lower half. Yet she stayed conscious, and the voice of her mind rhythmically chanted her song. She focused and let it pour out from her. It was her story, her dream of how it could have been, the way she wished life for the Olomnri had been.

It was a song born of hope, a dream for her people to awaken from a nightmare and find themselves. She sang a song filled with passion for unity and peace, a song sung by one who had seen through the lies and fear ruling their lives. It was a fluid, rhythmic melody of all she believed her people could be. The song was her release, flowing and comforting her. It blocked the pain, and soon it was an extension of her very own life's energy. Her song never ended, even as she drifted in and out of consciousness. And then, even as she expired, the song kept going. She did not know it, but her inner voice telepathically reached out to every Olomnri. It filled their minds and cleared the fog of rage that blinded them from seeing the truth of what they did ... and the awakening began.

This chance connection with the hidden telepathic ability, which all Olomnri inherently possessed, saved them. Her song and its strength permeated their thoughts with such passion that soldiers, commanders, and leaders of entire regions all stopped in midmotion and midsentence. Missile-launch countdowns halted in their final seconds, and the extinction of the Olomnri was averted.

They froze as ideas of peace and calm entered their minds, cleansing them of the hate and fear that had for too long driven them to ruthlessness, and in this moment, they experienced an analytical awakening and saw every truth.

Tears fell from their eyes as they looked to their brothers standing on fields littered in lifeless bodies—corpses torn limb from limb—where, until now, generations of ceaseless battle had been waged. Many dropped to their knees, with heads in their hands. The reality of what had been and what they had done fully setting in.

Some stood in disbelief of who they had been. Their bodies covered in the gore of those lying at their feet, and as the clarity of the brutality and senseless carnage settled into every one of their minds, a feeling of great sadness, guilt and humility washed over them.

Lighnia sang of how they would sustain a state of peace while confronting the pain locked deep in their hearts. They would take hold of the suffering and fear from so many generations and cast it away. She repeated this commitment over and over rhythmically, unknowing her link with every Olomnri and swept away every insanity for a new clarity.

Her out of mind flow gained strength, transfixed continuously, and finally, when a feeling of fulfillment was there, she let go, releasing her connection to the physical realm yet somehow maintained a state of conscious awareness, one beyond the link to the physical plane.

A unified Olomnri emerged in a turning point in their existence, and with it they all saw how close they had come to causing their own extinction. Somehow her name emerged, a subconscious name for the awakening of their people and to speak it was to remind of their dark history and their solemn vow to never return to such ways. "Lighnia."

Tranquility became the new reality. The Olomnri searched for knowledge, strove for peace, and found enlightenment. Three generations passed before the technology to leave their still-crippled world emerged, and as it did, they renamed their mother planet to honor the voice that had saved them all: Lighnia.

An age of insightful reflection and ingenious discoveries arose, and soon they discovered how to extend their lives beyond centuries. Incapable of hostility or irrationality, their civilization spread like wildfire. Hundreds of millions of planets were terra-formed, and their numbers exponentially grew. They cultivated and discovered knowledge hidden behind the gates of their now-conquered violent madness and by this, they found spiritual immortality.

For more than a million years, they spread throughout their galaxy, growing to hundreds of billions and then trillions of Olomnri—until everything changed.

The feeling of utter safety and peace ended as suddenly as it had begun so very long ago. Emerging from beyond the outer edges of their galaxy, an evil entered into Chronlia: a swarm of world-eater creatures emerged from a dark ripple in the fabric of space and time, and with them came destruction.

First contact was made when massive moon-sized creatures with black carbon shells flashed into space in a solar system on the outskirts of Chronlia. Monsters with tentacles reaching out for hundreds of kilometers, crackling with dark energy; thorn-covered crablike legs twitched along their long wormlike bodies and the sight of them sent a cold hush into the minds of everyone.

There was nothing they could ever bring to their own defense against such an enemy. They had forgotten their ways of making war, they had left their ruthless cunning long in their past, all in exchange for this new civilization.

The dark swarm of creatures was sudden, ruthless, and devastating. They moved through ripples of time and space, leaping across the vast distances at faster than light travel. When they arrived in the inner zone of the solar system images of the enormous monsters streamed live to every planet in the galaxy. No one knew what to think. Huge, heavily armored beasts floated ominously in the orbit of this planet's atmosphere. Pictures and videos flooded social networks on a galactic scale and for a time, everyone froze not knowing what to do.

It started as suddenly as when the creatures arrived. Trillions of Olomnri across the star-scape of Chronlia watched the destructive force unleash its power on their people's world. The swarm left a few satellites that provided various angles of this first attack. The video feeds did not last, though, and soon, all real-time communications were cut off. After that, only thoughts could be felt and heard by those telepathically connected to the few Olomnri left on the planet.

Then, with a chilling finality, every last telepathic connection was gone—leaving only the thoughts describing how their planet was being ripped apart; thoughts of how there was no hope; thoughts of despair, fear, and panic; and then a silence that meant nothing had survived replaced it all. Every mind living on that world was gone.

Normally, when someone died in their culture, the energy of that life could be felt transcending beyond the physical plane. In their culture, death was peaceful and spiritually enlightened, and in many cases when Olomnri died, they would stay and talk transpathically to friends and family before shifting to the next life. This time, though, from those who had been in that system there was only silence.

The disappearance of so much life left them all in disbelief, and soon the seeds of fear emerged. A feeling of loss saturated the plane of telepathic thought, and everyone felt it.

It started as a trickle of emotion, a sadness felt in the heart of every Olomnri, and it took root; it transformed. And grew into a storm of confusion, outrage, panicked emotion that permeated their interlinked mindscape to its very core.

The fear was amplified when in the system under attack the very star disappeared from the galactic map. This was no trivial thing. In the beginning of their technological revolution, their scientists discovered a subdimensional filament that allowed for a real-time view of everything in their galaxy. It was what enabled them to travel across limitless space instantaneously. This map tapped into that window, and when a star went missing from that map, it meant that it no longer existed. The map was central to their society and was displayed as huge three-dimensional projections in every city center.

Now, where that star had been, there was something else: there was an inky cloud of darkness, a darkness seeming to be spreading slowly throughout that system, and as they watched it happen a feeling of doom gripped their hearts.

Some hoped for the best; some even tried to deny it, but deep down they felt the truth. Their long-cultivated way of life was now threatened by a force none believed they could defeat.

Fear of where these creatures would appear next boiled in the subconscious networks of their culture. It happened so fast—viral ideas jumped between individual minds as hysteria. "Have they left the destroyed star? Where will they strike next?" Everyone waited; wondering, speculating, and dreading the idea that they could be the next victims.

Three standard solar cycles passed before another system raised the alarm. Ready this time, video broadcasters put out distress calls, streaming images and videos of the creatures. On every world in the galaxy they watched their sky's and in this new place they captured bursts of dark swirls rippling beyond their outer atmosphere. Footage of thousands of them arriving around the habited planets streamed out to every corner of Chronlia. Every one saw, compared to the last attack, these new images, showed nearly unmistakable—the swarm had multiplied, and this time creatures raced forward in the attack.

Tendrils of plasma lashed out from the dark glossy creatures as they targeted and destroyed every defense installation and satellite in the system. In this case, this star system had defenses. It was routine for them to destroy asteroids heading for their worlds, and they targeted the creatures with everything they had. Their very best proved to be of no consequence, direct hits showed little to no effect. This time, the creatures destroyed all the real-time satellites in the initial strikes, cutting off the live feed broadcasts with quick finality. Yet those who were mind-linked still received descriptions of what was happening, until, as suddenly and as brutally as before, the connections cut off, leaving a silent, empty void of lifelessness.

The swarm seemed driven by an insatiable hunger. They moved from system to system, leaving only darkness in their wake. Somehow, it seemed the monstrous creatures consumed even the stars themselves but they had no way of truly knowing.

They got organized and sent probes into systems gone dark and lost forever, but they never lasted long. Glimpses of the creatures and their faint iridescent tentacles were captured, along with huge storms of energy that always ended the video feeds before they ever got to far.

Unsure of their enemy's true face or its reasons for coming to their corner of the universe, the Olomnri named this swarm of destruction by the same name given to the most evil of their own kind, from the days of killing, from the days of their darkest hours, from before the great shift. They called them *Sethree*, the gods of death.

Timiat

The pillars in the hall shook as thundering energy crashed down from beyond the sky. Rippling waves of crackling plasma rolled across the landscape, and buildings toppled to the ground. The air filled with shattering glass, chunks of concrete, clouds of dust, and bursts of fire, all rising into the sky. Plasma shrieked down, ripping whole sections of smoldering planet crust into space, where waiting creatures rushed to devour it.

On the horizon, Timiat saw flashing tendrils of flame lash down to his planet's surface. A group of creatures beyond his planet's atmosphere were lancing arches of energy, smashing apart his world's crust into smaller sections. They were larger than what he remembered seeing in the footage of the last planet's destruction. *Death is getting closer,* he thought, the reality of it weighing heavily on his heart and thick in his mind.

Looking up into the sky, he cursed the attacking horde. There were thousands of them up there and he knew there was no place safe to hide, nothing he could do except, prepare for the end, and with purpose he found an inner peace.

He considered the reality of what was happening. This solar system was doomed to a fate undeserved by any, much less one with so much beauty and life. Whole systems of stars with planets hosting billions of Olomnri were gone, lost to this very same horde. They were a swarm of destroyers, creatures bent on the destruction of worlds and stars and now, here they were to take his home, his planet and he shook with outrage at it.

He stood on the balcony of a building high up on a ridge and watched it all unfold in front of him. On a normal night he would have seen a great coastal city with a vast ocean horizon. High up in the clear night sky, the display would have been majestic. At this time of year a beautiful purple world and its three moons would be cresting the horizon in a fantastic cosmic display. It was a sight he longed to see just one last time. He thought of the festivals, the gatherings, warm humid nights, and long tropical days.

The games, he thought, and with it, a feeling of disappointment washed over him. "The final match will never be played!" He cursed. "Oh, what a rivalry they had. It would have been the greatest match." Sadly, he whispered again, "It will never be played." Normally, the Olomnri of this world would have spent their time at ease, relaxing, celebrating, and taking in the climax of the warm summer season.

Sadly, in place of what should have been, there was a nightmarish and horrific scene, an exhibition of destruction and it was playing out right in front of his eyes. In the sky, half visible through smoke and billowing fire, he watched that beautiful purple planet and its moons shatter, as thousands of the creatures swarmed them. A tear dropped from his eye as he thought of all the dead and dying, and the thought of it sent a chill down his spine.

They were there—huge shapes among the destruction; glossy moon-sized beasts with tentacles reaching out hundreds of miles; crackling shards of galactic lightning were arching across them and he strained to understand. *Why was this happening to his people.* From where he stood he could just make out a row of thorn-covered legs writhing as a beast creature came over the horizon.

He calmly watched, contemplating what was to come. His eye went to a line of buildings off in the distance. The planet's crust fractured, and they crumbled to the ground. His senses escalated; his awareness piqued by his rushing adrenaline. The ground shook from continent-shattering impacts. And the skin on his arms crawled with the feeling of knowing death was soon to come.

On the horizon he saw the crust of his planet curl up and beyond that fire rose up into the sky. He nearly choked on his own breath. The scene was of rubble, fire, smoke, and lava spewing up into space. He barely stayed calm enough to keep his senses, accepting that his fate was impossible to prevent and with every new feeling of despair he let it go. As if the destruction in front of him was not enough, a panicked outcry from the minds of Olomnri on this world flowed through his subconscious. At the same time, an ever-growing void, an emptiness unnaturally silent in the realm of souls, chipped away at them.

Again—*boooooom!* Thunder from an impossibly ferocious storm. His eyes caught the arch of plasma rushing down from the sky and he watched it. The impact sent a shock wave rippling over the landscape, collapsing every structure inside a fifty-kilometer radius and the closeness of it got to him. His heart sank even lower. There was no hope! He knew it wouldn't be long now.

Again, another strike ripped into the surface of his planet, and closer buildings toppled to the ground. Fire slashed the air, thunder smashed the sky and another shock wave rushed past where he stood. His shaking got worse and with it, a fury and a fear to which he could so easily lose himself fought to take him over, but he could not! He knew he had to stay clear if he was to transcend consciously to the next life.

Each plasma impact slashed canyons into the planet's crust. He admired the sheer power of the enemy, as entire mountains were ripped up from the surface way off in the distance. He hardly noticed the cold tears dropping from his eyes.

Only a short time ago, this place had been a utopia; a paradise with tall slender buildings of polished white stone; a city of towers nearly ten thousand years old. Now, this planet was being torn apart and devoured by unimaginably powerful creatures. He could feel it, thick in the spiritual plane, it was death. All life on his world was ending. It was a sick feeling, a chill. Then a new feeling, something beyond, pulled at his mind: true evil.

More plasma from the creatures crashing through the atmosphere off the coastline, ignited the sea. A wall of fire washed over the mainland, expanding wider and closer as forked lightning lurched out from its sides. *Ionization*, he thought. The tears dropping from his eyes did not stop as flames wrapped around the chunks of his planet's surface now rising into the air. His planet's crust was beginning to break apart, it was falling away, crumbling into space. Yet somehow his hilltop vantage was still on the cusp of the destruction.

Thick, acrid heat washed over his face, and he reached out with his mind, patiently waiting for the end to this long yet shorter-than-desired cycle of life to conclude. The ground shook more violently this time, nearly knocking him from his feet, and as death came ever closer, everything seemed to slow. For him it seemed somehow unreal, and as his mind raced ahead of time, he realized this destroyer race was only interested in the raw materials of entire worlds.

He knew that his people were trying to make contact in every way possible, but there had been no reply. The creatures were oblivious and effortlessly sweeping all resistance aside.

He reached out with his mind to his family, all of them far from this danger condemning their home world. Farina, his fifth-born daughter, was the first to link with his mind. She felt him, and he her, the mind-to-mind connection spanning countless light-years, yet she felt so close. They understood that the rest of the family would be safe for long after today. He also felt that she knew of his approaching death. Suddenly, a flood of emotion swept over him. He felt his children, his closest friends, and lastly, with a great wave of strength, his wife, visiting her mother millions of light-years away. They were all there, linked to each other's minds in a cloud of telepathic thoughts, words, and emotions.

Confusion and fear were at the forefront of their initial reaction to the fact that he was about to die. "I will see you all in my next life, just as it has always been for generations," he reassured them, and for a moment, their fears were forgotten.

His family would live on, safe, on far-off planets and moons. They would live for many turns of their stars and do many things with their lives. With that thought, a silence took hold. This unstoppable evil, the Sethree—would they not do the same to all of Chronlia? Were they all doomed? What if this evil could never be stopped? A thought that they all seemed to have at the very same time, and with it came a cold fear that swept through the connection. He felt their panic enter his mind as the link filled with turbulent emotion. He knew there was no other choice and calmly issued his farewell before disconnecting, mentally shutting them out. He returned to the present moment. In front of him, the wall of fire was only seconds away.

He had to fight the fear with all his strength. With the end approaching, he searched his emotions and thoughts, preparing himself to go beyond the physical world of this lifetime.

Once again reaching out with his mind, he sent a projection of hope. He dreamed that someone, one day, would stop this inexorable plague sweeping across the galaxy. He put a seed of purpose out into the universe, wishing that somehow this evil would be stopped before it was too late and as the thought formed it hit him. The shock wave dried his tears instantly and in the same moment he was engulfed in flame—vaporized!

Separated from his physical form his awareness drifted up, rising away from the swirling mess of flame and carnage. He pulled feelings of tranquility and peace around him and embraced the shift into being a fully aware spiritual being. The transition was comforting and natural for the Olomnri. Long years of training and experience in the ethereal mind had prepared him for this moment, one he had experienced many times.

This time, though, this life was brutally cut short. As he ascended he felt a strange imbalance, a sharp pounding frequency in the plane of souls. It was harsh, and it was powerful, and as he drifted he saw them, uncountable wisps of those torn from their physical forms drifting in the spiritual realm. He felt them, transitioning from the physical realm into the sentient plane. But there was something else, a tug in the weave; it pulled at his being. It was a disturbance unlike anything he had ever encountered or heard of in any of his studies. Something was different, strange, and unfamiliar.

He saw a wave go through the billions of wisps, and then they were gone. "How could they be gone?" The sharp frequency was unnatural, a turbulent static energy pulsing from where the sky enveloped his dying world. It was pulling at him, ripping at his consciousness and then he understood; it was trying to take him. He sensed the others all around—uncountable souls rising, drifting—millions of Olomnri, who moments earlier lived in the physical plane.

They were being thrashed by a vast evil, a power that encompassed everything. The feeling went through him again and again; he sensed it before the full magnitude hit him, and then the shrieking of dying souls blanketed his mind. He saw the ripple; wisps vanished and then, even closer, a darkness took them. It attacked him, whatever it was. It searched for any fear or weakness, and when it found it, it feasted.

He fought with everything he had, straining to block it out, but it invaded his thoughts, and he quickly lost control but desperately a moment of clarity returned and he broke free. Dark tendrils latched on to his mind, and he fought it. He could see it. He saw the darkness consuming them, feasting on the weakened souls of his people. Not only were the Sethree devouring the minerals of the planets they destroyed, but a force beyond the physical plane was consuming the life energy of all who lived there.

"What kind of devils could feed on souls?" he questioned, fighting even harder to get past the next wave of screams pounding in his mind. He knew he had to regain his strength, he knew he had to find a way to escape.

When Timiat was a boy of this life, he studied the teachings of a great philosopher, a master of transcendence. He learned that, in theory, a fully sentient being was not restricted by space or time but only by the power of his mind. He had learned that when in a purely spiritual form, one could not cause an effect in the physical universe. But at the same time, while existing as a fully sentient spiritual being, one could move across the vast distances of the physical universe with no relation to time.

Not knowing precisely what to do, he focused his last ounce of strength and winked his ethereal body away from what would have been the end of his existence.

He shifted his position from above his decimated world, sending himself as far as he could reach and then farther. He consciously reached out past the edges of his galaxy, past everything he had ever known, stretching his mind, expanding beyond space itself And when he stopped, he looked back at the entire universe—every galaxy, every solar system, every quasar and black hole, all just a cluster of bright and dark glittering crystals. The decimation of his home world an undetectable spec in the vastness of it all. There was no frequency but his own, and, with relief, he felt safe.

He drifted, letting his instincts guide him on the currents of attraction. Something called to him, something fainter than a cosmic whisper, a feeling of hope and he could not avoid moving towards it. When he had it clearly in his mind, he reached across space, his consciousness shifting past billions of light-years in less than a moment of his own relative time. It called to him, the faint solar system on the outskirts of a glittering galaxy. There was just one water world, and on it he saw an adolescent form of sentient life. He reached out with his mind once more, this time with greater focus. *What a beauty, remote and young,* he considered. It was a place he would want to spend time investigating—and then, in a rushing motion of space and time, everything went dark.

Chapter 1

Earth Born

When John came downstairs for breakfast and saw the look in his wife's eyes, he immediately knew what it meant. Their child was on its way.

She sat at the table looking afraid and unsure, a look he had not seen since the times of unease and imbalance, a time before their marriage. He knew he would have to be extra gentle in his approach and tried to break the ice.

"Good morning" she sang out with a faked sense of ease. He could tell she was trying to hide her feelings and knew she was reluctantly aware they would be making a trip to the hospital today.

With a mischievous smirk, he replied calmly, "Good morning, darling. How are you feeling today? Ready for a car ride?"

She forced a grin. "I'm wonderful, but our baby seems to have other things on its mind."

Just then he saw the muscles in her face clench, and her jaw tightened as what he assumed was a contraction gripped her body. Immediately he was at her side. "How long have you been having them?" he asked, moving to help her toward their garage and into the back of the SUV. In his heart, he knew that this time it was urgent and smoothly buckled up before hoping in the driver seat and starting the car.

Until now, there had been no complications with the pregnancy, but life was full of surprises, and it seemed today was no different.

"John, I think my water broke," Susan whispered in a tentative, fearful voice. Her words sent a rush of adrenaline through his body that caused him to push the peddle down even harder.

She held on in the back and her mind reeled. *Was their baby really going to be premature?* She dreaded it! A few weeks earlier, their doctor had looked over the ultrasound and assured them there was nothing to worry about. But how could she not worry? This was her first child, and she had just turned thirty-five. Early or not, her baby was on the way, and there was no getting around it. She would be bringing a new life into the world in the very near future.

As they neared the hospital, John reached back and held her hand. He spoke in gentle tones, doing his best to calm her. He had a way of making her feel safe, always facing life with the attitude that everything would be all right, one way or the other. It was a big reason she loved him so much. His positive can-do attitude was contagious and sparked a new confidence, a drive to get through whatever she faced in life. His calm, strong perseverance helped her rise above an endless emotional roller coaster of troubles that kept her from her true potential.

In the days before they met, through college and after graduation, she was always stressed, confused, afraid, and unsure of who she was or what direction to take. It was a fear she never admitted to anyone. She had nearly resorted to drugs to overcome her emotional problems, but, by good fortune, John had swept her away. He had seen her in a coffee shop, introduced himself, and from there everything changed for the better.

Another contraction gripped her, snapping her out of the reverie. Her eyes focused on the approaching hospital sign. John's instincts had been correct, and she was thankful they had made it here before it was an emergency.

Once inside, everything went smoothly. It was an easy birth, free from complications, and when she finally held her baby, she swore she would never let him go.

Lying in her hospital bed, she cradled his tiny form. He was still wrapped in a bundle of soft linens and slowly wriggled. She was as happy as she could ever remember. John grinned from ear to ear, tearing up as their child reached as if trying to touch the ceiling.

Cradled in his mother's arms, he continued to stretch and reach with unexpected control. He was a very good-looking newborn, with dark blue eyes, thick tufts of dirty blond hair, and milky, almond-colored skin. After a time, he lay still, his eyes searching and unblinking, gazing up into theirs with a curious, thoughtful expression.

Dr. Jacobson showed his surprise at the condition of their child: "He is as healthy as any child would be expected to be, if born at the expected time, but he was six weeks early." There was no hiding his astonishment. He pointed out the controlled motor and vocal skills their baby was once again putting on display. He explained to them how extraordinary it was for a child only a few hours old—and six weeks premature—to have such a developed sense of control. "From our tests and every observation, the only explanation is that his development simply happened faster than average, and he decided it was time to exit the oven, so to say," he suggested in his most officious tone.

John could only laugh as he touched his own balding head while admiring his son's thick blond tufts. "So that's where it all went," he said approvingly and leaned in to plant a kiss on Susan's forehead.

"I love you," she whispered in a warm, soft voice, her eyes watching his as another tear of pride broke free to trickle down his cheek.

Chapter 2

Transition

Timiat was in full control, free, adrift in the spiritual realm, existing in a limitless state, a static energy in the universal drift. He enjoyed the freedom and power that came with being a fully conscious ethereal being, but physical life made things so much more tangible. He longed for the senses of touch, smell, the sound of nature, feelings that could only be felt when alive in the physical form. He watched and dreamed, analyzing the blue world, thinking that it might just be the right place to call home.

He was not sure he wanted a home. He felt safe, far from the danger, yet there was a cold feeling within. He felt a chilled dread creeping around his mind, images and emotions from a nightmare that seemed to have happened only moments ago. "Had they?" Horrifying thoughts pulsed through consciousness, flashing uncontrollably in waves of pain-filled energy.

Just as before, he pushed those feelings away and turned his attention back to the beautiful blue planet. From above and from all around, he looked in on a thriving and diverse culture. He questioned their patterns, confused as to why they all lived in such drastically different conditions.

For a moment, a feeling of the physical form gripped him, but he forced it away. Again, he felt the pull; he was linking to the start of a new life. He felt warmth, safety; he felt an honorable home and let himself be drawn in. It happened in a heartbeat, the shift from the ethereal realm into that of the physical. He joined in the moment of conception, the sentient energy of a new life on this small blue planet.

A blanket of darkness enveloped him, suddenly and without warning—a whoosh, a feeling of being pulled into a void, into a dark, confined space, from where there was no way out. This was different; his mind was trapped. He had just gone from a state of spiritual freedom and limitless ability to a sudden encasement, confined and surrounded by intangible walls. He did not know; he could not feel his ability to reach out and touch stars, whole galaxies, to push his consciousness across the impossible distances of the universe. He remembered the place before birth, but this time it was different, and oddly, the thought was lost to him. This time it was jarring and disconnected. His link to the spiritual plane was dulled, and slowly a manic claustrophobia took hold of him, and he started to lose himself.

He relapsed into states of claustrophobic dementia, finding peace in emptiness. It was as if a wall was built between his Olomnrian mind and this new physical form. Awareness returned from time to time, each instance seeming further and further away. When he did connect with his awareness, he focused with all his might, fruitlessly trying to hold on to memories that quickly faded.

His once-brimming mind was going blank. As time passed, his awareness centered on the sense of being cramped and the perpetually jarring motion from some outside force. His new existence had become a never-ending chamber of swishing and swashing, changing, but much too slowly and with that realization a sole purpose emerged. He must find a way to return to … something. Memoires from past lives, they were there in the back of his mind yet unreachable—a place he had once known, so much knowledge he had once, was now, gone.

Trapped, he strained to make something happen, anything at all, but it was slow. Long periods of empty thoughts were highlighted by rare moments of clarity. Escape! Focus! A mind commanding a body to grow and break free. On and on it went as the surrounding walls and constant motion filled his every waking moment. The one known as Timiat of the Olomnri people of Dorsalis-O was gone.

Finally, with a sudden rush, fluid slid past what was now purely a human child. He was squeezed hard, and unconsciousness took him. A moment passed, and he regained awareness and pressure from all around pushed him forward. Then he was squeezed even harder, squished and pushed. Pain came sharp and fast, pulsing with a strange drumming and a long, low hum. Sounds of effort reverberated from all around. He felt panic but could do nothing! Helpless and compressed, loud sounds pounded his mind. Then again, an even greater compression was followed by the sensation of being pushed. He was moving, inch by inch, and again unconsciousness took him.

Awake! A sharp pain brought him back, and he was blinded by a white brightness, a light that burned his still-closed eyes. More noises from all around blasted him as his mind lost all clarity. Large blurry shapes, and then he was touched and lifted. What was happening? He reached out with his mind, somehow instinctively unaware of why, but nothing happened. Helpless, he stared up at the large shapes towering above him. His eyes would not fully open, and his mind could not form a single coherent thought. It was frightening, but somehow it was safe. He felt a strange joy. He was no longer in the darkness, but who was he?

His sentient consciousness was totally lost to him. Eons of knowledge gone into a void of emptiness, a fragile newborn on a strange planet, far from the life he had known. He felt himself vomit as more weightlessness sent him spinning into unconsciousness, and he dreamed of nothing.

Susan and John Thoth brought their baby boy home two days after his birth. The doctors were astonished, a child premature like that would normally need to stay at least a week, but in this case, there was no need.

He was a calm child, except when truly confused or frightened, and in the early days he was prone to shrieking in ways truly hard to describe. His fits though quickly faded, and they all settled in. John and Susan easily decided on his name—Daniel Alexander Thoth, to remember John's fallen brother who died in the war; to honor an uncle of Susan',: a man who had been a big part of her childhood, nearly on the same level as what Dan had been for John. He had been the voice that pushed her to ignore the bullies and join with the kids of the library. He had nurtured her love for books and words and helped her mom when she saw tough times.

Daniel Alexander Thoth—born July 7, 2031.

Chapter 3

A New Home

As an infant, Daniel was well behaved, though his parents quickly noticed his way of directing a controlled focus towards whatever it was he wanted until it was achieved.

In the first months of their marriage, John purchased a medium-sized vineyard that had been left unattended for several years. The property overlooked the coastal town of Half Moon Bay, just south of San Francisco, a perfect spot for his plans. They demolished the old rundown house and designed a new one, their ideal place to settle down and raise a family.

Everyone gathered to meet the newborn baby boy. At only three weeks old, he was so small yet possessed surprising intention. Susan's brother Sam insisted that Daniel's full head of hair came from their great-grandfather. He was a legend to them, known for having quick wit until his last day at a ripe old age of one-hundred and twelve. He was also known for his near full head of hair until the very day he died.

Aunt Margaret went on and on about Daniel's deep blue eyes. "Like deep ocean water, so rich and enchanting," she said, giggling in her eccentric way. Daniel just gazed at her until he was passed on to the next family member waiting to hold and look at the newborn child.

John's brother Frank arrived with his wife and their twelve-year-old daughter, who was more interested in her new tablet than the family gathering.

Susan's eighty-three-year-old mother pulled up in the BMW X-2031 they had bought her last year, making an entrance as full of life as ever. She was always so young at heart and filled with an enthusiasm for life that was unmatched by anyone in the family. Thrilled to see her new grandson, her bubbly personality couldn't be contained, especially after the inevitable few drinks. A child from her daughter was something she had never believed would happen, and she was overjoyed.

After the initial excitement, individual family members came to sit next to him in his cozy blankets. They leaned in for closer looks, gently touching his tiny fingers. As they did, he studied them with an intense focus, as though contemplating what type of persons they might be. Most of his new family got the impression there was more to this baby boy than met the eye but it was never overtly expressed.

After dinner, John took their guests to show off Daniel's room. He had designed it as a test for the new technology he was pioneering. Puffy white clouds ringed the bottom edge of the walls and at the top of them a dark-blue sky faded to black, blending into the ceiling where an image of the Milky Way glowed. It looked like the paint was luminescent. In fact, it was the only light source in the entire room. When John explained the science behind how the walls worked, questions came from every direction. He had created a new type of display technology. It was a paint-based LED screen demonstrated by the nighttime theme all around them.

"It really is amazing. We engineered an atomic structure that aligns when the paint dries," John explained. "By doing this we can create a surface covered in wirelessly powered light-emitting particles that generate virtually no heat. The amazing part is that when you map the dimensions of the wall surfaces in the room into a software package we developed, you can then project images and video back onto the walls, which is how what you are seeing is created."

The Milky Way on the ceiling was captivating. The spiral galaxy in all of its glory, a glittering swirl of light, its form casting a faint glow into the room. The incredible image was rotating at a barely noticeable speed, but Frank's twelve-year-old daughter, Bridget, noticed it.

"Why are the sparkles moving, Uncle John?" she asked, momentarily distracted from the tablet in her hands.

John was happy to explain, "The image you see above is actually a real-time simulation of the Milky Way. It's a computer-generated representation using information from the world's most detailed astronomical databases." His tone relayed just how happy he was with the results.

Everyone knew that John had a huge passion for astronomy; it was his number-one hobby, aside from his work projects that became hobbies of their own. But when they saw the display on the ceiling and heard him tell of all the hoops he had been forced to jump through, they were speechless.

"Honestly, when we built the house, I knew it was going to be for our child, but I have spent hours and hours lying on this floor, exploring this map. This room, without a doubt, is my favorite room in the entire house," he whispered.

Using the room's tablet control, he zoomed in, showing how icons would popup menus over celestial bodies all linked to national space agency databases. The pop-ups offered options to view more information, such as pictures, planetary compositions, mass, distances, and so on. He continued the tour, telling them that this ceiling feature and the wall display currently illuminating the room was just one of the environments installed in the display software; he flipped through some of the other options.

With his extensive technology, engineering, and construction experience, John had found designing this custom home one of the most enjoyable projects of his life. He had known that one day they would have a child and, to Susan's chagrin, he had spent a massive amount of effort toward making a room beyond any child's wildest dreams.

The room was close to eight hundred square feet, and the software driving the PaintLED wall display system was designed to evolve as their child grew in body and mind. After flipping through the day theme, sunset theme and nighttime theme, they followed John to Daniel's crib, which hovered eighteen inches off the carpeted floor. The crib was held in place by a common technology found in many modern-day homes where panels with millions of field generators in the subfloors and ceilings of every room interact with similar panels on the bottoms of select furniture, enabling ridged levitation.

Daniel, at only three weeks old, was aware. From his mother's arms, he watched his father show the members of his new family the workings of his room, and he understood a few small things. He was so little and helpless in body, but in his mind he was awake, and he soaked up everything that happened. He saw his father move his free hand over the flat object held in his other and associated the movement with how the sparkling spiral in the ceiling changed. Everyone was captivated by the details above them, yet he focused more on the people in front of him rather than what was happening above.

He wished he could understand what his dad was saying; he watched as the ceiling zoomed into a cluster of sparkling points, past huge bright spheres and into a group of blue worlds. He wished he could understand what they were saying, but it was all just noise. He turned his eyes up to the sparkling swirl on the ceiling and gazed at what he would soon know to be stars and distant worlds, and an unfamiliar feeling raced through his mind. His awareness went somewhere else, his mind going somewhere far away from his tiny body. It was only for a moment, but it seemed like forever, and then, as his awareness returned to the room, a faint memory lingered, one that seemed so real yet so far away.

As he came back to present time, he discovered they were all watching his father reach down into the far corner of his small bed, and it slowly began to move. It moved above the floor toward a far wall. He had slept in this room for a few nights already, but this was something new. When the hovering crib got close to the wall, a window popped up with menus and icons. John flicked his fingers over the tablet in the crib, and a list of options appeared on the wall.

"One of the wall's display features, is to activate when the crib comes close to various sections in the floor," John explained. "Around the room, different windows and menus will appear in different areas. It's a labyrinth of learning and games that he will discover as he grows. In time, I will unlock higher levels in the system with new kinds of applications to explore."

Finished with the tour, John returned the crib to the center of the room, and they all filed out, most of them declaring that John was going to be the richest man alive when this amazing technology started hitting the markets. As the night ended, a warm feeling of family was felt by all.

Over the next few days Daniel thought of the changes he had seen in his room and wondered how he could control it like his father had. Each night after being put to bed, he would sleep for a time until waking and looking up. He would lie still, staring up at the swirls of glittery light above him, and that strange feeling would return. He had no understanding of what the swirls were or what those glittering sparks above him represented, only that every time he watched them the fleeting, distant feeling came, a feeling of a far too distant place. He would search the map of stars, finding additional details or a section he had not seen before, and he loved it.

At times he thought about how his father caused his bed to move, and he considered trying to figure it out, but decided it could wait, instead choosing the swirling mass of tiny sparkling lights above until he drifted back to sleep, where recurring dreams where he was traveling across the vast distances space, there were glowing forms sitting perfectly still, their legs crossed amid billowing white mists in temples that made him feel at home.

Weeks went by, and he felt he was not growing at all. The dreams faded away, as did the feeling he got when he looked up at the stars in his ceiling's display.

Weeks later, he and his father were back hanging out on the giant pillow in Daniel's room. There, they watched a video displayed on his bedroom walls. It was educational media meant for babies. Daniel understood it was called *The Happy Happy Show*. The colorful characters bounced around, sounding out letters and small words. They were bright, unreal, toylike characters that danced and pranced in a singsong way. The video quickly left him uninterested. It sent him into a state of complete boredom after watching for only ten minutes. By then, he understood what the sounds and symbols meant, but when he tried to make the sounds, he sputtered out confused and unstructured noise.

Rather than watching the video on the wall, he crawled over and pressed the tablet in the same way his father had. The sound stopped, and John regarded him with puzzlement. Daniel motioned with his tiny sausage arms, showing how his bed had moved, and then he looked to his father with a determined expression.

John watched as his little boy sat next to him, pointing at his crib and sliding his other hand through the air, showing how the bed could move. John was utterly shocked! He hadn't shown Daniel how to make the crib move. For that matter, how the heck did he know how to mute the sound on the video? How could he know? How would a child of this age understand something like that?

Thinking back, he realized Daniel was in the room when he was giving the family the tour weeks ago. *Impossible*, he thought, but somehow the boy had figured it out. Without worrying about how or why, he decided to show his little guy whatever he wanted. Getting on his knees, he picked up his son and lifted him into the air, flying him across the room to softly land in the crib.

Moments after showing his father what he wanted, Daniel was lifted across the room, feeling totally weightless, before finding himself lying in his floating bed, utterly under attack. His father's big hands tickled him, making him giggle uncontrollably, until finally the torture ended, and he sat up, expectantly. Daniel's expression said, "Thanks, now that we are done with that, can you please show me how this thing works?"

He watched as his father tapped the center of the panel at the end of the crib, and he immediately understood that doing so brought the screen to life. Four arrows and a grid with numbers appeared on the screen. He felt stupid for not thinking of that!

John hadn't expected to show Daniel how it worked so soon, thinking that it would be at least a year before his son was interested in learning about it. But to his surprise, the time was now, and so John demonstrated how to press the arrows and make the bed move, anticipating that Daniel would quickly take over but he didn't. John watched his son just sit there, looking at the screen in contemplation until the screen timed out. Puzzled, John reached down to restart it, but Daniel held up a hand and, in his baby voice, made a short, definite "Zaahh."

Daniel crawled over and reached up with outstretched arms, silently asking to be picked up.

Confused, John could only chuckle and picked up his boy without question. He carried him from the room to see his mother and maybe sneak a small snack before dinner. *Maybe he only wanted a ride in it or something*, he thought as they walked toward the kitchen.

A few days later, as they lay in bed, John and Susan talked of how amazing their son was turning out to be.

"Have you noticed how he picks up on things?" Susan asked.

"I know what you mean. He turned off the volume on the show we were watching the other day and demanded I show him how his crib controls worked. How is that even possible?" John replied.

"Should we be worried? I mean, how is he going to fit in? Do you think he will be one of those brilliant yet super-awkward people?" asked Susan.

"No question he may end up being brilliant, but he seems as normal as anyone. Look at the way he interacts with us, and remember how calm he was when the family met him. I don't think we have anything to worry about in that respect."

"You know, he is spending a lot of time in the middle of the night, playing with the menus on the wall display," Susan said.

"Really?" John questioned in surprise.

"Yeah. I woke up last night and checked on him. I guess he goes to sleep when we put him to bed and then wakes up in the middle of the night and explores the menus. I caught him trying to create the sounds as he followed along with a video—one of the teaching programs that sounds out the alphabet. He must have somehow figured out how to start and stop the learning videos using the crib's control panel."

"Well, at least he isn't howling and keeping us up every night, right? I don't think we need to worry, darling. Good night," he replied, kissing her before rolling over and drifting off to sleep.

As she tried to do the same, Susan considered smacking him for cutting their conversation short, but she knew it would only produce a grunt; once he was sleeping, it took a lot to wake him. She tried to figure out how their child was so amazingly gifted. *The speed at which he's learning is impossible,* she thought, and as wonderful as it was, it worried her.

There were rumors of organizations that seemed above the law, and it scared her to think her son might come to their attention. She dreaded the thought of having her son taken, like the alternative media were saying has happened to other families with special kids.

John was a fantastic father and one of the smartest people she knew, with his mind for engineering and technology, and she with her higher than average IQ. Between them there was no small portion of intelligence, but their son was beyond anything bestowed purely through genetic succession. Smart, they had expected, but Daniel was eerily smart.

Glancing over at her sleeping husband, she scowled and wacked him, producing the expected grunt. She felt miffed that he could sleep through just about anything. Her mind went back to the articles she had read on the internet, stories of families who claimed that black-clad agents pushed their way into homes and snatched up children without a word of explanation. The stories repeated in her mind, leading her back to the realization that each of the children targeted by these people were exceptionally intelligent, just like her son.

She had shown the articles to John, but after briefly looking at them, he claimed it was just a spoof, a writer using fearmongering to gain exposure. Finally she resolved to do everything in her power to prevent anyone from discovering how brilliant her Daniel truly was, and drifted off into peaceful sleep.

The next morning she woke, resolved to make things clear. At breakfast, she brought it up again, this time with more passion. "John, please. If there is even a remote possibility these stories have any truth, we need to consider them. What if our Daniel catches the attention of these people?"

None of the cases she referred to were ever officially acknowledged by any of the corporate media or by any branch of police or government. Many claimed these stories were outright lies, created by the conspiracy theorists, aligning with their all-too-common claims that some shadow corporations had taken control of the world's wealth and governments.

Yet she would not let it go. The reports from families that had lost children to these people seemed far too real for it to just be a hoax. There were videos of family members expressing genuine sadness, describing men in black SUVs and SWAT gear. Through tears they described how their locked front doors just swung open as agents covered in tactical gear flashed their golden badges too quickly for anyone to see. The articles told of how anyone who resisted received brutal incapacitating shocks, leaving them stunned and virtually immobile for hours. In one case, a mother was even killed as they took her child, the stun impact stopping her heart, the agents had just left her there. Somehow, in all cases surveillance systems were wiped clean and showed only static. For the alternative news groups conducting the investigations, it was a clear-cut case of advanced technology designed to disable monitoring systems, but to the corporate media, it was all far too unbelievable for them, and they suggested the people making these claims were dramatic attention-seekers.

She found a new example—a higher-profile case of a child being taken—and she brought it up on the kitchen table's touch-surface display. The video showed frantic parents speaking about losing their child. Major media had picked up the story, but of course they were owned by the shadow elites, people with unlimited wealth and in control of governments and banks all around the world. These people pulled the real strings, always dictating story lines for the masses to follow. In this case their puppets did not disappoint.

The corporate media figureheads spun the story to meet their agenda. They vilified the hysterical mother, claiming she was no longer taking her medications, while portraying the family as irresponsible and untrustworthy.

After watching this latest coverage, John lost all interest. Susan flipped through the other stories, determined to find some commonality. She noticed that whenever the families persisted in their allegations, the major media groups accused them of trying to cover up the disappearance of their own children—accusations that seemed to always lead to criminal investigations; in a few cases, charges against the families for child abuse and neglect were even laid.

She forced him to look, and he listened, knowing that if he did not give it proper attention, she would never let it go. He pointed out that the only media groups that seemed to agree with these families claims were conspiracy nut jobs known for always sensationalizing unsubstantiated rumors.

But even with his pointed critique, it was plain to Susan that something terrible was happening, and she wasn't about to let it go. After watching the interviews showing genuinely upset parents and children who claimed they witnessed their family members taken, John reluctantly agreed there could be truth to the stories, and he watched a few more before looking seriously at Susan.

"You're right; thank you for pushing this. If Daniel truly has the potential to become someone these people would want to seize, we should do everything in our power to protect him from being discovered. Obviously, we should not suppress his learning and growth, but I think it's important we keep him away from the public system as much as possible and maybe even dumb down his homeschooling test scores when we send them in for review."

Across the table, Daniel calmly ate his baby food, his attention drawn by the intensity of his parent's discussion. He paid no overt attention, attempting to have them believe he was not interested at all in what they were talking about. He really had no idea what they were saying, but he was starting to assign meaning to some of the words, and the rest he stored for later.

What could threaten me in a place like this? he wondered, understanding that much. He scooped another spoonful of the bittersweet mush into his toothless mouth.

A few days later, when his eyes opened in the middle of the night, and he set out to explore the walls of his room, he came across a learning program designed to teach hand signs. It showed actions he experienced daily, like when he was hungry or when he was dirty, thirsty, and many other signs for things yet unfamiliar to him. He was five months old and couldn't understand why he was still unable to verbalize the words that were so easy for him to conceive. Some of the simple two- and three-letter sounds he could pronounce, but any with multiple syllables, his voice just wouldn't do what his mind found so simple. The hand signs he understood instantly. He saw that they would give him the ability to communicate until he was able to make the words, and with this realization, he started spending every night learning them.

In less than two weeks he perfected the basics. His hands moved without having to think, and, with a feeling of pride, he felt ready to show off his newfound skill.

The following morning at breakfast, Susan sat him in his high-backed baby chair. He ate the mushy food and sipped the last bit of juice from his special orange cup. When he finished his juice, he slapped his hands down onto his highchair in two quick successive blows that caught both Susan and John's attention.

They looked up, surprised at his sudden outburst and Susan nearly started to scold him, but before she could begin, he signed: "Thank you for the food. More juice? Please."

Susan's jaw dropped. She had been studying the signs book for a few weeks, planning to start teaching him soon, and was just able to understand what he meant. John's expression was a virtual mirror to her own, and together they erupted in joyful laughter, showering him with admiration while completely forgetting the juice he had just requested. When they settled and realized Daniel was frowning at them, he made the signs again.

"Please, may I have more juice!" This time he folded his arms, wondering how these grownups could not even understand simple signs, and waited to have his simple request acknowledged.

Susan giggled and looked to John, who only shrugged with a grin and a disbelieving shake of his head. She brought over the juice and saw a satisfied smile emerge on Daniel's face. He nodded and signed "thank you." It was a stark reminder that Daniel was learning and understanding things faster than what was normally possible for any child. As they all returned to their morning meal, John and Susan shared another knowing look, concerned with the risks this presented to their family.

Along with studying signs he discovered a dictionary application and started spending a few hours each day learning new words—their meanings and how they were supposed to sound—by listening to the dictionary's audio feature. In doing so, memories from these past few months began having more meaning. For one, from the conversation he'd heard at breakfast a few weeks ago, he understood there was a possible risk of being taken from his family. He did not understand the reasons, only that there was some danger from a group that searched for the very brightest of children and then he saw it, he could never let strangers know his brilliance. With that understanding he decided he would have to learn faster and never forget anything in order to outsmart those who would do him and his family harm.

John and Susan quickly picked up sign language, enabling simple conversations with their son. Though the signs worked well enough, Susan and John encouraged Daniel to work on making the sounds of the words while signing what he wanted to say. He cringed as he tried and failed to pronounce the words, but they encouraged him, pushing him to make a real effort at training his voice.

His first birthday was exciting and eventful. The whole family returned to spend the long weekend at the house. They enjoyed the summer weather, lounging next to the pool, and enjoying food prepared by Aunt Margaret.

She was a fantastic cook and the owner and operator of a well-known catering company.

On the third day, as the entire family sat out on the deck after yet another incredible meal, they told stories, reminiscent of successes and of the challenges many of them faced growing up. It was a beautiful spot; the sun cast brilliant colors across the sweeping landscape drawing their eye's to a coastline and then out toward the distant ocean horizon.

In a moment of silence, Daniel chose to show off his ability to pronounce words. "It's beautiful, isn't it, Mom," he said with clear articulation. Everyone heard him, and all of their eyes turned to look with amazement. John's head whipped around to where Daniel sat, relaxed in Susan's arms. Over the past few weeks, they had been less focused on coaching him to sound out the words with his signs, making this a most unexpected surprise.

Susan saw the proud look on John's face and replied, "It is very beautiful, yes."

Susan's mother just giggled, her body wriggling in the recliner of which she was taking full advantage while nursing her customary glass of red wine.

"Has he been speaking like this for long?" Frank asked.

"He's been practicing the alphabet and some easy words, but never anything like this, not until now, the little rascal," Susan replied as she tousled his hair in a playfully affectionate display.

Chapter 4

Samantha

Susan and John's friends had all been blessed with children over the past few years. At first the new parents thought it would be perfect; Daniel was destined to have lots of playmates. She imagined that all their families would grow closer while their kids grew up together. But as they came to understand how different Daniel was, their thinking completely changed. There was no way any child would be on the same level as their son. It saddened them; Susan worried her son would miss his childhood and was tempted to take away all the computer time. But at the same time she didn't want to take away something he was so passionate about.

She knew it was important for Daniel to have friends, but where could they find kids who were even close to his intellectual level without risking discovery? They couldn't very well send him to a public daycare.

Robert Bradford and his wife, Charlotte, recently moved back to the area after spending nearly ten years living and working in Europe. In the past, they were two of their closest friends, and John and Robert, like old times, resumed playing golf on a regular basis. After a few rounds and some dinners out on the town, Robert confided in John the fears he had for his daughter, Samantha.

It turned out they too found themselves in a similar situation. Their daughter was blasting through homeschooling. "John, there are people out there taking kids. Charlotte and I … we think there is a pattern. They are targeting the smartest kids! We're worried about what might happen if she's noticed by the wrong people." Robert whispered as if someone might be listening. "We can't send her to public school, obviously, but we can't very well keep her from having friends. She understands. We talked to her about it. It scared her a bit, but she saw it for what it is. She even suggested that she could just act dumb around strangers." He laughed. "What do you think, John? Oh! And we registered her with the Wise Child Group. It is a program funded by people who stand for truth, for the freedom of mankind. They have a sanctuary for kids with exceptional abilities, and we believe they could be a big help in protecting Samantha."

"Wise Child Group?" John repeated. "Thanks, I think we will look into that. Daniel is only twelve months old, and he's speaking like a five-year-old. He loves to learn, and Susan convinced me of the same threat you're talking about. We really don't know what to do, other than keep him away from the public system. We could homeschool him, but like Samantha, where is he going to find friends? Could Samantha and Daniel be a good match? Why don't you bring her over and introduce her?"

Samantha was just turning five and already finished grade one. She was eagerly starting her grade two homeschooling package and was gaining speed. After hearing that Daniel was only a one-year-old, Robert was a bit worried that Samantha would not take to him. He described her as "past playing with baby toys," but he agreed it was their best chance, and John's description of Daniel suggested that he was not interested in childish toys either.

Charlotte, Robert's wife, was relieved to hear the news. "Maybe there's a chance. Maybe my daughter will find a childhood friend."

Samantha was more skeptical. She was an extremely smart five-year-old. When she first heard she would have to play with a toddler she was not happy. "Aw, Mom! He's just a baby. He'll be a nuisance and probably get poop on me."

But her parents hoped that Daniel was smart enough to keep up with her, and they convinced her to give it a chance: "Who else are you going to be friends with, Sam? At least this boy is in a comparable situation. Let's go meet him, okay?" Charlotte urged, using her most persuasive tone. She also did her best to plant the idea that Samantha could teach Daniel, convincing her that the best way to learn was by teaching others.

When they arrived, Samantha reverted to her original attitude. "Why did I come here? This is such a waste of my time," she scoffed as they knocked on the Thoths' front door.

It was like two cats meeting for the first time. Daniel, the smaller of the two, looked at Samantha, interested and curious. Samantha was standoffish and uncomfortable. She hid behind her mother's leg, holding her hand and trying to entirely avoid the situation. Daniel just sat there, lounging in his roller, a four-wheeled bumper car with a jumper chair that kept him upright in the middle and let him stand and bounce, enabling him to run along on the floor ahead of being able to walk. He calmly surveilled the situation. He watched her, trying to figure out why this little girl was hiding but realized the answer was not important. He chose instead to focus on a way of improving the situation through careful, well-measured tactics.

He looked to his father and then back to the strange, shy little girl and then back to his father. John smiled and indicated Daniel should play with her by a quick series of sign language. Taking the cue, he pushed his four-wheeled buggy forward, sending himself closer, and signed hello. Samantha looked at him at first with disdain but then with a faint glimmer of interest as she understood the signs. Daniel could see she obviously regretted agreeing to this visit but felt he could win her over.

"Hello, little baby boy," she said in her most petulant tone. She thought, *How am I supposed to find anything fun to do with this little baby? He can't even walk or talk!*

But Daniel, knowing she understood, persisted, signing that he would like to show her the walls in his room. She wondered what could be so special about walls, thinking the boy must have made a mistake, and she looked to her mom for refuge. Charlotte nudged her daughter forward. For a moment, Samantha thought to resist, to defy this arrangement, but then she thought, *Great minds are nothing if not explorers*, and she resolved to go along and find out what he meant about the walls of his room. *I hope we won't have to stay too long*, she thought, letting go of her mother's hand to follow the little boy now speeding away in the funny little roller. "To look at the walls? What a stupid waste of time," she contemptibly whispered and ran to catch up.

Susan briefly wondered why Daniel had not spoken out loud. Yet she knew he was a clever little devil, and whatever reason he had, it was probably a plan to find common ground with Samantha.

As they entered his room, the walls came to life, illuminating every corner of the space, and he saw her attitude change at once. His default environment started up and the walls shifted to display an ocean sunrise. The scene looked out over a tropical seascape; the walls increased in brightness and clarity as they moved farther into the room. Wispy clouds high up on the walls drifted slowly as the crystal-blue ocean shimmered with golden flakes of light. The warmth of the rising sun danced across the expansive panoramic view, and as Samantha turned she forgot her negative thoughts. The scene made it feel like they were standing on the edge of a white sandy beach, front row to a magnificent sunrise. As they stopped in the middle of his room, the sun slowed and came to rest just above the horizon.

Daniel walked his roller over to his crib and climbed in.

Samantha turned 360 degrees, hardly believing what she saw. For the first time in two years, she was stuck with nothing to say, she had no opinion, no evaluation, just pure amazement and admiration for the spectacle in front of her.

Daniel's crib lifted off the ground and hovered and then moved when he guided it toward the far wall, to the section he knew would activate the interface for the room's display list. When it loaded, he flipped through the environments until finding the one he wanted to show her, and with a practiced touch, he activated the theme.

This was a special one; it had been his first birthday gift and was by far his favorite.

Upon activation the room began to transition. The previous theme rose as they dropped below a shimmering surface of tropical water. The room went dark, simulating the initial haze of being submerged. Rays of light shot down from the surface of the water, and the scene slowly came into focus. The room brightened, revealing a coral reef filled with underwater life. Thousands of brightly colored fish filled the scene as far as they could see. The fish, although digitally generated, seemed like real life, and the beauty of it took Samantha's breath away. Schools of curious fish came up close and then darted away in sudden flashes. Daniel giggled, barely containing nearly uncontrolled laughter and as Samantha dropped heavily beside him he noticed her expression of dumbstruck amazement. "Whhaaaaaaooooooowww." She exclaimed as the spectacle moved with fluid reality all around them.

She took her eyes off the walls for a split second to look over at Daniel. When she saw the huge grin on his face, she snapped her eyes back to the walls, where he pointed to a dark area in the corner. The scene moved, taking them deeper into the shadows and as it went dark, a giant eel lurched lightning-fast swimming towards them. Samantha jumped instinctively, clinging to Daniel, who barely flinched in surprise. The scene followed the eel's path, leading back out into open water. Enchanted and excited, they waited to see what would come next.

They would nudge each other when they saw something and point to a particularly interesting fish or tower of coral as it slid past them in the immersive scene. They traveled through deeper places where very little light from the surface was able to reach to where glowing creatures and giant squids, eels, and strange flittering specs of light made their homes. The scene traveled back up and the room brightened, taking them through a lush coral reef and out over a huge ocean shelf. There they saw hundreds of hammerhead sharks, all swimming above a bottomless abyss. They passed pods of whales, and then along a shoreline, where sea lions and penguins chased the waves and smaller fish.

For an hour that felt like only a few short minutes—they hardly blinked. Eventually, their mothers came to the door of Daniels room and found them huddled against the side of Dan's crib, transfixed by the spectacle. To the mothers' relief, their children found friendship.

When they were finally wrestled away and brought to dinner, Samantha would not stop talking about what she had seen in Daniel's room. "It's amazing, so amazing! It was like we were really there! How can we make the walls in my room do that? It's so amazing!" she said repeatedly.

John had to explain that it was still a couple of years away from being available to consumers. He shared with them what a system like that would cost, something even five-year-old Samantha understood was far beyond what her family could afford.

John had invested huge sums of money developing the light emitting paint based display and custom software driving the PLED installed in Daniel's room. "It's not impossible, Samantha. The goal is to get to mass production, and the costs will eventually come down. I think you will have this technology in your home at some point in your lifetime."

Over the next six months, Daniel's ability to talk improved dramatically, and he and Samantha regularly chatted using video over the web. Up until now she hadn't said anything about her homeschooling classes, something she felt had to be kept a secret from everyone, but it eventually came out, and as she told him about how great it was to have so much to learn, Daniel's mood suddenly changed.

"What is this thing, home school?" he asked, wondering why he hadn't heard of it.

She showed him how she was learning to read and write new words every day, along with math and history studies.

Daniel was even more upset, and from her perspective, she could not understand why—until he started asking more questions.

"Where did you get it, home school? How come you get it, but I don't? It's not fair! I could have started it weeks ago. Why didn't you tell me sooner?" He sulked, showing a side of himself that rarely surfaced. He had no idea what homeschool was exactly, other than lots of stuff to learn.

Samantha tried a different tack, pointing out that he had the amazing room with the amazing walls, where home school was probably hidden in one of the widgets he had yet to find. She watched as the gears in his mind turned, and the sulking boy disappeared. His tantrum was replaced by a fiery determination.

When she was content that things were smoothed over, she began explaining more about the program, starting with the fact that he would have to wait before starting school. "Most kids don't start until they are at least four years old," she stated, not realizing her mistake until it was far too late.

She lost him again as he turned back into a petulant little boy. He told her in no uncertain terms that he would get school whenever he wanted, and then he abruptly ended their conversation.

When he hung up, she laughed, amused by his outburst. *Oh well*, she thought and started looking over her notes for the day.

He waited until breakfast the next morning, when his parents were together. Sitting in his highchair he spoke clearly, expressing his interest in the homeschool program. "Home school ... where is it? I would like to begin this school at once, please."

John was taken off guard. "Dan, you can wait another year before starting school. There is more than enough for you in the system as it is."

With that, Daniel went completely silent, giving his father the impression that the discussion was over. But, John did not notice Daniels resolve. As he returned to his breakfast and the morning news Daniel had not looked away. He was staring straight at him, unmoving and completely silent. He kept it up for over five minutes until finally John noticed Daniel's intense look. He immediately recognized the intention in his son's eyes, a look only seen when his son set his mind to something he felt was very important.

When their eyes met, Daniel quickly repeated his question. "There is no reason I should not start this home school today. I want to learn the words and the math and the history like Samantha. Please, can I have it?" For a moment, they stared at each other, unblinking.

Just then Susan looked up and caught the end of what Daniel was saying. She saw her son's look and knew he was not going to give up. She went to him, resting her hand on his shoulder. "What's going on, little man? Has something happened?"

He looked up at her, momentarily releasing the lock he had on his father. "Samantha has home school. She showed me her courses, words and numbers, and questions! How come I don't have that? I want to learn. I should have the home school too!"

Looking back to his father, the intensity returned, and John responded with a calm smile; he realized exactly what was going on. Reaching over, he put his fingertips on Daniel's arm. "Dan, after breakfast I will show you how to access the school application on your walls. You're right; it's fine. Thanks for asking so respectfully."

When they were done with their morning meal, John went straight to his office and made the changes to activate the elementary school materials.

When setting up the system he installed the limitations, thinking it would be better to let Daniel get a handle on the simple stuff first. His plan was to lift the restrictions as Daniel grew, but, as he knew now, that plan was backfiring.

It took only a few minutes to remove the tags in the code, tags keeping the elementary school materials from being activated. He stuck to the original plan and left the rest of the applications hidden. He was sure kindergarten through grade seven would be more than enough.

Finished, he headed down to find Daniel, who he knew would be patiently waiting in his room. After sitting down in his customary spot, enveloped in the giant beanbag chair, he showed Daniel the school app location on the wall display and watched Daniel as it activated.

Daniel learned from his parents that impatience and selfish blustering would get him nowhere. It was better, he learned, to present a calm, collected, and analytical approach to problems.

John watched Daniel flip through the kindergarten through grade seven homeschooling materials with a sense of pride. "How come this wasn't here before?" Daniel asked. "I have passed this part of the wall many times."

John explained his plan to lift restrictions over time, giving Daniel access to more applications as he grew, but as he said it, he realized what he had done.

Daniel spoke directly and immediately. His tone was one that left John feeling he had been wrong to hold anything back. "You have kept things hidden, haven't you? Yes, of course you have. Why? How will it harm me? Unlock them, please! All of them."

John was shocked by the ferocity of his son's look. It was nothing like what he had seen at the breakfast table; there was something else there. It wasn't disrespect or petulance; instead, he could tell that by holding things back, it broke an unspoken trust. He understood that after letting the cat out of the bag, he would have to make it right and unlock it all.

He raised his hands in surrender. "Sorry, son, I have to get to the office in a hurry this morning, but I promise I will have it done by tomorrow. You should have more than enough to keep you busy from now until then."

Daniel accepted the explanation, happy in knowing that if his dad said he would activate the rest, he could count on him to fulfill his word.

Over the next few weeks, a year's worth of course work flew by. He watched lessons over and over until completely understanding the information. In his studies, his goal was always to understand the concepts with confidence, duplicating what was taught, both verbatim and through practical application. He took the time to recreate the ideas and principles he was learning by applying them using his own concepts, and in doing so, in many cases, he found connections to other topics.

Susan would sit with him each day. She watched him as he studied, his entire body following the video displayed on the walls. She marveled at how her one-and-a-half-year-old child went through elementary school classes like they were just a review of knowledge he somehow already had. It worried her that he was not growing up as a normal child. At the same time, fear lingered in the back of her mind that, at any moment, men in dark suits could walk through the front door and take him. She thought Daniel's focus was amazing, though, and was happy that he and Samantha regularly talked on the video chats between actual visits.

While watching him study, she fell asleep, and later, when she awoke, she witnessed the two children in the middle of a video call. She watched undetected, seeing them talking like normal kids their age. Daniel especially sounded just like a two-year-old, and as she watched, she imagined him as a child just like any other. The idea gave her pause. *Would I want that?* she wondered, knowing what it was like to watch him develop just the way he was; and considered what a strange thought it was to have.

When Daniel signed off, she got up from the pillow and looked at him. "Why were you and Sam talking like that? Is it some kind of game you two play?" she asked.

He looked at her, thinking about what he should say. "It's probably better I tell you the truth, isn't it?" he said, seeming unsure. "Do you remember what you and Dad talked about that day at breakfast, you know, about the danger that I might be in if people find out how smart I am?"

She blinked, surprised that he had understood, let alone remembered. "But how did you know? You were only six months old." She let it go; it was unimportant. What was important was that somehow, he knew and was actively working to keep his and Samantha's secret out of the public domain.

"I remember what you said. I remember how Dad looked at you and then at me when he finally agreed there could be a very real danger for kids like me. I didn't understand you just then, but I remembered the words and how you acted. When I finally learned their meaning, I understood and decided it was up to me. I will get smart and protect us. Samantha and I have agreed that when speaking over the net, we have to talk as if we are ordinary kids. We even try making mistakes and play at struggling with simple ideas. Last time she was here we made a code for double meanings, like riddles, to get more complex ideas across by acting confused and silly," he explained, obviously proud of himself.

Susan looked at him, utterly amazed. She was speechless, shocked by her toddler's insight, and gave him a gentle pat on his head. "You're an amazing son, Daniel. I'm glad you are mine." A tear trickled down her cheek from the pride welling up inside her.

Later, she told John what Daniel and Sam were up to. He was surprised at first, and then he just laughed as though it was to be expected. They had worried and wondered how to talk to him about the danger, but now it seemed they would not have to.

Twice a week Samantha was dropped off at the Thoth house with a babysitter they trusted, and John, Susan, Robert and Tracey; Samantha's parents headed out for dinner in the city. Together, Daniel and Samantha played mind games and searched the net using John's second account, which he'd created for them to cover their activity.

Daniel caught up with Samantha when she was in grade four. Just over four months after starting school, he was excelling at an unnatural pace. His keen thirst for knowledge seemed to find new depths each time he completed a new topic. Math was one of his favorites, a subject that he caught on to with a flare of utter genius. He was turning two years old and was starting grade five, just ahead of Samantha. She felt a little jealous as he passed her, but by now she had come to accept that Daniel was more than a simple genius; there was something different about him, as though he had the unnatural gift to figure out anything he put his mind to. They were the closest of friends and the most trusted of allies in a world where being discovered as brilliant children could tear their families apart.

Over the next year, Daniel's progress appeared to slow, as he only completed up to grade seven. He discovered there were many more languages in the world other than English, and when he learned this, he decided to do his course work in both English and the two other most widely spoken languages, Mandarin and Spanish.

He started at grade one in both languages, working through the same classwork until he caught up to his English studies. At first the Chinese characters were impossible to remember, but with much practice it soon became easier, and from then on, after completing his classwork first in English, he would complete it in Spanish and Mandarin.

For his third birthday, his parents decided to invite only the Bradford's for a small family dinner to avoid the ordeal Daniel endured the last time everyone came for a visit. As a surprise, John brought home two black lab puppies and two Savannah kittens. Susan always said she wanted dogs, and he knew that the black labs were her favorite. The cats, though, were a special breed. They would grow up—big, be very loyal, and surely have allot of personality.

It wasn't their way to force Daniel to do anything, but they were concerned. They let him choose his path and find his way as much as he wished, but at the same time, they figured by giving him this distraction, he might turn to a more normal pace. They knew that if he kept up as he had been learning, it would get scary. Would he be ready for university by the age of five? They feared that no matter how well their son masked his intelligence, someone would find out, and when they did, it would mean the unthinkable.

A new very public abduction took place, and this time it was caught on video. Black SUVs arrived, and a team of tactically outfitted operatives entered the house. It happened in the same way the other families described it. The video was recorded by a secondary surveillance system hardened against advanced scrambler technologies, a surveillance system used by special forces all around the world.

The video of the black-clad figures swiftly putting down resistance was graphic and left nothing out. It showed that the mother, who attacked the lead man, was struck hard and then stunned. The father came on, swinging a golf club. It happened fast, each of them hitting the ground hard, unmoving. One of the assailants picked up the child, who screamed hysterically, and silenced him before they all turned, leaving just as quickly as they had arrived.

The family had been smart, uploading the video to torrent sites for days before sending it to every grassroots net broadcaster they could get through to.

The underground media covered the story for three days before every channel showing the video was taken down. When they came back online, there was no mention of it, and they refused to acknowledge questions from the public. For a while it kept popping up on various sites from people who downloaded before it was taken down, but they only lasted a few hundred views before quickly being blocked. To those paying attention, it was apparent those behind the taking of the world's smartest children wielded the power to do whatever they wanted, with entirely no fear of the law or the will of the people. It was obvious the corporate media was not going to tell the true story and did all they could to cover it up and distract from the truth.

Daniel found a video of the abduction and downloaded it as soon as it showed up on the web. He renamed the file and put it on a memory card to prevent any bots from finding it, and then he deleted it from his online system. After watching the clip a few times, he called his parents in.

"Hi, Mom. Hi, Dad. Sit down. I think you guys need to see this. Mom, your fears were justified. Here is the proof."

They watched it together and felt vindicated in their precautions. When the video ended, they looked at one another, hardly believing the graphic nature of the video, there was no denying how real it was.

"We will never let anything like this happen to our family. We must be vigilant and keep anyone outside our trusted circle from knowing about your gifts, Daniel," John fervently stated.

"John, I think we need to delete this video and get it out of our house!" Susan proclaimed.

Daniel looked at them with disdain. "Hold on. That would only help them cover up their crime! No way. We protect it and study it. Maybe there's a way we can see them coming by analyzing it."

John looked at his son and smiled. "You're right, Dan. I don't know if we can learn anything from the video, but don't delete it. It's the evidence the world needs, and the vested interests will scour the net. Maybe one day it will come in useful. For now, let's just keep it safe on that memory card, offline. Maybe we can make copies of it and anonymously mail them out to truth groups in a couple of weeks."

Samantha completed grade-five home school and her third year of basic Spanish; she had taken Daniel's cue to begin learning an additional language. She was way ahead of kids her own age and felt a sense of pride at her achievements.

When she came over, they shared secrets and talked about the kids who had been taken. They watched the video over and over, looking for clues to the identities of the black-clad figures, but of course they never did find any. One thing the two kids did know, though, was that these men were professionals, and the two made a game out of analyzing and zooming in on the footage in an attempt to break the story.

The two big cats were amazing for Daniel. As kittens, John and Susan made sure to keep them in Daniel's room. The idea was to create a bond between them that they hoped would last a lifetime. Susan loved to watch Daniel toy with the clumsy kittens and suggested he name them Tom and Jerry, after her favorite childhood cartoon characters. As they grew, he taught them to fetch and stand guard, building a connection beyond what was common for even these super-intelligent cats.

Chapter 5

Angelo

When Daniel was just shy of three and a half years old, an arrogant man with social services credentials unexpectedly paid a visit to the house. When he came into the living room, he saw Daniel sitting with the two big cats. Tom immediately took up a stance of protective hostility, in a near-silent shudder, as though he instinctively knew what the man was truly about. Daniel didn't know who this man was or why he was here, and so made a point of putting on the act of being far less then what he truly was.

Tom had his back up, and Jerry was quick to take up position between the man and their human. Daniel started to laugh in his most baby-like voice, saying, "Tawm! Gawrry! Silly kitties. Stawp, you silly kitties." Their reaction was immediate; the cats went from being completely hostile to docile, sniffing at the man's hand before sitting back on their haunches as if nothing was wrong. They could feel Daniel's intuition, and although they appeared calm, Daniel could sense they were still on high alert, completely aware this man did not have good intentions.

Still not introduced, the man stepped around the cats and patted Daniel on the head. "I have heard so much about you from your father, Daniel. He says you're a very special boy."

The man's tone and his words made Daniel even more wary. He looked up with an eager but dumb expression. "Hello, funny man," he said in his most childish voice before giggling like a three-year-old should. "Dan-i-el," he mouthed, as if saying his name was still a challenge. "Hello! He-he!"

The man looked over at John and smiled coldly. He had been expecting much more, and this? This was an embarrassment.

John looked him in the eye and said flatly, doing his best to sound as natural as he could, "I tried to tell you over the phone. There really isn't anything very special about Daniel. He's still just a baby. I don't know where you would have heard otherwise."

"Well, our program seeks out children who are abnormally smart. We need to protect them, especially with what's been happening. These poor families, having their kids forcefully taken from them. I can't bear to think of how hard it must be for them to cope. It came to our attention that your son might be eligible for our program and the protection it provides gifted children," the man said, and Daniel saw the way his eyes shifted when he spoke.

John asked the question again, this time letting his voice get cold. "And what was the name of your program again? I forgot, sir; who do you represent? Can I see your identification?"

The man in the gray suit smirked at John. "Well, that is of no importance anymore, now is it? Obviously, your son is of no interest to us. Thank you for your time and your hospitality, Mr. Thoth," he said, smoothly walking toward the front door.

Daniel watched him with sharp, keen eyes and saw a similarity in the way he walked and the way the agents in the video carried themselves. His heart seemed to stop, and he nearly panicked. *The man is walking away; maybe it's fine,* he thought and prayed he would leave.

When John heard the man peel off in what sounded like a high-end sports car, he turned, slowly leaning his back against the wall. In a single smooth motion, he sagged to the floor. Daniel watched his father, knowing that the danger they feared was just now far too close for comfort.

"It was one of them, Dad. I recognized his walk. It was one of those men from the video. I think we fooled him," Daniel whispered.

John's heart had nearly stopped; he could only stare across the room at his son, who seemed unworried by the afternoon's sudden events.

That night, when John told Susan what had happened, she was furious at him for letting the man into the house. It sent her for a spin, unwilling to listen to his explanation. It took a while, but when she finally calmed down and was ready to listen, John recounted the events from earlier that day.

He told her about the phone call from the person claiming to be a social services worker; the man had said he was on his way to do a routine checkup on their child's living conditions. He told of how the man mentioned that he heard Daniel was a very special child and was excited to meet him. He recounted how by the time he'd hung up the phone and gotten downstairs to warn his son, the man was already at the front door. He told her how he'd heard the man knock once and then heard the lock turn over.

"The man stepped inside our house just as I entered our foyer. There was nothing I could do, except hope that Daniel was not in the middle of his classwork." He gripped her hand, reassuring her that it had gone just as well as they could have ever hoped. "I couldn't very well have kicked him out; it would have just caused more unwanted attention. I trusted Daniel would hear us coming and switch to some kid's TV show. We both know how good he is at putting on the toddler act. When I asked the man for credentials the first time I tried to raise my voice a bit to give Daniel some warning, maybe that helped."

"We were lucky he was in the living room doing demos with toy blocks," Susan admitted.

"He put on a perfect act, and the disappointment in the man's eyes was clear. I don't think he'll be paying us any more visits, thanks to Daniel. The question is, who raised the red flag? Who put the call in to these people, or was it, in fact, just a random check?" John thought out loud.

Following the unexpected visit, John immediately started researching the Wise Child Group. A quick search on the net revealed that more and more people of status were joining the ranks of supporters behind the group, many of them from circles of wealth and influence. He wondered about their motivation and looked into their backgrounds. At first, he found scandals and attacks on their characters, many having numerous class-action lawsuits from various shady shell corporations. It was clear to him these people were of virtue. Farther down the pages in his search, he found charity works, deeds of good will, and awards from various colleges. These people were choosing to stand against those known as the *shadow corporations*.

He was impressed, seeing the names of people with enough power to live in extravagant anonymity, and for a moment, he felt that maybe they were there to scout out the very best—but he let that thought go. There hadn't been any abductions of children enrolled in the program, and besides, they were only a select group of billionaires fighting back against the group with unlimited funds and the power to direct entire counties' decisions. He admired them for their hope and belief that by protecting and nurturing the smartest of children, these next generations might sway the power and overthrow the few small groups feeding off humanity's suffering.

John made an appointment and flew down to Los Angeles for an interview with Philip T. Baker, the headmaster of the Wise Child Group. He wanted to enroll Daniel as quickly as possible. After John's description of his son, the first question was, "how old is Daniel?" John didn't hesitate and left the man momentarily speechless and at a loss for how they should proceed. He recognized that the Thoth family had an incredibly gifted child, one who, if not protected, certainly would be of interest to the groups snatching up children without a trace.

They agreed that Philip would request volunteers from the school staff to find someone interested in mentoring and examining the boy. They also agreed that John would return in one week to conduct a series of interviews.

When John returned he was shown to a quaint room with a desk and two chairs and began meeting applicants.

The first man to walk through the door surprised John with his size and stature. He was a big man yet likable and impressed with his official introduction. John went through the motions of the interview, but after the first few questions, he knew this was not the person for the job. Daniel, at his age, would need someone far softer, and the man's official posture gave John a sense of unease.

Next, a younger woman stepped into the room. She introduced herself respectfully, but there was something *off* about her. His first impression was that she was doing this more for herself. Her words were superficially enthusiastic and interested, but behind them he saw a hidden condescending personality, as though she had something to prove to herself or maybe to the world. Whatever it was, the feeling was there that she did it not to help others but only to benefit herself, and so he crossed her off the list as well.

Next, a short lady in her mid-fifties entered the room. Soft-spoken and intelligent, when she spoke he felt a deeply inspired intellect and genuine care. Julian told of all the children she had watched go through the program, emphasizing the teaching quality and success rate of her many years of service. She described her purpose—a dedication to helping children harness their gifts while giving them the chance to make the most of their lives.

As she left, John thought of her as a definite standout candidate, one who would give all she had to her job.

The next candidate was an older man with silver-tipped hair, sharp glasses, and a thick woolen jacket. He entered with a smooth, graceful stride and introduced himself in a humble yet intellectual tone. He began by describing his extensive education and past positions at universities across the country.

John read the man's name off the list on the desk. "Angelo Bonifacio." *A respectable man*, he thought, and considered the man's age.

"Ah, Stanford, I did my best to teach humanities in an attempt to prepare students for the real world. As well, I have always liked studying the sciences in my leisure," Angelo remarked with the demeanor of an aged doctor. Last, he spoke of the forced retirement fast approaching and how he would miss teaching.

John saw Angelo's spirits fade when he mentioned retirement. He saw the man's passion was teaching, and he wondered if there was something he could do.

As Angelo walked out of the room, John felt his heart go out to the man, and he knew that he would be the perfect fit for Daniel and his family. As he began to rise from the chair with his decision already made, the next candidate entered in a strange, blustering step.

It was a small, red-faced man, middle-aged and a bit chubby, with rusty, scraggly hair. John tried to inform the man that a decision was already made but was cut off before he could start. The contemptuous tone had John disliking him immediately, and his pugnacious voice was far too much to bear.

"Who is this boy I will be seeing? Of course, you will be paying for my flights—is that not correct?" he stated. His beady little eyes darted up and down John, as if looking for a snack.

John wasted not a moment more with the man. He stood abruptly and, without a word, walked around the table and out the door.

With the interviews concluded, he went directly to the headmaster's office and found Philip reviewing papers. He seemed a little surprised to see John so soon.

"How did it go?" Philip asked.

"Very well, thank you. You selected some very respectable instructors, except …" He paused before commenting on the last one. "Well, almost all of them except that last one—Shruber, I believe his name was. I am surprised you would have a man like that on your staff."

Philip laughed. "Mr. Shruber is on his way out. He will not last another semester at the school, and Mr. Shrubs—as the students call him—knows it."

When the pleasantries were finished, John made Philip aware of who he liked best. "I would like to select Mr. Angelo Bonifacio if possible." His announcement thrilled the headmaster, and with a great he smile nodded his head in agreement.

"I am glad you have chosen Angelo. It's a sad thing, this mandatory retirement age. He is one of our most cherished instructors at the school. He is as close to a scholar as any I have ever met. His knowledge of languages, astronomy, math, science, history, and philosophy are simply unmatched by any we have ever had on staff." After finishing his eulogizing of Mr. Bonifacio, he suggested that, if possible, John and his family might have Angelo and his wife move north as guests of the Thoth family.

Hearing this, John liked the idea and requested a second interview with Angelo. He wanted to extend the offer in an official yet personal setting.

An hour later they sat across from one another in the same room as before, this time speaking of more personal matters. John learned that Angelo, although financially stable, was distressed that his forced retirement would leave nothing to drive him in life. He explained that he and his wife of over forty-seven years lived in a nice part of the city but felt that it lacked the open spaces back home in Portugal.

John didn't hesitate in extending the offer to have the Bonifacios live at the Thoth plantation. Angelo would be Daniel's tutor, which would keep him connected to the school until the mandatory children's education grades were completed, at which time Angelo would fully retire from official school duties but continue to work with Daniel for as long as he wished. John expressed that Angelo and his wife would be free to stay however long they liked and have their own guest house, as part of the family.

When John presented his offer, the silver-haired man stayed silent for a time, fighting the wave of emotion obviously welling up inside. John watched as a single tear trickled down the older man's cheek, until finally, he raised his eyes from his tightly clasped hands and looked into John's eyes. "I would like to graciously accept your offer—with one condition. I need you to have dinner with us tonight and help convince Lucia that this is right for us."

John agreed and that night joined them for dinner. To his surprise, he found that Angelo had not exaggerated when he said his wife was a culinary genius. Even before John entered their home, he smelled the rich aromas of roasting meat and baked goods. At the table was an amazing spread of roast lamb, dumplings, and cabbage rolls, and quickly learned this was a common affair at their household.

At dinner, Lucia told stories of how she had grown up on a farm in Portugal, where she worked in the kitchens, cooking, prepping, and cleaning for more than thirty people. "Angelo visited his family—they were partial owners of the plantation—and by the grace of God, we met and fell in love." She looked at Angelo with loving eyes. "It was love at first sight. We understood we would spend the rest of their lives together from the very first time we met."

She recalled when Angelo went back to America to continue his studies and then told of how she followed him there. She described arriving in a strange airport, afraid and alone, and recalled Angelo walking out from the crowed to take her in his arms, "that smile, that gentle smile." She reminisced. "Every couple of years we returned to Portugal and spent time visiting our parents, enjoying the rustic lifestyle and vibrant culture of our home town." Then, her voice went soft. "But then the last time we returned, we watched our parents slowly lowered into the ground. They were killed by mobs in an uprising.

"We stopped visiting after that, and since then, time seems to have flown us by, day after day. We never truly feel happy here, but what else is there to do? We have considered heading back and living in the countryside but with the instability of the government and the rise in crime rates, we just stay here and live out our days, safe and content, happy enough, I suppose." There was a sad contentment behind her words.

Lucia was a short, plump woman with a vibrant exuberance. Her thick dark hair fell in waves off her shoulders, and her rosy cheeks dimpled when she smiled. Her sparkling eyes accentuated her radiance—eyes that made John feel right at home. He saw a resemblance to his mother in the way she moved and spoke, leaving no doubt in his mind that these two kindred spirits were indeed the perfect fit for his family.

He recalled the days before his parents were lost in the crash—that last day when his mother held him and kissed him, telling him they would be back after the weekend. The plane crash took them when he was only fifteen, leaving him and his brothers alone with their uncle, a memory that seemed to never fade.

Seeing the two of them and listening to their stories, he knew destiny had brought them together. He would make their retirement comfortable. He thought of how Lucia would enjoy cooking meals and tending the gardens, and he was curious as to how Angelo would react when he found that Daniel was just three and half years old.

When he told Susan, she was more than a little surprised. "I've never even met these people! Why in the world are we having complete strangers move into the guesthouse, John?" she loudly scolded over the phone.

He had called to explain the situation, but her reaction made him realize that telling her this over the phone was a bad plan.

She prattled on and on at her husband for not consulting her before making such a huge decision. "How do you know if these people are going to be right for our family and our son, John?"

He deserved the rebuke, knowing full well that he should have talked to her first, but something had told him that in this case, it was better to ask for forgiveness rather than risk missing the chance. As penance, he promised to design and build a new guesthouse for when family and friends came to visit. "Susan, it might just free up some of your time, Lucia will want to help out I am sure. You can pursue more of your hobbies; you know, all those things you've had no time for."

He intentionally left out that Lucia was a master cook, knowing how much Susan would enjoy learning from someone of such culinary skill, but he knew as well that it was something she would have to find out for herself.

After leaving their apartment in the hands of a man John sent to handle the Bonifacio's' move, the two new hires flew from LA to the San Francisco airport, where they were picked up by the limo John also arranged. In the back of the modern vehicle, they sat comfortably, looking at each other, hardly believing how suddenly the direction of their lives just changed. They wondered if they were crazy for giving up everything to live with these strangers, but something told them it was right.

When they pulled up to the Thoths' house, they could hardly contain their tears of joy at the realization that this was their new home. They arrived just as the sun was setting over the ocean, and it was beautiful. The sun's dwindling light cast an orange and purple glow across the wispy clouds high up in the sky.

As they walked toward the front door, they saw into the courtyard and backyard, where an infinity pool ran from a big deck out toward the horizon. A large mosaic surrounded the pool, spreading out over the multileveled patio to a terrace and a larger deck with furniture and umbrellas. Behind that, a large grass area stretched out to where a line of trees marked the edge of the vineyards and orchards.

Lucia could hardly believe her eyes as the reality of their future solidified in her mind. Tears ran down her cheeks as she took in the amazing views, gardens, and buildings of this beautiful property—the place they would now call home.

When the doorbell chimed, signaling their guests' arrival, John watched his wife as she fought to control her rising anxiety. At the front door, they made their introductions. Fortunately, Susan's worries quickly disappeared, replaced by an enthusiastic and gracious feeling that came as she understood what John saw in these two lovely people.

The lasting love between the old pair and their genuine passion for life was plain to see. Susan stepped close, brushing her hand across Lucia's cheek to wipe away a lingering tear, and smiled. She considered the older woman's eyes and felt a trust kindle within. "I'm Susan. We're happy to have you. Welcome to our family! I hope your flight was comfortable."

"Oh yes! Thank you, Susan, very comfortable! We feel very fortunate to be here," Lucia replied.

"Can I meet Daniel now?" Angelo asked. "Is he around the house somewhere?"

"Oh, probably in his room, learning something, guarded by his two evil cats," John replied. "Let's wait and surprise him once you two are settled, all right?"

Just then the two black Labs trotted through the living room, gaining speed as they came. John gave a quick command, causing the two exuberant dogs to pull up short. They dropped to their haunches, tongues hanging from their mouths and whining to be freed, eager to greet these new people.

John laughed. "Don't worry about these two. They're just a couple of big baby boys who can never get enough attention."

Angelo was taken aback. Labs had always been his favorite dog. He loved them for their smarts, their loyalty, and of course their sleek, elegant look. He looked up at John with a question in his eyes. John knew full well what the older man would ask and nodded his approval. Angelo dropped to one knee and called the dogs forward. They came quickly, licking his hands and bumping their sides up against him. They circled him, sticking their noses into every nook and cranny of the old man's body. Angelo beamed with delight and spoke in Portuguese. praising the dogs for their beauty. "Cães bonitos, animais majestosos."

At dinner, Daniel, unaware of their new guests, was finally introduced to the couple. "Daniel, this is Angelo. He will be your personal tutor and examiner for the education certificates required by the state," Susan said as she introduced the man to her son.

Daniel frowned a little when he saw Angelo's expression and understood that he was not what the older man had expected.

Looking to John, Angelo asked softly, "I was not aware your son was so young. How old is he?"

"Daniel is very young, yes, he is three and a half."

Before John could continue, Daniel cut in. "You are to be my teacher, old man?" he asked in lightning-fast Mandarin. He had spoken harshly, with the tone of a petulant teenager, as though he had spoken the language his entire life.

Astonished, Angelo looked to John and then to Susan, searching for an explanation, but found the same knowing grin on each of their faces.

"Daniel, you know the rules. English only at the dinner table," Susan scolded, but Daniel ignored her. His eyes were locked on Angelo, analyzing him in an attempt to find out what type of person he might be.

Oh boy. One surprise after another, Angelo thought and then skillfully replied in perfect Mandarin. "Yes, child, you are correct. I will be your teacher."

Expecting a childish reply, he was disappointed when Daniel only maintained his gaze until finally, in a challenging tone, Daniel replied, "We will see who teaches whom."

Angelo watched the young blue-eyed golden-haired boy calmly returned to his food as though nothing had happened. The feeling that he was in for some major surprises lifted Angelo's spirits.

The dinner table was silent after that. Angelo hardly tasted his food as his mind raced with the wonder of how a boy this age could have learned Mandarin at such an advanced level.

The next morning John came downstairs to start his day just as the sky shifted to twilight. As he walked into the kitchen, he was surprised at the scent of freshly brewed coffee. He poured himself a cup and turned toward the bay windows overlooking the east-facing patio. He saw Angelo in one of the deck chairs, along with the dogs, Bill and Ted, who were sitting intently on either side of him. John sipped the coffee, noticed it was different, and walked out onto the deck to join the other man.

"Good morning, John. This view, this place—it is amazing," Angelo said, greeting him without turning to see who it was.

For a while they sat in silence, watching the sky slowly brighten until the sun finally crested the distant hills and cast its brilliant orange light over the rolling landscape in front of them. As the sun lifted above the horizon, John stood and invited the older man to go for a walk around the property.

"I am sorry we didn't warn you of Daniel's age, but I'm sure he will be enough to keep you interested." John's voice trailed off, refraining from giving the man advice on his son.

"John, it's as though a higher power has come to our rescue. Before you came along, it seemed we would be relegated to monotonous lives. This place ... it's like we have come home but to a safer and better version. We can't thank you enough for giving us this chance. I will admit I was shocked by Daniel's age, but I have a feeling he will be an entertaining and challenging pupil. How does he know Mandarin? How does a three-and-a-half-year-old know how to speak like that?"

John stopped and looked at the man. "You are welcome. We are happy you and your wife have chosen to join our family, and, to be honest, I have no idea how Daniel is doing what he is doing. I kinda hope you might figure that out."

They walked on in silence, Angelo wondering how far along Daniel really was. He couldn't fathom the child being past grade five- or six-level exercises but wasn't sure what to expect.

When they got back to the house, Angelo thanked John for the tour, and John replied with a radiant smile. "I know it's a lot. It's a tremendous change for both of you but a good one for all of us, I hope."

After breakfast, Angelo followed Daniel to his room, where the boy returned to the math problems displayed on his room's wall. He liked to start his days with a problem solving exorcise of some kind. Angelo watched as Daniel sat on the floor, picked up his tablet pen, and began scribbling as the video presentation resumed.

Tom and Jerry, who had been curled up, looked at the man they had seen only yesterday, and both quickly rose to their feet. Tom began his low growl, followed by Jerry, who always copied Tom's lead. Both big cats took on predatory postures, their ears pinned and their eyes locked on the trespassing stranger. They were both loving cats but at the same time instinctive in nature and capable hunters, with killer instincts.

Daniel looked over and spoke crisply. "Cats, be still. Eeet's okay, boys; eeet's okay."

At Daniel's command they quickly went to their bellies, perked their ears, and whipped their tails, showing the agitation they both still felt.

Angelo, no stranger to animals, knelt and allowed each cat to sniff and rub their noses against his hand. They soon became agreeable, and he ran his hands over their backs, giving them each a couple hard pats that triggered short, gratified mews.

"Great cats," Angelo said, as the pair of twenty-five-pound Savannahs sat up on their haunches, audibly purring now that they felt comfortable with this newcomer.

Daniel looked over and called Jerry to him. The big cat got up and trotted over without pause, his lanky figure giving him a unique attitude not seen in ordinary house cats. His mouth hung open as he stood in front of the boy. Daniel scratched under Jerry's chin and picked up a toy. "Would you like to fetch, Jerry? You wanna get the toy?"

When he tossed the stuffed toy across the room, Jerry bolted, nearly catching it from Daniel's hand. The cat pounced for the kill before bringing it back. The big cat dropped the toy at Daniel's side and sat there, expecting more play, but Daniel had done it for Angelo's benefit and laughed at the cat who, knowing Daniel's expression, went back to lie next to Tom.

With everyone properly introduced, Daniel asked in Spanish, "What will you teach me that I cannot find on the net?"

Angelo sat on the large leather beanbag and formally introduced himself. He spoke first in fluent Spanish, transitioned to Mandarin, and then continued in English. "I spent some time studying at Oxford, where I earned a PhD in history while always dabbling in advanced mathematics, alchemy, and the sciences."

He noticed that Daniel listened intently with a calculated eye, as though evaluating his achievements. He pushed on. "When I completed my studies, I pursued a tenure back at Stanford University and instructed there for twelve years before joining the Wise Child Group. I have a passion for languages and speak thirteen dialects fluently. I see you already have started and seem to be well on your way. I am impressed." He saw a spark of genuine interest ignite in the boy's eyes.

Daniel was amazed and said so, forgetting about the grade-eight math lesson still in progress on the display in front of them. "I am honored to have you as my instructor, Angelo." Saying it without loosing eye contact with the man.

"Thank you, Daniel. For a child of only three years, having even the smallest interest in learning, let alone learning three languages—now that is someone I am honored to meet as well."

They spent the next year becoming great friends. The boy raced through his classwork, surprising the man with his ability to understand and retain what seemed like unlimited amounts of information. Angelo told him more than once about his first impressions, recalling his initial reaction that first night at the dinner table. He had been filled with a sense of disappointment, shocked that his new pupil was so young. Then, he reflected on how, after the first week of watching Daniel learn, he realized the boy could prove to be one of the greatest students he would ever instruct.

Sometimes he felt that Daniel already knew the answers, as though a wealth of knowledge was somehow hidden inside the boy. He half wondered if there was such a thing as past lives and entertained the idea that Daniel could have been a scholar or a scientist in some long-past existence. Angelo tried his best to teach Daniel lessons beyond what he could learn from textbooks on the computer, and Daniel requested that Angelo teach him German and Portuguese in small amounts while he finished learning Spanish and Mandarin.

Samantha still regularly came for visits, and while Daniel focused on complex study problems that he insisted on figuring out for himself, Angelo helped Samantha with her studies.

That year a child under the protection of the WCG was taken. Luckily, every child enrolled in the program was given an untraceable advanced tracking system implant, which led the authorities to find where the abducted child and a group of other children were being held.

They found them in a training camp—a high-tech facility with great comfort for the children, along with advanced learning centers. Some who had been there for a long time were resentful at being found and released from their captor's custody, while others, newly arrived, rejoiced at being reunited with their families.

It was a revelation to the world. Over thirty children were recovered, all of them free to tell their stories to the media. But it ended there; the facility's ownership was so enshrouded in shell corporations there could be no tracing of those truly behind it.

Daniel's fourth birthday came and went as he finished grade nine and started grade ten. Angelo, seeing his young pupil's brilliance, introduced him to new academic resources on the net.

Daniel saw the value of this resource immediately and made it a goal to watch and learn every video on the site.

Angelo, hearing what Daniel planned, was surprised but knew he shouldn't be. "You are going to watch them all?" he asked.

To Daniel, it was a simple thing—start at the beginning and continue through to the end. So over the next three years he committed himself, and each day progress was made.

To the delight of everyone, Samantha's visits began involving less study and more outdoor activities. When she came over, the two went out and ran the back yard grass, swam in the pool, and explored the vineyards, sometimes venturing to the rock piles on the outskirts of the property. They imagined themselves as captains of huge spaceships in a fleet battling an unrelenting alien horde. Daniel's imagination seemed limitless, and Samantha's enjoyment at playing along with the scenarios was admirably enthusiastic.

Daniel described huge creatures come to devour Earth, creatures he described as moon-sized beasts with tentacles reaching out hundreds of miles in all directions. He described them as a force nearly unbeatable but insisted they had to try. They imagined fantastic battles, always nearly losing, but in the end, they always introduced a secret weapon to overcome the overwhelming odds against them.

These were some of Daniel's favorite moments. On a hot summer's day, after running in the fields and swimming in the pool, they sat with their feet in the water and talked.

"Sam, what do you want to be when you grow up?" Daniel asked.

"Me? Well, I want to be a scientist, of course. I want to work with plants and animals. I want to cure disease, and help people live longer by fixing our genes. What about you, Dan?"

He hesitated in silent contemplation. The silence stretched on until Sam nearly asked again, but just then he turned to her. "I want to have all the answers, Sam. I want to help the world heal itself. I am going to fix pollution, and feed the hungry, and help educate those who don't have access to education. I want to save everyone who wants to be free of oppression in third-world countries. Education for everyone, Sam. There are so many minds lost to poverty. I want them all to live the life we live—or better!"

Just before his seventh birthday, Daniel completed all three thousand training videos on the online academy website and blew through the rest of the high school curriculum, all the way up to graduation, scoring 100% on his personal final test papers. He was nearly fluent in four languages, thanks to Angelo's constant conversations, and he pondered which one he would tackle next. Angelo could not help but notice how easily Daniel learned anything he looked at.

On his seventh birthday, they celebrated with a small gathering of their closest family and friends. Susan's sister Margaret could not believe how fast Daniel was growing up and expressed amazement at his mature nature.

The fact he had completed high school was a close-kept secret, one they agreed to keep for at least a couple of more years.

Later, after everyone left, John asked his son a serious question, one he already knew the answer to but felt the need to ask non the less. "So, what are you planning next? You gonna take some time and be a kid, or are you going to continue charging ahead?"

Daniel thought about it for a second. He thought he knew the answer as well but had never put it to words before. His eyes focused and with confidence he described his plans. "I don't think I can hide forever, and I have a feeling that I must confront those in the shadows at some point in my life. I would like to find other kids like me and continue to learn, so when I do have to confront evil, they will be no match for us. I think I will spend some time studying computer languages, programming, engineering, and the applications of advanced science. There is a severe void between the advancement of technology and the ability for computer languages to keep up, so I will address that as my first goal. In the process, I hope to make some money so I can help pay for university."

John, Susan, and Angelo were completely stunned at hearing this. They were left wide-eyed, they were speechless, and when the shock finally wore off, John was the first to speak. "First of all, you never have to worry about paying for school. Never mind the fact you are far too young to be thinking about university. Dan, you should have some fun; live a little. Don't worry about confronting and fighting the world's most powerful and most evil people just yet!"

Angelo continued to be invaluable in assisting with Daniel's studies. Along with his new interests in various programming languages and advanced sciences, he began digging into Latin, Arabic, and Hebrew as a way to search history for clues as to why mankind was so fractured.

Daniel found that Stanford University offered free online video lectures for entire semesters in the computer science program, starting from the very basics all the way up to programming software for artificial intelligence, designed to solve complex weather systems, genomic mapping, and particle physics solutions. With this discovery, he dove right in, asking his father to order the textbooks needed for the assigned studies. As he grasped the implications of computer languages, he saw a whole new realm of unlimited possibilities and was inspired.

His aptitude for math, science, and programming continued to amaze his tutor, but at the same time Angelo felt that a strong dose of history and current world politics would be healthy for the boy. With some effort, he managed to wrench him away from the online coursework for a few hours each day, and they walked outside to talk of philosophy, history, and the importance of having balance in one's life.

During these times, Angelo told Daniel of past wars, empires collapsing, the Romans, the Greeks, the Egyptians, and how they had fallen because of greed and corruption, making sure Daniel saw their common mistakes. Daniel listened to Angelo tell of great leaders and great revolutions. Angelo told of how the world had come so close to being free from corruption, yet in today's world there was no shortage of it, to be sure. When the stories returned to the here and now, though, Angelo always saddened, reflecting on how the good people of earth were losing ground to the loudest, most corrupt few.

Angelo always spoke of a family that had been orchestrating events for over five hundred years—a group that had split into six families, all from of the same bloodline but under new names, and now, with their influence and assets, they accounted for over 80% of the world's major wealth, along with indirect ownerships of every country's debt.

Angelo told of their impenetrable and limitless power—a group capable of raising or tearing down entire countries. Daniel, who understood they had to keep his brilliant mind hidden from the world, saw the further implications of how powerful these people and their corporations really were.

Whenever they got into talking conspiracies and shadow corporations, Angelo always got very passionate, often repeating stories from his childhood. He recounted what had happened to Europe long before Daniel was born. They had systematically bankrupted country after country, taking control of their governments through the offerings of huge loans that the countries and their people could never hope to repay. When the loans came due and the countries were unable to pay the banks, corporations owned by the financial institutions seized the natural resources and inserted their own governments to enslave the people.

Daniel would always notice the pain in the man's eyes as he described the events that had plunged the citizens of countries into poverty. He would tell of how inflation rose along with crime rates and the anarchistic chaos that took hold of entire cities.

With an angry tone, Angelo described how his parents and extended family were killed by looters and rioters, people starving and desperate with nothing left to do but prey on the weak to survive.

On a day when Angelo got particularly passionate about the topic, Daniel asked, "Why do people let this happen? How can nearly all of humanity allow such a small number, just a greedy few, to ruin our world?"

"Because of fear and power my boy. They have the system played; they are the ones who created it." He stopped and closed his eyes. "The only way to change it is for the world to take a stand, and when that happens, there likely will be a bloody revolution. Let's face it; the ultra-rich will bunker down and let those who choose to stand against them die off in one last world war before emerging to sit triumphantly on the ruins of those who saw the truth."

"So is there any hope at all?" Daniel asked.

"Hope." The older man chuckled. "It's a funny thing, my boy. The governments who helped those manipulators take control of the currencies and build their fiat systems—they have become the slaves of those they had hoped to join. Many of them, I am sure, want desperately to break free, but they can't. The only hope is for people to go through life without attracting the attention of the shadow corporations. That is the only hope I see."

"But what about innovative technologies that could replace the ones these corporations and evil people have control over? Couldn't the people supply themselves with food, energy, and medicine?" asked Daniel.

They walked to the gazebo in the middle of the vineyards and sat, looking out over the ocean and the distant horizon.

"Every time a brilliant inventor comes along with a revolutionary technology or medicine that could displace the balance of power, they disappear, snapped up by police, puppets of those who are completely untouchable." Angelo smiled wryly. "I bet the puppets are starting to realize their folly in supporting the suppressive people, and I bet they wish they had stood for what is right when they had the chance. Now, though, it is far too late. There are far too many loyalist insiders. And those who now seek the truth are finding themselves more and more pushed to the outside. Things that could have helped humanity break free from the shackles of suppression have been confiscated, and the inventors in search of alternatives often have fallen to accidents or have been ruined to the point of having nothing left but the shirts on their backs and the streets to call their homes."

Daniel looked at the silver-haired man with his bronze complexion and focused eyes, silently staring off into the distance. *Something needs to be done!* he thought, making a silent promise to somehow make a change in the world. He sat looking at the ocean, dreaming of unmasking those who lived free from accountability, and a sense of exhilaration washed over him.

Over the next eleven months, Angelo helped Daniel work through four years of university-level computer science. By the end, Daniel had completed and patented a software package designed to analyze any software's hardware integration code and modify it to more efficiently work with the newest hardware. He submitted it to the Stanford computer science faculty via their open submissions policy and felt a sense of satisfaction at the achievement. Their reply was filled with praise, recognizing its potential and publicly announcing its viability in the ever-changing landscape of technology and software.

He followed his software success with a crash course in business and then incorporated his first company. He created a net-based storefront for his algorithm and, nearly overnight, received hundreds of orders. It became evident that the sophisticated artificial intelligence could save software companies thousands of programming hours needed to keep current with the quickly advancing world of technology. Daniel's algorithm was designed to analyze raw code, assess requirements of current hardware specifications, and update the software line by line, while maintaining full functionality and optimizing for different operating platforms.

As word got out, sales climbed, netting D. T. Software $3.5 million in the first six months. Seeing this, John, Susan, and Angelo could only shake their heads at Daniel's brilliance.

"Well, son, maybe I will let you pay for your own college education after all," John proudly announced after hearing these earnings numbers.

Chapter 6

Stas

Stas Dimitrievich Gurkovsky and his parents lived in a small condo on the outskirts of Aleksin, Russia. Throughout his childhood, instead of running the streets with the other kids, he spent hours in the nearly deserted library, where he found a passion for computer languages. He and his parents always lived in the same one-bedroom apartment, doing whatever they could to eat and stay warm during the cold winters but Stas had plans to change that.

His parents quickly recognized his passion for programming and the potential for him to escape their lower-class lifestyle and so they did what they needed to. It was a hard choice; they had saved the money to move away from the impoverished town, but instead they chose to buy Stas a laptop, hoping he would make a better future for himself—and for them, in the process.

The laptop fueled his interest, and soon it evolved beyond just a hobby. He quickly found the dark web and linked up with various hacker clans. The first thing he learned was how to create and farm web bots, little programs that infiltrate people's computers and steel passwords for all sorts of accounts. His web crawlers and spam campaigns installed subroutines to steal credit card information and filtered half a percent from all online transactions into his own hidden accounts. He built online gambling websites, making commissions on people's transactions, and things began to get better for them.

His internet Ponzi schemes and hacking-for-hire contracts paid real money—cash that helped them live without worrying where the next meal would come from—and a new feeling of prosperity entered their lives. He made a few friends on the nets, even learned the name of one guy in China. A math wizard and genius in; Python, C/C++, Java, Perl and LISP. He and Jimmy teamed up a bit, imbedding codes in images and conspiring to survive among the sharks of the dark web.

Stas knew he and his family needed to leave their city and some where people don't kill each other for their food or get beaten half to death for walking alone in the wrong place at the wrong time. Crime was rampant in their city, and no one was safe. A new kind of drug was on the streets, and it was creating a plague. Many of the poorest areas in the world, where the drug was in wide use, looked like an apocalypse had taken place.

Finally, when Stas and his parents had enough money, they moved south to the western coastline of the Caspian Sea. It was warmer and safer, and Stas saw a real change in his parents. Real happiness replaced their state of constant struggle, and for him, seeing his parents happy and safe was the greatest gift of all. Life was good; they had turned the corner, and things were going to keep getting better.

The padlock on their front door popped, and the door silently swung open. Large figures, clad in black SWAT gear, moved like ghosts into their new apartment's living room. They were sitting together, watching a show on their new flat screen, and were completely unaware of the intruders until it was too late.

As they entered, his father, Alex, rose to object, but before he took two steps, the lead armored figure shocked him, and Alex dropped to the floor. His mother started screaming, and just as quickly, she was cut off by a shock round to her chest. She curled into a ball, her scream changing into the sound of a deflating balloon as, like her husband, she lost consciousness.

Stas watched in mute disbelief. He looked at his mother and then his father, fearing the worst, and a cold feeling gripped his heart. One of the armored men knelt beside his father and felt for a pulse. To Stas's relief, the armored figure nodded. "Alive." Stas hadn't moved—he couldn't—and then, as suddenly as it had started, he too was stunned and sagged into the couch, unconscious.

When his eyes opened, he found himself strapped to a chair in a room with walls of smooth gray concrete and a single bulb hanging above. His head throbbed, and a dizziness filled his senses. He fought to stay awake. His vision blurred, and his head spun as he struggled to regain clarity. He vomited, nearly passing out, but somehow, he pushed past the nausea. When he finally regained most of his senses, he realized there was a person standing in the darkened corner of the room.

The man stepped closer, just beyond the light, and watched the boy's eyes track his silhouetted figure. A high-level request had come to his branch, instructions to pick up the boy and take his parents as insurance. Isaak had sent one of his more elite squads on the job, and, as expected, here the target was, just like many before him, faced with a choice: cooperate or suffer.

Isaak held his silence, eyeing the boy, impressed that he had not called out and even more impressed that he remained conscious. Most captives, when they opened their eyes for the first time, dry heaved, and just as quickly passed out again, some repeating the cycle as many as five or six times before regaining their senses. The energy weapons with which the company equipped their teams were one of a kind and did beautiful work.

He admired the fury in the boy's eyes, not uncommon for a person in his situation, but this boy had real fire. Isaak knew how it felt to be hit by one of the energy weapons and what it was like to wake up hours—if not days—later. He had been taken when he was just a boy, and they had used the weapon on him nearly fifteen years ago; it was still a memory that felt like it had happened only yesterday. He recalled the nausea and disorientation as he drifted in and out. He vomited each time until there was nothing left, and his body just heaved, with his head swimming for what seemed like hours.

Stas was big for his age. He had survived the streets by fighting to win. Strung-out men and women could be dangerous, and more than once he had fought to survive. He knew many of the beatings he had given to the filth of his city were fatal ones, and he was strangely okay with it. He knew that if he had let them live, a woman surely would have been raped or a weaker person killed at the hands of those who had tried to make him their victim.

He stared hard at the dark shape standing in front of him. He shook his head, struggling to keep the nausea and blurriness from creeping back in. He was determined not to be the first to speak and stubbornly waited for his captor to break the silence. The smell of vomit from his lap was the worst part. Its putrid odor nearly sent him spinning more than once, but he kept his composure and waited, unwilling to show any weakness.

After what seemed like half an hour of silence, the rage at being strapped to this chair and the memory of how he and his parents were attacked finally got the better of him, "Show yourself, you coward!" He shook the chair, pulling on his wrists and legs, but it was no use, and he went still, realizing he was at this agent's mercy. The figure, whose features were still hidden beyond the light, just stood there, stone still, and it frightened him.

Isaak spoke. "I am very impressed, my friend. Not many people stay conscious the first time they wake from a shock weapon's effect."

"Who are you? What do you want?" Stas rasped.

"I am your friend. As for what we want, I will be getting to that soon enough. You are charged with extortion, identity theft, and the illegal breaching of company firewalls, among a list of other crimes for which you will be held accountable."

Stas understood. His work had been going so well that he had come close to having enough money to quit the illegal stuff, but now it was too late. The hand of authority had come, and he was done. He cursed under his breath, remembering when he had felt he was winning too much. The one saving grace, he thought, was that his parents would be able to use the money from the hidden accounts—the ones that no one would be able to trace. Then it occurred to him: What if they had his parents?

"You have two options. We charge you and your parents with the crimes I have listed. Your parents ... well, let's just say it will not end well for any of you. That's the first option. Second option: We hold your parents at a comfortable facility where they will not be harmed unless you stop cooperating. You will go to America; you will be enrolled in a university; you will get above-average grades; and when you are finished, you will work for us. It is simple, so what will it be?"

Stas saw no way out. Why not work for these people? But his parents? "How do I know my parents will be safe?" he asked.

"We will allow a weekly video call if you meet our criteria," the man replied, stepping into the light so that Stas could see with whom he was dealing. "You will be well compensated, and your life will be comfortable—that is, if you do what we say, when we say. In time, you will be reunited with your parents and provided with a large house, where you will live well in whatever city of the world we choose for you to work. Your parents are already at the facility where they will stay, if you accept our offer. If you choose to fight us or go against us in any way, we will kill your lovely parents and not quickly. They will suffer, and for you, we will accept our loss and send you to a work camp, where your life will not be comfortable in the least. In fact, it will be a place where you'll be forced to work hard every day until it finally kills you. So I ask again: What choice will you make, boy?"

The decision was easy, but he stalled, holding out just long enough to force the main to step forward, he looked up from where his eyes lingered on the floor.

"I don't see any choice; of course, you win. I will do whatever you want me to do. May I speak with my parents? And may I choose the university?"

He heard the man sigh inwardly and wait a few moments. Then, without warning, he stepped closer, letting Stas know they had a deal. Stas considered this agent who had stolen his life and hoped that one day he could kill this man.

A few days later they let him see his parents via video call. When he saw they were safe, he was relieved, and happy to hear they would live together in a comfortable cottage. He told them the deal, and his mother cried. Stas watched as his father tried to comfort her.

The meeting with his parents ended when guards came and took him by the arms. They did not force him, but he felt that if he had resisted, they would have made him regret it. From there, all he knew was that he was in some type of van. Hours went by, and he slept, waking when they finally stopped, arriving, as he soon found out, at an airport.

As he got out of the van, a twenty year old good looking girl greeted him. "Hello. My name is Anna, and I will be accompanying you to America. I will help you get settled and enrolled in the university," she said with a sad smile. He was happy to be going to America, yet in the girl's eyes he saw so much pain, and in that moment, he understood just how evil these people could be.

Chapter 7

University

Daniel's eighth birthday came and went without major fanfare. John installed yet another new theme for his room's display and surprised everyone by the complexity of it. This time it was a world history artificial intelligence, one Daniel could play forward and back to view recreations of cities and civilizations in beautiful photorealistic 3-D simulations.

A few days later Angelo lectured him on the future directions he might want to pursue. He fervently pointed out that at his age, Daniel should take time to enjoy life and be a kid, yet as he said the words, he saw Daniel was not interested in simple pursuits.

"I think it would be a good idea if you started researching universities you might like to attend," Angelo suggested. "Figuring out which programs might interest you would be a good start—that is, if you truly are not interested in being a child. Are you?"

"I have completed all of the research I intend doing on that subject," Daniel replied. "I will apply to Stanford. I did just complete their online computer science program, after all." Daniel paused and then said, "I will challenge necessary bachelor certificates and then apply for graduate programs." He passed a data file to Angelo's tablet. "Have a look. It's a list of studies I'm interested in."

When the file opened on Angelo's tablet, he saw a list with far more than he would have anticipated: advanced computer sciences, astrophysics, photonics, chemistry, genomics, mechanical engineering, particle physics, aeronautics, mathematics, materials sciences, nano materials research, and energy research. He stared at the list before looking up, open-mouthed and dumbstruck. "This is a lifetime's worth of study topics, boy," the older man laughed. "Have you decided to become a scholarly hermit so soon in life?"

Angelo knew full well how brilliant this little man was. There was no doubt he was the quickest learner he had ever met, and his ability to understand and retain information at an unnatural rate was uncanny. He looked back at the list. *How long would this take?* he thought, trying to work out how many years a typical person accepted into each program would need to accomplish this. *Yet this boy—who could know what is truly possible?*

"Daniel, it might take lifetimes to complete these programs." With those words, he saw the unmistakable determination rise in the boy, an intensity that caused Angelo to involuntarily step back.

Daniel looked fierce, daring Angelo to tell him he could not do it. His expression made it clear; he knew exactly what he was getting into. He knew it would be hard, maybe impossible, but he believed he would overcome the challenge, and he planned to exceed all expectations.

With the help of Philip T. Baker from the Wise Child Group, Angelo pulled the necessary strings at San Francisco State University to get Daniel an acceptance interview. Daniel needed enrollment in a whole host of degree programs. He would need to submit final papers and attend exams in every subject before he would be permitted to apply at Stanford.

At the University, Gerald Anderson, the dean of the school, thought it was a joke when Daniel and Angelo first entered his office. In fact, he nearly laughed them both out. Fortunately, Angelo's presence brought the seeming charade some respectability, and as the dean paused to let Angelo explain, Angelo took control of the situation.

"Sir, Daniel has completed advanced levels in mathematics and physics, among others, exceeding all course requirements for the credits he is here to challenge. A level of respect surely is due, and it would be best that you disregard his age."

Gerald's initial smug look disappeared. "Angelo, come now. We both know each other. You are a respected academic, and if what you say is true, which I honestly am not sure I believe, Daniel will do very well here." The dean then acknowledged Daniel with a new level of respect.

"Hello, sir. I am very honored to meet you," Daniel said.

The dean considered the recommendation from the head of the Wise

Child Group and looked over Daniel's papers where he noticed the method of payment. His eyes paused, looking again at the check. Clearly, it was the boy's very own account and signed with his own elegant signature. He concluded that the boy's parents must have had everything to do with it.

Reviewing the list of certificates, he was astonished by how many there were, and inwardly he chuckled. He would be happy to take the family's money and watch as this overly confident kid failed.

Daniel breezed through the exams, finishing ahead of everyone in every examination. In each case, when finished he confidently stepped to the front of the room, curtly nodded to the exam hall supervisor, dropped his papers, and turned to walk swiftly out.

Stanford

With successful program challenges and the GPA needed for eligibility, Daniel started filling out application packages. When Angelo looked them over, he noticed the start dates on each application were all the same. Knowing Daniel did not make blatant mistakes, he was quick to question it. "Are you actually planning to take these programs simultaneously?"

"Yes. I want to gain as much knowledge as quickly as possible. The benefit of encompassing so much at once is that there will be things I find and apply across each subject. I won't have any issues completing term papers and meeting workload requirements. I will complete thesis papers and research presentations in all the disciplines ahead of schedule. At the same time, I will concentrate on my primary goal of gaining the knowledge I need to get to the next stage in my plans."

Angelo tried to explain that students were not permitted to float between graduate programs, but seeing that unmistakable look in his young friend's eyes, he didn't push the matter. Instead, he chose to let things play out as they would. Angelo knew reality would set in when Daniel's applications were rejected. The boy would realize life was not as malleable as he imagined, and a part of Angelo looked forward to it. Then it hit him: *What did he say? The next stage in his plans?*

"Daniel, what plans are you talking about?" he asked.

Daniel smiled. "It's time to change the world, Angelo. Remember the stories you told me on our walks? The stories about the world's imbalance and how the few create war, disease, and poverty to control the masses? It made me see how I can help the world break free."

Angelo just smiled, knowing that if anyone could do it, this amazing boy would be the one.

When Daniel told Samantha the news, she got sad. They had become very close friends, spending almost all of their time together, and felt a connection that was strange and indescribable to her. She feared it would be lost when he went away to university.

"I want to learn genomics and biology," Samantha said. "I want to find a way to modify grass and trees to give them the ability to grow faster, taller, and with less water. Maybe by modifying some plants to enable them to feed on pollution in very arid climates, we can fight global warming." She avoided the news that Daniel was planning to go away as soon as he got accepted into school.

"I agree, Sam. Something needs to be done to help reverse mankind's effects on the world. I have a few ideas myself, one of which is to fund your research whenever you are ready to seriously begin."

When she heard that, she was thrilled and forgot her worries about his going away.

"You know, we need to find a way of somehow overturning those working from the shadows, those controlling the money, food, energy, and health services. They suppress every emerging group that threatens their power, and I believe they have serious plans to depopulate the planet." Daniel confided.

He admired how driven Samantha was. He felt she was the only person near his age who could even remotely keep up with his thinking.

She, on the other hand, felt their sharing of ideas was more a time where Daniel reflected on his own thoughts. She cherished the way he allowed her a window into his mind. He always tried to describe complicated concepts in simplified ways that she could comprehend. Sometimes he would describe his thoughts and ask her if she thought he had missed anything or if she saw a way he could look at it differently. He always waited patiently, waiting until she thought of something.

She feared he might think her perspective juvenile or stupid, but almost every time, after hearing her viewpoint, he went silent, pondering her answer. She enjoyed watching him think hard and loved the way he looked at it from her viewpoint. More times than she could remember, when he had considered her comments and applied it to his thoughts, he would say, "And that is why you're my best friend, Sam. You think of things from a point of view that I often miss."

He promised they would stay friends forever; they would talk over video chat as much as possible, and he swore they would reunite when he was done at the university.

Sam was still sad. She knew he would be too focused on studies to allow for their regular conversations to continue. When he told her about all the programs he was planning to do simultaneously, she knew for certain she would become a distant memory. She feared he would never get around to even thinking about her, let alone talking with her, but at the same time she understood that what he was attempting to do was nearly impossible, and something inside her knew they would come together when it was all done.

She planned to focus on her own studies, to spend most of her time researching and taking extra courses after finishing her required schooling. She used it to push away the sadness, and she held on to her faith that their friendship would be interrupted only for a short few years.

Daniel submitted his applications to Stanford a week later, sending off twelve packages to different departments with the hopes of being accepted into all of them.

Within a week—and to everyone's surprise—he was granted interviews with the department heads from each program to which he had applied.

Angelo was flabbergasted. He thought for sure they would have declined at least some of the applications. *Interviews for admission in every faculty?* Apparently, Daniel's reputation was becoming known. *Maybe they were thinking to convince him to commit solely to their department. Or maybe they were unaware that he had applied to more than one program.*

Angelo knew how universities and their faculties worked. Something totally out of the ordinary was happening, but even so, there was no way Daniel was going to be admitted into more than one program at the same time. Chuckling to himself, he headed to the guesthouse to fulfill his promise and join his wife for some personal time.

They sat on the porch of their private guesthouse, with an amazing view—from a quaint and private terrace overlooking the distant ocean horizon. Sunset was their favorite time of day, a time when they sat with wine or tea and watched the light spill over the landscape, watching as the sun dropped below the horizon. There was so much peace here, and they felt so grateful for the generosity of the Thoth family.

Over the next few days, Daniel replied to all the pre-acceptance letters, confirming he would attend interviews with each department.

When he arrived to meet the department heads, he saw their disbelief. He understood full well they had not grasped how young he really was and laughed inwardly at their reactions. In every case, though, he quickly changed their views by speaking with articulate insight on each subject, and from one interview to the next, he gained more and more confidence.

They all had the same first question: "In what order do you plan on tackling the twelve programs for which you have applied?"

It was a question he expected and wasn't afraid to be honest. He would pause for effect, as if to give it thought, and then say, "My plan is to complete all twelve graduate programs over the same time it would normally take an honors student to finish one. I don't mean to seem overly confident, but I feel I likely will complete the requirements and produce discoveries in many of the programs."

After stating his intentions, he would observe their reactions. He felt he could see their minds mull over what seemed the insanity of a naive little boy and tried to keep up with their thought processes. In each case their initial response was similar. One after the other, they explained how it was impossible for anyone to do what he was proposing, and in each case their answer was that they would never allow it.

Once again, he had expected this reaction and came prepared. "Yes, to you it must appear that I am just a naive little boy with dreams of grandeur, some of which, in fact, is true. I admit I dream big and may not see every obstacle I will face. But I did complete eight bachelor's degree challenges and obtained one of the highest grade point averages in the country in less than five months. So let me spend my money and take this risk, and if I can pull it off, then you will be the ones who saw brilliance and allowed it to strive for greatness. If I fail, then of course you can say that you warned of the risks. I assure you the likely outcome is that Stanford will be the home to something that has never happened and likely will never happen again." He'd spoken in a scholarly tone that left each panel from each department silently convinced.

It was a sight none of them ever had expected—an eight-year-old boy sitting in a big wooden chair, his feet comically nowhere near touching the floor, but when he projected his voice, the intelligence and confidence was unmistakable. Even though it was the voice of an eight-year-old, high-pitched and immature, the verbal composition, inclination, and delivery was captivating, to say the least.

Program heads from each department called him back for second-round interviews. This time they quizzed him and repeatedly explained that just a single program took years, with no time off for even the best students to meet the requirements. They described the demanding schedules that just one program entailed, hoping that it might dissuade him from venturing too quickly into waters far over his head.

As usual, Daniel had done his research on these very issues. He came up with statistics on study schedules and final-paper submissions. He used accurate assumptions to estimate start-to-finish times for students at the top of their programs and knew he could do much better.

With this information, he guessed he would need less than a quarter of the time the other students required. Something inside him said he was on the brink of unlocking a limitless cascade of knowledge, an existential database lurking somewhere in his subconscious.

He showed his statistics to the interviewers and convinced them he would not have a problem meeting requirements in any of their programs. Angelo, his chaperone, was always seated at the back of each session and, for the most part, went unnoticed. He observed the proceedings silently as Daniel handled the questions with a calm and confident ease.

Daniel welcomed his mentor's friendship and guidance, never thinking he would have wanted it any other way. In fact, Angelo proved time and time again an invaluable friend. His past position as a respected professor at the university opened doors only someone with his experience could do, and Daniel knew that without Angelo's support and presence—always reassuring department heads that Daniel was everything he said he was—he might not have had any chance at being admitted to even half of the programs in his sights.

After the second round of interviews, a week passed before the response was issued. The first letter was a selection of grants and scholarships they were prepared to offer him—*a good sign*, he thought, but he would not require them. With his recent windfall from the sale of his software company, along with the licensing and patent rights, he had over $250 million. The second envelope was filled with acceptance letters, and when he saw them his heart leaped with the realization that he really had made it.

Daniel was accepted into every program to which he applied. Angelo could hardly believe it. Susan cried. John laughed and laughed, and Daniel was so happy he almost missed the single stipulation.

He was accepted but limited to start only half this year. In two years, if he was able to stay ahead, he could start the other six programs, if he still chose to do so. The letter also stated there would be no leniencies. Last, the acceptance letter required him to choose which studies he would start first, requiring he notify them within fifteen days. It wasn't an easy decision, but after a consultation with Angelo, he chose to start with mathematics, advanced computer sciences, energy research, particle physics, materials sciences, and nano materials research.

Before starting classes, he purchased a house near the university, a refuge where he could set up a proper study to work on things in private. After seeing a few places, he purchased a house overlooking the Stanford University golf course and began to get the new place ready.

It was a medium-sized home, recently renovated, with an open floor plan on each of the three levels. In the backyard there was a lap pool, his favorite form of fitness. The best feature of the house was the rooftop patio and its view of the golf course and the main campus in the distance. When he first stood up there, he imagined all the discoveries and achievements he would pursue, all the goals he would achieve, and the steps he would begin taking on the march towards save humanity from its current downward spiral.

The basement was perfect. It was one huge open space, ideal for the PLED display system he planned to install. Angelo and Lucia moved with him, Angelo insisting they would not wish for it to be any other way.

When John and Susan learned he was planning to move into a house near the university, they talked long into the night, debating whether or not they should live with him on a permanent basis. After a long back-and-forth, they decided it would be okay to spend a few weekends a month visiting, and leave Daniel to tackle this huge undertaking with as few distractions as possible.

Everything Daniel had accomplished up until this point was by his own determination. It seemed to them he possessed a knowingness of where he was heading and what he wanted—a motivating purpose that did not require their attention or approval and a drive that would never let him fail. They knew deep in their hearts that Daniel was beyond the normal level of humanity. It scared them, but they accepted it, while wondering where it might lead their family.

A few days before he started at the university, Angelo dropped off Daniel for orientation. The older man had expected to accompany him, but when they arrived, Daniel asked if he could go it on his own.

"I understand, Daniel. Confronting things on our own sometimes is how we grow the most. Text me twenty minutes before you are ready, and I will come pick you up. Back at this same spot, right?" He smiled with approval as Daniel got out of the car, proud of a boy he had watched grow into a small yet mighty little man.

As Daniel walked into the courtyard to meet his orientation group, he saw a dark-haired girl holding a sign with his name on it. She sat waiting at the entrance to the Main Quad building in the Memorial Courtyard and, from a distance, he thought she looked nice.

He, on the other hand, stood out like a sore thumb, and when she saw him, she smiled and waved. "Hello, little boy. My name is Brittney, and I will be your orientation guide." She had a kind and intelligent voice and reached down to shake his small hand.

She was the lucky one, selected from a group of top honors students to give Daniel Thoth his orientation. It was a historic day! A boy genius was set to join their ranks as one of Stanford's elite class. It was a huge achievement for any student to be accepted into a doctorate or master's program, and a-part of her thought it might just be a big hoax, but her curiosity pushed her to find out and so she proceeded with the tour.

As they walked to the first building, he looked up at the school's crest above the main entrance and read out the German words. "Die luft der freiheit weht," he said, pronouncing the words with a perfectly inclined accent. Then, without pause, said, "The winds of freedom. Do you know where the unofficial motto for Stanford came from? He was a sixteenth-century poet, scholar, and the leader of the imperial knights of the Holy Roman Empire. His name was Ulrich von Hutten."

The way he pronounced and projected those words surprised her. That was all it took; she was convinced he was most certainly the same boy she'd read about—an eight-year-old who breezed through undergrad essays and final exams like they were college entry forms.

For the remainder of the tour she observed how Daniel took everything in with a silent intensity. When he wanted to know more about something, he asked directly, in a decisive tone that seemed far too sophisticated for a boy his age.

When they completed the tour, there was no doubt in her mind that this boy was one of those brilliant savant kids, the kind you read about but never get to meet. As they walked, she watched how the professors looked at him with awe and respect, welcoming him personally to their programs. It was amazing, she thought, how they acknowledged him with deference, as if expecting to receive his final papers right then and there.

"Daniel, it was a pleasure to be your orientation guide today. I can see that you are someone with unlimited potential, and it would be my honor to be your friend. So if you need anything—someone to talk to or something—just send me a text or an email, and I will help you any way I can."

Over the next three months Daniel completed papers and presentations, proposing what he planned to pursue in all six programs. He took advantage of every available hour, structuring each day with precise sleep and nutrition schedules of exactly eight and a half hours away from study for sleep, food, and exercise in every twenty-four-hour period. Angelo, Lucia, and his parents started getting worried, but as they had agreed at the outset of their son's evident pilgrimage, they let him determine his own patterns.

They found that the best time to talk with their son was over food, an occasion highlighted by Lucia's artfully prepared dishes. They didn't make it down as often as they would have liked, but when they did, they were always eager to hear how he was doing. To their relief, they consistently found that their son was the same person he had always been. Even with the extremely regimented, self-imposed schedule, he was still calm, collected, and analytical with his characteristically unique intellectual charm.

His first papers detailing what he planned to research captured the attention of the academics instantly. Faculty members assigned to monitor the phenom and report on his progress came running to the offices of those who decided what was possible.

Eyes throughout academia—more than he could possibly know—scrutinized him. Academics at the highest levels debated the feasibility and sanity of the concepts he put forward. Behind closed doors, in the smoking rooms of those long standing authorities, Daniel's lack of reality was scorned with cold animosity.

"His theories in particle physics are not possible," they said. His energy research involved elements not found on the periodic table, and his claim that he would solve the holy grail of mathematical formulas, the unifying theory, was too bold.

In an abstract paper, he presented a theory that at the lowest known levels of all particles there was a filament of dark matter holding everything together. He put forward that in those currently undetected frequencies, there could, in fact, be the keys to all matter and potential gateways for the transmission of information over unlimited distances with unlimited bandwidths.

Though, even to Daniel, some of his propositions seemed impossible and pure science fiction, he could not deny the feeling that something told him that there was a way. He focused his mind, searching for answers he knew were there, and rather than casting impossible ideas aside, he narrowed his eyes and opened himself to a limitless bank of memory he felt just beyond his reach.

Weeks passed as he covered mountains of information. He had brought it upon himself, and he rose to the occasion. Exhausted, his head sagged, and his eyes fluttered closed, then opened, as he fought to stay awake; he had to proofread the paper he was writing on quantum well structures. His mind drifted into a haze of exhaustion, and he saw the answers, pieces of the impossible puzzle. Symbols for sacred geometry combined, forming the frequencies needed to peer into the hidden realms of dark matter. It came to him in a moment of unconscious clarity—an array of filaments, their coordinates at the subatomic level moving in a viewport reflection of space, matter moving to any position, anywhere, instantly. "Teleportation," he blurted out, his voice bringing him back to his basement study room.

When his mind cleared, his eyes snapped open, and he swept the desk-sized tablet screen clear. He created a new document and started illustrating what had come to him in feverish scribbles, symbols, combinations, and equations never seen in any textbook. It was beyond anything he ever expected.

When academia saw his latest theoretical postulates, they held nothing back in tearing him down. More than just a small amount of resentment came from his professors. They sat him down for a talk and used their most professorial demeanor. They made it clear he would need to stick more to reality and less to the hopes and dreams of boyish science fiction to continue his studies in their programs.

Daniel saw the tragic truth. He had been terribly naive. It made him realize a plain fact, it would be prudent to keep his most profound findings, theories, and inventions to himself; this decision was made for him. From now on, he would continue his most advanced research in private. The time he spent peering into the dark corners of his mind, exploring ideas of impossible science, and researching what seamed feasible to him, yet impossible to academia, would be his and his alone.

He spent hours each night away from unwelcome onlookers, his eyes locked on the PLED display system covering the walls and ceiling of his downstairs studio. He worked out equations and built simulations, created new particle compounds yet undiscovered, and intensely focused on finding the pieces he would need for the next stage.

As his final computer science program submission, he designed an artificial intelligence research assistant. He named it the Analytics AI, and it provided a way to scan vast bodies of information and isolate key concepts. It also continuously searched for new accredited articles and white papers, parsing them in near real time, cataloging the key data, and notifying him with summarized reports. His AI was invaluable, helping him stay current with any number of subjects he assigned it to research.

He knew he had to continue reaching for the concepts and ideas whispering in the back of his subconscious, but for the academic authoritarians, he presented only their vision of reality. He gave them perfection as they saw it. For those indoctrinated in what they knew, he found it simply a matter of duplicating theories and principles they expected only the most brilliant could understand. *Child's play*, Daniel thought as he finalized yet another paper demonstrating full understanding and insightful perspective on genomic manipulation. In his thesis, he hinted at the usefulness of mapping algorithms to develop effective genetic modifications of human DNA for the prevention of disease and cell degeneration.

But what he hinted at in his final paper only scratched the surface of what he uncovered. What he wasn't telling them was that he created a fully functioning beta amino with an algorithm to analyze and correct cell deterioration. He tested it on his own genome and watched as it modified his cells nearly unnoticeably with just the slightest correction. The beta amino taught his cells to resist the most dangerous diseases. It was an amazing breakthrough, something the world needed, but his inner voice told him to wait.

This would be something to roll out to those joining the movement, and he knew if Big Pharma caught wind of this too soon, they would attack with all their might. In his final paper, he left out the groundbreaking discoveries, only including a portion of his detailed working formula. He deliberately chose to provide a road map, breadcrumbs that one day the most brilliant of open minds might follow, but he did not give the final answers.

His personal experiments constructing the frameworks of concepts that, if fully realized, would one day change everything on earth inspired him to push even harder. The papers he handed in were insightful and on point, sometimes implying potential for greater things but never making claims too far outside the establishment's reality. He would not be so foolish as to repeat his earlier naïveté.

After yet another long day of research and postulation, he quit an hour early to have dinner on the upper deck of his house. When he finished eating, he watched the sun fall behind the horizon, and his mind drifted, relaxed and content.

It was a peaceful night with no wind, and as the sky darkened, he cleared his mind and watched the stars appear. He let his mind wander free and found himself contemplating the far reaches of the universe. It was a topic to which his mind often went when he was fully at peace. He imagined star systems with life-abundant worlds. Images he knew he had never witnessed seemed so clear in his mind. He thought of the stars and their infinite possibilities, their vast distances. An idea came alive as his eyes scanned the clear night sky, and a plan to bring it to life formed. It would be a perfect way to apply research from nearly all the programs he was bringing to completion. It would be a symbol for all those who believed in him and supported him from the very beginning.

The venue was important, and after a short search, he found a huge auditorium with no bookings for weeks. He convinced the owner that when he installed his revolutionary holographic display, there would be people lined up for as far as the eye can see.

Over the next few weeks he fine-tuned software to populate the hologram and calibrated a zero-point light emitter that he'd invented to project the three-dimensional display into midair.

For the computer science program, he developed a real-time, to-scale, spatial map of the Milky Way galaxy. He used the concept his father had used on the ceiling of his room, but he took it to entirely new heights. For this version, he first created an AI to continuously search every information source in the world, seeking out and covertly infiltrating every space agency database and private research program, while staying anonymous by using his personally designed, infinite IP-masking algorithm.

He coined the package *Astros*. It's most impressive feature was a unique characteristic he developed just for this new AI. It learned and improved tracking models for the positions of every known cosmic body in the Milky Way and beyond. Astros, while analyzing and cataloging the immense amount of data, created the three-dimensional models of everything it processed. Using the immense amount of information it captured while crawling the networks of space agencies around the world, Astros populated the real-time three-dimensional map, accurately representing star systems, planets, moons, black holes, and even the asteroid belts in every region where data was available. The very moment anything new was added to any database in the world, Astros listed it, analyzed it and updated the holographic real-time galaxy map. The point cloud it created was filled with billions of clusters of light, atom-sized specs of zero-point energy, all rotating on the axes of their own stars, while slowly rotating around the center of the galaxy.

His holographic projection system utilized the infrared spectrum of light to work magic. It sent out a wall of light in wavelengths completely naked to the human eye until passing exact coordinates in three-dimensional space where different wavelengths crossed, shifting into the visible spectrum for the fraction of time it took to illuminate trillions of unique sparkling atoms of light in midair.

He used the most advanced 3-D printing technologies available to create the orb-shaped projector. Its surface was packed with billions of particle-sized full-spectrum projectors, each capable of casting billions of spatial illuminations using his patented zero-point light-generation technology.

The orb in the center of the auditorium floor was a miracle of technological advancement, and he knew this alone would be a crowning achievement.

It was his way of saying to the world, "Even though an idea seems impossible, it does not mean it is unattainable."

The holographic presentation was astonishing. A three-dimensional map filled the 120,000 cubic meters of the auditorium's airy interior. It sparkled faintly, rotating at the exact fraction of speed relative to its scaled proportions. The hologram maintained a radius of forty meters, an exact replica of our very own spiraling galaxy, all rotating around a central cluster of stars and black holes.

People came in droves, excited to have an intimate experience with the Milky Way. Students, faculty, and professors from every university were the first to have the pleasure of seeing the spectacle, and as they posted their experiences to social media, it became national news. The venue began drawing the attention of major media from across the country, and then the story went international.

After the first few weeks, lined-up crowds snaked through the campus, all of them drawn by his installation. More and more people arrived, and many camped out, waiting for days to get in.

It forced the university's hand; a nationwide news broadcast was issued. Access was restricted to those in the scientific community, and only scheduled viewings for university groups and scientific agencies would be permitted until further notice. Head astronomers, astrophysicists, and program heads from top space agencies around the world came to spend hours studying the map.

At first, their skepticism was palpable toward Daniel's claim that his display was the most accurate representation of the Milky Way on the planet. They worked to see if the data was in any way inaccurate or artistically altered, but after days and days of observations they could verify only that it was as current and perfect in its scaled format as it ever could be. After weeks of analysis, the head of the International Space Agency was quoted as saying, "It matches the most precise measurements the world has on file for location, scale, and mass of all known cosmic bodies in the Milky Way, including some we still do not understand." And then the question came: "How did this preteen university student have the information to create this perfectly accurate representation of the galaxy in the first place?"

The fact that Daniel's star map display contained information that leading agencies had not even analyzed yet—and likely would not begin processing for months—raised red flags. All the space agency directors knew they were behind in processing data and were all too aware they were constantly falling farther and farther behind as data dumps from hundreds of explorer satellites constantly arrived. Thousands of hours of information dropped into databases every few minutes, and with some small knowledge of what these untapped databases contained, there was more than a little confusion about how this display seemed to contain all of it—and more than anyone was even aware.

When the space agency scientists confirmed that somehow Daniel's system showed information not publicly available, they called him into a private meeting.

He knew what they wanted before they asked and was fearful as to how they would react. He decided to be completely honest and told them about the AI he'd developed to run the system and how it accessed the data they believed was securely collecting dust.

The initial reaction from the directors of the space agency to finding that he had hacked their systems was to shut down the display and charge him with securities theft and illegal breaches of secure networks, but before they called it in, they listened to what he had to say. He helped them realize that with this system they could revolutionize how they analyzed their data, and they were smart enough to see that what he was offering was a huge step in the right direction.

After privately expressing their rights under corporate law, making it clear that they could charge him and seize his technology for the breach of their secure networks, they publicly congratulated him with a formal request that he continue his work, and they thanked him for assisting them in better understanding their universe. He was given commendations from NASA, Stanford, and the International Space Confederation for the accomplishment—but there was one stipulation. He was required to license them the patents so they could construct similar installations at their own private facilities at no cost.

The amount of attention that came his way was far more than he wanted. The media vans began parking on campus, and their reporters adopted tactics of lying in wait to interview him between his labs. As well, they frequently pounced on him when he was traveling to and from the school, and it quickly got out of hand.

Angelo was a godsend, always there to push them back, forcing them away in fast and often angry Portuguese. When Daniel was mauled on his way between buildings by a group of overzealous journalists, the university finally stepped in, officially banning the media from campus, but it didn't stop all of them. He finally made a public statement, making it clear that he was not going to take any interviews, and when they refused to stop swarming him between campus and his home, he pressed harassment charges against specific news organizations, making an example for anyone planning to continue their campaign of broadcasting his life to the world.

Finally, with the legal action and the university's backing, the media reps backed off, leaving him to return to his bubble of academic anonymity.

From then on, he kept to himself around the university. He stopped looking to make friends or engage in conversation with any of the students or faculty. Angelo was always there, just like a loyal guard dog, making it difficult for anyone to approach him uninvited, and for a time, Daniel found comfort in his solitude. It was not because he did not want to interact with others; in fact, there was a part of him wanting nothing more than to find friendship. But the focused drive inside him made that a difficult proposition, and so he continued on his path with as few distractions as possible.

He still wished he could find a true friend at the university, someone like Samantha, but they all seemed so overly awed by his accomplishments, only interested in picking his brain to find out what he was planning to work on next, and so he avoided them. Days passed, and he forgot about it, and then out of nowhere he discovered he was not the only kid genius at Stanford.

He started attending a lecture series covering logic for advanced artificial intelligence by a professor whose insightful approaches to solving critical problems in software architecture resonated with him. In the first lecture, he noticed a first-year student, who he discovered was Stas Dimitievich Gurkovsky, a Russian national of fifteen years old. Daniel watched and listened, learning that Stas was way ahead of everyone in the class, and it piqued his interest.

He hacked the school's database, masking his identity with his infinite IP generator, and found that Stas was sponsored by a Russian exchange program that appeared, on the surface, to be much like the Wise Child Group.

The big Russian spoke decent English with a distinctly thick accent and seemed to practice never making eye contact with anyone.

Daniel half listened to the lecture while browsing the school's database to find out more. He dug into the academic scores and saw that Stas was nothing short of brilliant. The lecturer was eloquent and worth listening to, but the revelation that there might be someone he could befriend brought him back to the class much more frequently than he had otherwise planned.

He caught conversations after class, overhearing other students speak in awe and jealousy of the young Russian. They spoke of how his insights and ability to understand concepts came too easily. Apparently, there was rumor that Stas was having such an easy time that he was pre-studying two semesters ahead of schedule.

After attending his fourth lecture in a row, Daniel waited after class. Stas was hunched over, focused on whatever it was he was working on, and Daniel knew it was time. He approached, unsure of how he would introduce himself. Finally, standing right next to where Stas sat, he waited and was surprised that Stas kept his head down, even though obviously noticing Daniel standing right next to him.

Daniel coughed, trying to get his attention, but there was no response. When it started to get awkward, however, the Russian boy whispered, "I am busy. Go away."

Daniel pressed forward and said in perfectly pronounced Russian, "Hello. It is very nice to meet you. I understand you have an exceptional ability for understanding programming languages. Are you willing to take a moment out of your busy schedule to make a friend?"

Stas looked up, grinning, and reached out his hand. "Good to meet you too, Daniel. I know who you are; who doesn't? Your accomplishments at such an early age are inspiring. Yet I am confused. Why are you interested in a freshman's academics?"

Stas laughed. "There is not a single person on campus who doesn't know who Daniel Thoth is. I know you have been watching me, and I have been anticipating this moment. There aren't too many genius kids out there who haven't been snatched up by the shadow corporations, after all. We might as well team up, right?"

From the start of their friendship, Daniel noticed Stas got a little stand-offish whenever asked about his past. There was something he was afraid of telling, something he did not want anyone to find out. Instead of pressing for information, though, Daniel left it alone. He chose to focus on the here and now and worked at building trust. He pursued a course of common interest and the exchange of forward-thinking ideas, and as a team they began looking outward from their bubble of insightful ingenuity.

Over time, Stas noticeably let go of his paranoia, as he saw that Daniel was not seeking to uncover his troubled past. They bounced abstract and impossible concepts off one another, finding solutions to problems that might have taken much longer in the absence of their new collaboration.

Stas was extremely talented at writing artificial-intelligence software, specifically targeting autonomous robotic systems and algorithms for developing code that learned to modify processes and solve difficult engineering problems on the fly. New hardware with configurations mimicking the human brain presented incredible potentials for AIs, and Stas was at the forefront of development for these new platforms, even beginning to challenge the commercial complex with his revolutionary analytics.

Unknown to Daniel, Stas constantly thought of the day his parents would be returned to him. He worried about where he would be sent and who he would work for, hoping for one of the big space exploration companies or a robotics manufacturing company. As long as it was programming for orbiting satellite maintenance drones or asteroid mining and prospecting projects, he felt he would be happy. But he knew deep down that he would always be at the bidding of the people who held his family, and he resented them for it.

When Daniel finally brought Stas to see his personal research and development studio in the Palo Alto house basement, Stas was absolutely blown away. He had heard about this PLED technology, but seeing it firsthand was incredible, and he was honored by Daniel's trust in him.

As they stepped into the room, the polished floor, walls, and ceiling came alive. They sat in recliners facing the main display wall, and Daniel started the tour. He showed things he had never shared with anyone, and when he activated the newly installed holographic projector, symbols, sacred geometry, packets of code, and strings of DNA appeared in front of them.

"Stas, I am going to need your help with the company I am forming. I trust you as much as my family, and let's be honest—where else am I going to find someone with your kind of talent for developing software? Sure, I am good at it too, but there are other things I need to focus on, and there is a lot to do. What do you think?"

Stas was silent, his mind going straight to the invisible hand holding his family hostage. *Who knows what they will require of me?* he thought as a cold feeling went through his core.

Countless implications ran through his mind. He realized the magnitude and possibilities. It would potentially be the greatest opportunity of his life, but at the same time, the cold feeling held him back.

What if they ask me to betray my friend? The question bounced through his mind. He knew they would ask, and then he would have to do it! "Oh dear!" he said aloud, realizing too late that maybe he had slipped up.

Daniel was startled by his friend's reaction. He regarded him with an inquisitive, knowing mind on full alert. Something was not right. He watched Stas lean forward in his chair and put his head in his hands. A nearly imperceptible shudder came from him. *Maybe it's time to dig into his past,* Daniel thought; he knew his friend feared revealing it. Daniel watched and waited as Stas silently sat there, holding his face in his hands. A low moan rose from deep inside Stas. Daniel reached out a hand to touch his big friend's shoulder. "It's all right, Stas. Forget it."

He felt his friend shake and knew it was now or never. "What is it? What's bothering you? You don't have to accept my offer. It's fine, man. Don't worry about it."

At first, Stas was angry, looking up with fear-filled eyes. "They will kill them, Dan. They'll kill them. No one can know; no one can find out. I have to do everything they say, or ..." He trailed off, his head going back to his hands with an uncontrollable shudder.

Stas knew Daniel was the most brilliant and trustworthy person he had ever known, and after a few more minutes, he mustered his strength and told the whole story.

Chapter 8

Thomas Stiedly

The cold, hard man reclined in his big leather chair behind his large dark-mahogany desk, his feet propped up on it. A feeling that his world was about to crash down all around him filled his mind. He stared up at the ceiling, his thoughts churning. Anger, fear, a keen killer's instinct—these emotions had been set loose by a phone call that ended over an hour before. They had called. Those from whom he was never supposed to hear. *When you hear from the directors, you know your life hangs in the balance.*

Through clenched teeth he cursed, "How? How could this have happened? This prodigy, this fountain of innovation—how could that boy have slipped through our nets?"

Too late; it was far too late for them to act now. The boy was far too public. "Damn," he swore. "Gad damn!"

A large bottle of eighteen-year-old Macallan sherry oak scotch sat empty next to an ashtray filled with the stubs of fine cigars. Today's revelation had called for one particularly special Cuban, its final embers still sending a thin trickle of white smoke up into the room's high, dark ceiling. He stared, bleary-eyed, recalling every detail from the call. It had been short and to the point. They were not happy at all, not one bit. A chill went through him as he recalled those cold, harsh voices.

It was worse than just a small mistake. People contracted around the world to catch genius kids like this, were depended on, and when deemed negligent in their duties, they would pay with their lives. Entire families would find themselves bagged and tagged, shipped to whatever sad fate awaited them, all because of an indirect connection to the organization and the need of those in the shadows to punish any who failed them.

People with contracts from his organization enjoyed a surplus of money and privilege, but the penalties that went along with these benefits were swift and severe. *Well*, he thought, *the bastards deserve it! They've been lazy and negligent.* This was no small screwup. This was no ordinary kid genius. This kid was unnatural, and the reports said the boy had groundbreaking ideas with the ability to make them a reality—ideas that would jeopardize everything the corporation and its founding families have controlled for the last handful of centuries or more.

They could kill the boy, they had said, but with so many people protecting him and so much media surrounding him, they decided to wait. Somehow, the boy was in Stanford University. "That damn school and their altruistic ideas of protecting those with foresight and goals for ethical business," he cursed. It was one of the few schools of higher education that was aware of their organization and actively working against them.

His people were always trying to infiltrate the university, but nearly every one of them had been identified and persecuted, charged with fabricated crimes that somehow the authorities of the university always made stick. It seemed they had real backing to stand up to the organization, backing that could effectively resist. "The Wise Child Group," he murmured. The directors had been clear; he was to monitor the boy as closely as possible and flag anything he was working on that threatened their control.

Thomas knew he was lucky to still have his head and would do everything they asked of him, no matter the cost. Terrible things would happen to people because of this mistake, but he knew that if they wanted him dead, a wet squad would have shown up already.

For now, people with eyes on the boy would be kept as high-priority assets. Satellite surveillance was being put in place, and on-the-ground surveillance would be established off campus near the boy's temporary house. They would be everywhere.

Over the next six months Daniel noticed changes in the people around him. It seemed they became suspicious and watchful of his every move. Something told him they were looking for things he might not be including in his papers, and he decided to streamline the completion of his programs, keeping anything beyond what science said was possible, hidden away in his head or fragmented as abstract details in various papers.

A few weeks after Stas told Daniel the tragic truth of his past, his big Russian friend came to him at his personal study with terrible news.

"They know we are friends, Dan. They know everything, although I don't think they know I am here right now or that I have told you my secret. They want me to spy on you! They want me to tell them what you are working on and what you have planned. I don't know what to do! If I don't do what they say, they will hurt my parents!"

"Don't worry, Stas. Tell them everything. Don't hold anything back. I am serious; you can even tell them I have asked you to come work for me when you're done with school. I'm sure they will love that. We will feed them some misleading information and you can promise them my most hidden secrets until we are finally ready to free your parents." Daniel confidently responded.

Before wrapping up his house in Palo Alto, he spent two months virtually downloading an entire bachelor's degree of corporate business law into his mind. He knew he would need the preparation before setting up the corporation that would be the vehicle in achieving his first set of goals.

He turned thirteen and completed his scholarly adventure, a display of brilliance that even those who knew of what he was capable thought completely impossible.

When the move was done and Daniel was back at the family house, Susan handed over a box filled with envelopes—letters that had started arriving months earlier from large corporations and agencies all around the world. Daniel looked at his mom with an inquisitive eye.

"We thought it best to wait until you were done with your studies at least. This way, you can look at them all at once." She paused and then said tentatively, "And we are hoping you will come home for a while and take some downtime before running off to conquer the world."

It was true; the box of letters proved to be full of offers for all sorts of positions in the most prestigious research facilities around the world. Some of the salary offers were far higher than could be expected by the most veteran and most brilliant scientist working in the private sector, but he was not interested. There were government agency letters stating he was required to provide white papers on all of his processes in order to have patents approved, and he laughed at their demands.

Then one of the envelopes caught his eye, one that he didn't throw on the garbage pile. It was stamped with the symbol of the Pentagon, representing one of the highest levels of government, and he pocketed it before letting anyone see.

Stepping into his old room for the first time since leaving for university was the best part about coming home. The moment he crossed its threshold the walls lit up, loading the newest environment—one of his very own designs. A vibrant luminescence jumped out from the walls, an effect that always awakened his mind. A sharp blue-on-black stream of database displayed, as lattices of connections between node-based information packets flew past. He voiced a command: "Stanford," and the ocean of information turned with a smooth easy flow. The display stopped in a quadrant where the program he created to manage everything he worked on at the university was located. Daniel smiled. It was nice to be home!

After a few days, he found himself sitting on the back patio, relaxing and enjoying the sky as the sun crested the horizon, its light casting a wash of color that brought a comforting feeling only this place could do. He thought of the offers from various agencies and companies. To him, it was a joke. He knew that aside from a very few, they were all linked to the ones he wished to topple. He considered the money they offered and thought about where that money came from.

A sound from the kitchen caught his ears and snapped him out of the daydream. He stood, shook out his legs, and lazily walked back into the house and into the living room, where his parents, Lucia, and Angelo were all deep in conversation.

He paused in the entrance and was aware that he had gone unnoticed. He slowly stepped further into the room and watched. Who would notice him first? When they turned, he saw that his mother had been crying. She had dark smudges under her eyes and her demeanor made it plain to see that she was very upset.

She wiped at her face. "You're running off to work for one of those big fancy technology companies, aren't you," she accused.

Daniel was surprised but held his tongue and smiled. "No, Mom, I was thinking about staying where I belong and starting work on building a technology company of my own right here."

Lucia burst into rapid Portuguese, exclaiming what a wonderful moment this was and how everyone was going to be back together for good. "Oh boy!" she said. "We will have a feast, we will have wine, and all of our friends should come!" On and on she rejoiced, though only Angelo and Daniel really understood a single word of it.

John, hearing the news, fought back tears of his own. He felt a rush of pride for his son and was excited by the prospects this new project would bring. Susan gripped his hand, her sadness turning into tears of joy. She looked to John, and together they knelt to embrace Daniel, their genius son.

When the embrace ended, he explained his plans, and they all noticed his assertive and decisive tone. Susan knew that whenever he used that voice there was little that would stand in his way.

"There was one letter," he began, "a letter that we should handle as soon as possible. It has a summons to a meeting that I feel is very important for me to attend, and I would like you, Father, and you, Angelo, to accompany me to the White House, where we will meet and speak with some very powerful and important people. As well, my future is here. I want to build a tech company to rival the largest in the world. I want to see those who use their power for corruption lose their hold on the world, and I want to see humanity awaken and be freed from their uneducated chains."

He pulled the envelope from his back pocket, the only one from the countless pile he planned on acknowledging. They saw the document with the seal of the president of the United States, the head of the FBI, and the stamp of the director of the Department of National Security, all clearly marked at the bottom of the page.

He explained briefly the implications of the letter, and as they listened, they all noticed how he spoke like one with worldly experience.

The letter stated clearly that Daniel would be allowed six months following the completion of his studies at Stanford University to reply and attend a closed-door meeting with the director of the FBI, Mr. Gregory Sylinger; the head of the Department of National Security, Mr. Ryan Brennan; and the president of the United States. He was summoned, it said, to discuss Daniel's intentions, and he would be an honored guest. It concluded by stating that Daniel was considered possibly one of the brightest minds ever born into humanity, and it hinted that Daniel might be at risk of being targeted by those who viewed his potential as a threat to certain interests.

It was agreed that Daniel, Angelo, and John should immediately call the White House and arrange travel. They were given a chartered flight to Washington, D.C., and were scheduled to attend Daniel's summons.

Daniel, in the company of his father and Angelo, arrived at the White House guest reception gate in a government-issued SUV less than two days after reading the letter. When they arrived, and after a thorough security scan and secondary authorization, they were admitted into the White House and guided to the room where they waited for the meeting to start.

It was the intention of the president, the FBI director, and the head of the Department of National Security to make the meeting with Daniel be restricted to just the four of them, but after Daniel made his case, an agreement was made that John and Angelo could attend with stipulations. The first was that they were to say nothing unless directly addressed by the three men conducting the meeting, and the second was that nothing said in the meeting was to be repeated to anyone, including their wives or closest friends.

When they first entered the boardroom, Daniel was instructed to sit in the single chair on one side of the dark hardwood table. His father and Angelo were pointed to chairs lining the wall directly behind him.

Fewer than ten minutes passed before Mr. Sylinger, the president, and Mr. Brennan entered from the door on the far side of the room.

Mr. Brennan began the meeting formally by reminding everyone that what they were about to discuss fell under the strictest and most sensitive of nondisclosure agreements.

Mr. Sylinger cut in. "Son, we want to make sure you are safe. We know about the kids who have been taken; the world's governments know, but there is very little we can do. The ones who take them convert them into their own highly motivated operatives, who then infiltrate all levels of law enforcement, education, and government. They have been doing it for years, and their power is not something any of us can risk going up against."

Before Mr. Sylinger could continue his description of the dark and scary backstory of those controlling the establishment, Mr. Brennan started again. "I have been following you ever since your enrollment in the Wise Child Group, an organization all three of us support in every way we can. I even went to the trouble of making sure your public file stayed ordinary, to prevent you from being targeted by those we cannot rightly confront due to the power they truly have."

Hearing this, Daniel realized part of the reason he had made it this far was because of these three.

Next, the president reinforced what his fellow patriots so adamantly presented. "Son, we want to make sure of your continued protection and safety, but now that you have become a brilliant public figure we do not believe the same covert tactics that have been so effective up until now will do any good. It is our recommendation that, for whatever course you choose to take, you hire a private security firm, one that you can trust and one that will be committed to protecting you, your family, and your friends."

Mr. Brennan queried, "What are your intentions, now that you have finished your academic career, my boy? We know you have received countless offers from major corporations, so what is it that you plan to do? Our one major concern is that you keep your tech on our soil. We would not like to see other countries get hold of your groundbreaking advancements before our own military complex and tech industry get first crack at it."

Daniel calmly replied, "Before answering your first questions, I would like to thank you for informing me about the kinds of risks my family may face moving forward. Thank you for helping me stay under the radar up until now. My plans are to continue research into new forms of energy generation, information transfer technologies, environmental cleanup technologies, and advanced 3-D printing techniques. I see a bright future for the world and humankind as a whole. I want to take away the power of those manipulating the world's financial markets, creating war and poverty, and manufacturing disease and mental disorders, all for their own financial gains and all at the cost of so many suffering people."

John and Angelo saw the three men of influence all nod, changing their postures from authoritative to accepting. They listened to Daniel describe his long-term plans to take down those pulling the strings of their government and nearly all governments of the world, and they liked the sound of his goals.

They won Daniel's trust from the very beginning, and so, as they neared the end of their meeting, he decided to bring up Stas and his parents.

"My friend's parents are being held captive to control him. He is a genius and a close friend who I want to have as a big part of the new tech company I will be starting this year. I promised Stas that I would never betray his secret, but I trust you. I need to get them out of captivity so Stas can be free to work with me in taking down these criminals and their organizations!" He described everything Stas told him, detailing where he had been taken and where his friend's parents might be.

The three men looked at one another in a silent consultation. "We will do what we can, son. In fact, I promise you that we will get them back," the president vowed in a serious tone and with the resolve of a man who knew what it was like to get pushed around by those controlling his government from the shadows. "We will get Stas's parents back, Dan. We know of their facilities and have had our sights on several of them. They are targets we have wanted to take down as a way to covertly strike back at the Russian arm of this organization. We will need some pictures of them, of course, and likely will be ready to move within the next two months."

After the meeting, Daniel, John, and Angelo left the White House with a sense of urgency. It was obvious they needed to contract a security firm right away, and at the same time, all three of them felt a sense of triumph in the knowledge that Daniel had the unofficial support of these very powerful figures.

When they got home, Susan and Lucia peppered them with questions, and they gave the scripted answers to cover up what they truly had discussed. The idea that the president, the head of the FBI, and the head of the Department of National Security just wanted to meet and talk with Daniel was more than enough explanation. They described the White House and the president in every detail, telling of his stoic secret service agents and the extensive security checkpoints they experienced. Lucia, uninterested with it all, decided they should all have something to eat and pulled Susan toward the kitchen.

The next day, Daniel got straight to work on finalizing the new tech company's registration. He chose United Earth Technologies as the name, a name that held a lot of meaning for him. It reflected his vision to change the world, and as he wrote it, he hoped he would be successful. Next, he and his father contacted the three security firms Mr. Sylinger recommended and set up interviews.

Samantha finally came over, and together, along with the ever-inquisitive cats, Tom and Jerry, they spent the hot summer's day walking around the property, catching up and laughing about old jokes only they knew. They talked of times and moments that stood out while Daniel was away and speculated on what their futures might hold.

He told her stories from his time at Stanford, whispering conspiratorially about how some academic leaders tried to direct him toward sticking to only what they thought was possible.

She told of the few boys she hung out with and laughed about how she lost interest just about as quickly as anyone could.

He told her about Stas and how he would join them soon. He paused and then forced out the next words: "As soon as he completes his program." He thought it best not to speak the hidden truth. The two big cats followed them everywhere, playfully chasing one another through the lines of trees, disappearing and then pouncing from behind hedges, excited to be back at the family property.

It is so nice to be home, he thought, realizing just how much he missed Samantha and the wide-open space.

Two days later the interviews with the security teams began. John, Angelo, and Daniel sat in the field house on the northwest corner of the property and waited. Each team was given an exact time with GPS coordinates in their invitation package as an easy prerequisite for attending the interview. When the first team arrived, four large men, led by a silver-haired leathery-skinned man, silently walked in. They came across as very professional and highly recommended by Mr. Sylinger and Mr. Brennan. It turned out, though, that their teams were engaged in several projects, which gave Daniel and his father pause, and so they declined to put forward an offer.

The next team arrived in two large six-door trucks with tinted windows, huge tires, and aftermarket suspensions, giving them that beefy off-road look. The team members piled out and set up a perimeter, all of them wearing full kits: body armor, assault weapons, dark gray Kevlar, and carbon padding along their arms, elbows, and legs. Two of the group broke off and entered the small building, the leader lifting his tactical helmet from his head to hold it under his arm before greeting Daniel and his father and the other, who stood firm at the door.

Dillon Samuelson's chiseled features and eyes seemed to bore right through them and impressed both Daniel and John. John though, immediately felt familiarity in the man; he stared, unable to put his finger on why he recognized him but the feeling just would not go away.

Seeing John's eyes, the man smirked and gave a knowing look. Slowly, John opened his wallet and slipped a picture of his brother Bryan's special forces team out from behind another card. In the picture, they were clad in their gear and ready for their next mission, polished and crisp. It was the last picture taken of his brother before he was killed in action more than fifteen years earlier. It didn't take long for John to recognize the strong, hard-nosed man standing next to Bryan in the old picture, and when he looked up and saw the spitting image of the man now waiting to be addressed a wash of emotion nearly broke through his stoic and professional attitude.

Bryan used to talk of his team and its leader, telling how Dillon Samuelson was one of the best he'd ever worked with. He was proud to be on a team whose leader went to bat for his guys and, whenever possible, stood for doing what was right. John decided to stay silent and slipped the picture back into his wallet. He realized it would be best to keep the recognition to himself, and let Daniel conduct the interview with an unbiased view.

Dillon's team turned out to be a very capable bunch, all of them having served in Delta Force, Navy SEALs, or SAS Special Forces before moving on to the more lucrative private sector. "My team is currently looking at several options. We prefer clients needing protection, rather than the all-too-common clients with unethical motivations." Dillon didn't hide the fact that in the past his team had been involved in those kinds of contracts, which always meant more money but also meant more risk. "We are all here because we want to give back and help those who would otherwise be the victims of those with no problem seeing innocent people get killed to protect their bottom line," he stated with finality and confidence.

When they left, John told Daniel that he'd recognized Dillon and expressed how impressed he was with that group. Daniel looked at the photo and then back to his father. "This is a picture of your brother, the one who died in action, isn't it?" Daniel asked.

"Yes," John replied. "Bryan always trusted Dillon with his life, and I think we can trust him with ours." He remembered the letter from Dillon that told of the firefight—a nighttime action with a band of insurgent rebels; they'd been pinned down with no chance, when Bryan bravely sacrificed himself to save them all from capture, torture, and death.

Daniel went silent, thinking. He liked the men from the security team and felt they would be a good fit. He knew it was right and made the decision before the next team arrived. When the next group walked in, he wrote a check covering their expenses and explained in no uncertain terms that a decision already had been made.

After returning to the main house, he went to his room and positioned his new hover chair directly in front of the video call application on his wall display. He called Dillon on the personal number given to him at the end of the interview. Moments later, Dillon was looking back at him with a professional yet surprised expression.

"I thought it would be your father contacting me," Dillon commented.

Daniel smiled. "I can understand why, Mr. Samuelson, as I am aware of the history you have with our family, but if you choose to accept my offer, I will be your employer. I hope that is all right with you."

"You know, I had a hard time not bringing up your uncle in the interview. Bryan was a good friend, and he is still missed. I saw the recognition in your father's eyes almost immediately. Of course, it's strange to be taking orders from a thirteen-year-old, but your reputation precedes you, and yes, we will accept the offer. Thank you."

Daniel nodded, acknowledging Dillon's acceptance, and explained more about the job. "I don't expect there to be very much excitement in the short term, but who knows what to expect, right? We will need anti-surveillance measures immediately to keep unwanted threats from looking in on us. Of course, you and your team are professionals, and I am sure you will take care of all that. I hope this contract won't be too boring for your highly experienced team."

Dillon smiled. "To be honest, my boys could use a contract where they are not being shot at from sunup to sundown, and yes, we will take care of everything. When do we start?"

"You just did. I'd like to have you onsite today. Please supply your own covert accommodations for the time being until the main campus is ready."

"Agreed," Dillon replied, and they ended the call.

Daniel felt even more confident in the decision. He felt the Samuelson security team would be able to effectively secure his company's technologies and, at the same time, provide excellent protection for his family and friends.

Dillon's men moved in covertly on the first night, starting at over five kilometers outside the property's perimeter, watching, listening, and slowly moving in. On the third night, they identified a caravan parked up on a hill with an elderly couple. They were fronting as retired travelers, which proved to be a lie, and were instead revealed to be an advanced monitoring and recording team. Their instruments pointed at the house and fed everything into a real-time satellite uplink. *Someone out there is seriously keeping tabs,* Dillon thought as the call came in, and he gave the order without hesitation. *Better to kill off the roaches before they multiply,* he thought.

The covert enemy team was taken silently, and their caravan was stripped and burned. Unknown to any of the Thoth family, the two evidently highly trained operatives were interrogated until they finally confessed that those who were interested in the Thoth family were above any of their pay grades. When they broke and gave up who they were and why they were there, they lashed out, threatening the men inside the interrogation van. "All of your lives are now forfeit, just for being involved." The restrained man cursed and subsequently got a firm fist to the face for his trouble.

Daniel, from the outset, ordered there was to be no killing unless absolutely necessary, and so when the interrogation was complete, two of Dillon's team secretly transported the two spies out of the country, leaving them wearing only their underwear in the slums of Haiti.

Dillon reported his findings in a meeting he requested with John and Daniel, following the interrogation and disposal of the offenders.

"We caught two people conducting surveillance on your property from the high road. They were trained operatives and, by the sounds of it, contracted by an organization we have found to be as dirty as they come. I will be honest; I didn't think this job was going to be all that exciting, but after finding these two, seeing their gear, and hearing the threats they offered, I think we may be in for some excitement after all," Dillon respectfully conveyed.

"Where are they now?" John asked.

"Oh, don't worry; we didn't kill them. We just sent them to a bad place. They'll probably make it out, but they might not. One way or the other, their employers will not be happy with them," Dillon replied.

The next stage in getting things rolling was to find office space for the new tech company. Accompanied by his father, Angelo, and Dillon, Daniel toured facilities throughout Silicon Valley and up the coast into Washington, Oregon, and even more inland. After searching for days, nothing seemed to match up with what Daniel was looking for.

"It would be better if this main office was a little closer to the family's primary residence. We need to avoid splitting up the security team, after all, and don't you want to spend your nights at home, Daniel?" Dillon offhandedly pointed out.

With Dillon's suggestion, Daniel realized how blind they had been. The idea was for him to be home, not off in some facility or living in yet another house far away from his family.

That night over dinner they discussed the dilemma. John sat silently, thinking of the implications of this new venture his son was pursuing. He thought that maybe he should try to talk Daniel out of it. Their family did not need any more money; they were very well off. His PLED installation company was doing more business and growing faster than expected, and Daniel's software deal brought in more than they would ever need. Deep down he wanted to persuade his son to just be a boy and do things a child would do. But he knew the simple fact; Daniel was meant for greater things, and so instead of trying to convince him to forget his goals, he chose to help solve the puzzle of finding the ideal location for a facility to house his son's future inventions.

He looked up. "What about that huge parcel of land up the road, Dan? There's that old rock quarry and areas of that landfill that are no longer in use. Wouldn't it be better to design your own facility? I mean, you could custom build it, and my old friend's industrial construction company is looking for work. I hear things are slow these days, and it's less than twenty-five minutes from our house!"

It would cost more to build a custom facility, but he knew how much Daniel was making off his patent royalties, and his son had over $500 million in his accounts, which likely would be more than enough to purchase the land and complete construction. After proposing his idea, Daniel's eyes lit up with the realization that it was by far the best option, and with that, they all agreed that tomorrow they would find a way to make it happen.

Over the next few weeks, they purchased the abandoned rock quarry and adjacent parcels of land, right up to the borders of the local landfill. Dan didn't hesitate in getting the design started for the new facility, and after walking his new property to get the lay of the land, he threw out the first design with the realization that it would be far better to excavate and bury the facility underground.

He designed a five-story fortress, each level with over one hundred thousand square feet of research-and-development space. Down the center he incorporated a top-to-bottom atrium, an airy space that would carry sunlight down into the deepest depths of the facility.

Construction started right away. The excavation went quickly, and soon structural steel was being placed. They hired an army of contractors to work day and night, installing plumbing, wiring, lighting, and environmental controls. Teams of technicians from companies supplying the lab equipment scurried through the facility, installing, calibrating, and testing the expensive 3-D printers, server systems, and particle-manipulation chambers. They managed to finish it in only six months of construction, and Daniel paid out huge bonuses to the contractors who played the biggest rolls in completing it so quickly.

When finished, the only evidence of the underground facility was the curved nickel glass panels that encased the entire top floor along with the thirty-foot bay doors, which would receive large deliveries of equipment into the lower levels.

The landscape around the facility was leveled by pushing the excavated materials to the perimeter, where a huge berm was formed around the entire property. Along the ten-foot-wide top of the berm they planted two rows of Leyland cypress trees, which would grow three feet per year and fill out considerably as they matured. Three small modern homes were built in the central area of the property near the dome of the main facility. The last critical build was the gatehouse and security gate, which a team began manning twenty-four hours a day.

Natalya Gurkovsky rolled out of bed and softly walked down the hall of her comfortable cottage home. She and her husband had been in captivity for nearly five years and were accustomed to it. There was nothing to complain about; they were fed well, didn't have to work, and enjoyed walking the trails in the sections of forest inside the fence.

But they were still hostages, held captive to ensure their son did everything those holding them asked him to do. They missed seeing Stas in person and looked forward to the thirty-minute video calls once per week, but it wasn't enough. As she washed her face and brushed her teeth to start yet another day, she thought how she would give up the comfortable living and healthy food for just one day with her son. As she turned to head back to the bedroom to force her husband out of bed, the walls shook from an explosion in the main square of the compound.

Alex was at her side in a moment. Machine gunfire bursts came from outside, and they held on to each other. In a panic, they crawled across the floor and into their bedroom, finding a corner beside their bed to wait out whatever was going on. The clapping noise of a helicopter cut through the gunfire, and another explosion shook the small cottage. They looked to each other in the hope that the other would figure out what was happening, but neither could hazard a guess. Moments later, their front door crashed open, and men wearing unmarked SWAT gear rushed in.

"Are you Alex and Natalya Gurkovsky, parents of Stas Gurkovsky?" the lead armored man called, stepping into their room like a professional accustomed to this kind of action.

"Yes. What has our son done?" Alex responded in a contemptuous voice as he craned his head up to look at the man who spoke in strangely accented Russian.

"Please—we don't have a lot of time. We are here to take you to him. Come with us, please. Come quickly," the lead man said.

There was no hesitation from the elderly couple. They sprang to their feet and followed the team out to the chopper, where they climbed aboard, noticing other choppers at some of the other houses. Then Alex looked toward the central building, where their jailors lived. It must have been the most recent explosion; the main building was engulfed in flames, and the bodies of their captors lay unmoving throughout the yard.

As they lifted off, Natalya looked at Alex with satisfaction, and Alex looked back with vengeful delight. "We have been saved, my darling," Alex silently mouthed. Neither of them with any clue why or how this had come to pass, but they were happy to see their captors lying in their own pools of blood. It was a good day.

They were transported out of Russia to the United States and found themselves housed in similar accommodations until finally being reunited with their son.

Daniel found out when Stas and his parents arrived on the doorstep of his family home, just weeks after construction of the new facility was completed.

Daniel looked at his friend with a serious expression. "Good timing, Stas. We just completed construction. Your parents can pick one of the houses on the main compound, and you guys can call that home. Trust me; you will be happy. They are as modern and well finished as they come. Glad you and your parents are safe. I hope you are ready for what is to come."

Chapter 9

United Earth Technologies

Two weeks before Daniel turned fourteen, the new facility went online. Stas was even more excited than Daniel, eagerly anticipating the moment he would first log into the supercomputers in the belly of the building and begin developing their platform.

During the construction, state-of-the-art servers boasting over 125 Zeta FLOPS of processing power, one trillion terabytes of local random-access memory, and three times that in storage were installed. The hardware for the servers alone cost more than the entire construction of the facility, but they both knew it was worth it and would be crucial in their efforts to achieve their goals.

With the new facility up and running, Daniel and Stas went straight to work. Daniel's first order of business was to get the facility off the grid by designing a new power source. From the beginning of the facility's design process, Daniel's goal was to power it from the inside, rather than paying for electricity from the grid. Below the sub-basement, below where the mainframe computers hummed, a bunker was built to house the future power source, and Daniel was eager to put it in place.

He spent a week working on the design; his mind feeding him groundbreaking advancements whenever earth physics principles stopped him from achieving the impossible. He spent hours visualizing, brainstorming, troubleshooting, engineering, and calculating the exact resonant and magnetic formulas for fields that would drive this new kind of power cell.

When Angelo came to see what he was working on and, after looking over the designs. He proclaimed that what Daniel postulated was impossible.

"These ideas of yours, Daniel! For a person who knows the laws of physics like the back of his hand, you should see that the most basic principles prove your designs impossible. You can't have perpetual motion, my boy. It just cannot be done."

Before Daniel kicked him out for being a skeptic in a place where the word *impossible* was strictly forbidden, he clarified that just because it did not work based on the known laws, that did not mean he wouldn't find a way to make it work. "I will force the laws of physics to bend and break while navigating the realms of impossibilities."

When the design was ready, he headed to the second floor and called up the digital blueprints on the main 3-D printer display. When the three-dimensional printing system finished calibrating, carbon powder and metal gasses began fusing into incredibly strong components for the device. The housing was designed to hold in place various electromagnetic resonant frequency emitters and super-strength permanent magnets. The framework of the housing would lock the magnets in place in an exact configuration, creating overlapping fields to drive the reaction and as the prototype neared completion, Daniel saw in his mind exactly how it would all work.

Angelo, skeptical as always, knew something about magnetism and re-peatedly reminded Daniel of the respect he needed to give these natural forces. He also didn't hesitate to remind his young friend that what he was attempting was the same free-energy trickery people had been chasing for decades—quackery never amounting to anything more than conspiracy theories and black boxes that never delivered as advertised.

With the housing for the magnets finished, Daniel used hydraulic arms to place each high-powered magnet in its slot and wired up the resonant frequency emitters. With the magnets in place, the central frame was then lowered into a chamber, where three inches of magnetic shielding of his own design was applied, followed by ten minutes in a chamber that bombarded the powder coating with a host of frequencies designed to align the atoms and solidify the particles, to further restrict the massive magnetic fields from passing beyond the interior of the device.

"So now that you have sixty magnets equaling an aggregate total of three hundred thousand pounds of force, I guess you will want to keep every kind of material with any magnetic properties well away from it, right?" Angelo asked, seconded by Stas, now standing well outside the room and peeking around the doorframe with a very wary look.

Hearing their fears, Daniel laughed and grabbed a handful of steel ball bearings from a jar on the far wall. He looked at them and smiled, turned, and threw the balls on the floor toward the new contraption. Stas and Angelo could not believe their eyes; they watched as the ball bearings literally rolled to the base and bounced off.

"I figured out a configuration of carbon using an exactly tuned lattice of nickel, iron, platinum, and silver, all vectored to block the field from affecting metals and electronics outside of the generator," he boasted.

It didn't stop their fears, though, and jokingly, Angelo spoke in rapid Portuguese. "Okay, okay, so that's a near miracle, but the issue still stands: perpetual motion is just not possible."

Daniel frowned. He walked over to pick up one of the ball bearings off the polished concrete floor, turned, and looked them both in the eyes. "The magnetic field is inert outside of the power cell, but inside it is powerful. I have configured the array of magnets so that the magnitude of pull force is exponentially greater than the aggregate force you pointed out." He paused just long enough to let his words sink in and then turned back to the device where he slapped the ball bearing through the single opening at the top.

They looked to the wall displays that showed streaming footage from an array of three-thousand-frames-per-second cameras installed all along the interior of the torus chamber inside the device. They watched the ball begin zipping around the chamber's interior, and within a few seconds, there was only a streak of acceleration. After fifteen seconds the streak became a solid line, wrapping around the entire inner chamber, until suddenly a loud crash punched through the room as the steel ball broke the sound barrier.

They watched as the line started to glow. The device screamed as the bearing turned from a ribbon of metal into a string of molten steel. Then, the noise dissipated as the solid molten band grew brighter and brighter as the particle speed neared twenty thousand meters per second. As the reaction neared half the speed of light, the plasma inside the chamber turned to dust, and the reaction ended.

They all stood looking at one another, shocked by how quickly that had happened.

For a moment, it was hard to breathe, as acrid black smoke billowed out of the top opening on the device, but within a few minutes, the ventilation system cleared the air, making it comfortable for them to analyze the data collected during the impromptu event.

Angelo and Stas shared a mutual sigh of relief, letting out the heavy breaths they had held since the beginning of Daniel's stunt. They looked at him, both unable to form the questions racing through their minds. Angelo's eyes said he was not happy with the risk Daniel had just taken, and Daniel saw it.

"Perpetual acceleration! *Voila*!" Daniel paused, knowing their thoughts. "I am sorry, guys. That was reckless of me. The device is not decompressed, so with the atmosphere inside the chamber, when the steel ball began looping into perpetual acceleration, it reached a velocity that burned it up. Like a meteor entering the atmosphere. The trick will be to create a vacuum inside the chamber and remove all atmospheric particles that cause friction, and then by using a precisely balanced compound I am designing as the catalyst, an overlapping electromagnetic resonant field will push back against the accelerating compound, constraining the acceleration and harvesting enormous amounts of energy."

Stas and Angelo just looked at each other with expressions of disbelief. "The heck you say," Stas blurted out, a little miffed by the danger they had just been in.

Angelo's eyes went to Daniel, but he said nothing; he only held him with a stern expression and saw that Daniel understood. The pair of them turned to leave in the hope they would not find themselves sucked into a black hole or torn apart in a powerful reaction gone wrong and as they left Daniel called after them, "guys, I'm sorry, alright?".

Daniel shrugged as they left, eager to return to his work and set his mind to the task of configuring the nanoparticle assembler. There was one last modification he needed to apply to the 3-D printing system in order to fabricate the catalyst compound for his power cell to work exactly the way he envisioned.

By taking osmium, iron cobalt, gold, platinum, and neodymium particles, he found a way to produce perfect spheres with incredibly high magnetic and conductive properties. Before turning in for the night, he queued a production of fifty-five-millimeter spheres for tomorrow's first tests.

In the morning the spheres were ready, and he considered doing the first test with half of them. He loaded the insertion module and ran the decompression cycle. The power cell whooshed as the inner chamber purged every atmospheric particle, achieving a perfect vacuum seal. His fingers flashed as he punched in the command to begin the reaction, and the spheres dropped into the chamber.

The moment they entered they snapped to the center of the chamber's inner magnetic field, accelerating just like the steel ball bearing had done the day before. He started typing, quickly activating the resonant field generators designed to constrain the acceleration and harvest the energy. He watched the streaming video out of the corner of his eye and saw energy lance out of the accelerating spheres. Tendrils of white energy flashed into the walls of the chamber, looping the energy down into storage banks.

He was relieved. The opposing force harvesting the energy was working to stabilize the reaction, and he wondered if he could increase the amount of energy the device was outputting. He stepped up the load on the resistant field and saw the energy output triple. He was amazed; the spheres acting as the catalysts of the reaction were traveling at nearly half the speed of light with no visible rise in temperature and no atomic destabilization. He watched the video feeds as arcs of the energy powered into the chamber's inner walls, the swirling glowing tendrils crawling through the air between the balls and chamber walls were hard to look away from, but he did, and then his eyes went to the numerical readouts.

When he brought up the graph showing the energy output, he did a double-take. The current reaction in the chamber was generating 540 gigajoules, enough to power nearly half of Silicon Valley, and he knew he could triple the number of spheres and double their size without any modifications to the setup. He punched in some numbers and saw that if he were to do that, it would exponentially increase the output to where just one of these relatively small power cells could run half the country.

He watched for a while, observing the small fluctuations and ran numbers through a simulator to check for any chances the device would eventually require a restart. He ran one more set of calculations as a one-hundredth blind check. Satisfied, he left the device with the AI designed to keep the reaction stabilized and went to find his friends.

As he walked up the central stairs, Daniel considered the implications of this latest success. With only a dozen of these power cells, United Earth Technologies could corner the entire North American electrical power industry. It was an exciting thought, but he knew it was too soon. They would need to gain a foothold and create enough wealth to stand against the vested interests before making that kind of move. The controlling factions would stop at nothing to block such a revolutionary shift, and he knew they would have to be ready.

He chose to take his time going up the steps and enjoyed the open space of the central atrium. The air was perfectly balanced to feel like a spring day and the space was vibrant and alive, illuminated primarily by the huge curved panels of glass at the surface working to refract light down into every corner of the underground facility.

Samantha, whose passion for plants was unmatched by anyone Daniel knew, had taken on the responsibility of populating the facility with greenery. As he walked, he considered what a splendid job she had done, recalling the first few weeks as she selected the wide variety of plants that now brought so much life to the space.

When he got to the second floor, he found Angelo and Stas in the main developer's suite in front of the circular 180-degree PLED wall display. "I wonder what these guys are up to," he said as he entered the room. "So we all survived. How's it going?"

"All done?" Stas asked.

"It seems so, yep. We will be running completely off-grid and have a surplus of power that could run half of Silicon Valley with just one of those puppies," Daniel replied.

Angelo just shook his head. "So what's left? What's next? Are we going to invent new kinds of space travel and colonize distant worlds, Daniel?" Angelo asked, rolling his eyes.

"Probably, but I think it's time for a little R&R, don't you think?" Daniel replied, smiling. "Why don't you guy's cut out early and come spend the rest of the day by the pool at the main house."

For the next few days, they left the office empty and enjoyed the comforts of the outdoors. They went for a hike around the vineyards and spent hours at the pool, theorizing, imagining, and being free. They spoke of the many things they could achieve and toyed with ideas even they considered science fiction. Daniel enjoyed watching Samantha inspect plants and explain their cycles of life, durability, nutritional characteristics, and how they fit into the sensitive ecosystem of nature.

When they returned to work, their first order of business was to connect the new power cell and take the facility off the grid. That task required help, so they called John, who brought in some trusted contractors to get the contraption down to the basement bunker. Stas went to work putting in security measures on the network, while Daniel began writing the foundation of an advanced AI that would be a building block for their future.

A month passed, and all seemed calm—until a train of black SUVs arrived unannounced at the outer gates of the United Earth facility. They drove up fast and stopped just as quickly. From the lead vehicle, a tall, thin man, wearing a black suit and sunglasses, stepped out. He was followed by two larger men wearing black SWAT gear and carrying assault weapons. The three very FBI-looking men walked to the intercom and demanded the front gates be opened to allow a full inspection of the facility.

Dillon replied to the demands of the thin man through the microphone speaker system in no uncertain tones. "First, what is your business here? We are a private corporation and have committed no crimes, nor have we done anything to warrant a hostile search. Second, could you please identify what branch of the FBI or Department of National Security you are representing?"

The man in the suit smiled like a wolf surveying a herd of sheep. "In accordance with the National Security Act, we have the right to investigate suspicious activity anywhere on American soil," he proclaimed, presenting a dubiously suspicious warrant stating his full authority to conduct a search-and-seizure of the entire property if in any way deemed a threat to national security.

There were twelve SUVs in the train, each capable of carrying six heavily armed men. Dillon questioned the warrant again, demanding this time to see agency identification, but in return he received a threatening, authoritative response. "The agency I represent does not need warrants for entry and will not be trifled with."

Dillon decided it would be best to stall and keep these thugs outside the gate until he got more information, and he wanted Daniel to be involved in any final decisions.

When Dillon's chat window popped up describing the situation at the front gate, Daniel flipped to the security camera feed and set it to full screen. To him, it looked like an entire army, and he instinctively felt a surge of panic. He fought the feeling down by concentrating and thinking objectively. "What can we do?" Then he remembered his friends in the government. The number was still fresh in his mind, and he made the call to Gregory Sylinger as fast as he could.

He got lucky. Sylinger answered on the second ring. "Hello, Daniel, it's nice to hear from you. How can I help you today? Have you called to share some new tech with us, perhaps?" he asked.

Daniel cut straight to the chase, explaining, with obvious fear in his voice, the situation at his facility's gate.

Sylinger listened and then assured him there were no warrants or legal notices issued for the United Earth properties. Daniel worked quickly and sent Sylinger an image of the man's face. He spoke the man's name without pause. "Thomas Stiedly is a known operative working as a corporate security agent, Daniel. These guys should not be pulling a stunt like this. Wow, they sure are getting bold, aren't they? Twelve SUVs loaded with men, you say? I will take care of this, Dan; don't you worry. There is no easy way of knowing for whom they are working, but they have no right to be doing what they are doing. I am going to make a call." And when the line disconnected, Daniel felt better, knowing that another player was on the board.

He got on the radio to Dillon and let him know that the thugs at their front gate were not associated with any official agency. If they did not stand down, Dillon could expect to use force in turning them away. His eyes were locked on the surveillance footage, watching the intimidating group posturing, as if to make an assault on the gate. He prayed Sylinger would get through to these mercenaries before all hell broke loose.

The pale man wearing the expensive high-tech Kevlar suit reached into his pocket and pulled out his phone. Stiedly raised the phone to his ear; everyone in the control room saw the short conversation and knew by the man's body language that something had changed. They watched him put his phone back into his inside jacket pocket and order his men back into their vehicles. Thomas paused and looked back in a slow, calculated move. The anger in his posture was evident, and they watched as he lowered his glasses for those watching to see the cold, unspoken promise. *This was just the beginning.*

Dillon audibly scoffed at the man, remembering when his firm had worked for him on two black ops missions back when they were first starting out. Knowing Stiedly was involved brought a new level of risk to the playing field, and he knew he was going to have to talk to his guys. This job had just gone from being a boring gig to something that could get serious, really quick.

His men had been grumbling a bit these past few weeks with the lack of excitement, and he had found their complaints tiresome. Many of them were making more money than any other security posting. This new revelation, though, made it plain; they were here for a reason, and he mentally recommitted himself to do everything in his power to protect the boy and his family. *To be sure, there will have to be a meeting with the team later tonight,* he thought. Everyone needed to know that their employer was stirring up some pretty big sharks, which would undoubtedly mean big trouble to come.

Shaken, Daniel considered the shadow organizations and their power. Their influence saw no bounds, and it was apparent they had no issues using any tactic necessary to stop those competing against them. He saw the danger for what it was and feared things could end in terrible violence against him and those close to him. He sat looking out over the ocean from the back patio of the main house, deliberating on what more he could do to protect his friends, family, and the technologies he was creating.

He understood that only a handful of people controlled the largest international organizations, central banks, and governments—the untouchables, those lurking in anonymity. He was afraid. He feared that he and his friends were too few. How could they stand up to people so insulated, people with the power to dictate the course of world events? He thought about how so many people in society were unaware of the truth, and it sickened him.

He recalled conversations with Angelo when they had walked the vineyards. He remembered Angelo's telling of the ways these families cleverly empowered themselves. "Daniel, they take control of the money systems, communication and information systems, food, health care, energy, transportation, and governments. Over decades, by war and commerce, seat by seat, they have inserted their own people in positions of authority all around the world. Of course, many companies independently produce products and deliver them to the markets, but they are only allowed to exist because those in the shadows profit from the interest on money owed to them by the same companies."

Daniel saw ways to free the people from this suppressive group but feared what it would cost. He knew from history what happened to entire nations that fell out of favor.

As he sat pondering the possibilities, weighing the facts, and imagining all the different outcomes, Dillon walked up the steps from below the pool and sat next to him. "Pretty exciting day, right?" he offered in his gruffest voice. Daniel had come to trust this man and his war-scarred nuance. The big man's presence reassured him, and he fought the feelings racking his brain, thoughts of every way things could go wrong.

"I am afraid," he admitted. "I am afraid people are going to die. I mean, if we stay on this path, is it worth the risk? But at the same time, if we don't try, what will happen? Humankind will never be free. We will never rise as a species. Can we just leave Earth's people virtually enslaved?" The questions were directed as much toward himself as to his respected friend. His eyes never left the horizon, searching, looking to the distance for the answer: Could they do it?

"Son, I watched one of my best friends sacrifice himself to save our entire squad: your dad's brother. I have sent men to their deaths to achieve objectives that needed achieving more than once, and believe me, I still feel those days to my core. My point is this: In life, having the ability to make the hard choices is what sets us apart. I don't know what you're doing, but something has those snakes riled, and let me tell you, if I must give my life to have the carpet pulled out from under them, I'll gladly do it. Our world needs a change! There has been far too much pain, far too many lies, and far too many innocent people killed. I want to see them burn even more than you do, kid, so please, please don't quit. Do it for everyone. Be decisive; be aware; see from every viewpoint; investigate the unknown; imagine limitless possibilities; and believe in yourself and those around you."

They sat in silence for a while until the grizzled man stood, gripping Daniel's shoulder. "I hope you find a way to topple them, Dan. I truly do, and I don't mind if I go down because if you can't do it, I don't think anyone ever can." He turned and walked back down to the pool area and into the quickly fading light.

Back at Stanford, while researching particle physics, Daniel privately laid the groundwork for creating what seemed to be a completely undetected superhighway for wireless energy and information. During his research, he tinkered with wireless energy and data transmission, and in a moment of insight, he found a way to tap into what he could only describe as the infinite realm of dark matter. In his tests he found he could send enormous amounts of data and energy through all sorts of materials known to block radio waves of every kind. He sent the frequencies past the most sensitive detector arrays he could get his hands on. There was no trace or effect to the transmission, and the bandwidth was seemingly instantaneous and limitless.

At the time, he realized the magnitude of the discovery and quickly covered it up. He deleted every clue and memorized the steps along with the order of frequencies needed to gain access to the spaces between matter. To the academics, it was yet one more unsuccessful attempt at finding what he postulated must be there.

In the United Earth facility, he easily remembered how to recreate the same experiment and was relieved to find he had not forgotten the overlapping frequency pattern and atomic structure of the fabricated material that made it all work. He 3-D printed a series of dime-sized transmitter receivers, assembling and ordering the atomic structure in an exact way to fold the frequency waves of space, and began testing what would be his first major volley against the shadow corporations.

The first thing he did was unplug the power cable and data connections to the computer system powering his room's display and replaced it with a wireless power plug containing the small transmitter receiver chip. He was uncertain if it would work, but when he turned his room's system back on, he found there was no difference. For the next few days he tried making it fail. He loaded processor-intensive applications and environments, pushing the graphics display to run at maximum levels for hours, searching for any deficiencies in the transfer of electricity from his facility to the power plug in for his room's system. He sent terabytes of data back and forth between his home computer system and the servers miles away and found that instead of having to wait as he normally did, the data transfers were now almost instantaneous.

After testing it on the wall display in his room, he patched another transmitter receiver into the main power line of the house and set up tests to see if he could find a signal between the two properties. He ran diagnostics using various antenna arrays at locations between the house and the facility for two weeks, and as he expected there was no evidence of the wireless network.

The next thing he wanted to figure out was if there were any limitations in the distance this wireless technology could effectively transmit energy and data. In order to answer this, he designed a battery data card to replace the one in his tablet and 3-D printed it.

A week later, Daniel chartered a return flight to the Dominican Republic and sent out flight tickets for family members to fly into San Francisco the day before. He planned to rent a beach house for the entire family and insisted that everyone come for vacation. The timing could not have been better. Daniel was about to turn fifteen years old, and what better way to celebrate than to have the family flown down for some sun-filled fun in a tropical paradise.

Dillon, though, was not keen on the idea after the recent run-in with his old handler. He objected, but in the end, he gave in. Dillon imagined that a smaller team would attract less attention, and the last thing they wanted was to leave the facility unsecured. Dillon's four man team checked the plane for explosives, tracking beacons and ran diagnostics before declaring it safe, and they all boarded, excited for this reunion.

When they arrived at the villa, it was straight to the beach for a dip in the warm ocean and then some relaxation in the the palm trees' sun-speckled shade.

Daniel shied away from the hot blond sand, where many of the family chose to bask in the sun. He looked out over the ocean from his shady refuge and watched as Samantha and her parents splashed in the water, his uncle and their kids running along the beach and his parents find refuge in the pool. Angelo looked so content in a reclined beach chair, sipping on an umbrella-topped drink, and Daniel marked this moment as one of the best.

He reflected on how much his silver-haired friend had helped and supported him over the past few years. Without Angelo, he knew he would never have learned so much of language and philosophy, subjects in which he might otherwise have found very little interest. In Angelo and Lucia, he saw how two people could live their lives as partners, happy and in tune, knowing one another's unique ways like no one else. He admired them for it and could not thank his father enough for bringing them into their family.

He snapped out of it, and his mind went to the task that inspired this trip: the task of finding out how well the wireless network would do over longer distances. Sitting up, he reached into his backpack and pulled the tablet, he smiled seeing that it was still using power from the California facility. He activated the status window for his chip and observed the readings. Before they left the house on the way to the airport, he'd installed an application to continually move a 10.5 terabyte folder with various file types between the tablet and the servers back home. The tablet was equipped with a sixty-four-terabit solid-state hard drive, and as the files went back and forth, the software tracked the exact amount of time it took for each transfer to finish.

The chart was surprising. He swiped back to look at the graph for the time when they were in the air and saw no drop in the connection and no change in the transfer times. Next, he brought up another software package designed to analyze the integrity of the data and checked for any corruption in the files. There was no error rate at all.

The tablet was fully charged, but the question was, how much power was available over this kind of distance? With another program designed to measure available energy, he checked the readouts and was unsure if he could believe what he saw. It showed that he could receive the maximum output from the power cell if there was something on this end to patch that much energy into.

Excited that it worked beyond his wildest expectations, he deactivated the screen and slipped the tablet into his backpack before heading to the pool for a swim and some time away from the science and the planning.

After dinner they sat in comfortable deck chairs, sharing stories from the past few years. Daniel's mind felt free, completely relaxed, and as he half listened to their stories, a part of his mind drifted off onto other things.

Everything has gone by so fast, he thought. It was a blur of focused effort, with rare moments to look up and enjoy life. Now, though, with the first set of goals realized, the future was looking bright. He watched Angelo, Stas, his parents, Samantha with her parents, and the rest laughing and reminiscing in this perfect tropical setting. It felt so safe, but then he remembered the security team maintaining a perimeter around the villa's property. They were out there, he knew, silent, invisible, and essential. He let that thought drift away, once again taking refuge in his family's and friends' merriment.

Finally, after thirteen days of enjoyment, it was time to leave. The Bradford's, his uncles Sam and Frank, accompanied by their wives, and his aunt Margaret all loaded into the SUVs he'd rented to shuttle them back to the airport. The last group to go was Daniel, Stas, his parents, Angelo, Lucia, and Daniel's parents, with Dillon's security team in two Jeeps, one in front and the other behind their stretch SUV.

It happened on the last side street before turning out onto the main road. Two black SUVs rushed in, blocking them on both sides before men in black SWAT gear piled out of the attacking vehicles. There was no warning, the assaulting squad opened fire on Daniel's security team.

Jake was the first out of the lead Jeep and dropped to one knee, opening fire and knocking one of the black-clad thugs off his feet, but before he could find another target, he was thrown back as multiple hits ripped into his body. Three short bursts from the attackers tore his chest plate open, and his blood sprayed high into the air. Over the next few moments, the air filled with fully automatic fire from all sides. Dillon and his men put up a fight, but they were outmanned and quickly put down with an efficient finality. Pools of blood spread out from where the fallen lay and an eerie silence briefly swept over the scene.

As the smoke cleared, the assailants encircled their SUV, and with a swift crack, the lead man smashed the central passenger-door window, showering Angelo with glass. Something snapped inside Angelo, and as the pebbles of glass bounced off him, he lost all self-control. He screamed, hurtling curses through the now-open window at every one of the attackers.

He cursed them, calling them evil dogs, worthless swine, and worse. Daniel had never seen Angelo lose himself so completely; the rage and fury in his eyes made him look like an animal cornered by attackers. Daniel felt a chill go through his body as he watched the lead man reach in and jerk the door open with a force that nearly took it off the hinges.

Angelo kept yelling, seemingly unaware of the danger they faced. With a sudden motion, the lead attacker gripped him and dragged him out. Angelo's voice cut off in a squeal of pain, followed by a cold hard voice from the one holding the older man.

"Let this be an example to you. If the boy doesn't turn over his tablet with all of its security features disabled and the password reset window ready for me to enter my new password, we will drag you all out, and you will die just like this man." Without hesitation, he pushed the older man to his knees and shot him twice through the back of the head.

Lucia screamed, losing herself just as Angelo had, sobbing and cursing in rapid Portuguese. She lunged out the open door toward the man who had just killed her husband, and her speed surprised everyone. But she only made it two steps before getting chopped down by the hand of an even bigger man. He picked her up by the hair and dragged her, kicking and screaming, to where her dead husband lay. The huge man pulled her to her knees and put his visor-covered face close to the back of her head. The rest of the hit squad chuckled as he held her there, letting her struggle and fight against his iron grip. Everything seemed to slow; seconds felt like minutes as the fight drained from her.

She gave up the struggle, her body sagging as realization of what was going to happen set in, and the big man pushed her down, closer to Angelo's body. Her sobs were the only sound, her voice rising and falling, long and sorrowful, as the loss tore at her soul. It stretched on, all of them watching her. And then when it had been far too long, the one who held her raised his shotgun and pulled the trigger. Torn by the impact of the blow, her limp body dropped to lie atop Angelo's corpse, and as one, they passed on. As the terror of Lucia's murder ended, the black ops figures turned with practiced cunning back to the SUV limo, where the rest of their prey huddled in fear.

Susan began to scream in panic as her dear friend was dropped, but John quickly reached over, he wrapped her up in his arms and covering her mouth. He feared she would be next and looked to his son to do anything they asked.

Daniel didn't hesitate.

"You can have it. Please don't hurt anyone else!" he shouted, his voice cracking as he fought uncontrollable emotion.

He switched the tablet's screen to the window showing the chip status and the data transfer statistics and then typed in a command to bring up the password reset window. He held out his bag and the tablet. "Please, just take it! Nothing is worth killing for."

The closest man reached in and took the tablet, lifting it to view the screen. Daniel watched and shuddered at the cruelty these people displayed. The man in the helmet saw the schematics and status bars of the chip and, more important, the password reset window. He typed in a new password and chuckled. From there he quickly slipped it into a tactical bag and secured it on his chest webbing.

The man loomed in the open door of their vehicle and, in a cold hard voice, thanked them. As he turned, his team followed, and in the next few moments their vehicles peeled away, leaving only a cloud of dust and the bleeding bodies of those who lost the fight.

Stas stared hard at the door where the man had stood only a moment ago. His mother swore in Russian, comparing them to the worst secret police that would frequently terrorize people with complete impunity.

John reached out and slammed the door. "Get us out of here, now! Get us to the airport as fast as you can!" he shouted to the driver, who immediately put the vehicle into drive, leaving the bloody scene just as fast as their assailants.

Susan went hysterical. "We can't just leave them there! We have to go back for them. How can we just leave them there?" she shouted as tears rolled down her face. She loved Lucia like a sister and seeing her executed like that was more then she could bear.

John knew they couldn't take the time to retrieve their friends' bodies or wait for the police to show up. They would be able to recover the bodies through his business connections once they were out of the country, but if they waited, they would be subjected to endless interrogation and put into custody for who knew how long. It was better this way, he knew. Spending weeks in a prison awaiting release would be far harder on everyone than simply getting out of the country and asking for forgiveness later.

As they reached the airport, he finally got through to Susan that the best thing they could do was to make it through security, get on their plane, and make it safely back home to California.

She barely kept it together as they passed through security. "She has food poisoning, sir," John explained to the guard at the gate. "Once we are on board our chartered plane, she can take a sleeping pill. We have lots of room for her to lie down for the flight."

Once in the air, John went to Daniel and whispered, "Can you give me an explanation for what just happened?"

Daniel was still coming to terms with the fact that their entire security team, along with the person he respected most in the world, plus Lucia, whom his entire family loved so much, had all just been murdered in cold blood right in front of them. The attackers were there for only one thing: his tablet. "There was no way they could have known. There was no way! They must have been ordered to take my electronics by force, thinking that they would score something, maybe plans. How could they even know what I am working on?" he mumbled, just loud enough for John to catch a few things.

Daniel looked to his father. He hadn't told him about the encounter at

ОшибкаНе

the facility gates a little over two months ago, and he wondered if things would have turned out differently if he had.

They went to the forward cabin, where they could speak in private, and for the next two hours, he told his father the entire story—the technology he was working on; his plan to release it as an add-on for every wireless device in the world; how he envisioned undercutting wireless network subscriptions by a quarter of their best prices and taking the entire market share. He told of how he disconnected the facility from the electrical grid and then the house and the plantation.

As he finished, he thought of Stiedly, the man who led the group that day at his facility. He remembered the voice and those last words. None of the voices from today's attackers sounded anything like him, though. They were all gruff and highly trained mercenaries. Thomas spoke with an air of intellectual superiority and a clearly cruel inclination. There was no way of knowing for sure if the attackers were sent by the man or by a completely different organization, but he swore he would find out, one way or the other, and take his revenge.

When Daniel finished telling his story, John looked concerned but felt like his mind was clear, considering the events of the past few hours. He looked at his son and paused before asking his first question. "What are you planning to do about the technology, now that it is in the hands of the enemy?"

The reality of what just happened was heavy on Daniel's heart, but his father's question triggered a knowing smile that broke through the tears.

"They will try to block all signals coming to and from the stolen tablet, but what they don't know is that my wireless data transmissions cannot be blocked by any known technology or material. The other thing they don't realize is that just because I unlocked the tablet and gave them access to assign new passwords doesn't mean I can't wipe the hard drives, which I did the moment we lifted off. The prototype chip they have in the device is useless without the frequency algorithms making everything possible. Even if they could figure out the algorithms for the frequency, the exact order of assembly in the particle assembler to recreate the chip's unique ability to tap into a dimension of space that has eluded science for so long, it is simply something that would be nearly impossible to replicate unless you know it's code. To them, the chip will seem like an ordinary composite. I think I am very lucky they didn't kidnap me. Pretty stupid of them, really," Daniel explained as his thought process brought him back to the loss of their loved ones.

When they finished saying all there was to say, they went back into the main cabin and answered some questions for the rest of the family. After that, the remainder of the flight was somber, as the reality of what had happened truly set in. Susan shook, sobbing uncontrollably as John did his best to comfort her. Stas's parents spoke in fast angry Russian, and Samantha huddled with her parents and the rest of them just looked shocked.

Daniel was devastated! Cold tears ran down his face as images of Angelo's last moments flashed through his mind. The screams of horror from Lucia and the panicked terror he had felt haunted him. Someone on the plane was saying something, but whatever it was it did not make it to where his mind had gone. A flood of guilt and sadness overwhelmed him, and for a time he was lost to the pain of it all.

He considered that maybe the best thing to do was to give up. Who was he to stand against those who are untouchable? And as his mind went toward despair, a memory from when he had first met Angelo emerged.

The memory played back in his mind. He had been only four years old and had fallen to his knees, causing a trickle of blood to run down his leg. He remembered that when he'd seen the blood, he panicked, crying out in agony, as though all the world was coming to an end. He remembered that Angelo had watched him until his upset ran its course, waiting until Daniel's outburst settled before helping him up. Angelo had not used a comforting voice but instead one of knowledge and insightful reason.

"Can you breathe?" the old man had asked, watching Daniel with caring yet analytical eyes. The question snapped him out of his panic, and as he caught his breath, he heard Angelo's voice in his mind like he was right there, "A person's character is not judged by his ability to make it through life without falling but instead by his ability to get up and learn and keep moving forward, stronger than before."

Angelo always talked of the loss and struggles in his life and how that made him who he was. Over time, Daniel grew to admire this quality in the man.

As the memory faded, the sadness was replaced with anger, a hot hatred for the people who took his friends. He wanted to strike out at them, and he began to channel the emotions of the loss into a need for revenge. *I'll kill them all*, he thought, imagining every way he could ruin them.

Stas said little the entire flight, but when they were off the plane, he walked with Daniel to their waiting vehicles. They got into the BMW together, Stas waving to his parents, with whom he apparently already had discussed these arrangements. As they pulled onto the highway, Stas finally broke the silence. "We can't let this stop us, Daniel. We have to use it. We have to feed on the pain they have caused us and fight back. We can't let them win, Dan."

A tear rolled from Daniel's eye and down his face as the magnitude of what happened rose to the surface once more. He looked to his friend, "If we go ahead with this, will any of us be safe? Won't we be putting everyone we care about at risk?"

Stas stayed silent, thinking about it as they sped down the highway. "Will anyone ever be free if we don't do something?" he finally replied.

A dangerous look washed over Daniel's face, and he spoke with a cold tone Stas was unfamiliar hearing from his friend. "We are going to take from them what they hold most dear, Stas: their wealth, their power, their influence. We will strike at them not with force but with intelligence and leave them with nothing. We will unmask every one of them and see them fall."

Chapter 10

Survivor

He was still unconscious; his shoulder was smashed to pieces where the bullet had torn through. Near the top of his helmet there was a gaping hole where a large-caliber shell glanced off. It had thrown him from his feet and knocked him out, likely saving his life. On the way down, he was struck in the thigh, grazed in the ribs, and took a round to the chest that hit on an angle, tearing through his vest and leaving a deep flesh wound and broken ribs. The impacts kicked his body as he fell back, but, he was alive—barely.

His eyes fluttered open and he gasped. He looked around instinctively, scanning the scene before making any move. There was only the dead. He knew he needed to move, he knew it had to be immediately. He had to! He fought through the fog, nausea from the concussion tearing him down, he pushed aside the urge to close his eyes. The pain from his wounds were beyond anything he had ever endured; his ribs were shattered, his leg was limp from a bullet wound, with every move his head pounded, a splitting pain on the cusp of knocking him out. He was losing blood, but somehow, he pushed through it.

His vision blurred, and his body gave him nothing, but he wouldn't—he couldn't—give up the boy! What had happened? He saw Jake, Patrick, Brad, Raffi—all dead, broken by the fully automatic armor-piercing rounds. His head dropped for a moment as he mourned his fallen brothers and steeled himself to the task of crawling away. He knew there wasn't long; if he was still there when the police arrived, it would go very badly for him. The men who hit them were pros, and the same people who made it happen likely paid off the police. He dragged himself, pushing with his one good leg and pulling with his one good arm toward the main street.

It was as far as he could go, and he collapsed, his back against a fence between two garbage cans. He might go unnoticed for at least a little longer, he hoped. Across the street he saw a cab, and with his last strength, he reached out his good arm in a bid for help.

Antonio always drove the same route, and today was no different. He took pride in his taxi; it was clean, it ran well, and it was his property. He had finally finished paying it off and was no longer obligated to pay out a portion of his fares to rent the cab ever since going private. Normally, he stayed away from trouble, sticking to the safest routes and avoiding pick up of rowdy or dangerous fares. When he saw the tactically armored half-dead man, naturally his first instinct was to drive off, but there was something about the man's face. The way he lay against the fence, partly concealed among piles of garbage, the way his hand was outstretched toward him—it gave him pause. *There must be a reason God parked him here*, he thought. He stepped out of his cab to walk across the empty street to where the man lay in his own pooling blood.

"Please," the man whispered, "I need to save the boy." It was all he had left, and with it, his eyes closed, unconsciously.

Antonio could hear the sirens getting closer and considered leaving this to the authorities. Yet he paused; something inside said he must help this man. He ran back to his cab and executed a quick U-turn, parking it right next to where the bloody man lay. Antonio was a big man, strong from his days working for his uncle, when he carried sacks of grain all day, every day. But even so, he needed every ounce of his strength to get the limp man into the back of his cab. "You will be paying for new upholstery," he muttered, shutting the door and jumping into the driver's seat. He hit the gas.

Moments later he reached the far corner of the street and looked in his rearview mirror. Police cars, followed by black SUV SWAT vans, raced into the alley, heading for the beach houses, where this man must have come from.

Antonio headed straight for his house, where his wife, fortunately, was on her day off. She was only a first-year nurse, and he wasn't too sure what she could do for the man, but he knew it was his only chance. When he arrived and went in to ask her for help, though, she was not happy to hear what he'd done.

"Are you crazy? You are bringing trouble into our home," she barked and nearly called the police.

"You know I have seen many people in need. I always leave them. I have always steered away from danger. But when I saw this man, something touched my heart; God has called on us to help this man. I think he is a soldier, and he fights for truth—one who protects those who need protecting. We have to help him," he insisted.

"How do you know? What if he's not? What if he's just another mercenary who kills for the highest price? What then?" she demanded.

"He isn't. I can feel it. Please help, please," he begged.

After nearly twenty minutes, he finally convinced her they needed to help. She followed him outside to where the badly injured man lay slumped in the back seat, and her look of disgust only got worse. He was barely conscious, not fully aware of what was going on. He groaned as Antonio opened the door, and when Sofia finally saw him, she gasped.

"Look at all that blood; your cab it's ruined. Why is he not dead? He should be dead, Antonio! This is bad—very, very bad!" But when she saw the man's eyes, she understood why her husband had chosen to help.

Dillon saw her look and heard her words. "I'm good for it. My chest pocket it's yours." He grunted, putting on his best smile and coughed hard, his face betraying his real pain.

"We are going to help you," Antonio promised, and together they helped him out of the cab and into the bathroom of the house.

Sofia never personally treated gunshot wounds on the job, but she watched the doctors at the hospital handle patients with wounds like these all the time. They used Dillon's combat knife to cut away his armor and clothes, doing their best to clean his wounds and stop the bleeding as they went. Dillon gave instructions for his shoulder between bouts of unconsciousness, until finally they left him lying on the floor of their bathroom, covered in their blankets and sleeping, she did her best to build a splint for his leg and wrapped his chest, "If he makes it, it will take a while for him to heal," she whispered and they both said a short prayer for the man.

That evening they saw the reports on the news. There had been a gunfight just outside of the Palms Resort. It was reported that a squad of four men attacked an SUV leaving the resort. The reporter was interviewing a SWAT team member from the alleged security team that saved the family and killed the four attackers.

Seeing this, Sofia wanted to contact the police immediately, but Antonio felt that there was something wrong about the man giving the interview, and he persuaded her to wait. They had both heard Dillon's constant muttering from the floor of their bathroom. "I need to save the boy and protect the family." There was no way he could be putting on a show for them, and it was enough for Antonio to convince her the news story was a cover-up for whatever really happened.

After three days Dillon was able to sit up, and they helped him move from the hallway floor to their bedroom. They gave him their bed and told him he could use it for as long as it took him to recover.

Dillon was more than grateful, insisting they take the emergency cash in the chest pocket of his vest.

Antonio looked through the vest and found the fold of money. After counting it, he found there was an even $20,000. It was more than Antonio would make in six months.

"Take it. It's for exactly this scenario, and when I get home, I'll send you more. You deserve it. The boy will be more than grateful to find out you helped me survive."

Antonio ripped out the upholstery from the back of his cab and burned it that very same day. In the morning, he took his cab to his cousin's shop to install all new leather seats and carpeted floors with just a small portion of Dillon's emergency cash.

As Dillon got better, Sofia convinced him to tell the entire story—how he had come to work for the Thoth family, the holiday, the attack, and deaths of his men, right up until he was knocked unconscious. The last thing he remembered was the painful crawl toward a taxi that seemed so far away.

Daniel didn't bother applying for real patents for the universal chip technology, a term he decided would fit well with where it was headed. Patents, he felt, were unnecessary, simply because of the plain fact that, to the science community, his device was impossible, but he did humor them. *An Array of atoms and frequencies designed to resonate with the vastness of subatomic dimensions,* it read and was all he ever gave them.

The first thing he did when they got home was begin expanding the facility—excavation and the construction of a new fifteen-floor bunker building to house the servers and future 3-D printing operations needed for them to become a global internet service provider. This was necessary to bypass paying major providers for access to their networks. Once again, they hired John's friend's industrial construction firm, and within a week, an army of skilled tradesmen were working around the clock in the north corner of the facility grounds.

Daniel didn't like it, but he had to get financing from his father's friends, as they did not have another $500 million lying around for this new rushed construction. They came in as angel investors, with a guaranteed payback, plus 50 percent over the next two years: a time frame he knew would mean nothing in the coming months. It was necessary; they wouldn't be able to pull off hijacking the wireless marketplace without a double-capacity server system as a starting point. His father's connections jumped on the opportunity, privately committing to fund the construction with an open-ended clause under the same terms, and everything continued as planned.

Daniel, accompanied by his father, spent weeks in meetings with expensive lawyers. They needed to prepare for the inevitable court battles. John knew the plan, and Daniel was no fool. They needed to be protected; lawsuits would begin as soon as they started taking market share and refusing to license their technology and having decisive action plans would limit the impact.

It took almost six months to get everything in place before launching the new product. The new building had enough servers and data storage to download the entirety of the world's cloud networks four times over. They put up an online store front, where people could create accounts, enter their payment information, and order the chip-enabled battery type for their device. The wireless package they were offering was unbeatable. It guaranteed customers infinite battery life, unlimited worldwide calling, unlimited worldwide data, voice mail, and call display for a flat rate of twenty-five dollars a month, anywhere in the world. It did not matter which device you had, and anyone could sign up.

The fourth floor of the main facility and the top three floors of the new building were jammed with five hundred 3-D printing and packaging stations, all fully automated to fill orders as soon as they came in. Each station could complete up to one thousand orders every twenty-four hours, and not one stopped for the first four weeks.

In first month they delivered fourteen million network battery chips, making $350 million in subscription fees. Daniel saw the demand would continue to grow and knew they would need even more facility space as the world's population converted to this disruptive technology. Seeing the future demand, yet another underground facility was commissioned, this one to a depth of thirty floors, double the size of the recently completed server building.

Phone manufactures made appointments to discuss what kinds of technology advancements they could pursue in order to exploit the new data transfer rates and power bandwidths of the universal power and data chip. Hearing that tests showed bandwidths all the way up to teraflop per-second transfer rates without any noticeable slowdowns, the developers blinked in amazement and disbelief.

Publicly traded stocks of companies in direct competition with United Earth plummeted as their revenue streams began dropping off. Daniel knew this move presented substantial risk; there was no doubt those in the shadows were watching and would be aware that U.E. was now a real threat. World news continuously commented on the fact there were no patents on the technology, questioning why not a single third party was able to solve the riddle to this scientific breakthrough taking the market by storm.

It didn't take long for the wireless service providers to submit lawsuits, accusing U.E. of takeover tactics and monopolizing the market. Huge corporations, some too big to fail, were at risk of going out of business as people dropped their expensive contracts. It became obvious that everyone with a phone, tablet, or portable computer was moving over to the universal chip.

The expensive lawyers Daniel and John prearranged were, thankfully, up to the task. In court case after court case, they decisively withstood the onslaught of accusations posed by the corporations.

Daniel laughed to himself one day when a representative from a major telecommunications provider stood and pointed his finger, saying, "How dare you monopolize this market and make these services cheaper than we can possibly do?" It was funny to Daniel because the telecommunication industry had been monopolized for years; there was no real competition between the big companies. They were all owned indirectly by a single group that always seemed to remain behind the scenes and out of sight. They just rebranded and franchised patented technologies all around the world.

The legal battles were expensive, but the fact was Daniel had left the door wide open. There were no restricting patents stopping competitors from duplicating what he had created. He always said in court that if they could figure out the technology, they would be free to join the network and move in the direction of progress.

With the help of his father, the newly christened vice chairman of the U.E. board of directors, and with the assistance of John's friend's contracting company working to finish the third building, they purchased newly constructed warehouses all around the world. In these newly acquired buildings they installed refrigerator-sized energy cells and additional server farms to back up the main facility and stay ahead of the ever-growing number of U.E. accounts.

Stas created a security AI that managed the accounts and crawled the servers: its job—to search and destroy the constant attacks aimed at the U.E. wireless networks. Daniel tried to show his gratitude by giving Stas and his family millions of dollars, but Stas wanted nothing more than to apply his skills as a programmer, and his parents loved nothing more than spending time with their son and walking along the coastal beaches. Stas himself enjoyed the challenges Daniel set in front of him and was proud to be a part of what Daniel was trying to accomplish in the world.

It took longer than he would have liked, but after five weeks of rest and easy training, Dillon regained enough strength to attempt a homecoming. Before leaving, he went through his torn armor and cut away the stitching where the checkbook Daniel had given him was concealed. He had promised to make sure they were rewarded when he got back but figured it was better to take care of it now.

Daniel had issued him the checkbook after the encounter at the front gate, making it clear that in the protection of his family, no expense was too great. He wondered what would be appropriate and decided his life was not cheap, so he wrote out a check for $2.5 million and presented it to

Antonio and Sofia. "Thank you both. You saved my life, and I think the boy can afford it."

Antonio dropped him off at the airport. Dillon was dressed as a typical tourist, and as he stepped away into the crowd, Antonio felt he had helped someone truly worth helping.

When Dillon entered the airport, he made a call to Brice back at the main facility in California on the prepaid cell phone Antonio got him a few days earlier. When Brice heard Dillon's voice on the other end of the line, Dillon felt the man's surprise and joy as if he were standing right next to him. Brice had a business-class seat booked for his friend on the next flight out, and six hours later, he was safely in the air.

On the call, he asked Brice not to let anyone know he was alive, wanting to surprise Daniel and the rest of the team when he arrived, and his friend grudgingly made the promise.

Daniel was on the R&D level in front of a huge PLED wall that wrapped around one end of the entire room when he felt a presence enter the room. As he turned, he recognized the silhouette. It was the ghost of a man he swore he had lost, yet not a ghost, and as it registered that Dillon truly stood in the doorway, Daniels voice caught in his throat.

"I am sorry, sir," Dillon said in a repentant voice.

"You're alive." Daniel hardly believed it. "I saw you get cut down and made very dead!"

"Yes, I was grazed in the head and knocked unconscious in the beginning of the fight. I awoke a few minutes later, and everyone was gone. I crawled away and found a cab driver who helped me. You will notice a tidy sum from the expense account when the cab driver and his wife cash the check I gave them," he explained.

Daniel walked over to the man, who looked like he had lost a lot of weight. "What's important is that you are alive, my friend. I was starting to wonder if your team would be up to the task of keeping things safe around here without you."

"Have there been any threats since you got back?" Dillon asked.

"No, things have been pretty quiet, except for the lawyers and legal matters that seem to be a never-ending battle," Daniel replied. He told Dillon of the developments in the company's business over the past few months, emphasizing his renewed resolve to dethrone those behind the attack.

A year passed as Daniel worked, building the next phase of his plans. He turned sixteen as United Earth Technologies joined the highest grossing corporations in the world. After literally taking over the mobile service market, their monthly revenue reached $10 billion. When his father came to him with the news, showing him their monthly earnings, Daniel just looked back at him with hard, cold eyes.

"We have hardly scratched the surface. They must be feeling it a little, but just wait. Soon there will be nothing they can do. We will take everything from them, and humanity will rise from the darkness in which it has been trapped for so many generations."

Chapter 11

The Shadows

On the two-hundredth floor of a corporate building in Beijing's downtown business district, a meeting was under way. The upper echelon of a group long thought of as the five families, or the Illuminati, gathered in person. These were the people controlling the world from the shadows. International banks, trade, energy, food production, communications networks, governments of every nation—they indirectly owned and controlled it all.

Each of the families had accumulated their power and wealth over the past six hundred years. They used misdirection, manipulation, and double-dealings as their primary methods. Their descendants started the modern banking system, the creation of fiat currency, collecting interest on fabricated loans. They created money out of thin air, adding zeros to ledgers with no physical backing, yet no one ever called them out.

Those who saw their greed and demanded answers always ended up the victims of accidents and the targets of aggressive propaganda campaigns. The Illuminati used tactics that left no roads leading back to who or what they were, and they always won.

The reason for this rare gathering was the up-and-coming U.E. Technologies, a new upstart owned by a boy with the ability to uncover the secrets of the universe. This mere sixteen-year-old was taking control of their telecommunications and wireless information monopolies around the globe. Something needed to be done about it.

The oldest, a grizzly man with jowly cheeks, purple lips, and deep, dark sockets where his eyes hid from the dim light of the room, spoke. "You fools.

We had the chance to kill the boy and his family! But instead we listened to the weakest of us, convinced to wait and steal this boy's secrets for our own, rather than snuff him outright. He is growing stronger, and we must act decisively!"

The group instructed their agents to purchase the new U.E. product, yet their top-level scientists scratched their heads, unable to unlock its secrets. No one could find the frequency or even decipher the unique order in which the atoms of the carbon chips were assembled. Their only answers for their masters were that this was something outside of the world of possibilities.

The consensus around the table was that they had to destroy the United Earth corporation at all costs. For a start, they planned a slanderous campaign in the hope that it would cause people to return to their old providers. They would advertise that people could restart their old plans with no activation fees and even introduce cheaper unlimited data. If that didn't work, they agreed what the next step would be—they would kill everyone connected to the Thoth family, once and for all, and destroy every facility the company owned and was currently building.

The following week, major news networks, owned and financed by the very people threatened by the United Earth movement, began showing reports that the new U.E. device was causing major health concerns. They manufactured false scientific evidence that demonstrated how the U.E. wireless network was extremely hazardous. The big media introduced fabricated stories that the power supplies emitted trace amounts of radioactive waves. They even brought in firsthand accounts of people claiming extreme headaches, nose bleeds, and seizures from exposure to the so-called wonder technology. In parallel to the slander campaign, the U.E. website was hit by teams of hackers, sending billions of requests per second against the servers. The attacks caused the site to freeze and crash, preventing people from requesting refunds or accessing the help desk where U.E.'s own scientific evidence could be found.

The people's reaction to the slander campaign was not good. Most believed the reports. While the media spread their lies, millions of people returned to their previous subscribers and for Daniel and his friends, it was hard to watch. It was impossible for them to counter the accusations via the media, they wouldn't even return his lawyer's calls. They were going to pay, he knew! Making blatantly false accusations and using manufactured scientific claims while ignoring the facts was something his lawyers would make them regret.

Thankfully, before going to market they had commissioned rigorous tests on the device, paying consulting fees to leading members of the scientific community. Various third parties—Google, Samsung, Tesla, and two leading medical corporations, all wanting a piece of the action—commissioned safety analysis tests under full NDA agreements for future legal use. His lawyers insisted it was paramount that he prove there were no unexpected side effects under third-party unbiased tests, citing examples of exactly what was happening now.

At the start of the cyberattack, the hackers tried crashing the security system while inserting viruses. Fortunately, the AI that Stas created to protect against these sorts of attacks was way too clever. It allowed the digital mercenaries just enough access, letting them think they were getting in, before locking them out and archiving the attackers' IP and sending back a virus of his own design.

Stas, an experienced internet pirate himself, saw the DOS attacks coming and designed a way to fight back. They could have shut down the DOS attackers in the first hours, but he convinced Daniel to wait and allow the attackers time to believe they were winning. He wanted them to reveal themselves as much as possible in order to return the most decisive and effective final blow.

They waited a week and a half before deploying the search-and-destroy bots. Billions of IP addresses were stored, yet most would end up being proxies, decoys hackers used to hide from detection. Stas was used to these tactics, and by using an undetectable trace of his own, he pinpointed every last attacker before deploying what he called Haast's Eagle. It was his pride and joy, a Trojan virus named after the largest and most dangerous eagle ever known to exist.

His eagle was equipped with an algorithm beyond anything he had ever known before. He designed it to get past any system's firewalls, while staying completely undetected. When it was in, it deployed a second Trojan that began transferring everything on their hard drives back to the U.E. servers, while at the same time distributing another algorithm that would run if his eagle was detected. Upon detection in the enemy's system, it wiped everything and triggered every piece of hardware to overclock, running at multiples of their maximum levels. Their hard drives would fry, memory would cook, and CPUs would melt as they ran at ten times their maximin rates.

Haast's Eagle was a counterattack that would destroy their entire setups. Once she was in, it didn't matter if they pulled the power. As soon as they powered their systems back up, his eagle was waiting to finish the job.

When Stas began parsing the data retrieved from the attackers' hard drives, he found some of them familiar, old acquaintances from when he was just like them—a hacker for hire, living off scams and political contracts. Other records collected by Haast's Eagle showed they were hired to attack U.E. servers by people with very deep pockets.

Stas felt a little sorry for them, as his eagle wiped their systems and destroyed most if not all of their hardware. *But,* he thought, *if they want to play with the big boys, it means they are going to get a full dose of their own medicine.*

Soon, after the counterattack, the DOS attackers were neutralized, and the U.E. websites came back.

Daniel posted presentations of intensive tests, proving the absence of any safety hazards, along with proof that the major media corporations refused to receive the third-party evidence, refuting their false claims.

His lawyers worked quickly, submitting numerous class-action lawsuits against every media broadcaster who distributed the slanderous information while ignoring factual data made readily available to them.

Daniel tried to get in touch with the FBI director and the director of the Department of National Security. He left messages at the Pentagon, asking for assistance against the hacker attacks and false information being distributed about his company, but he got no support. The reply was that all communication with the U.E. corporation was forbidden until the company shared its secret technologies with the world.

Days later, Gregory, one of the only people from whom Daniel expected to hear back, sent a private message from his daughter's friend's phone: "Daniel, all I can say is that the most powerful people in the world are out for you. Getting help from the FBI or any other law agencies will be tough from here on out. Get in touch with the Donald Macready security team. They are trustworthy and hardnosed. They have enough reasons to want the corrupt bureaucrats and greedy figureheads brought to their knees and will be very loyal to your cause. Good luck, son. Please don't contact me again."

Macready and his team showed up at the main facility twenty-three hours after Dillon made the call. He and his team of thirty specialists came in three privately owned Black Hawk helicopters, loaded with gear. Over the following week, they set up shop in the security house next to the front gate and toured the facilities. They were a welcome addition to the Samuelson team, which was down to just five members after the attack in the Dominican Republic—the deaths had caused some to decide to get out before it cost them their own lives.

Chapter 12

United Earth, Phase II

John walked into Daniel's bedroom and sat in a newly purchased leather reclining chair. Ambient pastel light filled the room as the swirling PLED walls subtly shifted.

"Dan, you know I'll support your choices, and I admire your goals, but I am concerned. Is it the right choice? Are we really the ones to do it? How could we stop an army of goons from rolling in, killing all of us, and taking everything? These people will stop at nothing, you do know that, don't you? And if that did happen, God forbid, it would give them even more control than ever before."

Daniel sat across from his father in silence, memories of their family's loss rising within. The way Angelo's eyes looked just before he lost his life flashed in his mind. A tear trickled down his cheek as he held back the flood of emotion. He mourned their loss for days after the funeral, but even now, after more than six months, there were times when the loss was still hard to confront.

John saw the boy's strength and wondered how his son was now a young man with so much potential. *Can my son truly make real change in the world?* he wondered.

Daniel collected himself and spoke directly to the issues his father bought up.

"In our world, there is imbalance! A selfish few hold power over the many. They control the basic things we desire and need. They are nameless and untraceable. Father, we can heal the world! Imagine our species if all of humanity got good education along with inalienable rights. We can provide things people use, with improvements in functionality, at a fraction of the current costs. I will see those who hurt us brought to their knees. Someone must stand up and help the world break free. Mankind has potential to achieve a far greater existence if we simply find a way to work together. War, crime, illness, poverty, ideology, and fanatical faiths are all manufactured by those using misdirection and fear to feed their power."

John stared into the pastel swirls slowly drifting on the walls of his son's room until Daniel finally snapped him out of it.

"Dad, you get what I am saying, right? We can't let this continue!"

"But what if going up against them leads to the loss of more of those we love?" The words came out before he realized his near-sighted thought. Realizing it, he shook his head and apologized. "I am sorry; it would seem whatever sacrifices need be made are worth their cost if real change in the world can be achieved."

The things Daniel wanted to accomplish were what people only dreamed of and wrote about in fiction stories—tales of how the world could be "if only people would unify under the banner of growth and prosperity." He was not only achieving milestones in this crusade but taking his achievements to constant new heights. Life for humanity was a struggle, while the wealthy few lived in luxury and ease. Even the middle class was unable to access good education systems, and the corruption of the elite became clear decades ago.

Looking into his father's eyes, he promised to do everything in his power to protect their family and friends, even though in his heart he knew it might not be enough.

Stas was overworked. It was just him, along with the assistance of the AI's they created to do a lot of the work. He was alone in supporting United Earth's networks and wanted help. After taking down the attackers and analyzing the data listing identities of those involved in the attack, he was relieved to find that a few from his past were not in the list.

Over the last few weeks, he'd thought of his old friend Jimmy. He wondered how he was doing and hoped he had avoided being picked up by the people who got him. To his relief, there was no evidence he was involved in the attacks. He also thought of how good it would be to have Jimmy on his team. Jimmy was the equivalent of five people when it came to high-level math, along with having an uncanny ability in network security and AI development and his well-rounded knowledge in the main five computer languages. He also knew that if Jimmy was on the other side, the attacks would have been far worse! And so, with the hope that he might find his old friend, he began a search.

After doing an initial sweep, using a web crawler he designed to search every social media site and dark web hub, he found no sign of his friend. At first Stas feared the worst, thinking he was either dead or enslaved for going against shadow corporation wishes. When the AI came back with a possible match, a glimmer of hope came to life, he couldn't believe it. Apparently, Jimmy recently signed up for a U.E. wireless data plan with a fake identity. He found him with the facial recognition search, and when the image popped up on his screen, Stas recognized him right away, it was like one of the same face cards they used to use when passing codes.

Using one of his own untraceable alternate web identities, Stas sent a private message, asking his old friend if he would be interested in a new opportunity. He attached a garbled picture of himself and nested fairly obvious codes that only Jimmy would know how to decipher.

Jimmy, his long-lost friend, was living in mainland China and barely scraping by. Normally, he would never open spam offers and advertisements on his device but the syntax of the title, // U, main E, []{(JimJim, big opportunity, come join!)`* return STAS; <1>`}, had him clicking in with excitement. When he saw his old friend's picture, he teared up. He was alive! He looked closer at the picture and found barcodes, symbols, and numbers in the garbled sections of the picture. It was the same code they'd used for bank accounts, addresses, and phone numbers. It was a pleasure decoding them—it brought back memories of good times, and when he was done, he followed the instructions.

He was a small young man, appearing to have gone without a good meal for far too long. Stas remembered him as a math genius and programmer prodigy. He was a person who loved contemplating physics and the possibilities of impossibilities. Jimmy always impressed him by how incredibly smart he was; he could solve complex problems quickly, like no one else he'd ever met, other than Daniel. When they worked together, hacking various corporations and banks in search of extra cash scams, things had never run better. Life, though, had not gone well for him since those days. Jimmy was forced into working as a factory cleaner to survive, hiding from those who wanted to take him away.

Ever since his Russian friend's disappearance, Jimmy kept his identity off the web. The factory kept him off the streets and allowed him to save a little. The work hours were long, but at least he had remained unnoticed.

Daniel was skeptical at first. "You want to bring on a factory worker from China?" he asked in his driest tone. But Stas convinced him, and Daniel authorized it. The security team did extensive checks on the teenager for any questionable affiliations, and they made the arrangements. After he arrived and was introduced to everyone, Stas brought him up to speed.

Hearing about his new role with U.E., Jimmy was overjoyed and told Stas about all that happened since they'd last spoke.

"I don't know how to thank you, Stas. After you disappeared that day so many years ago, I felt like I needed to get away, like I was somehow at risk. I think I was very lucky. It was a strange day. I remember feeling like something was wrong, and when I came home, instead of going to my computers, I crawled out my window onto the roof of my family's apartment. It was only by chance! A few days earlier, after you stopped replying to my messages, I stashed a bag with food and clothes up there. Anyway, when I got up there, I sat and looked out over the city for a while. And then I lost my parents. When I was about to head back down, I heard shouts and saw flashes come from my apartment. Men had come, and I knew I had to run! They were there for me, I think, and in China, life is not as cherished as it is in other parts of the world. I knew my parents were dead. Ever since then I have been hiding, working where I can to survive, and keeping my identity off the net, but I kept learning. I never stopped learning. I vowed that I would build the biggest, most destructive virus ever known to man and hurt those who took my family from me. But I can't find out who they are. I have sent out web crawlers from internet cafés, looking for clues, but those who sent the men to take me—they are invisible. They cannot be found! Then, you contacted me, and here I am."

Stas just stared at him, amazed at the story. He thought of how similar his story might have been if he had escaped that day they came and took him.

"Jimmy, I know you want revenge; we all do, no one more than Daniel. But if you are going to be a part of this team, you must abandon your mission and follow the vision Daniel has for us. Trust me, my friend, whatever effect your virus would have if unleashed is nothing compared to what Daniel has already done, and it is only the beginning. We are going to ruin them. We are going to take away their power."

Jimmy nodded, knowing that U.E. was far bigger than anything he had envisioned for his retribution. He swore himself to the cause.

The lawyers made short work of the media corporations who blatantly ignored the truth. Instead of paying out $300 billion in legal settlements that would have left paper trails back to the the shell corporations behind everything, Daniel gave them a second option. During prime-time news, every day for three weeks, they publicly repeated the same message: "We apologize for misrepresenting the facts in regard to United Earth. In light of new scientific evidence, the United Earth wireless technology is proven to be completely safe, and we retract all claims otherwise that were previously made." He made them dig their own graves.

As a result, there was an initial surge of reactivations, while at the same time those on the fence chose to sign up for their own U.E. wireless accounts. The initial effect of the negative PR campaign had hurt them, but with the media retracting their claims, it reversed the flow. Those who orchestrated the entire scenario brought on their own demise. The negative sentiment got everyone's attention, got everyone talking about it, and then the story flipped on its head, creating even more demand than expected. Within the second month after the media's retraction and public apology, U.E. income broke $25 billion a month. Subscriptions steadily climbed and before long they captured nearly all the world's wireless markets.

With the new success, Daniel gave Dillon full authority to triple his team's size. The call went out to all his old friends, brothers in arms all, with strong feelings against the establishment and their worldly manipulation. They built a ten-foot-tall perimeter wall around the main house property and posted teams to new strategic positions. With the new security, Daniel felt ready for the next phase.

The plan was to build out the wireless energy chip to the automotive industry. They would market the product by offering the conversion of any vehicle from combustion or battery pack at no charge. With the U.E. power pack, people would never have to worry about recharging. Their vehicles would receive as much power as was needed, and the user would be billed accordingly.

The cost savings and convenience for people was unmatched. Daniel and his father, who was an incredible asset in planning and implementing the business strategy, set the next stage into motion. John put in place a management team to take care of handling the thousands of shop licenses and training materials needed to get distribution to a global scale, along with a payment structure for shops doing the conversions.

The problem of where to do all the conversions was simple enough. Existing automotive shops were contacted and offered licensing and training, giving them official status as U.E. conversion locations. As they came online, more and more shops applied to gain the new business opportunity. The U.E. corporation purchased warehouses in every city in anticipation of the parts removed during each conversion. Though the conversions were free of charge, the indirect payment was that all parts removed in the conversion would become U.E. property. Once everything was in place, Daniel and his close group of family and friends watched with excitement as the world made yet another paradigm shift.

Daniel sent legal teams with offers to the automotive companies. He wanted to give them the opportunity to order the chips for cars on their manufacturing lines at no cost. The only stipulation was that people purchasing those new cars with the U.E. technology would automatically be enrolled in the U.E. automotive energy subscription.

The major companies who still built a lot of gas-powered vehicles all declined. It was expected. The big car companies were likely controlled by the very people he opposed. Some of the smaller car manufacturers, those breaking into the market with primarily electric technologies—were eager to join the movement. They saw the benefit of not needing to install expensive battery packs in their new vehicles, a cost savings that would allow them to drop their prices, while at the same time increasing their margins.

As the new program rolled out, major media refused to broadcast U.E. commercials. It was of no consequence; the world was now primarily using the U.E. wireless cloud, and blocking broadcasts over social media and streaming video sites on the U.E. network was impossible for anyone but Stas and his team. The global censorship of truth was at an end.

Things moved very quickly. Every shop licensed to conduct conversions put in requests for continued delivery of chips, and hundreds of new shops requested training packages every day.

Two weeks after the automotive campaign began, a call came in on the security line, requesting clearance for a chopper to land on the U.E. headquarters landing pad. Dillon was in the control room, as usual, and received the call himself. *Why shouldn't Air Force One come for a visit?* he thought after the pilot identified himself.

"That will be fine. Put her down on pad two, please," Dillon officially barked into the channel.

United States Secret Service agents in full SWAT gear were the first out of the chopper; then came the president, Mr. Brennan, and finally, Mr. Sylinger, the three men with whom Daniel privately met just after finishing his studies at Stanford.

He had been in the lab all day, working to develop a personal protective field emitter. He wasn't quite finished when Dillon's message popped up on his screen. Daniel's reply was short. "They will have to wait. I am finishing up a train of thought. I'll be about an hour." He did not rush, but when he found a suitable stopping point, he wrapped up and headed up to the top-floor sunroom, where the men sat comfortably, patiently waiting.

They stood as Daniel entered, showing the same level of respect he recalled from their first encounter. They shook hands, and the president respectfully asked if there was a private place they could talk. Daniel showed them into the library across the hall from where they had waited, and they sat at a modern boardroom table.

"Well," said the president, "thank you for having us. We are still fans of what you are doing, but those who pull the strings of world affairs are rattled, and pressure is being put on us to shut you down. The powers that be, if you will, are taking a strong stance against what your company is achieving. They want you to share the designs or face major consequences," he solemnly stated.

Daniel smiled conspiratorially. "Everyone knows there are no patents protecting what I have created, and people are free to it, if they can figure it out. And, might I add, my company is now one of the biggest global earners in the world. Have you noticed how much tax we are paying? We have used no tax shelters. We pay top corporate rates. Why? Because, as we discussed in our first meeting, as long as my company benefits America, then I should be protected. Correct?"

The president sighed, looking tired. "You know as well as we do that no one has the slightest idea how the U.E. technology works, Daniel. We don't want to see you or your family get hurt. Please come to the table with them! Tax money only goes so far. These are the most powerful people in the world, Daniel. You are taking away their control."

Daniel felt anger rise inside him as he recalled the deaths of Angelo and Lucia. "What about my friends, who we left lying in the street in the Dominican Republic? Is giving these people what they do not deserve honorable to my lost friends? What about the places in the world where people die for lack of water or suitable food? What about the constant war in this world and the uncured diseases—so easily cured, if not for the pharmaceutical profiteers?"

"Yes, we are all sorry about that, Daniel," Mr. Brennan cut in.

"Even though the U.E. corporation is in good standing, there are factions of the government demanding seizure of your energy technology on the grounds of national security, and we can only stop their lobbying efforts for so long."

"The second most important reason I am not going to share the secrets of my technology is because the world can't seem to live in peace," Daniel explained. "There's always war, and every country continues to expand its military force. It seems to me that our people are continuously working on better, more efficient ways for killing. Most important, those you referred to as the people pulling the strings—if they get their hands on my tech, there will be no way to see our species elevate beyond the suppressed condition we have been stuck in for so many generations. I am sorry, gentlemen, but I cannot do what you ask."

Nodding, the president stood and began moving toward the doorway. Daniel and the two other men followed a short distance behind. The president abruptly turned and put his hand on Daniel's shoulder. He considered Daniel's eyes hard and spoke calmly, yet with an urgent and stern tone. "I hope you will be safe, but I cannot promise your safety when the rest of my government votes to move against you. For your sake and for the safety of your loved ones, please consider sharing or making peace with those that would otherwise see complete destruction of what you have created, rather than have their empires end."

After the unexpected meeting, Daniel thought on the matter and discussed it extensively with Stas, Dillon, and his father. They concluded that in order to survive long enough to tip the balance, they would need to offer a financial compromise. There would be no sharing of formulas. Instead, they would set up foundations to help those losing their jobs. They would also make a public offering to supplement lost income for the multinational corporations, just enough to keep them at bay. They just needed a little more time to see it through, to make it to where humanity was able to use the tech in everything new.

To the wireless companies, Daniel offered a 15 percent income share for the next twenty-five years. He laced his promises with suggestions that he might want to join their fold, giving them hope he would become theirs. He approached the power corporations of the world, the old monopoly holders over electricity, and offered a stern ultimatum. His proposal was for a 35% profit share for the next five years and an agreement that their manpower would do residential installations.

Daniel and his father launched the U.E. electric grid marketing campaign that promoted residential and industrial power chips for free to anyone wanting to sign up.

In the past, those working from the anonymity of the shadows did everything in their power to suppress and prevent anything like this from ever happening. But Daniel somehow slipped by, and aside from some sort of military assault on United Earth Technologies, there was nothing else they could do. After weeks of legal meetings, they saw that it was either a 75% reduction in revenue or a 100% loss.

Electrical contractors saw the biggest boom in business as entire cities ordered chips, while humanity embraced the U.E. technological offering. Another paradigm shift started.

Daniel turned seventeen as his company took full control of the world's energy supply. Coal, nuclear, hydro, solar, and wind were shut down everywhere, and millions of jobs were lost. Seeing people lose their jobs because of what he was doing, Daniel set up even more foundations, guaranteeing funds to pay for education and to support families for everyone losing their incomes that soon became known as the U.E. program.

Even with their free share, those losing their control were far from content. There was no way to ignore the substantial reduction in revenues; the elephant in the room was undeniable. United Earth Technologies was becoming unstoppable. The simple fact that the boy was outside their closed circle made the defeat much harder to bear, and the truth of his suggestions of joining them quickly was seen as obvious falsehoods.

What could they do? The people of the world were embracing the change. But the heads of power, the unnamed shadows of the world, looked down on humanity and refused to stand for the sheep seeing true prosperity. In their eyes, mankind was doomed, if not enslaved, under their control. The insane cried out in terror, and their greedy minions demonstrated a sick kind of madness as they shouted their lies over their unwatched corporate media networks.

Chapter 13

Antamina

The world at large accepted the energy revolution, primarily because of the U.E. foundations providing the very best funding for professional re-education programs, family support funds and the cold handshake Daniel made with international figureheads.

At the U.E. main facilities, Daniel worked tirelessly, perpetually locked in the third-floor R&D lab. Something was awake inside him and it called to search for secrets hiding in the realm of impossibility. He was looking for a way to instantly transmit matter over large distances. It was there—he could feel it, the knowledge he needed, just outside his mind.

In his search, he created a new magnification technique to peer into the bandwidth his wireless energy and data transmitting chip accessed. He searched, yet he found nothing, and he doubted himself. Closing his eyes, he whispered, "It's just not there. But it must be!" He forced himself to look again; he wanted to quit, but in that moment of weakness, he saw what looked like a dark ribbon. Excited, he zoomed in billions of times more and saw glimmering specks. Amazed and curious to see how far this new magnification apparatus could go, he zoomed in quadrillions more times. Discovering no real limits, he stopped to observe his findings and was left speechless.

What he saw reminded him of a galaxy super-cluster field—a tapestry of glowing mists, like the one illustrated by a leading team in the national science news; a map showing the location of the Milky Way and billions of other galaxies in the larger galactic currents of the universe. It was beautiful.

Eagerly, Daniel looked further. He zoomed even more, septillions of times more, again and again. He found no limits, and then, just as he thought it would go on forever, the zoom stopped. He was looking at the very filament he originally started zooming into.

The infinite zoom had taken him full circle, back to the exact atomic position he was looking through, except in a totally new subdimension of the very same space. He fell back in his chair with his hands on his face. "How is this possible?" he exclaimed, exhausted by his own personal drive to discover and push past impossibilities yet he would not take a break now.

He pulled up the modular application tool set and generated a program to scan, list, and codify a complicated carbon composite. When that was complete, he tested his postulate. He moved the position of the scanned composite in the filament viewport dimension using the codified data, and the object in his dimension changed positions. "Come, Stas! Come right now. You are not going to believe this!" His voice rang out over their wireless coms network.

When his big friend arrived and saw the composite teleport in front of him, his response was dry and mocking. "So are we going to start teleporting ourselves around the office now? Because you know we never leave the office anyway."

Daniel looked at him with incredulity. "Yes, Stas, that's exactly why I locked myself in my lab for the past three weeks, so you can get coffee without having to get out of your chair. What I think we need you to do now is write us some new software. We need the new software to look through this dimensional window and begin cataloging every energy signature of everybody of mass in the entire Milky Way and then the universe."

Daniel put the filament viewport up on the wall display. He imagined that by looking through this filament, this interdimensional reflection, one could move through space at a galactic, interstellar, or planetary level as quickly as moving a tool tip across a digital display. They could know what was out there and send things to and from places, farther than humankind could ever hope to travel.

Stas didn't believe what Daniel was showing him. It was as though the picture in front of their eyes was a mirage of limitless points. Daniel flicked the magnification zoom, bringing tens of thousands of galaxies into focus. He flicked to the side, and it scrolled, causing millions of galaxies to fly past. "Okay, so this is happening right now? How is this possible?" he muttered as he turned to head up to the developer's suite. "You can feed this subdimensional viewport to my office, right?"

"Yes, doing that now," Daniel confirmed, smiling to himself at how Stas always took a challenge in stride. He was decisive and brilliant and possessed a keen mind, a good friend.

When Stas got back to the lab, he took pleasure in announcing that everything was now on hold for a new high-priority task. "We need to write software to survey, track, and display the positions of every object with mass inside the Milky Way—and then, I would imagine, beyond. Daniel has found some wormhole, interdimensional, reflection viewport. You are not going to believe it." When he was in his seat, he linked up to the system Daniel was now streaming to the servers. He zoomed all the way until he saw their office. Then he saw himself sitting at his desk, and Jimmy gasped as he watched over his friend's shoulder.

A chill went through them as they saw the real-time feedback of their forms in an energy signature viewport. They analyzed it, and then, employing Daniel's algorithm to see into this window, they began compiling and cataloging just what was in the room. Jimmy was indispensable, assisting with equations beyond what Stas could easily understand.

With the software ready, they started. Initially, Stas wanted to create a single signature with the mass, size, and mineral composition for Earth, as was the plan for all other objects in the initial cataloging, but Daniel insisted they go the extra mile on Earth. He wanted them to use Earth as a world point cloud prototype. He also insisted they do this because he needed that information for another project.

With things moving along so well, Daniel wanted to move to the next stage and would need a much bigger facility. At first, he was unsure where to find a secure location. He wanted more than a billion square meters of floor space, enough to store materials and house 3-D printing modules large enough to print one-thousand-cubic-meter composites, while having a huge hydroponics division, where Samantha could work on developing new strains of plants to help fight back against the ever-spreading deserts of the world.

The world's forests were as scarce as they had ever been. Everywhere, deserts encroached more and more on the last of the forested regions, and he dreamed of seeing Earth return to a state of abundant natural life.

He consulted his father about what he was looking for, and before he was finished explaining, John had the answer.

"What about finding a huge pit mine nearing the end of its life? It's perfect. You're not looking for ore, right? You're looking for space. Imagine building a facility inside one of those huge abandoned pit mines, Dan. It would almost seem like too much space." Seeing what his son was achieving made this new proposition inspiring. "If we can find a project in the right location nearing completion, with environment and deactivation requirements, we could potentially acquire it and begin construction of a new facility immediately."

After hearing his father's proposal, Daniel was inspired and wrote a program to search out potential properties with the specifications his father described. They wanted the property to be an open pit mine, no less than five hundred meters deep and two thousand meters wide in both directions. Finally, he wanted to find a property at a high elevation, preferably three thousand meters above sea level or more, and located somewhere in South America.

Daniel personally reviewed the results of the search and short-listed the best few. After a brief scan, the Antamina copper-zinc mine in central Peru stood out as an obvious choice. He analyzed the energy signatures of the landscape around the pit mine through the filament viewport and, seeing what he was looking for, decided it was the best option.

Knowing they would soon be making international flights, they installed a runway on a new parcel of land adjacent to the main facility and purchased a Gulfstream G650 equipped with a U.E. power cell, giving it unlimited range.

Dillon, Stas, John, and Daniel flew to the Andes in Peru the following week. On the final approach, the plane circled the site a dozen times. Finally, when they landed on the property's private airstrip, most of their minds were already made up.

They toured the huge site, a mine that had produced copper, silver, zinc, and other minerals for the past thirty-two years. The project was six months from the start of its deactivation construction phase, and Daniel knew they could get it for a steal. At just over seven hundred meters deep, with canyon-like walls spanning a length of just over three thousand meters long and fifteen hundred meters wide, along with other side pits, there would be more than enough space.

At the end of the tour, they convened with the owners' representatives and put together an offer that would be hard-pressed to refuse.

When the purchase was complete, Daniel's very next step was to instruct his acquisitions team to approach the Peruvian government with a deal they too could not refuse. Daniel and his organization were world renowned, as nearly every country on earth was hooked up to the U.E. energy grid. Now, with contracts to U.E. for the energy powering their cities, it cost them less than one-tenth of what they had previously paid, while at the same time the change had ended nearly all carbon emissions worldwide.

Daniel's great friend and mentor Angelo Bonifacio used to speak fondly of Peru. He would tell Daniel that it was one of his favorite places in the world. The memory came clearly, and his heart skipped; he heard his old friend's voice as if he were there, standing with him. "Its people are so kind and passionate for life. Its mountains and coastlines are so majestic, and the culture, my boy—the culture!" he would say.

The landscapes that Angelo would describe painted pictures of pristine beauty—rugged and lush tropical countrysides, leading up to towering mountains that ran the length of the entire country. When Daniel was just learning of the world, he dreamed of visiting these places and felt a sense of satisfaction, knowing he would be spending a lot of time here.

United Earth Technologies was now a $2 trillion a year engine with no end in sight. Fortunately, the Peruvian people saw his interest in their country as an honor; what he wanted, though, was a very tall order. In the end, he offered them $1.5 trillion as a onetime payment for complete sovereignty over the land around the Antamina mine. However, the huge sum of money was to be paid under a legal agreement, binding them to pay off the national debt and create a trust to keep the country's financial balance from ever seeing debt again.

At first, they were shocked. The bureaucrats, with their vested interests and corporate media channels, all cried out at the nerve and pomposity of U.E.'s proposition. "No Peruvian official would consider allowing a new country to form inside their own borders," they proclaimed.

Daniel took it all in stride, laying out the details of the agreement publicly in ways the majority of Peruvian officials soon understood as beneficial to both parties. He needed a place he could legally prevent anyone from entering, and what better place than a remote mountainous pit mine?

The deal was struck, and U.E. took possession of a four-hundred-square-kilometer parcel of land with full sovereign title. Over the next six months, the employees at the mine received huge end-of-contract compensation packages in return for work in prepping the pit for its future construction.

Every day, seventy thousand tons of blasted rock was crushed, washed, and sent back to the pit as three-quarter grade. The grade rock was packed two feet thick on all primary levels and one foot thick everywhere else inside the site. The huge roads and flattened areas spiraling up the sides of the pit were packed and smoothed by teams of graders, dozers, and excavators as the freshly laid washed rock was layered on. Five thousand workers, now with tripled rates, worked in ten-hour shifts twenty-four hours a day, and the work went quickly.

As the grading of the pit's surfaces was completed, the mine workers trickled down the road that would soon no longer exist. Daniel flew back and forth from California to the site over the course of the preparation and felt the excitement at seeing the project's ground works come to completion. This new facility would be the jumping-off point in establishing off-planet operations.

When the prep work was complete, a new phase of resource gathering began. All around the world, huge transport trucks equipped with matter transmitters arrived at auto-part scrap-collection stations, there, they deployed conveyer belts and began loading up the scrap materials from months of conversions. Inside each transport truck, the scrap was scanned and then dropped into a second chamber, where it transmitted to coordinates one hundred meters above the bottom of the new Antamina raw materials storage area.

As the scrap parts arrived, they crashed down onto a pile that would continue growing until every scrap part from around the globe arrived. The next phase began. Daniel worked on a way to convert the raw materials into a carbon powder for a newly designed 3-D printing chamber critical to the assembly of the new facility and all future construction.

He found that for each unifying frequency in matter, there was an opposite, a resonant frequency that, if directed properly, caused the materials to shatter: a real-world atomizing frequency. He designed a chamber to direct frequency waves into raw materials and successfully tested the system on various compositions before setting up the storage system. When the raw materials atomized, the dust like particles moved outward and transmitted to storage tanks, where unifying frequencies recombined them into near atom sized carbon powder for the 3-D printers.

In the huge additional building in the north corner of the main campus in North America, they filled four floors with huge 3-D printers capable of matter-transmitting finished composites, along with rows of carbon conversion chambers, and as it all went into place, Daniel finished final designs for the new facility and construction began.

In the Antamina pit, sections of huge anchors arrived, one hundred meters above the floor, where the piles of scrap continued to materialize and fall to the ground. Each of the caps drilled deep into the walls, sending huge networks of beams far out into the bedrock. When the anchors were set, the structural beams started arriving. They latticed out in all directions, creating a honeycomb structure that gained strength with each beam's placement. The matter transmitters worked tirelessly, teleporting the structural beams to predesigned locations all around the base of the mine and then up to where the first platform was to begin bridging the gap for the first floor, which would span between the distant walls. As the mass of interlocking beams formed like an intricate jigsaw puzzle, the foundation grew more and more solid. Sections of the first platforms, where power cells, huge 3-D printers, carbon separators, and matter transmitters materialized in their designed locations and the first-floor neared completion.

While the assembly continued, Daniel perfected the matter transmitter to safely work with organic subjects, specifically people. Knowing it worked was one thing though, actually doing it scared him way too much to actually try. *What if it leaves my mind behind?* he thought fearfully, picturing hundreds of unacceptable scenarios. *What if I come out dismembered or blind?*

Stas and Jimmy stayed busy designing worker bots that were needed for detailed finishing tasks. Using the point cloud of the entire pit, they wrote AI for the robots, soon be the autonomous workers, builders, lifters, and finishers for the entire facility. Daniel considered marketing the bots but decided that for the good of the working man, he would keep them off the market for now. With their current revenues, there was no need for any further products; in fact, he felt it soon would be time to start giving back in even bigger ways.

As assembly of the facility continued, Daniel scaled up the power cell design and 3-D printed one large enough to transmit materials anywhere inside Earth's solar system. The latest power cell was the largest so far, and he found no real limitations in his simulated models. This single generator, if put on the world grid, would power the entire planet three times over, and it was only the size of a small SUV.

The third level of the facility's construction was soon complete. This level was a multideck layout spanning the entire distance between the canyon walls. The deck was over three hundred meters above the bottom of the pit, with its main level over four thousand meters across and ringed by tiers of other platforms that rose to the walls on the perimeter.

John, Stas, Dillon, and Daniel wondered how the bots would move about the facility. They considered using rubber tracks with magnetic buds to move up walls and along ceilings, but after discussing it in length, decided there had to be a better option. They didn't want the bots to be restricted on tracks or wheels, and just as they were about to give up for the day, Stas offhandedly remarked that it would be best if they could hover. "Antigravity, you know!" he joked in his thick Russian accent, his way of mocking his own idea. They all laughed when he said it, but Daniel's mind latched onto the idea. *There has to be a way*, he thought, giving the impossible concept real consideration.

When Daniel got back to his lab, Stas's remark about antigravity stuck in his mind. He looked at the digital wall and decided now was as good a time as any.

He started by writing out the equations for relativity, hoping that something would jump out at him. Then he wrote out the laws of conservation and illustrated a series of magnetic fields before jotting out Newton's law of universal gravitation. After that, he began scribbling and illustrating every known physics equation for gravity until he went through all of the most advanced equations mankind had ever contemplated. He hardly paused as a wave of new equations, along with images of objects encompassed by fields of circular patterns, came to his mind.

It was as though he saw it all through another's eyes—an innate understanding of every trick beyond the walls of humanity's sandbox. He filled the digital wall display with page after page of complex scribbles, symbols, and frequency waves, all describing the exact ratios, space displacement requirements, and mass offset variances. He wanted true antigravitational field technology, and it came to him. After hours of acting as a conduit to some unlimited bank of knowledge, he paused. Unconsciously, he began whispering a hymn, a song in a language not spoken on Earth—"Dyastyaaa, eYiyastyaaa, Dyastyaaa iyastyaaa." And as the song drifted out from his subconscious, his eyes closed. He curled up as though it was the only thing left to do and slept like he had not done in years.

The next morning, when he awoke, he found himself in his lab, at one with his favorite leather chair. He rubbed the sleep from his eyes and moved to get up, but as he did, the symbols and patterns on the screen caught his eyes, and it all came rushing back. Reaching to pick up the glass of water from its holder, he took a sip, and the previous night came back into focus. It was all there. He laughed at himself. "It's all there!" he rejoiced to the empty room. "AI, please run this new simulation," he commanded.

As Dillon, Jimmy, and John returned to the facility, they realized Daniel had not left the night before and instead of stopping on the second-floor developer's suite, they continued down to check on their friend. He was there, sitting dead-still, except for his fingers rippling across the keyboard in front of him.

The wall display was filled with equations of which none of them could make sense, and they each saw the simulation in one corner of the wall at nearly the same time. It was a strange field, pulsing and rotating as layers of energy appeared to slide through each other at varying speeds. Daniel often got into his work on an entirely different level than anyone else, and so, knowing it was better not to break his concentration, they left him to focus.

A few hours later a pop-up appeared on their monitors: "Drop everything. We need a stabilizing algorithm ASAP, using these variables. Make it quick."

They looked at each other, expecting some impossible task that would take days, but when they examined the variables Daniel supplied, they saw the principles were very straightforward. Within a couple of hours, when they finished the algorithm and after they tested it against the requirements, they passed it back to Daniel, excited to find out what the bigger picture of this project would be. They waited an hour before heading down to see what Daniel was working on. When they arrived, as expected, they found him sitting in exactly the same spot, as though time had somehow stopped on this level. The pulsing sphere was now in the center of the wall, surrounded by long strings of algebraic equations.

No longer willing to wait, Stas broke the silence. "What's going on, Daniel?" Daniel threw up his hand wordlessly, typing at a speed that would seem unnatural to most people.

Something told them he was close, so they stood and watched. The simulated orb on the wall stabilized; the violent pulsing was replaced by a smooth symmetrical flow. The display type changed, and they saw the layers shift colors. It was a rainbow of circles, all sliding along the surface of a sphere. Shades of red, orange, and purple shifted again, changing to cooler greens, blues, and purple strands. Daniel relaxed, sitting back in triumphant silence, just watching the simulation for a short time before turning to look at his friends.

"Hello! We now have antigravity fields for our robots—and for anything else we can think to use it for!"

Stas cursed audibly. "You know what the heck you are, Daniel? You're a freak, a darn freak!" And they all laughed at the unbelievable breakthrough.

After integrating the antigravity nodes into the drone design and applying a software patch so the bots could hover and work at the same time, the build description package was ready. The AI picked up the design, and using 3-D printers that were installed on the third deck of the Antamina facility, the first United Earth worker drone was printed.

The newly designed 3-D printers were calibrated to print incredible monolithic composites. Circuit boards contained every kind of semiconductor and sensor array, all were made from ultralight, harder-than-steel carbon and advanced materials in one single composite.

The day was going so well that Daniel thought he might take a break and relax outside for a few days, but Stas and Dillon gave stern looks. "Word is getting out, Daniel," Stas insisted.

"Our security at the new Antamina facility is nowhere close to what it needs to be. It is becoming world news! We are under surveillance by every special interest group in the world," Dillon added.

Stas followed Dillon's remark without giving Daniel time to interject. "Pictures and video of the Antamina assembly are popping up all over the net. The world is seeing videos of the structure, appearing piece by piece, without any construction crews on site. It's blowing people's minds man."

Stas brought up a digital display that showed the current satellite activity over the area. Huge drone traffic and a substantial portion of the world's military and government satellites were all directing their focus on the new United Earth Antamina property.

Daniel didn't see the problem at first. "What's the big deal, guys? So what if they can see how we do things? It's not like they are going to replicate our technologies."

"You have to see," Dillon argued. "Other countries of the world may be getting pushed by higher powers to test our borders, infiltrate our land, and conduct covert surveillance, if not military action against us. Not to mention that having this building seemingly grow up out of the ground is a bit much for people to come to grips with."

The reality of it sank in, and Daniel came to attention: He looked up sharply, remembering the tragedy that took place on their family vacation.

He turned on his heels. "Thank you both for helping me see this!" He swiftly walked to the end of the hall without looking back. He took the stairs at a trot, heading toward his lab, and called back to them over his shoulder.

"We need a new media presentation of goodwill for the world to see. Let's put one together and upload it to every video site on the U.E. wireless network. We need to make it clear to the world that our new facility is a peaceful installation to help humanity move in a positive direction."

Dillon looked to Stas. "Oh crap, I haven't seen him react like that in a while."

"Well, at least something is going to be done about it. The video is a good idea. I will pull some stuff out of the cloud and put something together. Could you do a recorded interview of yourself speaking about the prosperity we are working toward, Dillon? Thanks," Stas instructed.

Jimmy and Stas sent the message out to everyone on the U.E. network a few hours later. They used net crawlers to upload the public relations video to every site and forum in every language, as fast as the information could travel through the world's online networks.

No one saw Daniel for the next few days. He called up from his lab with requests for food, and when it was delivered, they found the lights off and no sign of him. Hours later, the plate would be gone, and then around dinner, when a new plate of food was brought to the lab, the previous one—now empty—would be there with a note, thanking them for understanding his need to have uninterrupted focus time.

No one knew, but he had taken the leap for the first time. He had thrown caution to the wind and matter-transmitted himself to the Antamina facility. There, he worked tirelessly in the newly printed research lab on the now-totally completed fourth level.

The thought that an imminent threat was looming sent him feverishly working to perfect a new device to protect them. He wanted to complete the personal protective field emitter he so nearly finished months ago. He remembered that he was missing something to bring it together, something not in mankind's understanding of the universe—and it was so close. This time, though, he was developing the field on a scale large enough to protect the entire Antamina property from both physical attack and unwanted eyes.

Daniel surprised Stas and Jimmy when his disheveled figured stepped into their lab. "I changed the frequency of the antigravity field and added a series of shifting zero-point electromagnetic forces to localize vectored frequencies. The field will deflect anything trying to pass through it. Up to a million-ton rock falling from the sky, that is," he announced.

To demonstrate the new field, he tossed a hovering chrome sphere into the center of the room and using a handheld controller, activated it. When it went live, there was a buzz in the room that made everyone's teeth feel funny. The shimmering sphere simmered and crackled less than ten feet from where they stood. He smiled at their astonishment and demonstrated how it worked. He took off his shoe and threw it at the shimmering field. When it hit, it bounced off like it was punched back multiple times harder than the shoe's initial velocity.

Stas stepped closer, a faint reflection of himself catching his eye in the orb's surface. The strange sphere shimmered and shifted as bands of energy distorted space.

"This is just the miniature version. The full-size one is already installed at the Antamina property. There won't be any more footage or unauthorized access from now on. The energy field enveloping Antamina extends to just a few hundred meters inside our borders, and nothing can get through," Daniel explained.

As soon as the protective energy field went up, blocking the eyes of the world, the powers that be, went from just curious to outraged. For weeks, they freely pointed the world's most sophisticated surveillance systems at the property. They watched and recorded streaming video of the structure that somehow grew itself into place, and then everything went blurry.

Dillon was the next person to transmit to the new facility, and when he arrived, he was utterly blown away. The interior of the dome-covered facility was other-worldly. His security building was incredible. There was polished concrete flooring, dark solid-wood paneling, leather couches, an amazing kitchen, along with the crowning centerpiece, the PLED wall, which was four movie theater screens tall and wrapped 180 degrees around one end of the five-thousand-square-foot room's circular wall.

Daniel and Stas were always busy developing AI to automate many tasks. For the Antamina construction, they developed an AI called the Architect. It was designed to take lists of requirements, dimensions, and finishing criteria, along with three-dimensional point cloud data of where the construction was to take place. Using all this, it generated a finished technical information model ready for the 3-D printers, matter transmitters, and drones to construct virtually anything they could dream up, wherever they wanted.

Dillon flopped down into the freshly 3-D-printed, ergonomic Italian leather hover chair, and a short orientation video started to play on the wall. It showed a team of recovery drones, a weapons room, surveillance drones, personal protection suits, and finally, the real gem: a personal transport vehicle.

His eyes nearly popped out of his head as the video showed the craft's specs. First, there was its speed capabilities—numbers that could not be possible. Next, he saw an array of anti-g-force regulators to keep the cabin of the vehicle at one G-force of pressure no matter what maneuvers were being pulled. The deflective energy-field emitters left him a little stunned by their elegant intelligence. After that, the luxurious interior was featured: red leather bucket seats with dark-brown stitching, dark mahogany panels with inlay chrome strip highlights, a huge LCD console equipped with a micro-holographic display projector for aerial views of surrounding terrain, and of course a matter-transmission drive for instant travel over vast distances.

From the outside, it looked like a race boat mixed with a large tactical SUV, and he could not wait to get his hands on it. When the video finished, he was out of his seat and heading across the room in what would be record time. As he entered the hangar and saw the vehicle, he gasped. It was beautiful.

He called Daniel to thank him, and as the call linked up to his ID, Daniel flashed into the room, materializing right in front of him. He smiled when the big man looked at him with forced indignation at Daniel's entrance.

"It would be best to wait a little while. Let's get settled in and wait for the eyes of the world to get bored of us before we start zipping around in flying saucers, okay?" Daniel suggested and stepped away. He winked. "Nice-looking place you have here. Check out the personal protection suits yet? Everyone should start wearing them under their street clothes. The protective suit will save your life." He activated the matter-transmitter panel on his forearm and, as quickly as he'd arrived, he flashed away.

Chapter 14

Conflict

A board a destroyer in the South Pacific Super Carrier battle group that was assigned to surveillance of the new U.E. sovereign land, the on-duty officer of the watch cursed when he was informed the feeds from the drones monitoring Antamina were a blurry mass. He slammed his fist down hard and cursed loudly. This was unacceptable. "Some kid controlling sovereign land in Peru?" He imagined the kid was creating weapons to take over the world and knew that the commander of the Nimitz-class carrier sailing southeast of his position shared similar feelings. They had been friends through training and always brought their families together when on leave. Deep down, he hoped that James Church would do something about this little brat and contemplated what they could legally do to neutralize this threat.

"Sir, we have three F-22 Raptors lifting off the *Gerald R. Ford*, with orders to investigate the surveillance feed issues, sir," the officer on deck reported.

"This day is about to get interesting," he muttered, having a hard time suppressing his satisfied grin.

The three Raptors quickly rose to their cruising altitude and punched their afterburners, accelerating past the sound barrier with consecutive sonic booms. Twenty-five minutes passed before they arrived at their objective, four thousand meters above sea level, just over five hundred kilometers away.

When they arrived, they didn't know what to make of what they saw and delayed in their report.

"Captain Michaels, report," the commander of the carrier gruffly ordered the lead pilot.

"Sir, it appears to be some sort of huge, shimmering sphere that spans the entire Antamina property. The sphere is blocking all visuals of the Antamina pit itself and appears to be stable. Please advise."

"Let's see what this thing is made of, Lieutenant. Fire a single tactical cluster bomb at the top of that dome," Commander Church ordered.

There was no hesitation; the lead F-22 sent a medium-range cruise missile loaded with a cluster payload that spread into a forty-foot-wide blanket of explosives that rippled across the shimmering energy field. The result was not what anyone expected. A magnetic shock wave, ten times greater than the detonation of the explosive shells, rebounded directly into the path of the two trailing fighters. A moment later, a wall of electromagnetic energy blew out their stabilization and fried most of their electronics. They spun out of control.

Dillon, sitting in his new office on the upper deck of the facility, watched the events from the very beginning. After Daniel left earlier in the day, Dillon had decided to play with the surveillance systems and see how they worked. There were hundreds of surveillance drones, and he sent up a group of the tennis ball-sized spheres to see what they could do. Each drone was equipped with long-range and wide-angle high-definition cameras, gravity-null field emitters, and basic force fields to prevent any kind of radar detection, along with the now standard-issue transmission drives. He sent some to hold positions at forty thousand feet above the facility and others to hover just inside the Antamina border, instructing them to scan the perimeter five hundred kilometers in every direction. The F-22s were picked up right away, and after looking at their flight paths, he had no doubt where they were heading.

When he confirmed their direction, he brought up the frequency-band scanner and patched directly into the fighter pilot's radio channels, not caring who might be listening. "Hostility is not recommended. Please proceed with extreme caution. Antamina is restricted airspace, and the U.E. is a peaceful corporation with aims to help humanity. Thank you." He received no reply—not that he had expected one—and knew the only thing he could do now was sit back and watch as the events unfolded on his massive display.

After the first flyover, he was relieved that nothing happened, but he knew deep down that something was bound to go wrong. On their second pass, something did! The lead fighter launched a missile at the dome. He trusted Daniel and knew the boy must have planned for something like this, but at the same time he was unsure of what would happen. In the few moments before impact, his skin crawled with the knowledge that this could end very badly for him and the facility.

When it was over, he wondered why he had ever doubted at all. There was not even a whisper inside the dome. He was familiar with the ammunitions they had used, and as he double-checked the shields-integrity monitoring application, he was even more surprised to see that less than a single percentage of disturbance in the field was registered on impact.

Though the missile had made no effect on the facility, the fallout was just getting started. His heart sank when he saw two of the jets spin out of control, and with zero hesitation, he activated four recovery drones to track and recover the men, who he hoped managed to eject before their planes hit the ground.

Seeing the third fighter peel off and head back toward the battle group at sea, he put on one of the personal protective suits Daniel recently had finished designing and jumped into the sleek all-atmosphere vehicle. He was itching to take it for a test drive, and the current situation more than warranted it. The controls were intuitive, and its ability to move was incredible. It could hit ten times the speed of sound in a split second without putting any g-force on the passengers inside, and he planned to push its limits.

Activating the null drive, he lifted off and raced toward the installation's energy field, knowing from the brief orientation that it would automatically sense the U.E. craft and allow him through. It felt as though he was sitting completely stationary while everything outside the vehicle's null field zipped past. He set the autopilot to fly directly to the closest pilot and checked the heads-up display to see what the drones were seeing. A sense of relief hit him as the first downed pilot sat up.

In the brief moments it took for him to arrive on the scene, he sent a broadcast radio message on the pilot's channel one more time, stating his old rank and that he would rescue and return the downed pilots to their ship.

It took less than a minute for him to arrive at the first pilot, who was visibly shaken and obviously unsure of the drones hovering a few meters on either side of him. Dillon came in at an angle and a speed that, to the pilot, must have appeared as a blur. He came to a nearly instantaneous stop, with only a loud humming sound, two hundred meters from where the pilot now stood, and he hovered toward him.

The pilot saw Dillon sitting in the craft and immediately threw up his hands in surrender. Chuckling, Dillon spoke into the microphone, projecting his voice outside of the null field protecting his ship. "Hey, pal. Don't bother with the standard surrender stuff. I'm here to help. Sergeant Dillon Samuelson of the Fifty-First, at your service. I work for the kid you all are trying to kill today. Hop in; let's go find your other buddy."

The man, who identified himself as Captain Travis Lee of the *Gerald R. Ford*, followed Dillon's instruction and carefully stepped into the back-seating area of the vehicle. Dillon activated a shield between him and the passenger compartment, just as a precaution, and lifted off at 60% of the vehicle's top speed.

The alarming rate of travel made Captain Lee gulp in surprise. "No g-forces? How is this possible?" he asked as Dillon slammed the vehicle into a dive toward where the other pilot was lying, hopefully only unconscious. "Holy crap, this thing can move," Travis exclaimed as he held on purely out of reflex.

They found the other pilot and revived him. His leg was broken, and after he was stabilized by the two drones, Dillon gave them a voice command to gently load the injured pilot into the craft.

As they lifted off, a voice came over the radio. "This is the captain of the USS *Gerald R. Ford*. Dillon Samuelson? You son of a gun! I thought you were dead," James Church said in his friendliest military tone.

Dillon recognized the voice from when he was enlisted in the service. He had been transported on an aircraft carrier and dropped in hostile territory. His team was en route to a mission that had left them stranded, and the memory of it brought up painful emotions. He knew it hadn't been the captain's fault, but it still stung, and he had to push the anger down. He smiled at the memory of repeatedly beating the man at chess, and then he replied, "Ha-ha! Good to hear your voice, sir. I look forward to putting my reigning title on the line if you would like a game after I get this injured man back aboard your boat."

"How bad is he?" Church asked.

"Just a broken leg. I guess he came down pretty hard. He was unconscious when we found him, but he'll live. Your other pilot is looking after him," Dillon replied.

"Well, I apologize for the trouble. I am personally giving you official clearance to land on the deck of my ship. What's your ETA?" Hearing Dillon's estimate of five minutes until touchdown, James laughed. "You are joking, right? You are roughly 650 miles out!" But Dillon assured him of the time frame and set the craft heading directly for the ship at nearly full speed.

Captain Lee moved forward in the rear cabin, leaving his injured brother-in-arms where he lay. He looked over Dillon's shoulder and saw what the cockpit of this craft looked like. The first thing he understood was the detailed holographic display that showed a point cloud of his aircraft carrier's deck and then the digital map that showed their progress and airspeed. He registered that they were traveling just over Mach 8, and when his mind finally accepted the readings, he was more than a little surprised.

"How is this possible? There is no way we are traveling that fast, are we? And how do you have such a detailed schematic of my ship's deck?" he asked.

Dillon reached out and touched a spot on the three-dimensional display of the aircraft carrier's deck. He tapped a helicopter pad. "Landing area alpha at 90% velocity," Dillon said to the craft's AI before turning to look at Captain Lee through the still-active field between them.

"Let's just say my employer is smarter than the average super-genius. Trust me when I say you guys really messed up by firing into our energy field."

Captain Lee just stared silently at him.

Dillon had the thought that James Church might have ulterior motives, *was he planning to ambush him once he landed on the deck of that ship?* A cold chill went up his spine with the thought. He would have to be cautious, he realized, and he set his sights forward, steeling himself for what was to come.

It took a total of four and a half minutes to travel the distance out to sea, and as they approached the group of warships, he made a call.

"Daniel, how are you, my man? We have had a bit of a mix-up with an American naval battle group this afternoon. Three F-22 Raptors buzzed the energy field, and one let off a shot. It ended badly for two of the jets. It turns out an old friend of mine is the captain of the carrier. So, I am transporting the wounded back to him. I will make sure everything is smoothed over. Would you like me to invite this old friend of mine, James Church, the commander of the aircraft carrier, back to the facility to sit down for a face-to-face talk?"

"Well, I am glad no one has died. If Captain Church and his staff would like to have a visit, we can send a pod for them. I wouldn't mind talking to them in person. It would best to befriend these people, would it not?" Daniel responded, surprising Dillon with his lack of concern.

The U.E. vehicle's approach on the naval radar was virtually undetected, coming in faster than a missile and landing with utterly no deceleration at all. From the control rooms aboard the ships facing Dillon's approach, captains and watch officers held their breaths as the streak of light flashed through the sky, heading directly for the flagship they were obligated to protect at all costs.

From the command center, high above the deck on the *Gerald R. Ford*, James watched it come in and feared the worst until the bolt of motion came to a complete stop on the designated landing pad. Standing with his hands on the rail, he stared down at the spot where the craft appeared without much sound at all. His knuckles were white, and he had still not taken a breath, when from behind him, he heard one of his officers ask, "What just happened, sir?"

James snapped out of his sudden daze and replied. "I am not really sure, son. I'm not really sure at all, but we are going to find out. I promise you that!"

Dillon stayed in the cockpit of his craft after landing, looking out at the nine hundred meters of deck spreading out in front of him. Men were running between fighter jets, loaders moving missiles, and fueling tanks, and then he saw them—three six-wheeled vehicles heading in his direction. He watched them, and the hope for a friendly reception dwindled. When they arrived less than fifteen seconds later in abrupt screeching halts, squads of men piled out to take up position surrounding his craft and he knew his initial instincts about all this were spot on.

He triggered the side door to allow Captain Lee and the medics to get the injured pilot out the back of his craft and firmly decided he would not be moving from his seat. The moment they cleared his vehicle, he activated the side-panel deflector shield once more and turned his gaze back to the nervous marines looking as though they would be happy to tear Dillon to pieces.

James came over the radio in his friendliest tone. "Don't worry, Dillon. These boys will take you into custody as a formality of your surrender and bring you up to the bridge, where we can talk in private. Your craft, of course, must be impounded, and you will be free from that brat you have been working for, once and for all."

"Sorry, old friend. I won't be turning myself over or relinquishing ownership of my vehicle. I don't think you want to see what this baby is capable of. The 'brat,' as you referred to him, has instructed me to extend an invitation for you to visit us back at the Antamina site. Will you accept that offer?"

James came back quickly. "I am sorry, Dillon. You will not be permitted to leave here, and if you try, we will stop you."

From the corner of his eye, Dillon saw a line of Raptors accelerating down the deck and lifting off in a practiced line. It was obvious his old friend's plan was to try to keep him busy while they got their birds into the air. He chuckled.

"James, did this morning's events not teach you anything? United Earth Technologies is a thousand years ahead of anyone else on Earth. We are certainly not going to share it with any of you war-loving, military-minded madmen. Daniel is not interested in conquest or world domination. We just want to spread peace and prosperity to everyone. He wants mankind to prosper as a group. He wants to heal Earth from the industrial disease of the past three hundred years. But first, people like you will need to give up your power, and those who benefit at the cost of the rest of us will need to step aside."

"Dillon, I repeat, if you try to leave the deck with that craft, I promise you lethal force will be used to stop you. I have received orders stating that you are to be taken into custody, and your craft is to be impounded or destroyed."

Dillon punched the controls to max and was gone from the deck in a split second. He shot straight up, traveling at nearly ten thousand meters per second, and maintained that speed for seven and a half seconds before coming to a stop at just over seventy-five thousand feet. He set the craft to hover and pulled up a scan of the area below. A swarm of Raptors circled the *Gerald R. Ford* and then, as suddenly as he had taken off, cruise missiles launched from the destroyers.

"What the hell are you doing, James?" he yelled.

"By executive order, the land known as Antamina has been deemed an international threat to be dealt with using extreme force. You would have been safe if you had stayed aboard, Dillon."

Dillon didn't bother replying to the man; instead, he got Daniel on the line as quickly as he could,

"Hi, Dillon. How are things going over there?" Daniel asked. 'Has Mr. Church accepted our offer?"

"As if you don't know! I find it hard to believe you have not been patched into the security surveillance system this entire time. Nearly fifty cruise missiles just launched from the battle group heading straight for the facility right now!"

There was a moment's pause from Daniel before Dillon heard his reply. "Ah, you got me! Yeah, I see them. Yep, no problem. There's a red button on the center console of your vehicle. If you press that, you will instantly transmit back inside the dome, to safety."

Dillon considered Daniel's last word: *safety.* "How in the world would it be safe to be behind a wall of energy soon to have over fifty cruise missiles impacting it?"

Daniel could have punched the missiles out of the air with pulses of energy transmitted into positions directly along the incoming flight paths, but he felt it would be better for those on the offensive to see firsthand the futility of using their weapons against his defensive shields.

He activated a new group of surveillance drones, some to monitor the impending impacts and others to record the ships and fighter planes first-hand. Next, he got on the phone to call a number he had hoped to never need in an emergency like this.

The president reached into his pocket and withdrew his phone. He paused, unsure if he wanted to take the call. He knew he would have to take it. Daniel, by his actions, had brought a lot of pressure down on his admin-istration—pressure from people and corporations only whispered about at the highest levels. They demanded the US government take steps—drastic, offensive steps.

They wanted his government to seize all United Earth properties and place Daniel Thoth under arrest for a litany of insane charges. The accusa-tions brought against him had an interesting effect. They created an insight-ful window into the minds of those Daniel was against. There were charges against humanity, claiming he was a traitor to humanity for keeping revolu-tionary technologies out of the hands of those who knew best.

Funny, the president thought, *Daniel was providing his technologies to the*

world, and benefiting everyone except those losing their monopolies. To him, it sure seamed they were the ones guilty of the charges they lay against the boy and his company.

He placed the phone to his ear. "Yes?"

"Sir, has the United States and its allies declared war on Antamina? There is a naval battle group scrambling fighter jets and launching cruise missiles at my facility as we speak."

The president recalled the executive order he had been pressured to sign and cursed into the phone. He had known that signing the document was a bad idea, but "pressure from the money," as his staff sometimes quietly referred to them, held a lot of power.

Daniel spoke again before the president could respond. "Sir, I am going to make an example of your battle group. I will do my best to ensure no one is killed."

"Daniel, I want you to hang tight. Don't do anything that will make this escalate any further. I will get this straightened out immediately."

"I am sorry, Mr. President. The world will see that I have been attacked and that I have every right to respond in defense of my territories! I am sorry; I hope we can stay friends." With a finality he intended to get across, he hung up the phone, leaving the president no opportunity to get in the last word.

The surveillance drones recorded the first ten cruise missiles hitting the deflection dome. The detonations were huge, their impacts creating electromagnetically charged shock waves exponentially stronger, straight back in the direction they came. The kickback smashed into a second wave of missiles on the tails of the first wave and it turned them into a roiling ball of fire and debris that rained down just inside the outer edge of the property. Daniel's eyes darted between feeds, watching the dozen videos from the surveillance drones capturing everything. More missiles were launched from the destroyers, and he felt a sense of vindication.

A rail gun slug hit the upper part of the dome, and the impact caught his attention. The amount of force it put on the protective field was significant and the blow back sent a storm of molten carbon shards spraying up into the sky. The integrity graph registered a 7% disruption. It wasn't enough to worry him, but the stakes were going up. It was time to put a stop to these bullies and their weapons. He knocked the next group of missiles out of the air with a carefully placed wall of miniature energy-field emitters and called up the only weapon he'd ever created. He transmitted the steel sphere to eye level of the aircraft command and control center, and then he waited, wanting them to see the twenty-foot-wide steel ball hovering at the center of their battle group before he set it off.

Tapping into their emergency radio channel, he made an announcement. "You must cease and desist all hostile actions against Antamina, or you will be disabled. This is your only warning."

As soon as he finished his message, the field's integrity graph registered another even larger impact. This time a series of rail gun slugs all hit the same place, causing the dome's integrity to drop to 35%. He shook his head and watched them. They fired on the steel ball floating at the center of their formation, its deflector field boiling with the impacts and Daniel watched the electromagnetic spectrum light up for hundreds of meters all around the device.

"These people are insane," he whispered and triggered the weapon with a reluctance he hadn't expected to feel. The electromagnetic pulse was massive, frying every system on the ships above the water line, while preventing it from going near the reactor cooling systems below. He also restricted the field from going above the highest points on the ships to prevent the aircraft from losing all control and crashing into the ocean.

Daniel dialed the president's number again and waited for the man to pick up.

"Daniel, I am talking to my military officials and having them stop whatever is going on."

"It's done, Mr. President. Your ships will be out of communication and likely will need electrical overhauls, but everyone on board should be unharmed. I know there is a sub out there, and if it attacks, I will be forced to destroy it. I would advise you to find out who was behind this and, for the benefit of everyone on Earth, arrest them."

The president hesitated and then said, "Daniel, I signed a document that may have precipitated these events. I am sorry about all this. There was little I could do."

"It's all right, sir. I understand. I will be uploading a video showing everything that has just happened over the past hour. The world is going to need to know. United Earth Technologies acted only in self-defense." Daniel wished the president well and knew he would not be able to return home for a while—if ever.

Now that the excitement was over, he localized the videos from the surveillance drones, and Samantha helped him quickly edit the series of events into a thirty-second clip. The footage was stunningly crisp and clear. It showed the initial attack and Dillon's rescue of the downed pilots. Next, the video cut to the impacts of the first cruise missiles and the subsequent launch of more missiles, a slow-motion clip of the cluster of rail gun slugs along with voice recordings of Daniel and Dillon's attempts to defuse the situation. Next came the footage of his counterstrike and last, a video of Daniel speaking to the world.

"People of Earth, I wish only to aid our people and bring about a world where prosperity and peace are the norm. Gone will be the days of war, lack of education and poverty, these terrible things we all so easily accept as the ways of life. But as I am sure many of you understand there are factions among us who do not want to achieve these goals. They will not benefit from a world with free energy, peace, and real cures to the illnesses from which they profit. Seek the truth and see past their lies. This video shows how they have just tried stopping me from helping Earth. Please pass this message along to everyone you know. We must not let them win, now is our time to awaken and rise to new ways of living. Thank you."

When the video was encoded, he uploaded it to the U.E. network and set the distributor bots to propagate it to the world's top video sites. Within hours it was viral, and his tensions eased.

Dillon hovered at seventy-five thousand feet following his hasty evacuation from the deck of the aircraft carrier, where his so-called friend's ulterior motives had become all too clear. Safe, high above whatever was going to happen, he watched as the full-scale attack played out and feared that all they worked so hard to achieve was about to get destroyed. But just as quickly as it had started, it was over.

He struggled to come to grips with what he had just witnessed. An entire naval battle group on the offensive in one minute, and in the next it was completely disabled.

He shook his head, thinking of the political fallout that would follow today's events. Yet he felt righteous in seeing the bullies get what they deserved. A sense of pride filled him, and the knowledge that he was on the side fighting for what was right brought him immense pride.

He looked at the red button on the console and pressed it. In the blink of an eye, he and his craft were transmitted to the vehicle bay in his new Antamina security building. A giggle escaped from within at the sheer glee he felt in that very moment, and he smiled like he hadn't done in years.

As he climbed out, he saw Daniel sitting in one of the leather chairs in the center of the Antamina security room where he looked up at the huge PLED wall display. "Guess we won't be taking any trips into town very soon, eh, boss?" he joked, walking across the polished concrete floor to join his young friend.

"Yeah, I suppose not. Don't worry; it will all get smoothed over. What are they going to do? Go back to using nuclear power? Ha!"

They laughed together, although with a sense of unease, as the distant feeling that what might come because of this might not be easy to bear.

Chapter 15

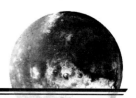

The Other Side of the Universe

In a binary star system far from the nightmare marching across their galaxy, six huge habitable worlds attracted many of the fleeing Olomnri. Billions of them arrived every day. Those unwilling to stand and fight from worlds closest to the ever-spreading darkness. Here in this sanctuary of spiritual transcendent practices, they gathered and joined in a collective meditation. They came from across their once-prosperous interstellar civilization, many consumed by fear and sadness. Yet they still believed that by being with their brothers and sisters, they would find peace, and from there—as one mind—they searched for hope.

The swarm of death devouring everything in its path proved utterly unstoppable. Hordes of the moon-sized planet-eaters mercilessly devoured everything in their path.

In many systems now lost to the unstoppable tide of death, brave Olomnri stayed to stand and fight. Millions of planets and their stars were consumed, and hundreds of billions of souls were lost forever.

In other parts of their Chronlian galaxy, entire solar systems built defenses, with plans to fight the impending darkness. Yet deep down they knew their efforts were in vain. A fighting spirit arose in some of their people, and a pride they had not nurtured for millions of years re-emerged, but it would never be enough.

In yet another torn solar system in the Chronlia galaxy, thousands of beasts drifted and consumed the shattered remnants of moons and planets, where no sentient life ever lived. They waited for their master to arrive. One planet was left; one with life that she desired most of all, and they loved to feel her joy for it.

A many-faceted diamond ship, larger than any star in this galaxy, materialized into this solar system's space. Its perfectly clean edges and smooth, glossy black surface slid between dimensions, and its very presence pulled the light from the system's sun into its surface. She came to take her next victims: souls.

Those she consumed would see their last moments among the living very soon. Aboard this nearly invisible giant ship, the dark empress of the Sethree—Shebra, Queen of Darkness, the Spirit-Eater—sat on her throne of solid gold, a throne sculpted to resemble a mass of tangled serpents, bones, and broken bodies, all of it inlaid with red ruby crystals along the accented contours. Long ribbons of dark red silk hung from an abyss of darkness overhead, the hanging silk forming a semicircle around the back of the gaudy throne, the crimson color framing the obsidian crystal walls and the glorious figure clad in her silken robes.

In her current form, she wore translucent silk embroidered with swirling patterns of creatures, like the ones she drove to destroy and consume entire solar systems. Behind the polished surface of the reflective obsidian walls of her immense cavernous lair, glowing, wispy strands of blue light shifted ever so slightly. They were trapped souls, those she had captured to keep for as long as she wished before feeding on their life energy.

In her mind, she saw the surface of the world she soon would consume. Her victims could do nothing to resist her insatiable appetite, and, with anticipation, she let out a long, terrifying sigh, a sound deep and enchanted, one not of any living world. Again, her anticipation echoed out into the immense chambers. It was the power of evil, limitless knowledge of the darkest kind, the tremors of one who has feasted on trillions of beings and basked in their fear. Her need to feel the sufferings of others could never be fulfilled.

There were nearly three billion Olomnri left on this tragically fated world, and she could feel their fear. When she was ready, she pushed her creatures forward, and, in a rush, they wasted no time ripping into the planet. The larger ones smashed through the planet's atmosphere, crashing hard into the planet's surface. Massive waves of energy lashed out, cracking the crust of the doomed world, while others swooped down, unleashing clouds of acidic gas. Soon the planet cracked open, and its inner core of molten lava splashed out into space. All life on this world was extinguished.

As they died, a faint shadow spread throughout the carnage. She'd come to take every one of their souls. Her victims rose from the hell that was once a utopian world, many unable to hold on to their spiritual conscious states after suffering such violent deaths. They knew nothing of what was to come. Some, though, were strong and attempted to flee or push past her all-encompassing form; those she enjoyed the most. For her, there was no ecstasy so pure as consuming life's energy.

Back on the ship her physical form sat stiffly, her eyes wide, glowing like red gemstones as her victims' life energy coursed through the spiritual and physical dimensions. A smile born of malevolent evil quivered on her face as the skin of her nearly nude body crawled with dark currents. Finished, she returned to her physical form and stood, enjoying the rush of new power. Her mind went out to her creatures. "Consume, multiply, spread our darkness to every corner of this galaxy. Feed!"

She turned to the walls of her inner sanctum, admiring the souls recently added, and laughed. Then, with a thought, her ship moved toward the star of this system.

The huge dark-diamond ship drew on the star's energy, pulling it in long tendrils over the huge distances of space, until soon there was only darkness and emptiness where once there had been light. Where once there had been so much life, the Sethree had come and consumed every bit of it.

Chapter 16

Fallout

Political repercussions from the incident with the US Navy battle group were not as bad as what Dillon initially expected. The video evidence proving they acted in self-defense went viral as soon as it was online. The proof of what really happened played out on every personal device all around the world, except the world's corporate media; there, they twisted the headlines and changed the narrative to portray U.E. as the instigators. The media did everything they could to implant the fear that U.E. was weaponizing its technologies and would soon attempt to enslave humanity.

The president of the United States was not happy. The document he signed weeks earlier, under the agreement it be used only in an emergency, had been applied as a free ticket to mount an assault on the United Earth's Antamina sovereign land. Politicians on Capitol Hill and military advisers had howled for action to be taken, and he had given them what they wanted. Now, though, the shadow government cronies in seats of power overdramatized their outrage at the United Earth's offensive actions against US military assets, and he knew he would need to make a stand.

The president felt responsible, and as a first step, he recorded an official statement. "Know this. Know that not a single American died when U.E. Technologies disabled the attacking vessels. Gratitude for our soldiers' lives should be given. America committed an act of war against an organization working to improve the lives of everyone on Earth. I believe it is time for those working to undermine our founding fathers' accomplishments, those working to undermine the sacrifices made to bring us our freedoms, they need to be held accountable for their treachery." He knew if he did not make a stand now, he would be remembered as the president who let the global shadow government win. The world needed substantial change. He saw how insane the loudest voices of the minority and their indirect rulers truly were, and he wanted to see it all changed.

An official summons was sent, requiring Daniel to attend an international hearing in Washington to finalize the legal inquiry into the incident that was tantamount to war between America and his corporation. Dillon didn't like it. He knew how much of a rat's nest DC was and feared this could have been their motive all along: to get Daniel into a trap where they could charge him and take him into custody.

On the day of the hearing, there was no sign of Daniel or his head of security in any of Washington DC's airports or hotels, nor on any of the thousands of cameras monitoring every major intersection throughout the city. The time and location had been made public by the media, and Daniel had published a short video confirming he would attend, but he was nowhere to be seen.

At first, they only played with the idea he might not show up, but it quickly got ugly. Each time they came back from commercials, they portrayed him more and more as a coward and a criminal who could no longer be trusted.

On Capitol Hill, where the panel of influential congressmen connected to global interests sat waiting for Daniel Thoth to arrive, the crowded room was loud, as those privileged enough to sit in on the day's scheduled events found their seats.

The hearing was set for two in the afternoon, and at ten minutes to the hour, there was still no sign of them. Daniel and his head of security, Dillon, stood together in the Antamina facility, making final preparations. They looked at each other, and Dillon smiled, thinking about how much this was going to stir the proverbial pot.

A moment later they flashed away and arrived in the center of the hearing room floor. There, they waited for the crowded room to realize they had just appeared.

"My God. How? Where did they come in?" someone loudly commented, as the rest of the room went silent, in awe of their sudden arrival.

Once they were seated, the hearing began. From the start it was obvious the panel was going to be hostile toward Daniel and United Earth. They focused their attack on why he kept scientific advancements of enormous importance from the people of the world. They listed the many innovative technologies and questioned why he was unwilling to share them with the world's governments in order to help solve the world's problems. They criticized him for attacking the naval battle group, claiming their navy had only defended itself from an attack by one of Daniel's militarized drones.

As the accusations continued, Dillon tried to interject, speaking out in his loud battlefield-hardened voice, but Daniel stopped him, apologized for his colleague's interruption, and asked the panel to continue.

A military official was called as a witness and pointed an angry finger directly at Daniel. "You, boy—you are a traitor to this country! How can we sit idle and allow you to walk free? Isn't it obvious? What other explanation is there for moving your operations off American soil and forming your own country? We should seize your properties and throw you in prison. It's the only way the world will be safe!"

The charges and accusations from the panel continued for three hours, their lies revealing to Daniel just how badly the world needed to be rid of people like this. It was nearly too much to stomach, waiting, sitting there, listening to these power-hungry, greedy, self-interested people of power, publicly lie and accuse him of things he knew were direct insights on their very own hidden sins. Yet he and Dillon dutifully, patiently waited for the panel to officially turn the floor over and allow Daniel to reply to their charges.

When they finally gave him the opportunity to speak, he nearly lost control of his emotions. He wanted to shout back at them, but he knew that was just what they wanted. He knew these people were connected to those orchestrating the attacks against him, and instead, he channeled his emotion into an analytical rebuttal.

"First of all, Antamina, as we all know, is sovereign land. It is governed and owned by my corporation. The video, which is public for anyone to view, shows that, without any doubt, we did not shoot first, let alone take any offensive action until it was made clear we had no other choice. The battle group at sea was firing volleys of cruise missiles and rail gun slugs, bombarding my installation's deflector shields. The so-called rogue attack drone was, in fact, my Senior Chief of Security, who is sitting next to me now. Mr. Samuelson went to the aid of the fighter pilots who lost control because of their initial attack on my facility. Dillon went to their aid and was cleared by the captain of the *Gerald R. Ford* to land on the flight deck of his ship so that medical crews could help the injured pilot. Would you like to listen to the as-yet-unpublicized recording of the communications between Mr. Samuelson and Captain James Church? Gentlemen? I am sure the people of Earth would enjoy it. Should I play that recording for you right now? No? I guess we should continue with these proceedings and leave that for later. Regarding the keys to my revolutionary technologies, I will not be turning them over to you. You, there, sitting atop your podium, clutching your righteous status with no hope of understanding why life on Earth is so bad for so many people, perhaps you do understand. Perhaps you are simply unwilling to risk your power to confront the reasons why things are the way they are. Well, it is no longer of any consequence. You are the perfect example of why the world's governments cannot be trusted with technologies such as mine. I fear there would be no world left after you militarized it and went to war among yourselves. You use misinformation, breed corruption, and covertly seed violence to maintain your destabilized playground. Well, beware! My vested interests are to see humanity rise from your ashes. After listening to your litany of charges against me, I only see people guilty of hypocrisy! You are the ones who have committed all of the crimes of which you have accused me."

Daniel saw clearly that these men and women of status did not like his words, and he saw them for what they were: puppets of the bankers and aristocratic manipulators of humanity. These sellouts were at the root of mankind's turmoil, and he considered how they would find ways to twist his words to their purpose. With that thought, he decided to close the session and leave them with nothing more than his directly pointed remarks. He struck his final blow.

"I would like to leave you with a few sobering thoughts. Earth will no longer be controlled by an elitist few. Everyone will get good education, and their awareness will grow. I will make sure of it. I have given the world clean energy at a fraction of the costs you would charge them, while reducing nearly all CO_2 emissions by 90%, That is how my technology is helping Earth and mankind. My organization also helped Peru pay off their national debt, allowing them to get out from under the control of these cartel bankers, who, I am sure, pull your strings as well. In the process, we removed all the corrupt officials who sat, much like you, high in their seats of power, imagining themselves untouchable. Your hold on the world is at an end; your corruption is played out. Military action against Antamina or any of the United Earth facilities will not be met with gentle hands in the future. I will not wage war; I will only defend the world against corruption. If I or my family and friends are attacked, the people responsible will be held accountable and prosecuted. Countries who wish to join our movement will have their debts paid, and as they prove themselves capable of sticking to a program of growth and peace, they will receive agricultural assistance, water purification and distribution systems, medicine, manufacturing, and advancements in their cities' infrastructure on a scale unmatched in our world's history. Thank you for indulging us and listening to what I have had to say.

"As a last note, there are a select group of people out there who control the world through financial suppressions and debt, war, drugs, energy, and education. They have even taken our children. To you, sitting in your high-backed leather chairs with so much entitled authority, is there any one of you who will stand against their agenda?"

As soon as he finished, he triggered the return function on both of their suits, and they flashed away. A second later, they stood back in the Antamina security building where they shared a knowing look and Dillon just smiled and shook his head, "You sure did put a line in the sand just now, I wonder if they cut the broadcast half way through your speech?"

They vanished in front of the eyes of nations. Their shapes dematerialized, leaving a faint ripple dissipating into the room. He was a teenager with words of potential, strength, and truth; a genius kid with the will to confront those with seemingly all the power. All around the world people watched the live broadcast, a broadcast that had been designed to publicly take control of the boy and his company. Instead, their plan had failed. Instead of taking control of Daniel and U.E., they got called out, and the people of Earth witnessed it happen.

John, Susan, and Samantha's parents sat in the living room of the Thoths' big house, watching the PLED wall display as Daniel spoke live on TV. When Daniel and his head of security vanished, they stayed silent until John cut the tension.

"Well, then. Now that that's settled, who would like some barbecue?"

The four of them looked at one another, deep concern dancing in their eyes. This was bigger than they'd thought. "How are we going to be safe?" Susan whispered.

Tracey, Samantha's mom, began to cry. "It's going to be like our holiday, isn't it? Except it will be all of us this time!"

After a few commercials, the broadcast came back on. It was an analyst summarizing and evaluating the events as they had unfolded. His tone and expression were of disbelief and incredulity, and they scoffed as he posed obviously scripted questions on how the boy and his head of security had appeared and then disappeared like that. The newscaster, an obvious puppet, struggled with denouncing Daniel's stance against the establishment-backed accusers. There was no hiding it; the world's sentiment toward Daniel's efforts was becoming a global movement.

John changed the channel, finding another broadcast showcasing a debate between two official-looking gentlemen. One of them was arguing for complete confiscation of the United Earth properties, while the other argued that someone was finally doing what was necessary to save Earth from the corrupted systems, and credit was due.

The Antamina pits transformation into a massive multilevel facility was complete. Nine of the lower levels were now filled with particle-assembly units, worker bots, assembly stations, testing chambers, and staging areas for deep-space matter transmission. The second lowest floor was a thing of pure technological beauty. It was filled with server blades, data storage banks, wireless transmitter stations, and six of the biggest power cells Daniel had yet created.

The army of bots and 3-D printers built a fleet of asteroid miners and particle separators, all designed to work in space for the first off-planet initiative—an undertaking that would see United Earth begin mining the asteroid belts between Mars and Jupiter and the construction of the first massive off-planet installations.

Plans were put into motion to free countries from unpayable amounts of debt, money owed to organizations that used economic espionage to steal wealth and enslave populations. In every government there were officials planted by the umbrella corporations to ensure their interests and control continued. It would be a matter of weeding them out while enabling people to break free from their impoverished enslavement.

Italy, Greece, Portugal, France, Spain, Poland, and Australia were the first to receive offers to join the United Earth movement and were quick to accept. Other countries would need to wait, as their governments had long since fallen to those working from the shadows. They would need these newly strengthened countries as examples before their people would rise against the establishment.

Stas created an AI that hacked into the records of every official in every country that joined the movement. It analyzed databases and private files, and, in some cases, it recovered deleted files that uncovered heinous crimes and corruption. Those with affiliations to the bankers, having taken kick-backs for pushing corporate approvals and huge loans against their own countries, were removed.

Meanwhile, Samantha took on the task of rehabilitating Earth's agri-cultural industry. Many crops had lost their ability to produce seed because of the big corporate control policies, and it was the first thing on her list to fix. For Sam, a genius biologist and geneticist, it was a simple thing to cor-rect genomic characteristics, and with Daniel's newest atom-based organic printer, she created billions of seeds, providing countries with crop strains that would grow in harsh climates and produce above-average, nutrient-rich produce.

She programmed the AI to transmit clouds of the seeds to thousands of locations all around the world, to where the deserts had turned once-forested countryside's and fertile farmlands into wastelands.

Daniel drew up plans using highly detailed topographical maps of the terrain where the seeds were being sent. He sketched water pipelines lead-ing away from where desalination plants would soon be constructed along deserted coastlines. Water would flow into the barren lands, and Samantha's seeds would start new, healthy forests and bring back fertile soil.

When he finished the requirements for the wasteland reclamation proj-ect, Daniel copied them to the central AI in charge of planet-side develop-ment. As soon as the schematics were loaded into the task list, drones were sent, foundations built, and desalination plants were printed and transmit-ted from Antamina. Pipelines were transmitted into place, and the water began to flow.

Finding U.E. low on resources, Daniel purchased every decommis-sioned power plant he could get his hands on, sending drones to dismantle and transmit the scraps into the bottom of the Antamina pit. The U.E. facil-ity's 3-D printers needed printing powder to continue production until the off-planet operations began.

United Earth provided countries with road maps designed to elevate their population's ability to improve their own lives. The message: If they committed to citizen education and ethics programs, beautiful buildings and more advanced infrastructure would be given to their cities and their people.

Daniel hoped that these steps would lead to a new state of mind and enlightenment of a kind he imagined he once knew. He could not understand the drive inside of him, a need to bring this new awareness to mankind, yet he knew that he had to do it.

A few weeks after the media event, Stas and his parents got together for their regular evening dinner. This time the main topic of discussion was what Daniel had done on TV. His parents hadn't come to the Antamina facility yet, and they asked what it was like. He told them of the pools, forested areas, and natural feel of the top level, where the living spaces and research labs were located.

"Son, we don't like it here. There are hordes of media vans outside the security gates, and we can't go to the ocean like we used to," his mother commented in a sad voice.

"Can we come to Antamina and stay there with you? We are afraid. We know what can happen when a government turns against you, and it frightens us that this government or some corporate thugs will come take us away," his father complained.

Stas didn't hesitate. "I will assign two security team members to help move whatever you want down to the transmitter platforms tomorrow," he promised.

After dinner, Stas used the self-protection suit he wore under his street clothes to return to the comfort and safety of Antamina, where he immediately went to the developer's suite.

"Hey, Jimmy, what's cracking?" Stas asked after transmitting into the middle of the room.

"Oh, very interesting, very, very interesting," Jimmy replied with the usually vague explanation he always used when he was totally zoned in.

"You ever going to sleep, man?" asked Stas.

"Yah, yah, sure, sure, soon," Jimmy replied.

Stas just shook his head, knowing it was a lie. He looked to his screen as he flopped down into his favorite chair. Swiveling the keyboard around to where he liked it, he began modifying an algorithm that would build a more in-depth 3-D model of the asteroid belt where they were about to begin mining operations.

His mind transitioned into a state of complete focus. He was one with the numbers, symbols, and syntax. His brilliance saw solutions, and he connected modular bits of code, modifying them at a speed that would seem unnatural to most.

On the top level of the Antamina facility, Daniel sat with Samantha in her lab. It was filled with plants of all sorts, growing under all kinds of lights in various soils and liquid solutions. "Sam, the seeds you engineered are working amazingly. In the most nutrient-devoid areas, life is sprouting up."

She turned on him with a look he did not expect and smiled in a way that told him she was not too pleased. "So what's next, Daniel?" Her tone sounded a little harsh, and he quickly understood why. She was stressed about the danger both of their families were in, and he didn't blame her.

"I know. I have invited them all to come live here for a while, but they are refusing. I don't know what else to do. You know how important the effort we are making to reverse the downward spiral mankind is in, right?" Daniel asked.

She looked at him with disdain. "Not all of us, Daniel. Without you, all of this would stop."

"I am going to go with Stas in the morning to try again. His parents are moving tomorrow. Maybe you should try to coax your parents into coming as well, or at the very least get them to wear the protection suits, so that if there is an attack, they will be saved," Daniel offered. As he stood to leave, his head spun, and he knew he needed some rest.

Chapter 17

The Shadows

They came together once more to meet in person, face-to-face, and resolve their setbacks. Helicopters swooped down toward the towering Hong Kong corporate building. It was a modern tower, owned by a multinational corporation with controlling interests in major industries all around the world. The five luxury helicopters landed on their respective platforms, each carrying one of the five heads of an organization that had, up until recently, controlled the wealth and power of the world for the past four centuries.

Prior to the helicopters' arrival, the top three floors of the building were secured by highly skilled paramilitary teams composed of cold, hardened men who were used to the task of carrying out their masters' orders.

When they were all seated in the boardroom, the air filled with their tobacco smoke, and after a few minutes of rest, a bald, ugly beast of a man spoke, his deep, rough, accented voice echoing with authority and outrage.

"How the hell did he get in and out of the hearing like that? We had people in place. At least one of those foolish kids strapped with explosives would have gotten him! Yet he just appeared, took the condemnations, returned some painful counterpoints. and then—*poof*—he was gone into thin air! How is this possible? We must move to the next stage. He must be removed at all costs!"

All around the table, shrouded in clouds of tobacco smoke, their heads nodded in agreement.

A silver-haired, golden-skinned man followed in a cruel and intelligent tone. "He said he knows who we are. And that he is watching us. I don't believe it for a second. This kid is nothing but an upstart who needs to be killed. His family, his friends—why did we not kill them all in the Dominican Republic? Why has this gotten so far without taking the required steps to stop it?"

A voice from the end of the table spoke in a cold, raspy tone, his silhouette barely visible. This was a voice even those at the table feared to hear. "Is the device in place and ready?"

"Yes, master, it is," the silver-haired man replied.

The shadow at the end of the table stood, sending a shudder through the rest of the room. A sliver of the moon's light cast through the plate-glass ceiling, and for a moment, they saw his face. He was old, yet there was youth to his presence. He was wrinkled and gray, with large dark-brown spots under his eyes. He looked at them. His eyes glowed white in the dim, smoky light, and his intention left them all with fear in the pits of their stomachs. "Have them watch; have them wait. When he is seen, end him and everyone he loves. A catastrophic failure of his technology, which obviously should have been left in the realm of science fiction for the good of mankind, will be what the media reports has happened."

All but one of the heads at the table nodded.

The fattest of the group, the youngest of them, replied with a different point of view. "Our scientists around the world still have not cracked the secrets that make these technologies possible. With his death, we will lose any hope of finding the answers. Should we not try?"

The man's voice trailed off as a gray hand rose into the air.

"This is not a time for questions of authority, Demetrios," the master snarled, and nearly as soon as the words were uttered, two large men covered in black tactical armor took hold of the fat man and violently dragged him out of his chair. They forced him onto his back, dragging him out onto the balcony by his wrists. He begged for mercy and kept on insisting that he only wanted to do what was best for the future of their organization. He pleaded with them to listen to reason, yet the gray hand rose even higher.

The black-armored man on the left pulled his combat knife from a thigh holster and thrust it through Demetrios's kneecap. This was followed by the other black-clad figure, whose knife slammed into the center of the other kneecap. The sound of crunching bone was clear through the man's screaming, and it sent chills down the backs of all at the table.

Demetrios shrieked with pain and begged, tears running down his face. They held him, letting him taste his fate. He screamed as the knives were pulled from his knees with quick tugs and then jammed right back into his shoulders. They held him for a moment, letting it sink into his head. The armored men punched the knives' hilts, and loud popping noises came from his shoulders; they came out of the sockets.

Everyone at the table watched, horrified, as a member of their very own—utterly untouchable group—was tortured and then dragged to the balcony railing. The two black-clad men tossed their three-hundred-pound victim up and over the railing, seemingly without any effort at all. The four remaining heads at the table listened to the scream fade away.

The gray man spoke again. "Will there be any other objections? This upstart will be ended at the earliest available opportunity. Do we all agree, gentlemen?"

No one spoke. After a moment, the man who began the meeting broke the silence. "Good, then, it is settled. Our little problem will be resolved soon."

Chapter 18

The Day It All Changed

In the morning, Daniel, Stas, and Samantha were in high spirits. They ate breakfast in a large glass-crowned pergola overlooking the upper platform of the Antamina facility, and they spoke of their parents finally coming to visit on this day. The vast upper level was quickly becoming a tropical wonderland.

From where they sat eating their morning meal and talking of the day ahead, they looked out over the tiered landscape carpeted with fast-growing trees. The forested areas were separated by wide, paved walkways that snaked between pools of both freshwater and saltwater. In the pools, newly hatched salmon, tuna, trout, colorful koi, and other fish explored their new environments. Among the newly planted jungle landscape, futuristic domes rose up fifteen floors. In the domes, various research labs and living quarters all were finished with modern amenities.

After breakfast, as a group they went over to the security building, where Dillon was looking over surveillance footage and catching up on world news.

"Morning, kids. Off on another adventure, are you?" Dillon smiled in a way new to his character.

Daniel, Samantha, and Stas, following Dillon's recommendation, agreed it would be best if they matter-transmitted separately, each covertly arriving directly in their respective families' houses.

"Don't forget; don't let them darn media types see you there," Dillon barked, just as they blinked away.

Stas arrived in the kitchen of his parents' house, where he found them waiting. Last night, a security detail had helped move some of his parents' things down to the transmitter station, and it looked like they were ready to go. When he got there, he didn't waste any time; they knew the plan and took the self-protection suits in stride.

Samantha arrived in the living room of her parents' house and shook her head from the slight nausea she always experienced when matter-transmitting. This was where she had spent her childhood, and she remembered playing with her father and working on her homeschooling right here on the floor of this room. After taking a moment to smell the familiar air and look around, she saw that not much of anything had changed, and without waiting for them to wake, she started silently up the stairs to their bedroom.

When she entered their room, she saw both were still fast asleep. She watched them for a moment, thinking of how much peace there was here, and stepped softly to the bed. Silently, she sat next to her mother.

After a few moments of listening to them sleep, she spoke, intent on waking them. "Mom, Dad, you guys waking up anytime soon?" she asked in her most girly sarcastic tone.

Tracey stirred, and Samantha took the liberty of bouncing up and down on the bed, just like when she was a little girl and wanted attention. Startled, they sat up in surprise.

"Oh good; you're up. I need you guys to put these on and come with me to Antamina for the day. We are having a nice family get-together. Everyone is coming; it will be fun," she said while enthusiastically, thrusting the two pairs of Spandex onesies into their laps.

Tracey looked at her daughter as if finally realizing this was not some kind of weird dream. "Dear, what time is it?" she asked.

"Time to get up and put this suit on, Mom!" Samantha replied.

"Sam, what's this really about?" her father, Robert, asked.

"Dad, you guys gotta come with me. You're at risk, and we need to get away from here for a little while, okay? Like, right now. It's no joke; I have a really bad feeling, okay? Please trust me!"

"Okay, honey, give us another hour, and we'll get into those things and go with you. By the way, what are those things?" Robert asked.

"Dad, we may not have an hour. These are personal protection suits that enable you to matter-transmit back to Antamina with me, right now."

"You mean like how Daniel and that man vanished into thin air on national television?" Tracey asked.

Samantha finally got them out of bed, after lying there for another fifteen minutes. Her mom demanded they all sit down for breakfast before suiting up. Tracey didn't seem too keen on matter-transmitting anywhere and avoided even touching the suit Samantha continually pushed her to put on.

When they got to the kitchen, Tracy remembered today's plans and started fretting about having to skip brunch with their friends. "We haven't seen them for weeks, Sam; it just won't do. We can't just take off because you are worried that something bad might happen without any real cause for it. How is something bad going to happen with all those media people out there? They follow us around everywhere, you know. Come on; let's be realistic, Sam! We are in no real danger at all," Tracy complained.

Samantha was pacing back and forth in the kitchen, nearly in tears. "Don't you understand? Remember what happened to Angelo and Lucia on our big holiday? This is serious. I really want you guys to get into these suits so we can go. Your friends will understand, okay? Please?"

When his parents had the suits on, Stas helped them with their last bags, and they headed for the matter-transmitter bay down in the main facility. When they got to the platform, his mother realized she'd forgotten a pendant that had been in the family for generations, and she took off back to the house to retrieve it.

Daniel materialized in the living room of his parents' home and saw his father sitting at the kitchen table, already into his first cup of coffee.

"Good morning, son. What brings you here?" John asked.

"Hey, Dad. I came to get you and Mom to come with me for a little visit to Antamina, where you will be safe until whatever is brewing out there blows over. You must be getting sick of all the media vehicles anyway, right?"

John looked at Daniel with sad eyes, "We are very proud of you, son. What you have done seems like an impossible achievement—free energy, paying off the debts of entire countries, giving them education and road maps for prosperity, while reclaiming barren landscapes lost to fire and drought!" John laughed, "Even just one of those things in an entire lifetime would have gotten you a Nobel prize, let alone your achievements in university."

"I know, Dad, but I really think you guys should get away from here for a while. Antamina is really nice. I think you and Mom will like it."

"I know, son. How are you going to get us there?"

Daniel pulled out the two pairs of black silk Spandex. "I need you and Mom to put these on. Make sure that it touches your skin everywhere—no underwear, 'kay? Can you get into yours, please? I want to go see how Mom is doing."

Daniel went to his parents' bedroom and found Susan fast asleep. As he walked to her, he said, "Mom, it's me. Can you wake up? We are going on a little trip today, okay?"

She turned over, opened her eyes, and smiled. "Can't go, Daniel. Who's going to feed the dogs and keep the dust off the shelves?"

"Come on, Mom. At least come for the day. Dad's already getting suited up. Come see the facility; tour my very own country," he playfully prodded.

John entered the room a few minutes later and placed a hand on his son's shoulder. "Let me talk to her, Daniel."

When Daniel got back downstairs, he walked into the living room and considered sitting on the leather couches, but the thought of smelling the outside air lured him to the back-patio doors.

He didn't think; he just stepped out onto the deck and took a deep breath. It smelled like home, and for an instant, he even forgot why he was here today. He walked to the edge of the pool deck and took in the view, recalling times he'd run through the orchards alongside Samantha and his cats. Thoughts of the days when he had stepped away from his work and lived like an ordinary boy came in waves, and he smiled, feeling free and clear.

On the high road above the Thoth property, a train of media vans and trucks stood at the ready for any sightings. They waited for the boy genius; they wanted to see his face, photograph him, and write articles speculating on what his next big plans might be.

When Daniel stepped out onto the back patio, the reporter on watch didn't spot him right away. It took a moment, but then, out of the corner of his eye, a movement caught the reporter's attention. It took less than a second to turn his telephoto camera toward the figure and zoom with its 1600 mm lens. The figure in his view was wearing padded clothing—it looked like a one-piece soft combat jumpsuit—and as the man registered that it was actually the boy, his voice caught in his throat. For a few brief moments, he choked and slammed his fist on the roof of the van. It was enough to loosen his nerves and he gasped. In a flash, word went out over the radio channels, and the entire media camp that was clustered around the United Earth compound burst into action.

And then it happened.

Frank Palings lifted the lid quickly, turning the key to arm the weapon, and without hesitation, he pressed down on the red button and held it there, knowing full well that this was the end. He had just activated two B-83 nuclear warheads, their payloads hidden in the back of the media van. The bombs were older models that normally would have had 1.2 megaton yields, but these were upgraded to exceed twenty megatons each. When set off, the land would be scoured of all life for tens of miles in every direction.

He thought of his family and the pictures the cruel-looking businessman had shown him, pictures of his wife and kids, all of them bound and gagged. The images of them kneeling in that dark room with meat hooks dangling above their heads burned in his mind. And the voice of the man telling him what was at stake. His family would see the same fate as those in the other pictures, he was shown images of the remains of those who had failed in the past. Pieces of human bodies that lay about in pools of blood; halved bodies hanging from meat hooks, just like the ones above his family. He had sworn he would do anything to ensure their safety.

They promised his family would be free; they promised his family would be financially taken care of. All he had to do was sacrifice himself by turning this key and pressing this red button at the very moment Daniel Thoth was confirmed, either at his parents' house or the underground facility next to where the big media van was parked.

A tear dropped from his eye and a hope for his family filled his heart as he released the red button.

Chapter 19

Reckoning

Two devastatingly powerful nuclear warheads detonated on the western seaboard of the United States. The blast leveled everything within a fifteen-mile radius. Anything that was flammable burned, while houses and reinforced concrete collapsed.

Samantha and her parents were still sitting at the kitchen table when it happened. It came out of nowhere. The kitchen was filled with a flash that momentarily blinded them. Luckily for her, the suit she was wearing identified the pressure change in the environment, as well as the intense blast of white light, and instantly generated a protective field around her entire body, locking her in place and shielding her from the flash as the room was torn away. She reached out, and time seemed to slow. Agonizingly, she watched the flesh of her parents turn to ash and blow away. A scream that no one but her could hear filled her senses, and she cried out in despair.

The floor was ripped away from below her as the shattering walls rolled over her protective energy shield. The field was pushed to its limit by the blast, but she held firm, watching the devastation unfold.

Tears streamed from her eyes, and she wished there was a way to deactivate the field. She wanted it all to end in that very moment. She wanted to let the storm of destruction take her, just as it had her parents, but she knew there was no real hope of that. Watching the fire roll along the landscape, she thought of how it would be better to live and see those who caused this come to justice. *I will never see justice if I am dead*, she thought. She triggered the emergency transmit function, arriving instantly in the security building of the Antamina facility. A moment later she opened her eyes and looked around, and she saw the stoic figure of Dillon Samuelson. Her heart beat hard—she felt it in her chest—and it all hit her. The realization that her parents were gone forever washed over her, and tears began to flow. She cried like she had never cried before, and in those tears, her resolve to seek vengeance hardened beyond every doubt.

Daniel stood on the back deck of his parent's house, right next to the infinity pool and memories of when he enjoyed swimming here danced in his mind. He had his back to the hills, where media vehicles surrounded the old rock quarry facility. When it happened, he only caught a glimpse of the flash before his personal protective field activated. It went 100% opaque protecting his eyes and skin from the burn of the nuke blast and locked him in place. When the flash passed, the shield's opaque setting diminished, and he witnessed what followed. The shock wave shredded everything around him. His body seized up, and a million thoughts raced through his mind. He could not understand. *What just happened?* But then he realized what it was, and his thoughts turned dark. The urge to trigger the emergency transmit signal was gone. *This is far too great a cost, and if it is my time, then so be it. Let the world return to its downward spiral*, he thought. *Maybe it's what they deserve.*

Pieces of buildings and debris from the blast flashed as they hit his protective field. He turned and watched as his childhood home was torn apart, splintered, and carried away piece by shattered piece. He turned again and looked out over the land, watching fires flare up as everything organic was charred. The air filled with dust and debris as the landscape was pummeled by the destructive force. He watched pieces of vehicles bouncing along in the wake of the shock wave. Nothing was left intact. It was like a scene from the very pits of hell. His fists clenched as he wondered if his mother had put the suit on in time, *O I pray Sam got her parents to get the suits on soon enough, why did I step out here and let them see me, how could I have been so stupid!* And with that thought, a heavy guilt that it was because of him, all this was happening.

Stas and his father stood waiting for his mother to return, and with a sudden, swift move, Stas stepped off and slapped the transmit button, sending his father and all of his parents' belongings back to Antamina. He jogged up the stairs to the top level and walked out onto the paved path. He was headed back to the house, where he knew his mother was probably still searching. He had taken less than three steps and a moment later he found himself sitting on one of the transmitter platforms next to his mother feeling like he had just been knocked on the head. They looked at each other and then over to another platform, where Stas's father, Alexei, stood with an expression of consternation. When the bomb went off, their proximity to the blast had been only a few thousand meters, and the intensity of the displacement caused their suits to activate immediately.

Daniel fought the powerful emotions building up within him and blinked as his eyes filled with tears. Vivid memories of when Angelo and Lucia were executed flashed through his mind. He wanted to return to see everyone safe in the mountain fortress of Antamina, but the fear and guilt that maybe it was all his fault kept him there. It burned inside him—the fear that his friends and family might not have made it because he had wanted fresh air. The idea that they might all be dead, it was far too much to face. Going back meant finding out who had been lost. He closed his eyes and fought the fear. He had to return. He knew it.

The feeling that this was all because of him filled every part of his mind. He had been the cause of this; if he had not tried so hard to help the world break free from the corrupt, the oppressive, and the greed-driven factions holding mankind down, this tragic loss of so much life would never have happened. He remembered what Angelo always said, "the deeds of others lay in their hands and theirs alone my boy." He smiled at the thought but still, he could not find the courage to face the cost of today's tragedy.

Another saying his old friend repeated so many times came to his mind: "In life, there will be dishonest people, those who will do anything to keep the majority believing what they do is for the people's benefit. What will define us will be how we stand up for what is right and rise against the manipulators of ideas and dealers of fear. How will they define you in the end, Daniel?"

A new kind of tear broke from his eye, and he reached to his forearm, triggering the matter-transmitter. In a flash, he returned to the familiar security building on the top level of the Antamina facility.

Stas was the first to see him standing on the platform, and Stas noticed his friend's look. "You made it. We were starting to get worried about you. What happened?" Stas asked.

Samantha stepped forward and wrapped her arms around Daniel. Her strong embrace snapped him back to reality. John was next, wrapping them both up as though to never let them go.

"What happened back there, Daniel?" John asked, still holding them in a tight embrace.

"Someone tried really hard to kill all of us—that's what happened, Dad. From what I can tell, a nuclear weapon was detonated right next to our home facility."

As they pulled away from one another, Daniel scanned the group and instantly knew who hadn't made it. Closing his eyes, he let out a sigh, as the reality of what was lost solidified in his mind and as it did a stream of tears dripped down his cheeks.

"The media likely will try to pin this on United Earth. I bet they make it look like some kind of facility meltdown. We need to find evidence to defend ourselves. There's no time to mourn our dead. We need to get to work!" Daniel commanded.

To Sam and John, it seemed like it hadn't registered with Daniel that Susan and Samantha's parents were dead.

Daniel looked directly at them. "I know. They didn't make it. I almost didn't come back myself. I wanted to give up and just let go of everything. You know what? That would be exactly what those behind this would want. For now, we need to use it as a driving force. We need to use it in the fight to make sure they don't win."

News of the disaster spread around the world in minutes. Big media networks all reported that a catastrophic failure of a power cell in the United Earth California headquarters was the cause of the explosion, and they declared Daniel dead. "The world reform he was trying to pioneer likely is over. What a tragic day for all the world," they pronounced.

"A boy genius, lost to the world; a tragedy and the death of a visionary. Why did he choose to step beyond what nature intended? Why did the world allow one person to play with technologies that should have been left alone?" Hit-piece headline after hit-piece headline was on every network around the world. It was sensational; it was tragic; it was their language!

The reports seemed unanimous, and to Daniel and his friends, they seemed scripted prior to the event. Every news station seemed to know for certain that the United Earth facility was the cause of the explosion. They jumped at the chance and called for every U.E. facilities to be shut down immediately. Media reports expressed remorse over the loss of Daniel Thoth and all those suffering in the areas around the blast site. At the same time, they took full advantage and pointed accusing fingers. They unabashedly laid full responsibility on Daniel for reaching beyond what science said was possible, and the world's populations believed them.

They showed footage from drones circling ground zero. They broadcast images of the devastated landscape and the crater, where they claimed the underground facility once was. From time to time they switched from the live news coverage to report on the world markets as they plummeted in the aftermath of the accident. It was obvious their mission was to vilify United Earth Technologies, and they did not pull any punches.

"Perfect. Now those bastards think you're dead and will stop bothering us," Dillon commented in his attempt to make light of the situation.

Daniel looked at him with a cold expression. "They want to shut United Earth down. They want things to go back to the way they were. It's not going to happen. We can't let them win."

Fortunately, Dillon strategically positioned one hundred surveillance drones above the two facilities after the incident with the US Navy, something he expected might come in handy if they ever got attacked and needed evidence to refute false claims just like these. Daniel brought up the footage from one of the medium-range surveillance drones that monitored the main campus in California and played it back. He accelerated the playback speed so that it was more like a time-lapse and started watching from when the media vehicles began arriving weeks ago. They watched as media vans crowded around the gates of the compound. As more arrived, they spread out down the south-curving road, heading back to the main house.

It only took three minutes before the footage got to the detonation. After it played out the first time, Daniel rewound, this time playing the detonation at half speed. The explosion played back once more, and, as a group, they saw the exact point of origin. Once again, he rewound the footage closer to just before it happened, this time setting it to play back at one-tenth normal speed.

When the detonation started, he paused the video, instantly stepping between the frames of just before and then just after the blast and carefully narrowed it down to the vehicle where the blast originated.

There was no doubt the bomb came from the media van parked along the outer ring road, in a position that ensured the greatest damage to the facility compound, while at the same time allowing the blast to expand out and down the sides of the hill to cause the widest amount of damage to the surrounding area.

"Stas, could you please bring up the best angle that shows the license plate on that van?" Daniel asked in an intense yet controlled tone. Everyone in the room felt it, a collective need for justice and vindication. "Dad, let's go look into some other information I've been compiling. Dillon will find out everything there is to know about that van and where it came from."

They walked to the other end of the room and sat in two chairs situated in the center of a stainless-steel half ring that hovered three feet off the ground. Daniel waved his hand through the air, activating a holographic digital screen that sprang up from the top edge of the ring.

"I have been tracking a group of people the world knows as the five families. Over the past few hundred years, they have taken control of the world's wealth, food, energy—you name it; they indirectly control and profit from it. I sent out millions of atom-sized sensors, cameras, and transceivers to follow and track these people."

Three-dimensional images appeared on each of the five screens, and he focused the playback to display footage of one from the group.

"One of their members was brutally murdered a few days ago, thrown from the top of a corporate building," Daniel continued, pointing to the screen playing the recording of the murder.

The video was dark and fuzzy, but it was clear enough to see the man get dragged out onto a balcony, stabbed in the knees and shoulders, and then thrown over the railing to his death.

"Unfortunately, they have some advanced technology that blocks the transceivers, preventing me from getting direct conversations, but at least we have their positions." He brought up lists of corporate holdings linked to accounts in central banks, majority ownerships in major oil and gas corporations, shipping companies, all the major media companies, and military manufacturing conglomerates, as well as all the tobacco and pharmaceutical multinationals.

Daniel looked at his father. "These are the people responsible! Their greed has led them to this. I paid the debts of those countries, knowing the money would go to them, and we followed it. I had hoped they would back off. But it's not about the money with them, is it? They want control; they want power; they want to make sure people don't rise and take control of their own futures. War, poverty, disease—these are their currencies. I think it is time to cut the head off this snake. Don't you agree?"

Murder was not something John wanted for his son, but these people had caused enough pain in the world to deserve the very worst fate.

Stas came back with the registration documents for the media van where the explosion originated. They showed it was sold to a man by the name of Frank Palings a few weeks before it showed up at the California facility. Stas paused and then, with a smile, showed the bill of sale. The previous owner was a security company run by the very man they all remembered like it was yesterday—Thomas Stiedly, the cold-heart who tried to crash the gate of the compound when they were first starting out; the very same person they all suspected of being behind the holiday attack.

With the link to this terrorist attack on American soil, every red-blooded federal officer in the country would be out for Stiedly's head. Of course, once his identity was displayed on every news feed, there was a good chance the masses would get to him first.

John, Stas, and Daniel worked on a media presentation using the high-definition footage showing the exact source of the explosion. One of the first things Daniel did at the start of their investigation was to order the surveillance drones conduct a high-resolution laser scan of the crater. What they found surprised them. Although the crater was deep, the lowest floors of the facility remained. The damage to the uppermost floors was total, but the lower floors were only collapsed, and at the very bottom there was little to no damage.

Daniel transmitted surveillance drones into the bottom floors of the three underground buildings to look around. In the bunkered lowest floors, the power cells the media was claiming caused the explosion were all still fully operational. The drones took video of the entire lower sections, showing the collapsed walls and rubble where whole rooms had caved from the pressure.

The evidence utterly exonerated his power-cell technology. To be sure, he programmed a worker bot to beat on a power cell with a huge piece of steel and then cut through it with a plasma torch while it was running. The video showed the reaction destabilize, there was some blow out, it was allot less than the force of a hand grenade, let alone anywhere near the scale of the nuclear detonation it was accused of causing.

When Samantha sent down the final cut, Stas encoded, and the web crawler went to work. Over the next few hours, it would upload it to every video website in the world.

Daniel decided not to hide from these people, and—against the objections of Dillon and his father—he created a video of himself, speaking to the camera.

"I am not dead! The nuclear weapon detonated next to my California facility killing thousands of innocent Americans, along with my mother and my dear friend's parents. It was an attack against all of us. The victims of this attack died because of the greed of those who will be named! The world's authorities will be called upon to act. The people who committed this act have lived in the shadows and controlled our world for far too long. They have done this by committing these kinds of crimes for centuries. This video shows evidence of the truth. It shows the true source of the explosion and, as you will see, information on the people behind it. I will not rest until they have come to justice—nor should any of you."

The video showed evidence that contradicted what the media preached as fact. When it was uploaded, it went to the top of the trending feeds, and as more and more people watched the presentation, a vindictive tone began resonating in the comments sections. The world's people were waking up.

More and more started to see past the lies of the corporate media, and the truth caught on like wildfire. Even major media groups, which had preached that all U.E. facilities should be shut down for the safety of mankind, changed their stories overnight.

Against the wishes of the broadcaster's ownership, those actually doing the work to produce content for the news shows began airing stories on private bank accounts worth billions, stories with documented evidence of how the central banks had orchestrated the fiat currency systems, a system that forced citizens to pay higher and higher taxes in order to cover the interest on debts created out of thin air.

Seventy-two hours after the tragic attack hit California, more and more evidence surfaced from various sources about a group of five who controlled 80% of the world's wealth. Daniel, Stas, and Jimmy sat in the software development lab, looking at a list of all the holdings, accounts, and corporations linked to the remaining four heads of what they referred to as the shadow corporation. They looked at the account records and saw the receipt of $2.5 trillion. It was the money Daniel had paid to erase the debts of those first nations. The payment had not even equated to a full percentage of the total worth of their holdings. Finding these things together, as a group, they were disgusted by it all.

"I know you guys have continued working on that R.D. virus that Jimmy developed before he joined us," Daniel said. "Didn't you use that as the base for the Search Out Trojan that helped uncover so much information on our enemies?"

They all smiled, and Jimmy nodded, his eyes showing a glimmer of anticipation. He dreamed of releasing it, and today could be the day. It would take everything from those using crime and hardship as tools to hoard the world's wealth.

"Good. How long until you can deploy it, targeting these four men's accounts and properties?" Daniel asked with cheery enthusiasm.

Stas laughed. "I would think a couple of hours, just to make sure we include everything they own, both directly and indirectly. What do you think, Jimmy?"

"Faster than that, Stas," Jimmy replied with a confident smile. "You are slow; I am much quicker." He felt a huge sense of satisfaction; the taste of sweet revenge was so close.

Within an hour it was ready, and Daniel came down to witness the send-off. The most sophisticated Trojan anyone had ever designed was about to be unleashed on the most corrupt people in the world. No one left the lab; instead, they pushed their reclining leather chairs out into the center of the room and watched. The wall display came alive with readouts of every action the Trojan took.

The virus hacked into every server with any connection to the four men. Cash accounts were liquidated, and the funds were distributed equally to every account below $50,000 on Earth. Corporate holdings were foreclosed, and their ownerships were transferred to nonprofit organizations with genuine interest in helping those needing it most. Secure databases were breached, accessing records of money paid to the security teams responsible for committing terrible crimes.

Daniel wanted to prevent an attack like the one that just killed so many people from ever happening again. He went to work modifying the atom-sized sensors, so they would function better when in proximity to advanced frequency disrupters. He also improved the geopositional sensors to enable hundreds of millions of them to work together and create much more detailed real-time three-dimensional point cloud videos.

Stas created a site to broadcast the dust drone footage and sent it out in a short video broadcast from the U.E. corporation. People who visited the page saw a new kind of online environment. It was a true-to-scale miniature of Earth but alive with real-time data. In the top left of the page, icons for each of the targeted individuals acted as links. When a person chose one of the links, the globe turned and zoomed to the targeted person's location. From there, the user was prompted to view pop-up windows showing live feeds from different angles and more detailed location information, including live voice recordings and lists of documented crimes.

Daniel wrote a quick subroutine to flag anyone who was communicating with the heads of the now-exposed shadow government. The routine targeted anyone linked to the criminals by sending new clouds of undetectable tracking particles to that person's location. The tracker would not go live on those persons until they moved to commit crimes, but the AI would be prepared to initialize public exposure as evidence that proved them as conspirators became clear.

Two days after the coup, Daniel got a call. "Daniel, it's the president. First off, I am glad you are okay, and I am sorry for your loss. These people have gone too far."

"Thank you, Mr. President. I too am very sorry for what happened. We are all still trying to come to grips with the loss." With the mention of it, Daniel felt the muscles in his face tense, and he teared up.

"Yes, well, I would like to thank you for how you have handled it. I am very fortunate to not have been involved with these people. You have put one heck of a scare into a lot of folks in my government, a lot of people with a lot to hide, I am sure." The president laughed. "It looks like the public is going to get their wish. I am not sure how you are tracking and watching everyone involved in the shadow government, and, quite frankly, I don't like it. It violates every privacy policy I can think of. Well, you have them on the run; that's what is important. I hear they are no longer wealthy, and a lot of people in the world have received tidy sums—impressive. So what's next for you, Daniel? I would request that you include America in your next wave of prosperity initiatives, please. I think you are clearly the way of the future, and we certainly would like to be a part of the direction you are heading."

Daniel stood, considered his tablet's camera, and eyed the president before replying. "Well, I suppose my next plans, Mr. President, don't need to be kept a secret. I want to help humanity spread out into our solar system and reach for the stars. We will see how things work out, I guess. As for my next phase in prosperity initiatives, once the weeds are removed from your administration, I would be happy to see America take a big step forward."

Before the president could reply, Daniel curtly thanked him and disconnected the call.

A few days later, Stas and Jimmy called Daniel to the computer lab. When Daniel arrived, they began the playback of a recording the AI captured when one of the people under surveillance got attacked. The video showed a mob converging on a man in a main street in London, England. Thirty or forty rough-looking English men and women came from both ends of the street and viciously went after him. The man was not one of the controlling figures but was identified as an enforcer. He must not have known he was being watched, as a day before he was recorded talking about killing a family for failing the organization. He was caught describing the way in which he and his team had ended the family members' lives in the most brutal ways—all of it uploaded to the net. Now, he was dead, beaten by a mob in the streets.

The AI did not tag any of the people involved in the attack, and Daniel did not directly notice. Stas noticed, but he held back from saying anything. He felt like the people committing these crimes deserved this kind of justice. Violent offenders were not on the list of people to track, and for the time being, Stas did not want to change it.

"I am sorry, but I enjoyed that a little," Stas said. "Only because the guy deserved every bit of it, though."

"We can't stoop to their level, Stas, but I understand how you feel. I felt it too. It felt like revenge for my mom and for Samantha's parents and Angelo and Lucia. Thank you for showing me."

For the next few weeks the watch map created more and more tracking icons for people connected to those behind the attack and those behind mankind's sad condition. Mobs in every city searched them out and took violent revenge. Communities in Europe organized very quickly. Militias searched out their oppressors with cunning, and icons dropped off the map just as quickly as they appeared. Some had protection—security squads that put up a fight—but as their money disappeared, dispersed by the R.D. virus, so did their protection.

Daniel finally considered the amount of killing going on and went to Stas and Dillon. "Guys, what do you think of what is going on? This is getting pretty cold-blooded, don't you think?"

"Dan, those who knowingly have gone along with tearing down the world's people deserve the swiftest and harshest punishment by the very people they have suppressed. But you're right; we need to make some changes and give fair warning," Stas agreed.

"I agree with Stas," Dillon followed. "Those who commit rape and murder and who conspire to cause atrocity need to be tracked, and recordings of their crimes should be made public. Some surely will be offended by this, but, like it or not, there will no longer be safety for those who commit these crimes."

Chapter 20

Into Space

Following the nuclear attack on the California facility, Daniel began transmitting a fleet of asteroid-mining drones, house-sized 3-D printers, particle separators, power cells, and element-containment chambers to the asteroid belt between Mars and Jupiter. Matter-transmitters around the perimeter of each deck worked nonstop, beaming the mining, processing, and printing groups to locations along the belt.

Upon arrival, the miner drones went straight to work. They matched up with huge floating rocks and chunks of ice, where they ripped off sections, collecting the ore and transmitting it to the particle-separator units. Inside the particle separators, the materials were scanned and buffeted with specially configured resonant waves that destabilized the raw materials, shattering and separating them into atomic-level gasses.

When the raw materials were separated, spatial frequency isolators matter-transmitted each mass of elemental gas into individual storage tanks stationed along the inner side of the Kuiper belt. There, the atomic-level elements were stored and sourced by the 3-D printing units for fabrication of more mineral-harvesting drones too expand the mining operations in preparation for the next stage.

The plan was simple: Stockpile elements for 3-D printing and then build a series of off-planet installations. Daniel's dream was to give people who wanted to make new lives the opportunity to do so. He wanted people to migrate off-Earth, and drastically reduce earth's population. The AI was tasked with exponential expansion of the mining and 3-D printing capabilities. He envisioned moon-sized printing foundries and stockpiles of elements on a scale large enough to print entire cities within the next four months.

To achieve this, the AI was given nearly total off-planet mining rights, but a few unbreakable rules were put in place. Unique structures were off limits and were to be catalogued. Everything was scanned for signs of life at the molecular level prior to processing, and dwarf planets were not to be mined unless approved by Samantha.

They all spent days glued to the live feeds of the drones tearing into huge blocks of ice and space rock, while maintaining a watchful eye over Earth's transition. The glaring problem, Daniel saw, was the terribly low level of education, along with an unacceptably high level of poverty in most of the large populations around the world. It was there—it was obvious—but he was stumped on how he and his friends were going to help these people rise from their accepted ways of living.

After breakfast at the Antamina facility—a morning event they liked to share as a group—Dillon, Samantha, and John headed off in an U.E. security vehicle to visit countries that were following the road maps and embracing the technology Daniel provided in this first phase of creating prosperity for mankind.

There was far too much on Daniel's mind, and he needed to find a distraction. After a short list of potential hobbies, he set his mind to designing a starship: something creative, a ship he imagined they would use to explore the galaxy or even the universe, once mankind was stabilized.

Right off the bat he knew it would be huge. After all, there were no restrictions of scale in space. He chose arbitrarily, typing in the dimensions as forty kilometers long, seven kilometers wide, and twenty kilometers deep. He imagined a central upper deck running the length and width of the vessel the entire area covered by a perfectly clear dome. He imagined the stars and spectacles of space glowing with brilliance whenever the lights inside the ship's primary living environment were dimmed to nighttime settings. The lower body was shaped like the hull of a sail boat, and on the top level, he sculpted a natural landscape. He added patches of forest, unique rock formations, and a cluster of buildings perched on a small rise in the land. On the central rise, overlooking a body of fresh water, would be the primary living area, built like a small, upscale resort.

He wondered what kinds of animals would be best, and after a pause to consider, he added a selection of birds, deer, rabbits, fish, reptiles, foxes, and others until he had a list that resembled a perfectly balanced petting zoo.

In the future, he wanted to use relativistic space-time to step forward in humanity's future. He wanted to see our people as a species expand out into the stars, while only a few months passed for those aboard the ship. He had not perfected it yet, but his goal was to find a way to travel at near light speed so that, by his estimations, normal space-time in relation to the time passing on the ship would be near a five-hundred-to-one ratio.

He worked on the space cruiser for most of the day, creating sketches of living quarters, laying out research and development laboratories, and creating the structural specification lists the AI would use to generate the technical 3-D models.

His two big cats, Tom and Jerry, who, to his relief, had moved to the Antamina installation before the tragedy in America, lay on a bed next to where he worked. When he stood, their ears perked, and they rose to follow. They insisted on going with him everywhere, curious to see the next place he would take them, and when he sat for hours, working on one thing or another, they seemed content to curl up and sleep. Sometimes, though, they disappeared for a few hours here and there, gone off to explore the upper levels of the Antamina facility, with its forests, fish-filled pools, and birds that Samantha artificially grew in her lab.

"What do you think, little buddy?" he asked Tom, who pushed his nose into Daniel's hand. He walked out of his lab, under the canopy of tall trees, toward one of the paths that meandered through the forest and then opened onto a meadow and a freshwater pool filled with big, colorful fish. As they walked, the two big cats watched the fish swarming the shoreline, anticipating a feeding.

Many people in the world, he considered, were a little like the fish in these ponds, existing without a worry of what went on outside their little space, never looking beyond what was in front of them, and most never believing it was possible to break free of the confines of their own immediate existence. He wanted to change that.

He walked along the path, no longer seeing the forest that had grown so much since they first arrived. He was consumed by thoughts of all the lives lost because of a small group of insane people bent on stopping him from helping mankind reach a new level of existence. His mother and Samantha's parents weighed heavily on his heart. He had loved them, and now they were gone. Gone because of what he was doing, and with that thought, the guilt crept in, a cold doubt along with a feeling of helplessness that pushed its way into his mind.

On the other side of the upper level of Antamina, Stas felt like a break and located Daniel on the filament map. "Jimmy, I'm going to stretch my legs. See ya in a bit, okay?" Stas announced as he stepped out of his chair. In mid-stride, he transmitted out of the room.

"Sure, Stas," Jimmy replied, unaware that Stas was already gone.

Stas jumped to a few feet from Daniel and greeted his friend. He immediately got the feeling that something was off.

"Hey, man, what's happening?" Stas asked as he patted Tom, who went up on his haunches, his front paws pressed to Stas's belly. He loved to try to rub his nose against Stas's chin. Stas couldn't miss the redness in his friend's eyes. "You okay? You got to stop dwelling on it, man. It wasn't your fault. It lies in the hands of those who committed the crimes, man; not you!"

Daniel looked at him, a small smile curling at the edge of his mouth. "Just thinking about all the things we've been through, where we are, and where we are heading. And well, yeah, I was thinking about all those people ..." He paused, looking off into the distance.

Stas looked into his friend's eyes and saw a look with which he was all too familiar. There was fire inside Daniel, and it gave him pause, knowing where it could lead. "Oh boy, here we go. I hope this doesn't mean Jimmy and I are going to be up for the next three days, working on some priority system you require ... does it?"

Daniel just looked back at his friend with a nonchalant shrug. Stas laughed and clapped him on the shoulder, steering him back toward the common house as the two big cats crashed through the ferns on either side of the trail.

"How are we going to get the impoverished populations imprisoned on belief systems that take away their freedom of choice Staz, how can we get them interested in a big change? How can we break through to these people?"

Stas just chuckled. "You know what, my friend? I have been wondering about that same thing. I thought about it for a while and started working on a solution. I call it the teacher bot. It's very similar to the surveillance drones, but I created a new AI that will learn about its pupils and tutor them. Here, let me show you."

They transmitted across the upper deck of Antamina into the software developer's lab and plopped down into hovering leather chairs. Stas activated the holographic keyboard on his chair and waved his hand through the air, his fingers flicking at the holographic keys. The holo-display in the center of the room flashed as the newly designed AI software appeared, displaying a three-dimensional structure of code packets. He moved through it with fluid expertise, showing off his masterful skill and knowledge of its structure. He showed Daniel the different modules of code he and Jimmy had incorporated and Daniel was impressed.

Daniel watched and recognized the modular packets used for the filament energy receivers, matter-transmission functions, and antigravity field emitter systems. He asked Stas to pause as a new packet came into focus. "It's a new algorithm. It learns about its owner and helps with any subject the person wishes to study, along with sticking to teaching mandatory basics."

Daniel was very impressed and listened to his friend lay out his plan. "I have been stuck on the idea that in order to rehabilitate Earth's populations, we need to educate them. I thought this would be an effective way to start. With the micro-monitoring clouds tracking crime all around the world, we can send bots to anyone who wants one. All people would need to do is raise their hand and hold it there until bots are printed and sent to them. So even people who do not have access to the U.E. network can get a teacher bot free and begin learning about the rest of the world."

"This is perfect, Stas. You are a genius! We should get this actioned immediately; it's not like it will cost us anything. Our mining operations in the asteroid belt are going far better than I had ever hoped. The elemental stockpiles are growing, and the mining flotilla is expanding fast. It is amazing how much rare earth metals are locked in that ice and stone floating in space."

Over the next few days, an army of the new bots, programmed to project a holographic message, were sent to regions where those still in poverty and isolation would receive the message and learn how to call for a teacher bot of their own. They arrived over villages, towns, and cities in the poorest parts of the world, hovering in place and displaying the holographic video that explained the offer Daniel personally recorded.

"Today we find ourselves with the chance to be free of oppression," the message began. "Let us not waste it bickering for superiority and power. Let us instead help our fellow man and prosper as a species. In many parts of the world, there is little education. Our aim is to correct that. United Earth is starting a program to give everyone an equal opportunity to educate themselves. We have designed a teacher bot, one that is now freely available to anyone who wants one. Hold up your hand with one finger pointing to the sky—like this—and one will be sent to you within a few minutes. The teacher bots will not monitor you or transmit information about you. Their sole purpose is to help you learn. Those who seek to use them to research ways of committing violence will find their teacher bot most disagreeable. I also would like to include in this message to everyone on Earth that my corporation, United Earth Technologies, has started a mandate of prosperity and unification. Packages are being sent out to governments and the media, describing in detail the requirements that need to be met in order for your country to be eligible. The major requirements are a reduction of crime and corruption and a visible display of self-improvement by citizens, something that should be helped along by the bots we are providing. Many people may already have heard of or seen the videos showing the changes in Spain, Italy, and Greece, formerly of the European Union. With United Earth's assistance, they have revitalized their lands and now have an abundance of fresh water, food, and new medical facilities capable of curing cancer and AIDS. These were the first countries we selected as examples. This is what the people and governments who work together to better themselves can expect. Thank you. That is all for now."

Daniel, Stas, and Jimmy watched the big wall display in the common building play back footage of people pointing to the sky, as nearly a billion people all made the sign to request a teacher bot at the same time. Bots arrived and scanned their new owners, introduced themselves, and explained their capabilities and purpose in every language.

Three weeks later Daniel finished the designs on a spherical five-thousand-cubic-foot space vehicle prototype, and the first thing he did was transmit it into the orbit of Ceres, a dwarf planet located in the main asteroid belt. He named it *Viewer One* and planned to take his friends on a tour of the wonders of their solar system soon.

When *Viewer One* left the lower deck of Antamina, instantly transmitting out over four hundred million kilometers into space, his anticipation for a first trip brought on a huge adrenaline rush, and he tapped the desk, waiting for a full diagnostic system check.

When the systems check came back, verifying the craft was fully operational, Daniel couldn't wait to get everyone together and transmitted up. In a momentary blip, he arrived in the lower viewing platform of the ship and took in the spectacle. He looked out into space through the walls designed to mirror everything on the outside of the ship at a resolution that made it seem just like transparent glass. For a time he just stood there, taking it all in and felt the magnitude of being the first, before transmitting up to the control room of the ship where he sat in the forwardmost command chair.

The view went on and on, an ocean of floating ice and stone, some with only trace amounts of minerals, while others had tons of valuable ore. He watched as glowing blue points of light blinked in and out from behind the array of space debris and noted with satisfaction the size of the 3-D printers and containment tanks floating nearby.

The AI was programmed to continuously increase the size and number of drones, 3-D printers, and containment arrays in proportion to the amount of stockpiled resources needed to proactively meet the future demand of construction projects. Plans were in the works for projects as large as entire continents back on Earth, and Daniel wanted to see them completed within the year.

He made a slight movement with his hand through the holo-field controlling the craft's position in space, and it zipped down to the surface of the ice-covered dwarf planet, Ceres. From his seat, Daniel's eyes tracked along the huge cracks that spread across the planet's surface, and he thought about the potential resource this ball of ice truly was. He knew there was water between the icy surface and rocky mantle in its center, and he wondered about what might be living there.

Satisfied, he looked down at the time and saw, to his surprise, an hour had already passed.

I wonder if anyone noticed, he thought and considered a short tour of the relatively nearby gas giants and their moons.

Europa was of great interest to Daniel, and when he flew over its turquoise baby-blue ice-covered surface, he thought of the discoveries people could make there. He imagined strange and beautiful fishlike creatures and an ecosystem so different from anything on Earth.

Viewer One's energy field easily resisted the gravitational forces that would have otherwise crushed the craft as he skimmed the outer edge of Jupiter. He had transmitted to fifty kilometers below the upper atmosphere of the gas giant before rising to only a few meters above the orange and purple gas. The orb ship *Viewer One,* shot along at thousands of kilometers per second.

After a few minutes of blasting across the sea of swirling color, he peeled off, up and away from the radioactive atmosphere on a heading for Callisto, one of Jupiter's moons. The large moon was hours away at his current speed, and so, after clearing the gas giant's atmosphere, he selected a position in the holo-field and activated the matter-transmission drive. *Viewer One* blinked across the empty space in an instant, entering a precise orbit above the cratered moonscape.

It was incredible, the number of impacts this moon had endured over time, as seen by the countless pockmarks. His eyes widened even more as what had to be the largest crater on the entire surface slid over the horizon and into view. This one he already knew about but seeing it firsthand was truly something to behold. Mankind sent satellites past these moons years ago and mapped these craters with fairly good detail. Valhalla crater measured at a diameter of just over four thousand kilometers across and was accented by a ring of jagged spires all around the entire circumference. His eyes teared as emotion welled up; it was so amazing, and he slowed the craft to take it all in.

He considered ending his tour and returning with his friends, so they could all share the experience of seeing these amazing sights for the first time. He knew it was the right call, and with that thought, he jumped *Viewer One* back into the orbit of Ceres before transmitting himself back to the Antamina site.

Dillon, his thick arms folded over his chest, sat in his leather hover chair, seemingly frozen in place. Not even a hair on his body moved. He had his eyes glued to the spot where Daniel appeared, and he let his opinion be known.

"So you're going to just head off into space without notifying your head of security, are ya, boy?" Dillon asked in a harsh tone before a smile he had been holding back replaced the stern look. He chuckled and then, in a more agreeable tone, asked, "So how was it? You could have at least invited this old dog to go along. Do you have any idea what a view of the stars from out there would mean to an old man like me?"

Daniel smiled innocently. "Yes, I know. I just went up to see the mining operations and then, without thinking, went on a little tour, but I thought of you guys and cut it short. I want to share seeing it all for the first time together. We all likely will get sick of being out there when we begin spending nearly all our time off-planet, you know."

That evening they sat around a huge stone-topped table in the common room for what felt like a family dinner.

"The teacher bots are having an incredibly positive effect in impoverished regions, people are learning, and everyone is seeing what is happening in the countries that have joined the movement," Samantha stated.

Dillon brought up an issue that had been in the back of Daniel's mind for days. "There are still pockets of radicals killing people with teacher bots. If we want to see a global change occur, these countries need to be included and helped to prosper. But the trouble is, they have become so militarized over the years ... hmm ... there must be something we can do."

Hearing this accurate expression of what he was thinking from one of his most respected friends, Daniel nodded in agreement. He felt that the peace forces were just not doing enough in those regions. "What if we militarize some of the drones, assign them to search out these people who are killing the innocent, and put them down with force?" he asked.

John shook his head. "We need to live and work for peace. We can't go to war against anyone. I think the best we can do is help the peace forces track these bad guys more accurately and help them be more effective in bringing justice. Unless the peace forces ask us for help, or we come under direct attack, we need to stay away from committing acts of violence."

John's response was well thought out, and the rest of the table, most of whom were on the side of taking immediate offensive action, saw the truth of it.

After dinner, Daniel and Stas went to the developer's lab to modify the watch map software. It would now create markers for anyone persecuting innocent people. Daniel brought up the concern with Stas that the Peace Corps and United Nation's forces should not be displayed on the public watch map. Understanding the need to protect these freedom fighters, they added a discrepancy to the AI, ensuring that the UN forces would not be made public or viewable by anyone other than the Antamina facility's mainframe database, unless their actions were red-flagged for cruelty or human rights violations.

They tested the update locally, and when they were satisfied there were no bugs, it was uploaded to the mainframe and integrated into the AI charged with watching over Earth's population. The two of them watched as the AI increased the number of micro-surveillance nodes exponentially, until finally stopping at just over ten trillion viewer particles. Daniel and Stas had not given the AI rules on how to go about its job, except for the parameters and objectives of identifying, following, and recording harmful and criminal actions. They knew what they had done was crossing the lines of privacy, but to weed out criminal elements in the world as quickly as possible, they felt it was acceptable. If people did not commit any of the crimes listed, they would have nothing to worry about; they would never be recorded.

Stas reflected on the reality of it. "What they don't know won't hurt them, right? It's not like these sensors and cameras can be seen by the naked eye, and only people who kill the innocent, control through fear and corruption, or commit atrocities are going to be tagged and tracked on the watch map. Let's face it; the world's population has been monitored by military and government agencies for longer than a lot of people have been alive. This is nothing new, just a necessary step to cure the world of its sickness."

Daniel looked at his friend silently and gave a curt nod before turning to leave the developer's suite. He had a sick feeling in his stomach. What they had done was justified, but the principle of it irked him. He feared they had done too much, but he kept his silence. A part of him knew this was integral to achieving their ultimate goals—their dreams of giving humanity the chance to rise to new levels of existence—and so he looked forward, on to what would come next.

In his idle time, Daniel worked on the design of the explorer ship. He still hadn't told them of this plan, unsure of how they would feel about leaving Earth to return a few hundred years in the future. He would invite them along, of course, with at least a hundred reputable scientists and world leaders to join on their journey into the far reaches of the Milky Way and possibly beyond. He just wasn't sure how to present it, and in any case, there was still a lot to get done before they could consider leaving mankind to its own devices.

John and Samantha continued working with the countries accepted into the prosperity program. From time to time they updated Daniel with lists of achievements, milestones, and especially the names of the newest countries completing startup packages. The primary mission was agricultural revitalization and mandatory basic education. Where it was catching on, the results were incredibly positive.

The United States was soon approved, and for them, Daniel created a special program focused on reforestation—the regeneration of their once-heavily forested countryside's, long since devastated by wildfires and drought. Newly engineered fast-growing trees and crops were scattered by hundreds of worker drones, while networks of pipe transmitted, creating lattice works of irrigation lines spreading out from newly installed desalination plants along their coastlines.

Daniel had neglected to check on the resources in the lower pit of the Antamina mine for a while, and when he did, he was a little surprised to find it nearly depleted. It was obvious they would need to begin transmitting stockpiles from the asteroid belt, where skyscraper-sized storage tanks were filled to capacity, waiting to be used. It was time to begin the next level of 3-D printing. It was time to open the nearly limitless distances of space to the expansion of mankind.

Before starting the off-planet expansion, though, he thought it would be wise to reinforce the Antamina foundations. He wrote a series of requirements, one being that the lower level be finished with engineered concrete slabs and carbon steel reinforcements.

He considered Mars, long a goal of mankind's adventurous spirit. For years various organizations on Earth had toyed with sending people to begin colonization, and admittedly, Daniel thought it was a prime world for future installations. The international space agencies had spent billions sending probes and rovers to Mars's surface, but they still had not completed preparations to send people on the long voyage. He chuckled to himself, thinking that they had never solved the problem of efficiently blocking out radiation while in space. So as the first off-world construction project, he decided to build an installation on the red planet before taking on the larger projects he wanted to see constructed.

Daniel brought the idea to the rest of the team, and they began brainstorming various wish-list items and basic requirements for the new facility.

To start, they all agreed the structures would need to house at least a couple million people. The next and most important thing was to figure out how to create Earthlike gravity, so as to maintain a home world aesthetic in the agriculture and design. They all agreed having Earthlike plants, trees, animals, and even insects to complete full-cycle ecosystems would be key to making peoples migration as effortless as possible. They planned modern living spaces, bodies of water, and big, open park areas with expansive views of the Martian landscape.

John, a lover of astronomy and planetary study and one who researched Mars extensively, picked a spot just south of the Valles Marineris canyon—a canyon on Mars many times larger than the Grand Canyon on Earth—as the site of the new installation. When Daniel saw the location his father picked, he was inspired. With this spark, Daniel called up the point cloud data collected by surveyor drones sent to scan every surface in the solar system, and he went to work designing the facility on the exact spot John had chosen. He enjoyed sketching an outline of where the installation would sit and found it a little hard to imagine the scale of a human in relation to the huge landscape.

The canyon was near four thousand kilometers long, and, for the most part, it ran east to west. The outline he drew put the future installation along the edge of the southeast corner of the widest section of the canyon, near the center of its length.

John and Samantha were especially creative in the list of design elements for the interior of the domes. They wished to include large bodies of water, floating walkways, and tall buildings scattered throughout the interior of the futuristic city domes.

This would be their first off-world installation. Daniel knew that his father, with his extensive experience in architectural design, and Samantha, with her keen eye for landscaping and agriculture, would work quite well as a team.

When he was content that things were going well, Daniel looked at his next task; he would find a way to unravel the riddle of 3-D printing organic life.

His mind drifted, seeing genomic blueprints and atomic structures with a clarity beyond anything he had ever experienced. Hours went by, feeling like only minutes, as he tapped into a place in his mind that seemed to hold the answers to impossible questions. When he woke up, he found himself slumped in his favorite chair, where he had spent every hour of the last day and a half, working out the solution to organic 3-D printing.

As Daniel's eyes focused, he saw a flashing green box on the screen in front of him. "Proceed with initial organic print." He clicked and was presented with a database of nearly every plant and animal known to man. With an astonished sense of anticipation, he selected his desk as the location for the newly printed item: "Sixteen-inch fish bowl, required ph. balanced saltwater, saltwater plants (sparse), three colorful seahorses." He closed his eyes and hit the return function, half expecting a lap full of seaweed and saltwater. When he opened them, though, his heart skipped, and he choked up. It was perfect!

"It works!" he shouted. Jerry, always the vocal one, looked up from where the two cats were curled together and meowed. "I did it, Jerry. It works. Can you believe it?" he said to the cat before panning through the filament cloud to Samantha's desk, where he sent a fully flowering white and pink orchid in a jade glass vase, along with a card that read, "From the depths of space, this flower was 3-D printed."

The next day he spent some time considering the asteroid belt mining reports and was surprised to see that it was past time to instruct the AI to begin building and sending new mining flotillas further out. The asteroid belt was just the start. When he activated the next phase, new mining groups were printed and assembled at an entirely new massive scale and sent to begin work along the inner side of our solar systems Kuiper belt.

Chapter 21

Earth's Emergence

Mankind's condition improved as crime rates dramatically declined. Everyone committing a high crime was recorded in 3-D point cloud video, and from that point on, their position was publicly broadcast. Those committing rape, grand theft, murder, slavery, kidnapping, and torture were tracked down. The righteous, in ways, became as ruthless and cold-blooded as those they hunted, but it did not last. A calm intellect rose from the turmoil, and those committing crimes were quickly and efficiently removed from society.

With the advent of the teacher bots and the United Earth prosperity programs, no one was left without education resources. In impoverished regions, food and water was sent regularly, along with holographic presentations encouraging them to continue on the path to prosperity. They urged the people of these lands to study, learn, and find ways to better themselves and their communities in exchange for the clean water and much-needed food. The world's populations found new meaning; all it took was basic education and new goals, and by these simple things a new awareness emerged.

Humanity's eyes were opened to a new more intelligent point of view. As a result, the mutual awareness and understanding gave entire populations the ability to identify evil and the courage to call it out.

For many, their outcry against the watching eyes was violent. Whatever was catching and recording every crime was in direct violation of the privacy acts of the previous century. The corporate media attacked United Earth with everything they had left, but it only solidified their end. They put out hostile propaganda campaigns, fabricating evidence and pushing their agenda, but there was no stopping the engine of truth that Daniel and his friends had unleashed on the world. The guilty cried out the loudest and accused United Earth of the very crimes they themselves were committing. But there was no turning back; mankind would find a basic goodwill, and, in the process, the lies and shrieking cries of evil's maddening fears and the outrage of their insane flocks would fade away.

In the rehabilitation of Earth's environment, it was impressive to see just how quickly the renewal of wastelands all around the world progressed. Where deserts had eaten away at once-thick forests, green belts of new growth lined irrigation pipes that continuously misted fresh water out onto the landscapes. New growth began. Life sprang up from of the ground with tenacity and the air quality improved. Communities on the outskirts of cities bordering these lands began to prosper and, for showing their drive to improve their own cultures condition and education, the AI rewarded them with community buildings, aquatic centers, medical facilities, and sporting facilities. Every time a reward was given, it came with the same message: "For perseverance in the pursuit of the betterment of our species, this facility has been rewarded to the people of this land." A rush toward knowledge all around the world began. The teacher bots pushed science, the universe, medicine, and the spread of goodwill as its main lessons and the people of earth awakened.

Weeks passed as the world continued on its new upward trend. New infrastructures to accelerate ecological rehabilitation on many of Earth's continents were completed, but there were still regions beyond repair. In some areas where generations of poverty had leaked into the ground, something more drastic needed to happen, and as long as the people still lived in these places, cleanup would be virtually impossible.

On Mars, all of the water for the lakes, natural dirt landscaping, plants, trees, and even the animals were printed using the new organic foundries. It was time to show the world what was possible.

Daniel finally invited his friends for a tour of their solar system and the construction on mars. Alongside them, he also invited a number of respected scientists and leading researchers from NASA, CERN, and other space and science organizations, including professors from top universities all around the world. He invited Mr. Sylinger, the president of the United States, Mr. Brennan, and a handful of other government representatives from countries leading the prosperity movement.

The invitation went out on specially designed marble-sized bots. They were modeled after the teacher bot, except much smaller and with one added feature—each messenger bot was equipped to scan and transmit the invited guest to wherever Daniel or the AI directed, as long as the guest accepted the invitation.

When the small spherical bot appeared, floating in front of each of the prospective guests, it immediately started a holographic invitation describing where they would be going and for how long they would be gone. At the end, it requested them to verbally except or decline the invitation. If they declined, the bot immediately transmitted back to Antamina; if they accepted, it then requested they notify it when they were prepared to leave. Not one person rejected the invite, and when they announced they were ready, the tiny orb scanned and transmitted them back to the Antamina security building.

Dillon sat waiting to receive each guest, and as they arrived he welcomed them, sitting each of them along the wall where they watched brief orientation presentations to prepare them for the day's events.

The group of guests quickly arrived as the message was received and accepted. Delegates and scientists from different countries all found familiar faces among the group. They energetically discussed what they were going to witness, while proudly commenting on being selected to see what Daniel Thoth and his group had in store for the human race.

After the brief orientation, Daniel stepped away from the wall, where he had been concealed behind a invisibility holo-field, and addressed them.

"Today, as your invitations explained, we are going to take a little trip off-planet and tour our first facility on Mars, one we have been working on for only a short few weeks. Please, everyone, spread out so that no one is closer than one meter before we transmit to the *Viewer One* ship."

They looked at each other, most with wonder in their eyes, as they shuffled to a distance from one another. Daniel waited until he was satisfied, pointing to some of them and telling them to step this way or that. "I would recommend you all take a deep breath on the count of three and hold it like you are about to have a dunk in frigid water. One, two, three." And in the next moment they were off.

In a flash, they found themselves standing in a room that seemed to only have a floor; the main viewing platform of *Viewer One*. The PLED coating on the inside of the ship's walls made it seem as though only a thin sheet of totally transparent glass separated them from the vast emptiness of space and many gasped in astonishment.

Their echoes of awe reverberated in their virtual silence as they came to grips with what they saw. They started moving in near-perfect synchronization, all of them pointing and commenting as though sharing the same exact thoughts. Daniel watched and laughed inwardly, understanding their initial reactions.

He glanced over to where his father stood, then shifted his eyes to Dillon, and then continued his scan to see that most had tears running down their cheeks. It was a sight none of them had ever expected to see. He smiled, remembering his first view of this place and knew what his guests—people who dedicated their lives to the study of places beyond Earth—must be feeling.

From *Viewer One*'s position over Ceres, the group looked out at the expansive asteroid belt, made much thinner by the army of miner bots hard at work. As they turned away from the belt, they saw the sun far off in the distance. It appeared smaller than they expected, just as a ball of light floating far out of reach, yet acting as the central beacon of the solar system.

Daniel watched them for a time before transmitting up to the control room, where he materialized directly in his command chair. He smoothly set a course for Jupiter, and the ship began to move. *Viewer One* went from its orbital course around Ceres to just over three hundred thousand kilometers an hour in an instant, leaving behind the asteroid belt and Ceres in a streak of blurred motion.

He let them experience space rushing past for a few minutes before jumping the ship into the upper atmosphere of the gas giant, just as he had done before. Racing along at nearly fifteen thousand kilometers per hour, he banked the ship back and forth, dipping down and submerging it completely in the swirling gas of the huge planet's atmosphere, before finally pulling up so that the huge mass of the planet fell away behind them. He punched up the speed to just over five hundred thousand kilometers per hour, and *Viewer One* took off.

The plasma thrusters on *Viewer One* could take the ship up past 0.4% the speed of light, but at that speed, space would begin to distort, turning the amazing view into a blur of indistinguishable streaks, not to mention there would be a noticeable amount of time dilation, and he didn't want these cornerstones of the political and scientific communities arriving home a few weeks later than he had promised.

Turning the ship, he vectored toward Europa, the fourth largest of Jupiter's moons. As they got closer to the famous ice moon, a geyser erupted from its surface, and he steered the ship toward the spectacle. He slowed to twenty kilometers per second as they passed the frozen cloud of crystalline particles spreading out into space. He hadn't said anything and wondered what his guests were thinking, but he wasn't going to break the silence just yet. Using the ship's computer, he transmitted John and Dillon up into the chairs on either side of him, and before they had a chance to say anything, he jumped the ship again into an orbit around the dwarf planet Pluto.

"Son, you gotta stop doing that!" John exclaimed.

Dillon just let out a whoop of exhilaration, obviously loving every moment of it.

This far away from the sun, space was dark—very dark! And even though he had pointed them toward the sun, now a tiny orange ball way off in the distance, it nearly blended into the tapestry of stars making up the Milky Way.

As their eyes adapted to the darkness, they noticed thousands of small points of blue light moving among the asteroids in the distance. There were hundreds of thousands in every direction, all going about the business of cutting and transmitting chunks of ice rock into the particle separators, where the ore was atomized and separated into individual elemental storage tanks. He waited to let his guests pick up on the bots before switching the outer surface of *Viewer One* from its matte white finish to a solid ball of light. It instantly lit up the surface of Pluto in front and below them, while quickly reaching the drones and asteroids in the nearby vicinity.

He flipped on the intercom and spoke. "We are currently orbiting Pluto, folks. As you can see, we have worker drones mining and collecting the minerals not only in the asteroid belt between Jupiter and Mars but also out here in the inner edge of the Kuiper belt. These mining operations are continuously expanding and collecting the materials needed to build off-planet cities we are planning on constructing in the very near future."

Looking over to John and then to Dillon, he saw both were utterly speechless, their mouths hanging open in disbelief.

"So, what do you guys think? Pretty cool, huh? Just wait 'til we visit Mars."

John and Dillon still sat silently, not knowing what to say, until John reached over and put his hand on Daniel's shoulder.

"It's amazing, son, truly amazing. Things people have only dreamed of and imagined in science fiction stories; things science thought wouldn't happen for hundreds of years—and that's a big if—and it's all happening because of you. You are making these things happen in a matter of a few short years. It's more than amazing, Daniel; it's a miracle for humanity. What you are doing will ensure mankind's survival and expansion. On Earth your technology is saving the planet and its people from the pollution and self-destruction that we, as a species, caused. It's just too much to believe, but seeing it in front of my eyes, your mother would have ..." He trailed off.

"I know, Dad. She would be so proud to see it all now. She has a lot to do with why I have pushed so hard to get here."

After a few minutes of silence, Daniel keyed in the coordinates for the Mars installation and jumped the ship, transmitting them into perfect geo-synchronized orbit, 130,000 feet above the newly finished facility.

When they all saw the huge structure perched atop the highest crest along the huge Valles Marineris canyon, a collective gasp swept the room of observers. On his control panel, Daniel brought up a holographic three-dimensional map of the planet and drew a line down around the domes of the new facility, over the canyon, and up to the back side of the largest structure. He leaned back and said, "Activate current course flight path; travel time twenty-two minutes." He stepped away from his command chair and transmitted the three of them back to the viewing deck.

As the ship moved along the preset course, the guests gathered at the front, eagerly watching the landscape *Viewer One* was descending towards. From behind them, Daniel began to speak like a tour guide educating a group on a sightseeing ride.

"As most of you probably already know, we are just above the great canyon, Valles Marineris, on Mars. As you can see, there is a newly constructed facility on the southeast corner of the central Malas Chasma, the widest section of the canyon. There are accommodations for up to five million people down there. Although, as this is the first off-world installation, the idea is to selectively admit people based on their outstanding work as humanitarians and as leaders of the new prosperity movement. My team and I have thought about it and believe that this can become the hub for our new world's leadership and most valuable contributing members. Those who are admitted to Mars One will have the freedom to travel between their new homes here and their current homes on Earth as well as future facilities. All travel will be via wristbands coded to your living DNA. The wrist bands not only will enable members of this installation to have free travel, but it will also protect them from most external threats. There will be other facilities to come, new larger ones designed to displace the overpopulated areas on Earth. For now, this will be the first step in humanity's journey to the stars. Are there any questions?"

Mr. Brennan was the first to speak. "How will these people be chosen and given access to this place? Will their families be included?"

"Good question, Andrew. The AI has already created a list of nearly one million people, including their families, who will receive invitation packages like the ones you received. For the first little while, it will feel a tad empty up here, but as more prove themselves, the AI will select them, and they will be given a place. I hope that answers the main questions you were thinking of. And yes, each one of you has been selected. In fact, you will be given the first choice of residence."

Viewer One pinged him as they passed within one thousand meters of their destination, and he looked down at a holo-sheet projected along his forearm. Daniel selected the group on board the ship and transmitted them into the main facility dome on Mars. They materialized on a stone lookout on the ridge of a hill. Daniel took a deep breath and then let it out, as if testing the air. "Oh, that's good," he pronounced in a somewhat relieved tone.

"What's good?" a young dark-haired physicist asked in his British accent.

"Oh, well, umm … well, the air is breathable, of course. You know, I really wasn't sure if we would survive this. You see, this is the first time any human has taken a breath in one of these facilities, and I, um, I was pretty sure, but had a small amount of doubt." Daniel considered the young man's eyes and asked seriously, "Are you feeling okay? No asphyxia; no spots in your vision? Dizziness? You don't feel faint, do you?"

Their reactions were priceless. He watched as they checked each other, their shock apparent. Daniel broke out into laughter, bending over at the waist to embellish his eccentricity at what he considered a very clever prank.

"Forgive me. Oh, I am very sorry; just a joke. I knew very well the air here is perfectly balanced. You will find it pristine compared to what Earth's air has become, although it is true we are taking the first breaths any human has taken in one of these facilities. It is perfectly safe; in fact, it's probably very good for you."

He laughed again at his joke and offered them free run of the place. "Please take an hour to explore the facility and claim your future dwellings. Your personal invitation bots will transmit you to wherever you describe, while ensuring that you stay inside the facility and they will answer any questions you might have. When the time is up, I will transmit you all to where we're having dinner."

A few moments later, nearly all the scientists and heads of state vanished, pointing to places they could see, urgently commanding their personal bots to take them there. Little did they know there was no shortage of high-level accommodations; in fact, there were more than one hundred thousand similar units at the highest level in this dome alone.

When those planning to go on their own searches left, Daniel addressed those who stayed. "Well then, shall we convene somewhere with a view?" he asked.

They nodded, and with deft skill he flicked at the holographic panel hovering over his forearm, and they transmitted to the rooftop of a tower complex near the center of the dome.

Alex Newman, a physicist from the CERN facility, was already there. He stood at the railing, unaware he had chosen to investigate the same location Daniel picked to show his friends and those preferring the guided tour.

"Alex, why don't you join us?" Daniel called, startling the older man, who turned in surprise and walked to where they stood.

"Boy, this place is incredible," the old man said. "I will have you know that I claimed my residence in a large, lofted space two floors down from this very deck. I think I will find this the perfect getaway for my family. Thank you for choosing me as one of the first."

Daniel nodded, acknowledging the man's gratitude. The group spread out, walking through the huge rooftop gardens to a large central pool. There were birds that seemed tame, flying close and landing on some of their shoulders. Chipmunks skittered up and down the trees, chirping and eyeing the newcomers who so suddenly appeared in their sanctuary.

Many of the guests vanished for a few minutes before returning with looks of satisfaction. After seeing this rooftop garden and hearing Alex's declaration, they were quick to claim their own top-floor units in this building. Daniel brought up the building on his hologram view and saw that in just the last few minutes, nearly all the residences on the upper three floors were claimed.

With everyone back on the rooftop garden, Daniel walked them over to the north railing and pointed out at the view. The great Valles Marineris stretched out in every direction. Down along the edge of the dome, it met the top of the canyon. A few in the group pointed to a large lake with detached residences, docks, and beaches, and Daniel transmitted them to the boardwalk that ran out along the dome's wall and along the lake's shoreline.

They walked along the floating boardwalk to an area with tables, chairs, and what looked like a bar, yet there was no one working. Daniel made a pointed example; he walked up to the bar and verbally ordered a strawberry and watermelon smoothie with vanilla cream. There was a faint flash, and a moment later his drink appeared on the counter in a three-quarter-liter glass cup. He smiled and stepped away.

"It is best to be specific with your orders, as the AI will do its best to match your request with common items, but in some cases, it will literally create whatever you describe."

They all took turns ordering drinks, some ordering beer, wine, or scotch, and others just ordering a juice or a simple cup of water.

Daniel checked the time and was surprised to see that nearly an hour and a half already had passed. Once again, he looked down at his forearm, flicked his fingers across his holo-control screen, and transmitted the guests to the dinner venue.

Moments later they were all high up in the central dome, standing around a huge, oval banquet table of white marble stone. As they took their seats, Daniel instructed the AI "AI, print one crystal goblet with mountain spring sparkling water for each person at the table," and as they reacted he smiled in delight.

Most had not seen the particle assemblers in action and were shocked when, without warning, the cups of water simply appeared. The others who had accompanied Daniel and his group on the guided tour were familiar with the replicator technology and did not hesitate to pick up the crystal cups for indulgent sips of the refreshing water.

"I hope everyone is happy with their chosen accommodations and has worked up an appetite. Here on Mars One, there are no farms or any need for harvesting food. Although it is not impossible to have a garden and raise livestock if you wish, we have particle assemblers that can create nearly any dish you desire, cooked exactly how you like it, and when you are finished, the same process will return the leftovers to their base elements and store them for future use. What you need to do is initialize the holographic menu, and pick whatever you wish to eat and drink. Trust me; the atomic structure and molecular makeup of anything you choose will be exactly as it is on Earth."

They looked at him with doubtful expressions, but he just smiled and nodded knowingly. "Yes, I know it's hard to believe. Let's face it; we are all sitting here at a table on a three-foot-thick stone disc that is hovering high above a tropical landscape under a dome on Mars. Is a particle assembler capable of generating any kind of food or drink so hard to believe?"

The members of the United Earth team were quick to start their selections, already familiar with the process. With their example, the rest at the table began searching their holographic menus and choosing their meals.

They all began requesting drinks and side dishes, some requesting specialty beer, scotch, wine, juice, and even sangria. Voices rang out—roast chicken, medium-rare New York steak, Ham and pineapple pizza, beef stew, sushi, and on and on until everyone had their orders.

In front of each of them, as soon as their selection was made, the organic printer synthesized the food—perfect medium-rare cuts of meat, steaming side dishes, bubbling soda, and even the twenty-year-old scotch Mr. Brennan ordered, complete with a perfectly round ice cube, exactly as he described, materialized.

Mr. Sylinger looked up from his steaming plate. "How can this be possible? Food that looks so perfect and smells so good—how could it just form out of thin air? It was like I could almost see atomic threads weaving together as it all formed, and now my senses unmistakably tell me to dig in!" He laughed with joy, picking up his fork and knife and doing just that. There were a few more exclamations of delight, but soon they were eating, and a silence brought on by the delicious food shrouded the entire table.

"Wow, it really is unbelievable that we are here. I don't think this kind of view could ever get old!" John exclaimed as he rhythmically clinked his fork on his crystal cup of water, a gesture that was joined by the rest of the group who looked up from their food with respectful nods toward Daniel in acknowledgment of his genius and achievements.

Daniel was pleased, seeing his friends, his father, and his guests so happy. It inspired him, and he stood to speak about his plans.

"I have an announcement to make," he said. "I have been planning a voyage of discovery outside of Earth's solar system. The purpose: to survey and discover all that we can of our beautiful Milky Way. On this voyage I would like for all the United Earth team, along with those of you here and any of your families who wish to come along, to join me. There is one thing you all need to understand, though; there is more than one purpose for this voyage. First, of course, is to witness the amazing places our galaxy has to offer, but the second and most important reason is to jump forward into mankind's future. We will use relative space-time to go into the future of our species and witness the expansion of our kind."

The audience shuffled, and many of them looked around, unsure. Daniel continued.

"By traveling at near light speed, we will dilate time and return to Earth's relative space-time far into mankind's future. We will witness the expansion of our species and our civilization into the stars. Of course, there are a lot of things we need to get into place before we can leave, such as; immigration programs to new off-world installations, education programs, and universal ethical ground rules. Our sole purpose should be to ensure the prosperity and unity of mankind. There is no place for the bureaucratic policymakers who breed corruption and confusion, those who manipulate and enslave. Ignorant policymakers will not be tolerated. Laws created simply by those in regulatory positions to gain more power will not be tolerated, and mankind's unity will be the norm. Troublemakers will find themselves relegated to lawless zones on Earth, or out skirting facilities with tight restrictions and routines if they choose rehabilitation."

He paused, letting his eyes go to each of theirs, one after the other, letting his statements sink in. He watched them as they understood his words.

He waved his hand over his personal hologram panel and entered a verbal key code. "Frontiersman." He said, and the command unlocked the designs of the secret ship he had been working on, "View in three-dimensional visualization display—center of table." He said, and a hologram of the ship appeared right where he requested.

They saw a huge spacecraft with a dome that ran the length of the upper deck and what looked like the hull of a sailboat dropping down underneath. He zoomed inside the dome, showing the landscape on the upper deck and the 360-degree view of space outside of the ship. He zoomed closer, bringing them to a complex of white-walled Mediterranean-style buildings, a style of architecture he was growing to prefer, much like the small groups of buildings along the lakes in Mars One. Below the group of buildings was a small turquoise-blue lake with well-groomed gardens, boardwalks, and white sand leading into the water. Beyond this central living area, a landscape of forests, hills, and small rolling mountains spread out from the central rise.

Dillon piped up as the hologram continued rotating. "Really, Daniel? Is this for real?"

"Yes, Dillon, there are no limitations of scale or design out here in space, and having the main deck feel and smell like Earth, with a wide range of ecosystems to explore, it will make our time more comfortable, perhaps even preferred. There is no cost to this; all the materials will be sourced from the asteroid belts. Currently a 3-D printer is under construction in the Kuiper belt, capable of printing the entire ship as you see it, including the living plants, trees, and animals, all as one single printing process. This new printer will have a one-thousand-kilometer internal printing area, possibly the largest printer we will ever need. Below the main deck, onboard element storage and 3-D printing facilities will cater to our every need. Along with that, there are fifty *Viewer One* crafts just like the one we toured our solar system in today, ten million probes the AI can transmit into areas we choose to more extensively survey, and thousands of miner flotilla seed groups, drone pods we will drop off in areas chosen for developing new mining outposts and locations for new installations. With this technology, the Milky Way will become our species' playground, and the expansion of our kind will reach beyond just a few small stars. We are going to make our Milky Way feel like mankind's backyard."

When the meal was done, and Daniel had answered a few of their more pressing questions, he made one last statement. "Please, share what you have seen here. Post your pictures publicly. I would like the world to see it and hear it from your own perspectives. Thank you for coming." With that, he transmitted them all back to Earth.

A few hours later, John came to Daniel in his sleeping quarters back in Antamina. His father sat in a leather hover chair and gazed out over the canopy of trees, he watched the birds swarming up and plunging down in search of food and smiled to himself, wondering if it was all just a dream.

"Have you seen the news, Daniel?" John asked.

"No, not yet." Then he smiled, guessing what had likely gotten the media excited. "The scientists and government officials are showing pictures and describing their experience on Mars One," Daniel mused.

John laughed. "Yep, they have video and pictures of it all. Social media is exploding. They are telling everyone that the only way to be granted access to Mars One is to be a leading figure in the prosperity movement. The media is saying that you are trying to subvert every government in the world and become the supreme ruler of mankind."

Daniel looked at his father with a smile and laughed. "Well, I suppose they are right. Up there, there won't be a government to manage the people. The people will follow basic human rights and do their required tasks in exchange for residence, or they will find themselves sent back to Earth's non-U.E. regions. Let them speculate for a while. The first wave of invitation bots have been sent out. Over a million people will have their bracelets coded to their DNA and then we will see the first wave of people arrive on Mars One. There will be more pictures and videos on the net. The reality of what the future holds for everyone will soon be common knowledge."

Daniel went silent for a moment, looking his father in the eyes. "I have been thinking."

"Oh, dear Lord. Do we really need another monumental shift in mankind's reality?" John cut in.

"No, seriously, I have been thinking about the people who truly need help, allot of people on Earth will not break free from their poverty unless given new opportunity. Their exchange for residence will be to study and improve intellectually. Of course, the rich and powerful on Earth will want to buy their way in, but we have no use for money. The resources in space are endless, and we have the means to utilize them without limitations. I am glad we decided to dedicate the Mars installations to those who prove themselves by working toward bettering humanity. We need to do something even more outside the box, though; we need to help those who, even with the teacher bots, are still trapped in poverty."

John looked at his son with a warm sense of pride. Daniel was truly doing all he could to reshape the future of the species. "Son, I think that is the best idea you have had so far." He laughed and wished Daniel a good night. Then he selected a destination on his forearm and transmitted away in a silent wink of light.

When his father left, Daniel returned to his thoughts, seeing mankind pass the proverbial threshold to a collective intellectual baseline that would allow him and his friends to venture out into the stars and trust that insanity would not creep back into humanity. His eyes wandered over the treetops until finally he closed them and drifted into yet another dreamless sleep.

Chapter 22

A New Civilization

Earth's population had grown beyond sustainability, ballooning past thirteen billion with no real signs of slowing. Many countries were enforcing a one-child rule, yet the less-developed parts of the world continued having high birth rates and increased levels of poverty, forcing mass migration and the destabilization of the free world.

Food and water shortages became commonplace; entire populations were constantly at risk of starvation. Floods of immigrants were turned away as many countries already had taken more than they could handle. Crime had significantly dropped due to the all-seeing AI, but there were still so many—too many—impoverished souls who lost their lives because they could not help themselves.

Daniel and his team saw all of this and vowed to put an end to the insanity. But the overpopulation, in Daniel's eyes, was not the problem. *The more people, the better,* he thought. United Earth's manufacturing capabilities were ready to build facilities faster than mankind could ever multiply. Humanity would see the greatest migration in history, a migration off Earth, followed by an exponential increase in numbers. The poorest and most impoverished would be the first to go. Billions would leave and find prosperity in the stars, and then—maybe then—Earth would have a chance to heal.

Back in his office, Daniel took some time to briefly look over the laser-scanned point cloud data of the asteroid belt. The massive holographic point cloud was truly something to behold, and he rotated it, exploring it with a fascinated and keen interest. As he went through it, his imagination began to tingle. He focused on a unique stretch where a few large asteroids floated in the emptiness of space. He imagined huge pillars and island-like shapes spanning along the arch of the belt's orbit, and he began sketching a design.

With this inspiration, he decided to go up for a firsthand look. Moments later, on board *Viewer One*, he triggered the craft's matter-transmitter drives, instantly arriving just a few thousand kilometers from the largest of the asteroids that sparked this creative adventure.

Picturing the huge pillars and imagining what he could create here, his mind raced with the possibilities. Inspired, he sketched out his thoughts, illustrating a sprawling metropolis floating in space. There would be huge central towers, thousands of them, and the floating islands along the arch of the belt would spread out for hundreds of kilometers in both directions. He knew this would be the place where a truly magnificent civilization would take root, the very first of its kind.

When he got back to his office in Antamina, he parked himself in front of his developer's desk and brought up the holographic control panel. The curved panel made of light pulsed as he deftly typed out commands. He called up windows, statistical charts, graphs, and compositional reports of the asteroid belt and set the viewer to the highest level of detail. The awesome expanse gave him a chill. The sheer scale of what he was about to begin was hard to comprehend, and it excited him.

The first and most crucial step of the construction was to create the foundations. He did rough digital sketches, typing in distances, quantity, and size of objects, and the AI did the rest by putting the huge 3-D printers to work. Thousands of ten-kilometer-tall pillars appeared in the central area of the city while millions of town-sized blocks appeared in all directions from the central pillars. Next, he programmed the AI to transmit gravitational nodes to the corners and structural midpoints of every object. Using these gravitational nodes, the massive objects shifted and locked into ideal orientations. He waited, imagining the 3-D printers fabricating and transmitting the huge islands and gravitational nodes to exact locations in space. Taking a closer look, he saw that in some cases there were kilometer-wide gaps between the pillars and noted these would be ideal for large city parks and sporting arenas in what he imagined would become the center of this bustling metropolis.

Long lines of smaller cubes and spheres were placed, stretching out from the central towers, as well as between the larger islands in the suburban areas, creating foundations for transportation infrastructure.

He sent out hundreds of drones programed to capture to record the facilities assembly and posted them all in streaming and archived formats to the United Earth video portal on the nets. The world went nuts. The media had no words and the people migrating to Mars One, all applauded the beauty of it.

While the gravity nodes stabilized and held every foundation in its place, they also created localized gravitational fields designed to match those of Earth, an important feature to prevent any changes in the physiology of those who would live their entire lives away from their home planet.

Daniel was a genius programmer, but the intuition algorithms Stas and Jimmy integrated into the new AI were incredible. As he checked the AI's expanded notes, he saw ingenious designs and details it added to the layout that otherwise would have taken weeks for him to originate.

Seeing the construction well under way, Daniel chose to do a short show-and-tell. He invited his friends and the presidents of India, America, and Peru to come up and watch the scene from *Viewer One*. Once onboard, they hovered fifteen hundred kilometers from the central columns and witnessed the enormous mosaic dance as the AI sorted and organized the ocean of floating, unrefined objects. He saw in his mind's eye a bustling tropical culture where people would become highly educated and find both peace and enlightenment. He hoped the future residence of the facility would grow as a group and embrace this new way of life, where disease, insanity, and crime would never exist. As the ocean of foundation objects settled into their final layout, the audience returned to their homes, excited by what they just witnessed.

Daniel spent a few more days finalizing the design requirements for the asteroid belt city, and in the last moments, he added a series of 3-D sculpture templates of sea creatures, elephants, and birds for the AI to incorporate into the foundations, landscaping, and finishing of the architecture. Drones arrived and carved out the landscapes, prepping the foundations and incorporating the sculptural templates by creating massive carvings that were so lifelike it reminded him of the Greek and Roman ages of affluence.

Throughout the floating city, every top surface was blasted, flattened, and shaped into multiple cascading levels, staircases, and foundation cavities. The AI submitted computer-generated previews of huge white buildings that would be printed in the Oort cloud mining flotillas and transmitted

233

directly into place. After inspecting them, Daniel found there was little to nothing he would have wanted to change. The AI did an incredible job of incorporating modern architecture with a dash of classical Mediterranean design. As drones completed their work, perfectly smooth surfaces with enchanting detail were left behind.

On another flyover review—this time with Samantha, Stas, and Daniel's father onboard *Viewer One*—one of the foundations in the network of islands caught Daniel's interest. The AI had chosen to use an octopus for its structural template, the intuition algorithms once again showing genius. Drones were carving out the entire top half, leaving huge towering tentacles, ten to thirty meters in diameter, sprouting up from the perimeter and curling in toward the center of the floating island. The tentacles gave it a feeling of a monster rising from the depths of the sea, and it inspired him. Curious, Daniel looked up the object in the database and read through the description the AI had assigned it. He found it was designated as a park, and in a moment of creativity, he appended the description with some of his own ideas. He added *tropical, jungle, humid,* and *natural,* and then, at the very bottom, he whimsically added *prehistoric* and *Jurassic* before publishing his edits and proceeding with the rest of the site-wide inspection.

Without realizing it, Daniel's whimsical addition inadvertently sent the AI on a misdirected task that would turn into an undertaking of immense proportion. The AI did not require approval to create new drones or start new survey missions. When there was a need for something, it was fully authorized to resolve the requirement however it saw fit, as long as it did not cause harm to any living organism or break the requirement for no mineral excavation on unique formations. It took the AI a split second to analyze its databases and discover the deficiency of prehistoric and Jurassic genomic 3-D printing information.

The AI set into motion the construction of a new foundry specifically to print surveyor drones and started searching the stars. Thousands and then millions of beach-ball-sized survey drones were printed and transmitted to nearby systems in an ever-expanding sphere of discovery. The survey drones were built with standalone power cores, matter-transmission actuators, antigravity field nodes, virtually impenetrable force-field generators, and an autonomous AI designed to intelligently collect data, scan surfaces, catalog temperatures, and record mineral compositions while streaming it all back to the central AI.

Every scan would be triangulated and added to the filament viewport maps until the prehistoric genomic materials required to fulfill the design criteria were located.

Stas and Jimmy were always hard at work. Lately, their focus was to repurpose the real-time holographic map of the Milky Way into something far more advanced. Their goal: a map of the universe using the subatomic filament viewport and a real-time communications network across unlimited distances. They imagined zooming into any galaxy with the ability to determine, by mass and energy signatures, accurate positional information of stars, planets, and space debris.

Jimmy was the first to notice the server's data loads. It was natural for hard drives and processing capabilities to need upgrading, and he thought the recent increase in data was attributed to the new universe map they'd just put online. Seeing the need, they decided to write a set of protocols giving the AI control to manage its own storage resources.

After creating a construction description for off-planet server design, along with locational specifications typical for any solar system in the Milky Way, they activated the new directions and let the AI do its thing. Within a few short hours, massive fifty-kilometer-wide orbs packed with processing and storage arrays were printed and transmitted to locations throughout Earth's solar system.

Stas was not one to worry, but after seeing the massive data increases, it got him thinking: What if it turned on them? The AI was fully capable of initializing tasks without requiring new packets of code. Were they at risk? After a few days of losing sleep over the fear of seeing humanity slaughtered by an AI turned against them, he went to Daniel and expressed his thoughts.

When Stas appeared on the holo-caller, Daniel invited him up to *Viewer One*, where he was spending most of his time these days. In a flash, Stas stood in the control room and saw why Daniel had been up here so much lately.

"So this is where you have been hiding. We've been wondering, Dan. Sam joked that you probably left the solar system and would return when we were all fifty years old."

Daniel chuckled. "I am sorry. It's only been a few days. What's up, big

guy? What's on your mind?" And then knowingly, he asked, "How do you
like the view?"

"Only a few weeks? Ha, yeah, man, you never stop. Okay, never mind.
Why did I come here? I am afraid, Dan. I am afraid for all of us. The AI—its
databases are expanding faster than anything we ever expected. I mean, this
thing is growing crazy fast. Jimmy and I gave it a requirement to manage its
own storage and processing hardware, with designs for off-planet server arrays, and it's been printing the massive things nonstop for the past five days!"

"What's gotten you frightened, Stas? Is something wrong on Earth? The
AI has not notified me of any threats or disturbances outside the normal
noise of humanity."

"That's just it—the AI," Stas whispered. "It's growing too fast, Dan! I'm
afraid it could become a threat to us—to all of us. What if it decides we are
vermin that need extermination? Oh God, now it knows what I am thinking!
Am I going to be the first it decides is a threat? Oh man. Oh shoot. I should
not have said this out loud. It's everywhere … isn't … it …" He trailed off,
visibly shaking.

"Stop it, Stas! That could never happen. When we first created the AI—
the base code for everything we have here—we included specific guidelines.
No AI could ever harm mankind or any other life unless protecting the
innocent from cruelty or insanity. You know that. You were there."

Before Stas raised an objection by pointing out the obvious flaws in
those instructions, Daniel continued.

"Stas, the AI's number-one mandate is to ensure life survives and grows,
no matter the cost to itself. Humans are at the very top of the survival priority list. I promise you there is nothing to fear from the AI, and even if
someone tried to alter these rules and turn the AI on us, that person would
be identified as a threat to the U.E. family and would be dealt with quite
swiftly. These core rules are unchangeable and set in stone, man."

"Thanks, Daniel. I should not have thought of these things. I'm sorry."

"No, Stas, sometimes fear keeps us alive. I'm glad our friendship has
stayed strong. You are the best in the world. If we'd never put these rules in
place, you might have saved all of us from falling victim to an AI bent on our
eradication. So please, in the future, if you ever have strange feelings about
anything, I want to hear about it. I need to hear about it." He paused, looking at the big Russian, who went from being a nervous wreck to somewhat

embarrassed for panicking the way he had. "Now, if you like, you can hang out for a while and observe what we have here."

Stas took a seat next to his friend and watched as Daniel bought up a hologram in the primary display. It was a perfect duplication of the landscape out in space. Daniel zoomed in, showing the drones working to finish the pristine landscapes. He zoomed closer to an area with polished concrete sculptures, smooth surfaces, and perfectly cut foundation cavities, ready for the arrival of buildings and organic finishing. He zoomed out again, and a section of finished town-sized asteroids went past the display. Stas saw what a masterful job the AI and worker drones were doing. Carvings of whales, turtles, and distinct types of fish were sculpted into the undersides of the floating islands. He panned the 3-D point cloud over an area where a cavity for a large body of water was carved out. Sculptures of elephants and dolphins lined the cliffs above where the huge lake would soon be and Stas could hardly believe it. They were designed to shoot long spouts of water out into the lake, a required feature for all large bodies of water in this installation.

As *Viewer One*'s course took them closer to the central towers, Daniel deactivated the holographic display so they could focus on the huge structures with their own eyes. He dialed down their speed, and as every moment passed, more and more details of the impossibly large pillars at the center of this floating city came into focus. The relief carvings, statues, and fountains in the outer areas of the project were stunning under the temporary facility assembly lighting, but here, on the columns and walls of these towers, the massive scale of it all was taken to an entirely new level.

Daniel piloted *Viewer One* ever closer to the freshly finished towers and they saw just how exquisite they were. Whales, turtles, and birds were carved into the pillars and walls of the majestic structures. They saw large bay windows and balconies, along with cavernous spaces, where forests and small pools would soon take their places.

When Daniel was done with this latest inspection, he pulled the ship away from the towering apartment-complex sculptures, and they viewed it all as a whole.

"How lucky am I to have had an urgent matter to speak with you about, right?" Stas commented.

Just before Daniel suggested they head back to Antamina, he saw a green square flash on his holographic console. The atmospheric retention field was fully calibrated—an atmospheric shield designed to keep the air in and the cold emptiness of space out, while acting as a temperature regulator by receiving data from a network of sensors throughout the habitat. It would act as the shield and the temperature regulator of the facility, as well as its daylight cycle lighting systems. Seeing the temperature was set, he looked over at Stas. "This should be interesting."

Foundries began synthesizing and transmitting air into the city, creating gusts of wind so powerful that drones working on the finishing touches of foundations were forced to put up their shields and hold their positions until the void was filled.

Stas stood to leave as the air's arrival completed. "You promise me you are going to come down for dinner tonight, will be sitting down in three and a half hours at the Antamina birds nest table." Stas said before dematerializing in a wink of static wave.

With the environmental calibration complete, living quarters started arriving in waves. White buildings transmitted from an array of foundries deep in the Oort cloud, and the city started to take shape. The buildings materialized in place on foundations prepped by the surfacing drones. With the atmosphere cleared for distribution of organic life, the AI started transmitting sheets of grass, plants, trees, and water. Then came the animals, fish, birds, and even the insects and microorganisms that would help keep the environment balanced and healthy, and like magic, the whole place came alive.

Every building that arrived was fully furnished as though a high-end interior decorator had received an unlimited budget and an empty canvas with only a few specific requests. Beds with linens of the highest quality Egyptian cotton were standard to every home, along with food synthesizers to create any dish a person could ever want.

Every wall in every home was an interactive display, programmed to provide more and more access to content as the inhabitants progressed further along in their educational and awareness programs. It was just like what Daniel's father had done when he was just a child, except this time, they would be aware of it and know that by working hard, they would gain more access, more privileges and their rightful place in this new society.

On Earth, regions considered third world were a hot topic among the United Earth team. They looked at the vast overpopulated areas and considered the diversity of cultures. How would they change how billions of people lived their lives, let alone bring them all together as one? Eight billion people, all living hard lives, suffering, dying, forgotten, and many stuck in medieval ideological belief systems.

In too many cases, people were born into poverty with no hope of ever escaping. Those who survived, living past the first few years of infancy, found themselves at life's end before reaching their middle teens, killed by infections, AIDS, drug addictions, or other children maddened by their lost and hopeless existence.

The United Earth programs around the world were helping, though. Large areas once rampant with poverty, crime, drugs, and disease were beginning to improve; yet they only created small islands of rehabilitation amid oceans of people beyond repair.

High above the Antamina treetops in an elevated atrium, Daniel and Samantha met to share a simple lunch and catch up. She described her concerns, going over her thought process of how to help all these people in need. She looked to Daniel for some suggestions.

"The main problem has always been how we can clean up these areas where billions of people live on top of each other," Daniel replied.

The intensity in his expression was plain; she knew that glimmer of genius dancing in his eyes, and it always gave her a warm sense.

"Sam, you're going to love this. I think we are ready to start moving people to the belt installation. It's beautiful up there. I just came back from an inspection. The climate is warm and fresh, like a coastal tropical city. There are forests, bodies of water, and modern buildings for over three billion people. It's a paradise, Sam, and I think we should give it to these people, those most unfortunate, those who have suffered for so long, those who for generations have died in poverty, where, no doubt, so much untold brilliance has been lost. They absolutely must be the first to migrate."

He went on describing a new series of standards, rehabilitation programs, and indoctrinations that people choosing to move to the belt would have to adopt and follow. Those who chose to join the new colonies would never want for food or suffer health issues ever again. Every person entering the colonies would receive the cure-all vaccination. They would find themselves enrolled in learning programs, starting from the very basics of math, common English, science, history, and music, along with required physical activities, both of which would be their job requirements for continued membership in the colonies. "Maybe we could even encourage the citizens to find a complete stranger every day and commit an act of kindness. Imagine the awareness and uplift that could bring a society and its people, Sam."

She smiled at him from across the table. "Can't we just release that cure-all on Earth and fix the problem of disease for good?"

"I suppose we could set the teacher bots up with the vaccination, but it will solve itself as people immigrate to the colonies," Daniel stated.

"And here I thought all of this was so insurmountable. It seems you have everything figured out now, don't you, Daniel?" she retorted.

He looked at her with a knowing smirk. "Are you being snooty, Sam? In any case, it is more important to revitalize the impoverished first. By educating them and giving them prosperous lives, we can stop losing people, who, if given a chance, could be the most brilliant of all of us. Earth has long been overpopulated. It is time to expand into the stars, and it's time for mankind to thrive."

She cut him off with a firm look and a few sharp words. "What about the ones with AIDS, Daniel? What about the ones with drug addictions? How are you planning to handle those people, Mr. Miracle Boy?"

"Sam, I'm not sure, but there is no need for that tone. We can solve it just like we have solved everything else we have come up against. The cleansing microbe will cure AIDS and detoxify the drug addicts, but you're right; many will be in a mental state that will require quite close monitoring. I think we will have to isolate the high-risk cases in temporary confined areas and prevent them from traveling to locations where those who are working to create better lives need peace and safety. I think many of the high-risk cases will choose the path of bettering themselves when they see how life can be, if lived with this new purpose of education and enlightenment. I hope they will embrace knowledge as the gift it truly is."

She smiled. "I fear this will be a little more complex than you or I can imagine. So where do we start?"

Daniel looked at her with relief. "First, I am going to have to create some internal barrier walls separating a section of the installation to isolate those who wish to emigrate but are deemed high risk. I know it's not ideal to isolate the most unfortunate, but let's face it; they will be isolated in a paradise looking out at the stars and wanting for nothing. If they die off, then so be it, but as most rehabilitate, they will be given full citizenship, just as they deserve. There is a bigger picture on which we need to stay focused. We are working to change billions of people's lives and, at the same time, change the course of mankind forever. Disease and drug addictions will steal some lives, but if we can weed that out of the overall group, then we will quickly see these people build a brilliant and healthy civilization."

As the next asteroid construction project started in the Trojan asteroid belt of Jupiter, the process of relocating people from the overpopulated slums began. India, a country with a population of over three billion, was the first.

Daniel drew up plans for massive gateways and transmitted them to locations along the outskirts of cities, where hundreds of millions of impoverished people lived. The gates were wide enough for nearly one hundred people to walk side by side into the chamber, where they would be transmitted, mid-stride, to processing stations in the belt installation. Around each gate he installed holographic projectors to show the landscape beyond, so those wondering where they would end up could see the other side. The migration began.

Daniel estimated that around five hundred people would pass through each gate every minute, meaning that it would take around three weeks for the expected three billion people to leave their impoverished homelands, as long as all went as planned. When the gates were tested and in position, Daniel stood in front of a camera in the main developer's suite and recorded a message for the people. He created a message that would repeat for as long as the gates stood. He wanted the people to know what was required. He wanted them to ponder if a life of study and betterment in a utopian civilization, where there would be laws to live by, was right for them. Some freedoms would be lost, but many new ones would be gained, and he hoped all would see and want to become a part of it.

"Utopia awaits you, a place where you will receive education, comfort, and food, where you wll live free of poverty and sickness. For those who choose to leave their lives here on Earth, I promise that you will find prosperity in your future. The conditions of entry and citizenship are as follows: Each person may bring only one bag of personal belongings weighing no more than thirty-five kilograms. There are to be no weapons of any kind brought along with anyone. People trying to smuggle weapons, such as guns, explosives, or chemical agents, will be shown no mercy and immediately will be transmitted not into paradise but into the void of space, where they will perish, alone and forgotten. There is no place for those who wish to harm others. Beyond these gates is for those who want to grow and be free of corruption, poverty, crime, and the fanatical groups that have plagued our world for far too long. Those concealing knives or any other handheld weapons will be transmitted to the back side of the dome, where they may choose to relinquish such items and get back in line or stay on Earth.

"Living quarters will be assigned at the processing stations when you arrive on the other side. Everyone will be scanned for disease and cured before being transmitted to your new homes. Please, I would like to stress that for those who choose to join this new civilization, you are in no way required to give up your customs, but at the same time you are very much required to work hard at your assigned duties and embrace your new lives. Citizens of this new colony will be assigned six hours of education per day until the standard level is achieved; after that, four hours per day thereafter as exchange for your citizenship. Until the minimum aptitude requirements are achieved, you will be confined to your quarters, aside from your daily activities. Please understand that these hours of study and probation periods are your payment for citizenship. Education will be the path to status and free travel throughout the United Earth colonies. Those who refuse to participate in the program will find themselves confined to their residences until the requirements of daily study are met, or you may choose to return to Earth's non-U.E. districts, where those unwilling to relinquish their disreputable ways will live unmolested. Lastly, in each residence citizens will find a code of ethics etched into the wall of their central family room. These are the rules of the land. Those who choose to commit theft or violence—those violating these rules—will be sent to rehabilitation. There you will either choose to renew your commitment to rejoin society as a respectable citizen or return to the non-U.E. districts on Earth."

The holographic message played for two full days before the entrances of the gateways opened. Food and water were sent to the hundreds of thousands gathered at every gateway, but Daniel insisted they listen to the message long enough to ensure everyone understood. Daniel watched them, amazed by how many people patiently waited and listened—and he felt hope that these people would embrace this new opportunity and way of life.

When the gateways activated, the holographic displays showing the other side flashed on. The huge crowds saw the landscape of the world that awaited them, and no one turned away. As the massive crowds moved forward, those on Earth's side watched as people transmitted to the brightly lit landscapes on the other side, where they kept walking toward the huge white buildings in the distance.

On the other side of the gate, the new arrivals were instructed to continue moving, making room for those who would follow. Drones equipped to scan for disease moved quickly among the arrivals, injecting them with the cure-all and providing food and water. Families were identified and assigned larger homes, while single people were sent to the central towers.

There were a few who thought they could smuggle firearms and explosives through the gateways, and in a few cases, radical fanatics strapped with explosives attempted to infiltrate the crowds. The number of people attempting atrocity and transmitted out into the emptiness of space for this crime grew beyond what Daniel ever expected possible. The AI continuously monitored each and every person to prevent these sorts of insane acts from taking place. But because the AI was programmed to allow people the chance to change their ways, it waited until the very last moments before transmitting them off planet, where they safely ended their existence in the silent vacuum of space, alone.

After the first two weeks, over two and a half billion people migrated to what was being called New India. Media choppers from every major network hovered over the crowds waiting their turns to pass through the "Gateways to Heaven," as they were now being called. The world watched with mixed speculation.

"It's too bad we don't have more facilities online, Dan. What about the other countries where people are living in poverty and need relief?" John commented as they all sat in the common room for a group meal.

"It won't be long. The Trojan belt facility is only a few weeks away, and the AI is scanning the outer reaches of the Oort cloud for other interesting formations for new installations. I was out there a few days ago; the views of the Milky Way are stunning."

"Oh, you went without me again, did you?" Dillon commented.

"Trust me, my friend. You are going to have your chance," Daniel replied.

Daniel held off personally speaking to the world after the first installation was opened, choosing to allow the unfolding events to speak for him.

China was the second country to receive gateways, something the Chinese government did not approve of at all. They claimed it was an act of war and attacked the gateways, but in every case, the millions of people moving through the gates were protected by energy fields, and the attacking fighter planes, missiles, and armed forces were transmitted to remote locations inside their nation's borders, preventing all loss of life. Their overpopulated areas emptied out as their people left for brighter futures; yet another migration was under way.

A week after China One opened in the Trojan belt, Africa began their exodus to a massive tropical landscape on the outskirts of the Oort cloud, where a sculptural masterpiece based on Africa's most majestic native animals received them. Within two months of the New India facilities opening, Earth's population was reduced by more than half. The poorest of mankind were now the kings and queens of off-world paradise cities, and the rest of the world could do nothing but watch it happen.

Cities where overpopulation and poverty was all people knew were now empty, and the cleanup drones wasted no time getting to work. Old derelict cities transformed into landscapes ready for renewal. Samantha was overjoyed with her task of designing the beginnings of futuristic green cities for those receiving full travel rights who wanted to return to Earth. She took considerable pride in her task.

Seeing the first steps of the transition well on its way, Daniel finally decided to create a new recording for those still left on Earth.

Smiling, he put on his most gracious face. "Hello. By now I am sure you have seen what is happening in the third-world regions of Earth. What you are witnessing is the first phase in a program to save and rehabilitate the neediest of Earth's citizens. Now I must stress that currently only the people of India, China, and Africa, living below the poverty line, will be admitted to the off-world projects. Those who try to violate this requirement will simply be transmitted to one mile on the other side of the gate. Our people have been confined to living on Earth for too long, and it is my goal to forever change that. The poorest of us—those who have lived in squalor, hardly noticed by those in the more developed parts of the world—they will have priority, and anyone wishing to challenge that may find their invitation delayed indefinitely. There will be more facilities ready to receive people soon, some of which will still be designated for those living at the poorest levels of society. I must stress, however, that there is no shortage of room in space, and in the future, those in the middle and upper classes will be given the opportunity to travel to off-world installations and even take up permanent residence, if you choose to join in the tenets of this new society. I hope everyone sees that this is a day of great achievement for all of mankind. Thank you."

Some would twist his words, he knew, but he didn't care. There would always be the cynics who needed to focus on the risks and feed off the fear and doubt of others, but as the global IQ increased, the skeptical minds would soon find themselves looking in from the outside, finding all their influence gone, along with the disappearance of yesterday's unaware populations.

Daniel, his father, Stas, Jimmy, Samantha, and the two big cats, Tom and Jerry, lounged in an all-glass room in a private United Earth suite in the Mars One installation. They sat on large pillows and soft leather recliners and discussed all they had achieved and where they imagined they and the rest of mankind were heading.

John spoke of his visit to the New India installation and described the respectful and courteous attitude of the new residents. "It's as though they have gone to heaven, and they have committed themselves to the code of ethics and required studies with all of their hearts. I wonder if they fear being sent back to the poverty and the garbage they left behind."

Dillon spoke up. "Now that this AI of yours is watching out for everyone and preventing anyone from getting a shot off, what, for Pete's sake, would you have me doing, boy? Should I expect a layoff any time soon? What about my teams?" he prodded in his deep, rusty voice.

Daniel looked at him and smiled. "You should take this lull in your career to travel, of course. You have access to a personal explorer ship. Go see things; go relax. Have some fun. Take your team and enjoy earth before we head out into the stars on a voyage that will be starting soon. I hope you and anyone you want to bring along will join us."

Daniel transmitted to his personal office in the Mars One facility in a top corner nook of the largest dome. It was an open-air space with incredible views of the Mars landscape and the fifty-kilometer-wide domed habitat below. After taking a moment to enjoy the view, he noticed an alert on one of his holographic screens. He brought it up and was left speechless. Somehow, the AI had located what looked like living prehistoric life on some far-off planet in a star system over three hundred light-years from Earth. He pulled up the AI's activity logs and keyed in a filter to isolate exploration missions. When he saw what the AI had been up to, he was dumbstruck, his offhand request for the New India natural reserve started a survey in an ever-expanding sphere out from Earth—and somehow, it had found living DNA matching the Jurassic period on earth.

He reviewed the survey in three dimensions, panning over an incredibly detailed point cloud of every star system the AI had scanned over the course of the search. He was amazed, impressed, and in awe at the achievement. At the same time, he was somewhat surprised he had completely missed it.

After looking over the surveyed point cloud, he noticed that the last upload was over six hours ago, and he wondered why. Considering it, he found that the AI stopped the survey, thinking its directive complete. Seeing how amazing the whole thing was, Daniel gave the AI a new set of commands, ordering it to continue its survey indefinitely, while limiting the expenditure of resources for printing surveyor drones to one hundred trillion active units at any given time. He flipped back to the readout, and read the list of the living dinosaurs that existed on the newly discovered group of planets and was amazed at just how Earthlike these worlds truly were.

He isolated the creatures he was interested in, listing only herbivores, and then picked the four he thought everyone loved most. First, he chose a duck-billed creature that would grow between one and one and a half tons. Next, he selected the all-too-common triceratops, observing that it would grow to between six and twelve tons. Of course, he had to select the stegosaurus, noting that it would grow up to twenty tons, and last, he selected a sauropod, one of the biggest dinosaurs to ever roam the earth. It would stand nearly sixty feet tall at its full height and weigh in at nearly one hundred tons. "Massive," he whispered, wondering just how much food one of these things would require. He gave the AI the list, adding a restriction to never have more than six of each type roaming the facility at any given time and then sent the instructions to have them printed and transmitted to the nature reserve.

Chapter 23

The *Frontiersman*

From *Viewer One*, Daniel and his closest friends looked out at the fifty-kilometer-long ship. The most prominent feature was the long glossy dome covering the entire length of the upper deck. Even after seeing it with their own eyes, it was still hard to believe it was real. They flew around it, inspecting the outside, and then *Viewer One* transmitted into the dome, where they flew over the interior landscape. Everyone was audibly amazed at the forested areas and rocky features of the distant landscape and by the diversity of the terrain. They soon flew over where the primary residences sat on a hill above a small group of lakes.

It was so exciting. Over the next few days they sent invitations to nearly five hundred scientists and community leaders. It was explained plainly in the invitation that the passengers on the ship would be aboard for up to two years of their own lives, while over two hundred years would pass in Earth space-time. Out of the entire group, only three declined, explaining that they would prefer to be a part of mankind's progress now, rather than returning to find all their friends and relatives long since dead and gone.

The travelers began arriving via the invitation bots on the main deck of the *Frontiersman* ship only a few days after the invitations were sent out. When everyone was aboard, Daniel, John, Dillon, and Samantha made an official announcement to the colonies and to those still living on Earth.

"We, the founders of the United Earth movement, along with a selection of scientists and members of society, are leaving on an exploratory voyage throughout the Milky Way. We will dilate time to jump ahead in mankind's future and return at various intervals to receive updates, with a goal of jumping ahead over two hundred years over the course of our journey. The AI will sustain all habitats on and off Earth, while maintaining the same levels of security and guidance, now an accepted and preferred way of life by most of us."

Over the past five years, life had drastically changed. With the increasing acceptance of the education requirements, gone were the days of government panels, for which regulators and overseers were paid to come up with more and more policies. Gone were the days of insanity and irrational addictions. Individuality, responsibility, and awareness were now a way of life for everyone in the U.E. confederacy. Even those with no previous education were knowledgeable and well read. It was creating an abundance of creativity and ingenuity, and a constructive, prosperous civilization emerged.

The message was given clearly: "We will be back, and while we are gone, be at peace, be creative, and procreate."

There was enough real estate in the colonies for mankind to triple in number, and even more facilities were planned for those achieving the highest levels of learning and enlightenment.

Once everyone settled in on the *Frontiersman*, Daniel went to the master control room and keyed in his passcode. It triggered the ship's dilation drives and, in a flash, an energy field enveloped the entire ship, transmitting them across the vastness of space near to the first destination where the ship accelerated to near light speed. They traveled at the extreme velocity for that last leg of the journey for just over twenty-four hours, effectively allowing a full year to pass back on Earth.

When they transitioned back into normal space-time, John, Dillon, Stas, and Daniel, along with the scientists and public officials, gathered in a perfectly round room the size of a stadium with walls that came alive. Clouds of interactive holographic footage appeared in midair, it was Earth and the colonies and all that had taken place over the past year.

The Mars installation had expanded; new domes at the far ends of the canyon were constructed to provide accommodations and opportunities to every person left on Earth interested in joining the U.E. way of life. By the end of that first year, mankind had fully embraced the opportunity to extend humanity into the stars.

The Russians made a huge effort to be at the forefront of educational programs, while at the same time actively promoting large families to help our species expand.

After a long session of catching up with mankind's first year of prosperity, Sam got herself into a *Viewer One* vehicle and transmitted out into the solar system they just arrived in. Daniel noticed she was taking off alone, and on a whim, he transmitted himself into the control room of her craft. When he arrived, he looked at her and felt something he was unsure was appropriate. *She's growing into an attractive girl,* he thought and awkwardly looked away.

"Hey, Sam. Excited?" he asked in nervous voice. To his relief, she smiled at him with a wink. "yea, aren't you?" she teased.

Aboard a *Viewer One*, they jumped into the atmosphere of one of the big green-and-blue planets in the habitable zone of this solar system and saw a very Earthlike environment. Daniel knew what this place was and chose to let Sam discover it for herself. She expertly piloted the craft down along tall red cliffs and Daniel pointed to the pink and white sandy beaches along the coast line bellow. They cruised along the eastern seaboard of a massive continent on this world. They both saw them at the same time—a flock of huge birds rising on the updrafts, way off in the distance. As they got closer, he knew she had to have recognized them, and he waited for her reaction.

"Pterodactyls," she whispered, "hundreds of them. How is this possible?"

He reached over to the control panel in front of her and triggered the cloaking shield. "Let's not startle them," he whispered.

She looked over at him. "Dan, what is going on here? Have you seeded this planet with Jurassic life and turned it into some prehistoric park?"

"Actually, it's quite the opposite. This is where the AI located the DNA we needed to bring those large dinos in the New India facility to life."

"Wow! It's hard to believe, isn't it? I mean, how on earth are there creatures like what lived on Earth millions of years ago, here, on this distant planet?"

"Maybe, life's blue print, a selection of perfect designs, a universal template if you will, patterns that repeat where ever life emerges throughout our universe is how," he whispered, in awe of the incredible beasts sailing on the currents of the updraft ahead of them.

That evening, after dinner, the environment on the *Frontiersman* shifted to the nighttime cycle. This was Samantha's favorite time of day, and as was becoming customary, they floated on their backs in the warm lagoon, looking out at the stars beyond the ship's dome. In the foreground, two of the huge blue-and-green planets framed the night sky; beyond, colorful nebula and distant strings of stars filled the picture, and the beauty of it held them in silent awe, but their minds were not silent.

When they floated like this, Daniel sometimes thought of her in ways he was unsure of. He knew they were natural thoughts; she was so smart, and he was starting to find her very attractive, but he feared that if he acted on these thoughts it could jeopardize their friendship in an irreparable way. After almost an hour, they swam back to the dock and headed to their separate rooms. He tried to act natural, cool, as though nothing like what he was thinking was in his mind, but at the same time he wanted to tell her. As they parted, Sam reached out and touched his shoulder.

"Thank you, Daniel. All of this—it's amazing, unbelievably so, and it's all because of you." She gave him a warm smile before turning and heading off into the dimly lit modern houses. His desire for her burned stronger than ever. He wanted her, yet it felt so forbidden, and as he walked to his rooms, his thoughts centered on what might become of their friendship if he gave in to these feelings.

When he finally lay in his bed, deep sleep came easily, and he drifted into a nightmarish dream.

The fire wrapped the air around him, yet he was untouched. It hammered the landscape in waves of flame. Everything that would burn turned to heaps of ash. It felt as though he was right there, standing amid unimaginable devastation. He saw bodies clinging to life; they writhed in the suffocating atmosphere of what seemed to be a once-lush world; a world now turned into a simmering hell; a world held in the clutches of darkness.

Tendrils of inky smoke floated hundreds of feet above the burning planet's surface. It was darkness, an evil with immeasurable power, its presence permeating every pore of those who would soon be its victims. Long strands of the smoke reached out from an even darker form of a beautiful woman, a form that seemed to watch with pleasure as her victims writhed, a sentient being with the power to step between the physical and spiritual realms. He understood that this dark being was feeding on life's energy, and he watched, completely unnoticed, as the inky form lashed out with thousands of dark strands. They slashed the air with strikes like lightning, crackling, flashing across vast distances. The tendrils latched onto physical forms, consuming the souls of those trapped under this dark blanket of misery. Death, fear, and apathy permeated this place, and there was no escaping it. He felt a panic rise in him. The cloying stink of it, the vile presence, and the hopelessness of those still living filled his mind. He felt he had to get away or he would go insane, and the fear he might be trapped forever permeated his awareness.

There was a flash in his mind's eye, and in the next moment, he found himself watching from a distant orbit of this splintering doomed world. He was to be a witness to what came next. The surface of the planet began to crumble. Lava burst up through fissures as the surface slowly splintered. The fracturing crust caused columns of magma to splash across the dying world's separating fragments. The oceans fell away, drifting into space, where giant sections froze, turning to huge clouds of ice crystals. Gravity was entirely lost as the planet turned into a cloud of rubble, and then there was a flash, a glimpse of a bigger picture—the solar system—and the horror that filled his mind's eye. And then he was gone.

He awoke with a sudden spasm as his mind returned to his body. He lifted a shaking hand and wiped his brow. He immediately noticed his blankets and how far he had gotten away from them. *They're getting worse,* he thought as the familiar tremors that followed these recurring nightmares shook his body, recurring dreams that felt like far more than just random unconscious nightmares. Then, as it always did, the dizziness came, and he shook his head in an effort to clear his addled mind. He couldn't let it slip away, he told himself; he had to remember, had to record what he could before his memory of the dream drifted away. "How can they feel so real? It's like I'm viewing some terrible reality somewhere out in the universe," he muttered as he gathered his strength and worked to control his breathing.

He fought to push down the adrenaline racing through his body, and after a few moments of focused calm, he reached for his tablet and recorded what he could remember. He sketched out images and scribbled descriptions of the feelings he had experienced and all that he saw, he sketched the dark inky smoke in the loose form of a woman; how the evil one seemed to enjoy the slow, drawn-out destruction of life. He sketched a diagram of the solar system as best he could recall—the medium-sized star in the center and the five planets all in stages of being harvested by swarms of glossy black creatures.

After finishing his notes, Daniel lay back, rolled to a new spot on his bed, and closed his eyes. He was determined to find his way back, hoping that he might return to where this dark one lurked in the depths of his dreams. He needed to learn more, but knew it would not happen tonight. He would not get his wish; he never returned to the same dream after waking. If there was something out there, something dangerous, something unknown, he wanted to find the answers. The dreams were horrific and occurred often, but he longed for them. Something about them felt far too real, and he wanted to know why.

After the first time, the first nightmarish dream, he forced himself to stay awake for days until the fatigue finally pulled him under. He woke up after hours of calm, uneventful rest, cursing himself for giving in to the need for sleep, but to his relief and surprise, there was no relapse. For a time he thought that first dream was a one-time thing, and returned to the strict eight hours of rest within every twenty-four he'd always stuck to. For more than a week, there was nothing—until, as suddenly as the first time, it happened again.

The second dream was much like the first; it came without warning, and he woke in a terror. But when he woke, his scientific mind saw the patterns and he felt more intrigued then alarmed. He went directly back to sleep but found only the calm, deep sleep to which he was accustomed.

From that point on, the dreams came randomly, and when they came, he documented them, making detailed notes to track and compare similarities from one dark vision to the next. The parallels were far too pronounced, and when details emerged, showing commonalities, the findings sent chills through his psyche.

When he got to the dining hall for breakfast the next day and sat down with Jon, Stas, and Sam, John and Stas awkwardly stood. Stas winked conspiratorially, and before he could say anything, they both headed off in separate directions, leaving Sam blushing and Daniel totally confused.

"What was that about?" he asked.

"Oh, it's nothing," she replied, smiling at him. As he sat, she noticed something was off, and it concerned her. "What's the matter? You look like you've seen a ghost or something, Dan. Are you sick?"

"Just a bad dream. Nothing to worry about, I think." He looked away awkwardly. "Are you planning on going on another *Viewer One* ride today?" he asked.

"Yes, in a short while. I wanted to wait for you," she teased, smiling shyly.

She sat across from him, watching as he requested his customary bowl of yogurt and fruit from the replicator. He felt her eyes on him and was unsure; his feelings from before were far from the front of his mind. The recent dream had shaken him to the core, and his resolve to avoid jeopardizing their friendship made him want to avoid it.

They explored the planets of this solar system for close to three weeks, allowing the enthusiastic scientists more than enough time to document the dynamic prehistoric ecosystem in all of its detail.

In the evening of the final day, they gathered in the central courtyard aboard the *Frontiersman*, all 115 of them. They spoke of what they saw and debated various conclusions. Many commented on how surreal it was, while others pointedly remarked against the decision to leave a place so soon where life was so nearly identical to Earth's prehistoric past. It went on for over an hour as the seasoned speakers and brilliant scientists made their cases and presented fascinating findings. Finally, Daniel stood and called for their attention.

"I understand many of you wanted to stay longer, and I apologize. The galaxy is filled with wonders, I would like to show you our next destination." He triggered the holographic projector in the center of the gathering. It was a nebula with which they all were familiar. "Ladies and gentlemen, may I present to you the Eagle nebula, a place all of us have seen in the images of astronomy and cosmology. Well, in just over a week we will be there, and over eight years will have passed in Earth's relative space time."

He waved to them and then looked down to his for-arm control holo, where he triggered the dilation drives, hurtling them into the United Earth Confederation's future.

Later that night, when all was still and the streaking stars shone through the outer dome of the ship's upper deck, Daniel closed his eyes and drifted into a deep, easy sleep.

A voice filled his mind, and another joined it; they were the cries of despair, born from desperate helplessness. Soon there were hundreds, then millions of them, each consciously projecting their minds in search of the one hope. They cried out in their very last moments, a level of affliction so overwhelmingly clear.

The voices, their tragedy filled his mind. As life after life was extinguished, harsh pain shocked his soul. It was an endless ocean of noise, thick with the desperation of those being taken. It was the darkness, and these were the voices of her victims, the echoes of their futile attempts to break free. He felt more then heard the cries of the countless! Their voices reached his mind and filled it, a defeated plea for a witness, a final, desperate hope. "Someone … someone save us! Someone stop the destruction of our worlds and our kind. Help us. Someone, please." It echoed in his mind, and his unconscious body twitched and shook.

The intensity of their voices increased, and his awareness moved, shifting in his dream to a distant view of a star and its planets, the source of these voices. Billions of tiny sparks flickered over the surfaces of three worlds, their light dying as quickly as they appeared. The space between him and the planets was filled with pieces of shattered moons and swarms of black crustaceous creatures, some the size of skyscrapers back on Earth, and others as large as moons.

The victims of this solar system had breached the veil preventing them from calling out into the spiritual realm. It was a small victory but with little meaning; there was nothing that could save them, and he felt each and every one of them knew it all too well. Each flash, he realized, was a life being taken, sentient spiritual beings consumed by a darkness, an evil with an insatiable hunger for life.

The three planets started breaking apart. Their surfaces shattered as the beetle-like creatures with long glowing tentacles fired ribbons of plasma. Floating, searching, hoping to find just one of the voices that somehow brought him here, Daniel found nothing. Silence was now absolute; they were gone. Only the calamity of destruction was left, a tapestry of havoc spreading through the vast distances. A malevolent finality filled Daniel's heart.

A ripple in space, a shimmer of substance—an obsidian diamond materialized in the center of this obliterated solar system. It was huge, even larger than the star. It came in a rush, a sense that was somehow familiar. There was a flash of light, and a strange feeling filled Daniel's awareness. Then his mind was filled with a shrieking trill. A foreign consciousness was in his mind, a powerful being reaching deep into his soul, and with it a cacophony of hysterical cackling ripped down through his awareness. The Dark One latched on to his presence, a cold hand pulling at his life energy. Just before all was lost, he was gone.

Back in his room aboard the *Frontiersman*, he snapped awake, wide-eyed, as the real feeling that he was still in the dream raced through his body. As his physical presence returned, his hand went to his chest, and he found himself completely drenched in sweat. He shook violently, worse than ever before.

They are getting more frequent and more intense, he thought and rolled to the wall, away from the puddle of sweat where he had thrashed only moments before. He reached to the shelf in search of his tablet. The tips of his fingers found it, and instinctively, he pulled it down.

He paused for a moment, fighting to slow the shaking. Waves of emotion submerged his thoughts, and tears dropped to his cheeks. Regaining control, he began recording, writing, and sketching everything he had just experienced.

As he made the notes, sketching images of what he'd seen in the dream, he flicked his fingers toward the far wall and triggered the room's PLED display.

The room's ceiling came to life with a detailed map of the Milky Way galaxy. He sat with his back against the padded wall and noted the moisture on his skin and the way his bed sheets were scattered. He sketched the diamond-shaped ship, the solar system's star, and its planets, marking groups of X's where the swarms of creatures had been. He noted the death of worlds, the darkness, the voices, and their last cries and how they lit up like sparks in last moments of life energy. He could still feel it—the way the aura of darkness sensed him and tried to latch on. The feeling of that tug came back to him, and his heart skipped.

When there was nothing left to recall, he put his tablet back and activated his command center screen. He had little doubt that these dreams were a window into a reality somewhere in a distant galaxy. It was undeniable, a faint sense of connection. He knew in his heart these dreams could be the key to finding some distant civilization, maybe one needing help, and so he went to work, reviewing notes and updating the timeline that tracked these dreams with an obsession beyond his customary tendencies.

A holographic display appeared, floating high in the big domed ceiling of his room. The sheet of light shimmered as it came to life. To an untrained eye, the activity on the display would seem incomprehensible—columns of numbers, icons cascading from data points, lists of newly surveyed star systems with corresponding columns showing planet sizes, types of life, habitability, areas of interest, mass, elemental makeup, and spatial coordinates for each astronomical object. He saw that over the past twenty-four hours, three hundred million new systems were scanned, and the overall number of planets with organic life was up to just over two hundred million. He saw a new maximum diameter in the water world class, over ten times larger than Earth. There were systems with multiple stars—huge rocky planets on strange elliptical trajectories that moved them in and out of habitable zones. The data was immense, yet Daniel saw the updates and registered them as quickly as the numbers changed.

He called up the custom software Stas and Jimmy created to track and compile his notes, and when the display finished loading, he started by looking at the chart that showed recordings of his vitals while dreaming. He analyzed the spikes in synaptic activity. As usual, he saw that his body temperature rose, and he viewed videos of the signature full-body spasms. It was hard not to see that they were getting progressively more violent with each episode. He rubbed at his sore neck and looked over the charts and graphs again. The length of his dreams were getting longer, and by monitoring and recording his cerebral activity, he saw definite similarities in the synaptic activity. He was sustaining higher and higher rates of mental bandwidth with each consecutive experience, each time sustaining the link longer and longer.

He knew there was no rational scientific explanation to justify the feeling, but instinctively he knew these dreams were taking him across the unknown distances of space to witness the destruction of entire solar systems. In his heart, he knew it was true. Somewhere out in the ocean of galaxies, he felt it. Those he witnessed in his dreams—he was connected to them, and it drove him. Somewhere inside, he felt a connection to a people and a place on the brink, a civilization in the clutches of a malevolent destroyer, and he knew that he was the key, their only hope.

His sketches and notes danced across the display. The first collection was disordered and scribbled, recorded before he learned to calm himself after returning to consciousness. It was not easy, waking in a state of complete confusion. Sometimes it took him a few moments to realize he was back from the dream. Yet he had learned to harness it and to look back at the dream and record it. His notes and drawings described a feeding ground, an unstoppable conquest of an evil far darker and more frightening than anything ever imagined. He never considered he was at risk while in the dreams, but the more he learned, the more it scared him, even as he became more and more intrigued and driven to find answers.

Nearly a year onboard the *Frontiersman* passed. Due to their time-dilating travel, over one hundred years elapsed for those in Earth's relative space-time. The scientists took great interest in reviewing mankind's growth, progress, and pitfalls. Family, sports, arts, music, travel, debates, and ingenuity were now the center of most people's lives. It was impressive to see how the people embraced their new lives and even more so in the growth and expansion that had taken place.

Chapter 24

The Fleet

On a planet in a distant solar system on the other side of the Milky Way galaxy, the human Jaxel was kicked awake by an extra-cruel guard. Then another horned and scaled beast came into the holding chamber, eager to inflict pain. This group of humans had been assigned to sleep in this cave only three hours ago, and now their rest time was over. The beast kicked the first man and stomped on the next. Another of the cruel masters howled, lashing out at anyone within reach. It was time for the humans to resume work, or die.

This system with a dozen Earth like planets is home to two very distinct races with sentient intelligence: human slaves and their cruel, lizardoid masters.

They are a super-intelligent reptilian species who walk primarily on two legs but easily transition to all fours. They range in size from seven feet tall to as large as busses and train cars and have strength enough to lift ten times their own weight.

These lizard beasts have long been a space-faring civilization and they rule over their human slaves with cruelty and disdain. Mankind has lived and worked here, working to survive in the mines on both the hot inner worlds and colder outer worlds of this system, and have done so for thousands of years. The more tropical worlds, those central to the habitable zone of this system are the paradise worlds of the Alaigeer.

Jaxel was on yet another shift in the mines. Today was the halfway point in this thirty-day turnaround. He was strong yet unsure if he would live through this one. He had to. His breeding partner would give birth to a third child soon, and he would only have a week to see it before the creatures took it away. Like every child, it would be raised in comfort, and taught the skills needed for their future lives as slaves. At age fifteen, the child would return to the mining colonies. If it was a girl, she would become a breeder like his current partner, and if a man, a worker in the mines, just like Jaxel. He looked up at the creature poised to stomp on him, and he considered resigning himself to it, having the life beaten out of him, but that was not his way. They fought to survive and were long since hardened to it. Reluctantly he stood and joined the haggard line of men, and in a line, they headed back out into the whistling hot air to work. Life was a constant, a grind to survive, and each moment was laced with the fear of being selected, singled out as an example for the rest.

They never went hungry; the masters even gave healing drink that made them stronger. But when it was time to work, they were solely at the mercy of their enslavers. The cruel beasts enjoyed inflicting pain. It seemed that in every major work area, punishment was always being carried out. Their victims suffered hours of torture, always ending with limbs being torn off and eaten as a reminder to every one of them: This is what they were.

Though they lived as slaves, they nurtured their own intelligence and never lost their humanity. As a single race, everyone of them held onto one undying tradition, the passing down of ancient stories of the home they were taken from generations ago, a history of their origins as tales from one generation to the next. Thousands of cities, all with millions of people destined to toil, breed, and die for their master's had ownership of only the legends of their past.

Back on the *Frontiersman*, those aboard the ship continued traveling in and out of time dilation, jumping ahead of Earth's relative time while visiting incredible areas in the Milky Way.

As a hobby, Dillon and Stas started to design warships, and when they were ready, they simulated mock battles, pitting their armadas against the other's designs in the huge hollo-deck in the belly of the ship.

They were like boys playing building blocks with near limitless technological possibilities. After destroying each other's simulated fleets over and over again, they began collaborating and integrating their best ideas to create more elite destroyers, battleships, and various attack craft. It was exciting to watch them put their newest designs up against hordes of the older models, always learning and improving their designs beyond anything they imagined when they first started.

After hundreds of iterations of the very best designs, they established seven classes of extremely formidable ships, all of them with thick platinum, topaz composite armor, and loaded with devastating weapons systems.

They were by no means specialists in the design of weapons, and neither was the AI, so in order to achieve the most effective tactical advantage, they hacked the quickly declining military industrial complex's and weapons developers' databases on Earth. The AI downloaded and added every design from the early twentieth century, along with the top-secret schematics of every known weapons design known, into the engineering libraries. With this new resource they pushed conceptual boundaries, forcing the AI to figure out how to assemble what they described using the available technological blueprints.

They designed rail guns to fire slugs weighing up to a few tons at speeds of more than fifty thousand miles per second and loaded with three- and five-megaton payloads, armor-piercing flechette rounds with thousand-spear packages designed to spread out before impact, and energy cannons to fire beams of electromagnetic plasma as hot as the surface of the sun. These were just some of the weapons they included in the battleships' arsenals.

It became a weekly attraction as many of the ship's passengers gathered in the big holo-room to watch as two separate AIs attacked one another until only one side remained.

Daniel watched and admired their passion, wondering why people always gravitated to destruction and weapons for entertainment. He did not mind, though, finding that a part of him enjoying the contests as much as they did.

When Daniel finally decided to tell his friends about his dreams, he invited them to a clearing far from the village on the main deck of the *Frontiersman*. Daniel looked them all in the eyes and spoke seriously. "I know this is going to be hard to believe, but please bear with me. I have been having some very disturbing dreams." He paused to look for a reaction.

"Go on, Daniel, please," his father said. "We all have noticed a change in you and have been wondering what it is. You have looked tired and worn out, while the rest of us are rested and content on this fantastic voyage of exploration. I think it would be best if you describe everything as well as you can."

As they listened to him describe the things he saw in his dreams, they were all shocked at the graphic nature and destructive images his words and when he showed them a small holo display of all of his sketches and notes taken about the dreams, it took a bit before anyone spoke.

Dillon was obviously shaken. "I will be damned if we go down because we didn't follow some crazy premonition from the person who has been the key to creating all of this. I think it is high time we build an offensive and defensive fleet. We are exploring the stars. What happens if we run into hostiles with similar technology to our own, and they chase us back to Earth—or worse, destroy us point-blank as we enter their solar system?" Dillon exclaimed in his most forthright tone. "I've been thinking about bringing this to you for some time now, but after hearing of these dreams of holocaust and planetary annihilation, I am going to have to insist we begin the formation and construction of a military fleet."

There was no argument from anyone as they all looked to Daniel, who was quick to bring up concerns, given mankind's history of violence. They collectively observed the many misguided atrocities. Was it worth the risk? If they built a war engine, would they not begin to seek war?

"I think mankind has come a long way, and we can always program contingencies into the AI that would prevent the fleet from ever being used against U.E.," Stas interjected with a conservative amount of hope.

"I think Dillon is right. If we come face-to-face with a real threat, we could be in bad trouble unless we have a trained military ready to defend us," John added.

"Well, I suppose we are all in agreement, then. The wise course of action for the survival and expansion of our species will be to build a well-armed fleet. Thankfully, Stas and Dillon have been designing ships of war. I would imagine we can trust your designs are practical and effective," Daniel said in an officious tone.

The two of them looked at each other with knowing smiles, "Oh, I think they will be a little better than practical, Daniel. More like devastatingly effective, if they ever get into a fight; isn't that right?" Dillon said with confidence while softly knuckling Stas in the shoulder.

The first ships of the fleet were printed and transmitted to just outside the far edge of Earth's solar system.

Dillon firmly believed humans had the power of mind to do things no

AI could ever do when in the field of battle, even with the best preparations. "Or 'algarithmictive' intuitives or whatever," he sniped. "No computer can take the place of a human when it comes down to a dirty street fight."

Daniel believed in Dillon's sentiment and was adamant that the best living accommodations and most state-of-the-art control centers be installed in every ship for live crews to take control, if ever the conditions became so dire they were needed.

Headline News! Join the Fleet, and Explore the Stars!

Adventure, it proclaimed! Exploration, it announced! Danger, honor, sacrifice, and commitment, it declared! The response was beyond anything they expected. Millions applied in the first two days following the announcement that a formal United Earth Fleet would be assembled. The announcement was very specific; only those with U.E. travel clearance and seventeen years or older were eligible.

Over the past 150 years, mankind multiplied to more than four times what their number had been when the *Frontiersman* commenced the time dilation tour. The human race had expanded to new installations in Earth's belts, the Oort cloud, and even more expansions on Mars. When Daniel and his friends left on their voyage, there were just over thirteen billion people. Many of them with less than a grade-one education. Now there were over forty-five billion, with most pursuing diverse college and university-level studies while designing and creating incredible innovative technologies, games, and entertainment.

New life sciences, pioneered by the many brilliant people of the colonies, were developed to regenerate cells in the body to prolong life. In this new ecosystem, one hundred years was considered only middle age. People, who would have otherwise been in the grave, looked and felt young.

Those accepted into the fleet went to newly constructed installations around Neptune and Saturn, where they found even more amazing amenities. Joining the fleet was a chance for adventure, an upgrade in quality of living, and the chance to go beyond the limits of colony life. Fleet membership meant new things to learn and new sights to see, but it came with the real commitment and training schedules associated with military life. The minimum term was ten years, a requirement that caused a small percentage of people to turn away, but there was no shortage of eager applicants.

It surprised Daniel just how many people were choosing to give up their lives filled with sports, comfort, education, and plenty. It encouraged him to find that an underlying eagerness to go beyond and step away from the comfort of safety prevailed among educated people. It called to them, the spirit of challenge, along with the innate need for purpose and glory. Only exemplary conduct would lead to positions befitting their commitment to the pursuit of knowledge and the protection of truth and freedom.

Daniel liked to think of how easily the paradigm among humans could be altered; all it took was to ensure basic education for everyone and resistance to suppressive dogmatic traditions. The world had changed; humanity was growing as one species.

Some opposed the creation of the fleet on the grounds that by building a military force, they would invite violence, based on the patterns of people's history. Though these feelings were rational and valid, even the most adamant of objectors saw that it would be better to prepare rather than be caught unprotected. They pointed out the risks of having a military force, while at the same time acknowledged how foolish being defenseless in the face of a malevolent enemy it would be. And so, the debate was ended by the very people presenting the cautions in the first place.

Along with many of those who accompanied them on the first voyage, Daniel and his closest friends resumed traveling, allowing another fifty years to elapse, while only two months passed for those aboard the *Frontiersman*.

On a day where the ship drifted along at only five hundred thousand kilometers per hour, with a spectacular view of a nebula's colors, it was as peaceful and enchanting as it ever could be.

Suddenly, the mood aboard the ship was disrupted. Red flashing lights came to life, and a loud klaxon sounded throughout the ship. Three surveyor drones had been destroyed by advanced weapons in a star system over seventy-five thousand light-years from Earth, far on the other side of the Milky Way galaxy.

Daniel, Stas, and Jimmy had been hovering in their control chairs high up in the central developer's chamber, focused on separate projects in different corners of the huge spherical room. The alarm brought them all to attention. It took only a moment for Daniel to switch the huge holographic view to the footage of the very first hostile contact.

Everyone who knew of Daniel's dreams feared that this could be it and wondered if they had found the ones destroying entire worlds. Dillon arrived at the top of the dome moments after the first alarm, materializing right next to Daniel.

"I am in contact with fleet command and have patched this viewport to their star map chamber. Is this them? The ones from your dreams?" Dillon asked, his voice hushed with a tinge of nervous energy.

They watched as huge pyramid ships the size of moons floated around blue-and-green water worlds. For Daniel, it quickly became obvious, these were not the demons from his dreams. "No, this is not them, this is something else." he whispered to his most trusted friends over their own secure channel.

"I suppose the good news is that the destroyers from my dreams are not camped out in our very own galaxy. The bad news, though, is that it looks like we have encountered a hostile shoot-first-and-ask-questions-later kind of space-faring species. Let's see what the drones find. Stas, Jimmy, let's make this system a priority exploration site and flood the place with surveyor drones. I want every grain of sand scanned and in front of us within the hour."

Dillon looked over at Dan with a smirk. "Command has already initiated a priority-one military-grade surveyor drone protocol, and we should start seeing the entire system within the next few minutes."

"Well, it's nice to know there are able and intelligent people making decisions at that level. Thank you, Dillon. I forgot how far we have come."

Millions of drones equipped with upgraded shields and hyper-thrusters transmitted to the newly discovered star system. The outer planets had next to no hostile forces, allowing the drones to lock into orbital surveillance positions and collect information. The drones' data formed a real-time, high-definition, medium-range network producing 3-D point clouds back in the holo-decks of the U.E. colonies. A short few minutes later, hundreds of millions more drones took up positions, transmitting reatime feeds of the system and its worlds that brought a detailed picture of what they were dealing with into focus.

Those aware of the new discovery were shocked to the core by what they saw—hundreds of millions, if not billions of people, all living on desolate outer worlds, slaves to a lizard-like race. The lizards' home worlds were blanketed in hot mists and tropical landscapes. Gaudy cities peppered with castles and temples made from artfully carved stone spread out over most of their lush mainland's. There were gigantic monuments and statues of what must have been great leaders, along with thousands of mountain-sized pyramids surrounding all of the largest cities.

Daniel, Dillon, Stas, and the military fleet commanders watched as the scans revealed humans, just like them, living in squalor and working mines on the outlying planets. The conditions looked dreadful. The mine worlds were on the inner and outer edges of the Goldilocks zone, where life hung on by the thinnest of margins.

As the scans came in, more brutal atrocities of this corner of the galaxy were unmasked. On a mining planet on the outer reaches of the system, they saw that humans were not only slaves but also one of the lizards' favorite foods.

As the drones infiltrated and scanned the central planets, they were effectively attacked. The reptile creatures were technologically advanced. They had energy weapons, along with ships capable of exceeding the extreme g-forces the drones pulled as they raced to scan and send as much information to Central Command before being destroyed.

With each new wave, the army of drones pushed farther and farther into the atmospheres of the central planets, where they captured a truly gruesome reality. Images of the scaly species appeared, and soon close-ups of the alligator-like figures loaded in command's holo-displays. The video feeds were graphic; humans were being tortured and eaten alive. Half eaten and partially cooked bodies lay on chopping blocks and tables in central squares where the hideous creatures came to feed. It was a dichotomy of sorts; for as advanced as they were technologically, they were equally as barbaric in the way they lived.

There were no doubts on the course of action mankind would have to take. Without a word, Dillon authorized U.E. Fleet intervention before transmitting himself directly to Central Command. He watched from outside their circle, an overseer who knew these men and women were competent and ready to make intelligent and emotionless tactical decisions. The military council agreed unanimously that a probing military force would be sent without delay, a tactic he thought was well measured. An unmanned contingent of battleships and cruisers were sent, transmitting to what was now being called the Alaigeer system.

The first wave of exploratory ships jumped to within combat distance of the largest enemy goliaths and engaged with a barrage of rail gun slugs, spear shot, and energy cannon fire. The enemy's huge ships, blistering with vast weaponry, were hardly damaged as the initial barrage was mostly deflected by Protective energy fields. After stopping the initial attack, plasma lashed out from the mountainous enemy warships, a barrage followed by thousands of small attack craft, all streaming toward the U.E. front line. Boiling energy lashed at the U.E. Fleet's defensive shields, and instead of being repelled, shards clung on. The plasma boiled, creating pockets of disturbance that allowed the following waves of smaller enemy ships to hit the United Earth armada hard. As the enemy attack craft made their first run, the instantaneous data gateways used by the AI and Central Command to control the battle groups in real time was lost. Those in Central Command watched helplessly as their first contingent of ships were pummeled. Once the battleships were torn to shreds by all manner of weaponry, the enemy got extremely aggressive at hunting down the remaining surveyor drones, and they skillfully cut all near range data feeds.

Everyone in U.E. colony facilities were soon aware of the situation. It took no time for word to spread. Contact had been made with a race that used people as slaves and as their primary food source, and before long, nearly everyone was watching live feeds off the central database.

There was an air of excitement; mankind's fighting spirit was alive and strong, and fleet personnel were anxious for a hands-on role in the battle. Now, after the failure of the unmanned attack force, they were going to get their chance.

Over five billion people joined the fleet over the past one hundred years. In their training, they schooled themselves in tactics and theory, playing war games among squadrons and cultivating the cunning competitiveness akin to the instincts of our species. They learned the physics of zero-gravity warfare and all its benefits and limitations. The fleet's largest battle cruisers required nearly two thousand personnel when switched to manned controls, and every crew was as ready as they would ever be.

An armada of over two hundred thousand fully crewed U.E. ships mobilized in less than two hours when the word was finally given—there was going to be a fight, and they were needed. The feeds now trickling in from covert drones showed an enemy that thought it had won. But as they would soon find out, they were sadly mistaken. Miniature stealth drones transmitted back into the system, and more and more live-streaming footage came back online.

They saw the huge lizards feasting in celebration of what they thought of as a great victory, and it sickened those watching. It was hard to watch fellow humans violently torn limb from limb as they fought for their lives against insurmountable force, but for the men and women of the fleet, gearing up for battle, it hardened their resolve. There was no doubt that their cause was just. There was a palpable pride as they prepared to put their lives on the line for a cause that meant saving so many of their own, and with that they plunged into battle.

Waves of destroyers, accompanied by fast attack ships, jumped into the hostile system where they engaged the enemy. Many took up positions among the outer planets and asteroids, where they swept aside the undermanned enemy outposts with quick and decisive strikes.

The admirals of the fleet watched and sent orders from Central Command in Earth's solar system. Their holograms shimmered as the drones continuously scanned their assigned areas, providing the information to perfectly replicate the exact position of every enemy vessel, every planetary body, and every fleet ship. They watched, planned, and positioned themselves to counterattack.

The human slaves watched their skies as silver warships destroyed Alaigeerian vessels just outside their atmospheres. The generals of the U.E. Fleet ordered attack drones down to these slave worlds, and they began hunting every lizard creature as quickly as possible.

Daniel took the initiative and sent holo-projectors to all the major population centers on the slave worlds, and he started communication. When they arrived, they activated, projecting ten-kilometer-wide displays showing members of the fleet manning the sleek battleships, along with a wider angle of human vessels moving in on the enemy hulks.

The enslaved watched their cruel masters fall, many of them not believing what they saw. The holo-displays let them know that humans from other worlds were here to save them, and as the reality of what was happening settled in, they started up a triumphant cheer. Soon they would be free.

From the beginning of their people's time here as slaves, it was told that long ago they lived on a warm blue world. They had flourished for generations, but then, long, long ago, pyramid-shaped castles in the sky had come and taken them away. It was the only tale they remembered, no one ever allowed the next generation to forget. Although the stories were sacred to their people, it still began to feel like a distant, impossible dream. On this day, though, their long-lost dreams awoke, and they chanted the song of hope and rejoiced that freedom had finally come.

The fight, though, was not yet over. Thousands of enemy ships rose from the huge tropical home worlds, the largest of them bigger than Mount Everest on Earth. Lush landscapes peeled away from mountainous war machines as they lifted into the air. The fleet and most of the U.E. citizens watched as hundreds of thousands of the massive ships rose through their steamy home worlds' atmospheres, accelerating out into space and coming for a fight.

They came to deal death and face it with fearless, godlike stature. When clear of their planet's atmosphere, the rising hulks wasted no time and charged straight into the offensive. Each of them sent out electromagnetic pulses in an effort to disable even the most radiation-hardened electronic and optical systems. They formed up between the large central worlds and charged. Their front line fired clouds of plasma that stretched into ribbons spanning millions of miles in all directions and in a flash the lattice work teleported forward, appearing within a few thousand kilometers of the U.E. front lines. As the wave of plasma approached, now traveling at over half the speed of light, the U.E. ships had little chance for evasive action. It was on them in an instant, and stringy nets of plasma lashed at the shields of the human armada's ships.

On the ships whose shields were hit hard by the plasma, their connection to Central Command was lost, but onboard, nothing changed, and their crews jumped into action. The ship's systems were undamaged, and this time they had a plan. They used barely detectable thrusters to mimic the last ships that had been disabled. They set a trap.

The electro-magnetic pulse sent out by the enemy neutralized the particle cloud scanners that provided footage from the central planets' surfaces, but the military-grade surveyor drones outside the plasma attack were left unaffected.

As the outer planets and asteroid mining camps were secured by fleet contingents, more and more ships positioned themselves to strike from every angle at the enemy vessels rushing to engage the apparently disabled United Earth main force. When the enemy opened fire on the decoy's, the crews onboard moved with speed and efficiency. They altered vectors, accelerating at top speeds, the entire enemy offensive to missed and left them out of position.

Though huge and hard to kill, the enemy ships were slow. In seconds the U.E. battle groups turned and opened fire. They struck with spear shot and millions of ten-foot-long incendiary steel shard explosives rippled across the the enemy shields. The impact disabled them for a moment. just long enough to allow the rail gun slugs following right behind them to tear into the enemy ships and detonate. The warheads ripped huge sections of the mountainous pyramid like vessels out into space, and more than a few of the enemy ships were crippled. With this kind of damage, it made them easy targets for the fleet's crews, who mercilessly pummeled them with everything in their arsenal. Hundreds of U.E. destroyers swept in to strafe the unorganized mass of enemy vessels, and they stuck with impressive strength. But the enemy had weapons of their own and even when crippled, their counterattacks caused devastating effect.

Ships were lost, and people died as the battle rose to a fever pitch. Nearly three months passed, and throughout the United Earth confederation there was little else talked about.

Whenever possible, damaged ships jumped away from the battle to distant shipyards, when they arrived, their crews were quickly transmitted back to their dispatch installations and reassigned to newly printed ships heading back into battle groups in line to smash the enemy. In some cases, after the crews were safely evacuated, the damaged ships were simply atomized, returning the elements back to containment chambers for use in printing new ships, while others had new parts transmitted into place and returned to service.

Some damaged ships arrived to safety, completely coated in the enemy's plasma. As dangerous as it was, it gave the AI a chance to contain it, store it, and study its atomic composition in search of ways to prevent it from clinging to the energy fields and disconnecting the real-time communications of their ships over the filament network.

The United Earth Fleet was like a cunning pack of wolves in a field of sheep. Their tactics shredded the enemy ships while taking minimal casualties. At the height of battle, nearly a quarter million of the mountainous, palace like ships had risen from all five of their planets to join in the battle, except a few, which, to everyone's surprise, vectored away from the fight and out of the solar system.

After witnessing more of the enemy ships head away from the battle, many of the fleet admiralty wondered if there could be more systems like this one in this region of the Milky Way. They considered it and saw how likely it was and so acted decisively.

Those charged with planning and ensuring the safety of mankind's future urgently assigned the surrounding area of the Milky Way top-priority data acquisition protocols, and, within a minute of the status update, 3-D printers sprang into action transmitting millions of military-grade surveyor drones into every system nearby.

Gateways to heaven were transmitted to locations around the slave cities and linked to brand-new facilities on three rocky planets in systems fifty light-years from Earth. The engineers in charge of terra-forming and expansion activities had decided to go completely over the top when designing these facilities, and even Daniel congratulated them on their inspiring work, both for their fantastic choice of location, with majestic nebula views, and the finishing's and overall design. Domes as large as entire continents were constructed and filled with tropical landscapes and highlighted by lakes, pools, forests, and emerald towers rising high above the canopies. Each lofty residence was in use as travel destinations for people of the colonies who reached beyond just the standard levels of education. On short notice, the entire network of installations was emptied out. There were many similar destinations people could go and as enlightened as these people were it was like a whisper in the wind, and as the last guests transmitted away, the first of the refugees arrived.

In this first system, where the initial contact was made, the United Earth forces rescued close to six billion human slaves while completely neutralizing the enemy. The lizard ships were destroyed to the very last one. U.E. light craft, crewed by small teams along with squadrons of militarized drones, scoured the large central planets in search of any remaining military installations. At the same time, they dropped points for transmission gates that arrived with teams of marines, who broke huge numbers of people out of what could only be described as cattle pens.

As the rescued humans arrived in the U.E. facilities, thousands of United Earth citizens volunteered to help the new arrivals learn and catch up with humanity's history and integrate into mankind's new civilization.

The data from the priority survey of the surrounding systems piled in. It didn't take long to find similar systems. All told, there were thirty-six stars with planets just like this first one. Solar systems with harsh reptilian masters and mining planets packed with human slaves. Some were not nearly as populated, but a few were more than three times larger and would prove to be much larger challenges to liberate.

Scans of these newly discovered systems showed more of the same and faster than before, the enemy became aware of the intrusion. Drones began dropping like flies and billions of microscopic sensors were deployed, sent to map the central planets of every Alaigeerian solar system. As expected, they saw the same atrocities; torture, mutilation, and signs that the beasts took pleasure in the pain they inflicted on their human cattle.

At every U.E. military facility, fleet personal went into full combat status for a war that was about to grow to an enormous scale. Three billion crew members were activated, and millions of new ships were printed in the days leading up to the invasions.

In Earth's solar system, out past Jupiter, a new massive holo-dome was printed to effectively accommodate the scale of this new campaign. A holo-display facility, with a diameter of 150 kilometers, was designed to fit all thirty-six systems at a resolution, allowing teams of commanders and admirals to track the action in real time.

The urgency of the fleet was impressive; no time was wasted in getting teams of analysts, planners, captains of ships, and their squad leaders into the holo-spheres to view their targeted systems and plan their strategies. It began just five days after the new Central Command dome was completed, and everyone had their orders.

Squads of fast attack ships with the most highly skilled crews were the first wave. They made runs on some of the smaller systems, aiming to take out perimeter defenses and knock out the ship-killing weaponry on the guardian hulks of each system. In deep space, all around the systems, over three million ships assembled, fully prepared to show these monsters the cost of their cruelty.

From the vast command sphere, top-level brass initiated fleet actions.

They sent out commands, sending battle groups to positions that protected the slave planets, while sending others to lure the hordes of enemy ships from their home worlds. Squadrons of battle cruisers, carriers, and fast attack vessels, along with newly designed cannon ships, transmitted into strategic positions as the clusters of enemy formations moved to engage. The U.E. Fleet struck fierce blows, hurting the enemy ships before they even got off their first shots.

Daniel transmitted into the main command holo-dome and checked his heads-up display to see where Dillon was. When he had his friend's location, he zipped through the holo-sphere using a personal cloaking device to stay hidden and pulled up to where Dillon spoke with a few of the admiralty.

Undetected, he watched and listened, periodically keying his controls to switch views on his personal holo, flipping between various regions where the fleet was engaged. One-star system caught his eye, and he zoomed in to take a closer look. He allowed Dillon and the admirals' conversation to drift into a distant corner of his awareness.

Nearly every enemy ship from all six planets in this system was forming up before any U.E. ships even entered their space. *Apparently, the warning is out,* he thought. They knew mankind was coming. He projected his display into the holo-deck panels in front of Dillon and the ones he was talking to, and he waited. It didn't take long before they all paused, unsure of who had changed their viewer's display, and then he watched them as the images caught their attention.

Dillon knew he was there the minute the display popped up in front of them, and he let it be known in his deep, battlefield-tested voice.

"Hello, Daniel. Come to watch some fireworks I see." he jeered.

At this, Daniel flicked off the invisibility cloak and acknowledged his friend, along with the group of young and brilliant commanders of the fleet. He respected them and in some cases considered them trusted friends, but now was not the time for catching up; there was a real battle to be won.

"Hello. How goes the war? Looks like we are a bit outmatched." he said with a chuckle, eyeing them with respect.

They saluted him, and he returned it before slipping back under the cloak of anonymity and transmitting himself back to where the *Frontiersman* floated in a peaceful and majestic region of the Milky Way.

When Dillon learned of the dreams, he insisted the *Frontiersman* be protected at all times, and commissioned a special armada that now surrounded it. Ten thousand heavily armed scorpion-class cruisers, commanded by the personal AI in charge of the massive explorer ship all took up positions at such great distances they were imposable to see with the naked eye, but non-the-less, standing by and ready to receive live crews, if ever needed.

Earth's fleet moved with cunning precision. They were lethal and hard to kill and hit the enemy ships from all sides. They lured the hulking pyramids, always picking away at them and their efficiencies made all the difference.

The U.E. Fleet took damage from the streams of plasma and walls of explosive steel balls thrown out by the Alaigeerian ships, but overall, they lost fewer than three hundred ships in the first month of the war. Many human lives were lost, paying the ultimate price for their bravery, but the toll on the enemy was far greater. The cannon ships, designed in response to how the hulking pyramid warships clustered together, fired three-hundred-ton slugs at nearly half the speed of light from their rail guns. Thousands of the slugs packed with incendiary-lined warheads came off the rails, hurtling toward the enemy and bursting into hundreds of shards that rained down against the massive vessels of war.

The campaign lasted a long six months, until finally each of the thirty-six systems were cleared of the lizard beasts. Many of the Alaigeerian solar systems were completely cleansed of the lizard creatures, while in the largest systems, where huge, super-sized planets orbited in Goldilocks regions, the U.E. stopped short of complete extermination.

It was decided in the last days of the war that it would be wrong to completely kill off this species. Instead, heads of the colonies and top military brass created an AI to quarantine them, installing layers of unmanned drone ships around each of the planets, with monitoring systems controlled by an AI programmed to destroy all technologies that enabled space travel and advanced weapons construction. These beasts would learn to survive without having humans in their diet, or they would starve to death.

Over twenty-five billion human slaves were saved, and another great migration into U.E. facilities of the Milky Way galaxy took place.

As the refugees found homes in the United Earth confederation they started the required daily education and group activities required of every citizen, Daniel sat in his personal office in the Mars One facility. His eyes danced across charts showing showing Genomic and DNA samples of these new members of the U.E. society. These refugee's DNA matched the people of Earth perfectly but with characteristics indicating lineages of humans from thousands of years ago and accounted for their strength from surviving as slaves to the cruelest of masters. but how? By all accounts, to him, it looked like these people were taken from Earth thousands of years ago. He closed his eyes and felt the air in the room against his skin, he reached out with his mind and got a feeling of the room around him in his mind and then a feeling of the landscape outside the domed facility. *It will be interesting to see how these people fit in,* he thought, stretching back in his chair and felt proud to have saved so many lives from further suffering.

Chapter 25

Discovery

Daniel; his father, John; Sam, who seemed different lately; Jimmy; Stas; and Dillon, along with the doctors and scientists wishing to accompany them on this next-time dilation journey, set out once again to see what they might find and allow mankind to jump forward in time. The message was given; they would make contact every five to ten years and return at some as-yet-undecided date. Many worlds in other solar systems sim-ilar to Earth would have their atmospheres terra-formed for future colonization, and the populations of United Earth were encouraged to expand. Our species is destined to spread out into the stars.

This time, Daniel and his team were more cautious. They had all learned from the recent encounter with the hostiles, and so they sent clusters of drones ahead to ensure new destinations would be safe. When regions were cleared for arrival, they went into time dilation, and all communication outside of the ship was cutoff. The *Frontiersman* slid through space, traveling in a state of nearly pure energy, just shy of the speed of light.

Daniel closed his eyes, drifting off after a day of hiking in the foothills of the huge ship's landscape, swimming in a beautiful lake, and reading some of his favorite literature from the end of the twenty third century. There was darkness as he fell into a deep sleep, and then it all shifted.

He saw it all as clearly as though he were there in physical form—a dual star system with seven huge blue-and-green worlds orbiting in the Goldilocks zones. They were, without a doubt, a glorious civilization that had prospered for thousands of years, yet their doom was now upon them. Like so many before them, their peaceful existence soon would be at an end. Clouds of glossy black creatures flooded toward those now trapped here and only able to wait in fear. From where he viewed the scene in his sleep-induced, out-of-body state, something else was there. He felt another presence and then saw it—a white wisp of smoke congealed, forming into the shape of a person, a wispy silhouette in the meditative lotus position. He blinked, and in the next moment there were hundreds of them, all in the distant corners of his mind. Everything felt calm as he drifted along, and for a moment the carnage in front of him was out of mind. Suddenly, it all changed.

His ethereal presence shifted, pushed to the surface of one of the planets, where buildings collapsed, and the ground ruptured under plasma impacts that rained down from creatures still outside the planet's atmosphere. He watched as bodies rose weightlessly, writhing in agony as their skin burned and melted from an acidic mist that completely saturated the atmosphere. The mist paralyzed them, trapping them in agony-filled stasis, while keeping them from dying and passing to the spiritual dimension.

Whoever was causing this had found new, slower ways to weaken the minds of her prey, by torturing them before sweeping down and feeding on their life energy as her creatures shattered and consumed their very worlds.

From where Daniel floated, he saw hundreds of millions of half-dead and blackened bodies, writhing in agony. They were blinded, and their skin pocked with sores as the pink acidic mist burned and melted them. Soft tissues were the first to go; eyes, lips, and ears eaten away, leaving blackened, horrid openings. By rights they should have died the moment they inhaled the mist, but as it entered their bodies, it changed and fought to keep them alive. As their exteriors were subjected to untold pain, their internal organs healed and rejuvenated. Daniel was there among them, floating at their level as the dream took him wherever it willed. He wished it would end. He fought it, trying to somehow take control and leave this horrid place, but he found no way to make that happen. And then the Dark One appeared off in the distance.

It was a black hole of consciousness in the spiritual plane, seemingly unaware of his presence. It floated through the helpless bodies locked in stasis and fed on their souls. As he witnessed the horror, a fear crept into his mind—a fear from the last time when he felt the Dark One latch on to his presence. The inky black smoke moved in sudden flashes of speed, pulling the life from its victims before snapping out of existence; the dark tendrils, the deep pounding throb saturated everything in Daniel's mind, but in a single moment, it was all just gone.

Relieved, his ethereal awareness scanned the landscape all around him, seeing and feeling so much death. The distant horizon rose up into the sky under yet another plasma impact, and in the next moment, his presence shifted. He found himself watching from thousands of kilometers beyond the outer atmosphere. The world's crust splintered under the swarms of the black creatures as they consumed the fractured remnants of the crumbling world, and a cold feeling filled his heart.

Suddenly, a ripple in space caught his attention; the diamond-shaped ship appeared, and he watched as the megalithic behemoth slid through space. The massive, dark, diamond shape moved toward the central stars of the system, and as it approached, the stars began expanding at alarming rates. In a flash, the nearest of the two went supernova, and as the massive release of energy expanded, it arched back toward the dark crystal-like ship. The stars' power funneled into a stream and curled towards the massive shape. The energy lanced across its surface and pulled in. Soon the other stars exploded and consumed, just like the first. He had never stayed in the dream this long, never witnessed the full end of an entire solar system, and then the cold fear overwhelmed his mind.

It happened in a sudden rush. She sensed his presence; the Draykon moved. In a blink, the space around his out of body awareness filled with the demon herself. As his fear took hold of him, the wispy forms on the edges of his mind wavered and a chilling laughter pierced his mind. It was the voice of a destroyer, an eater of souls.

"One who was lost, I can feel you but cannot see you. You hide in the shadows of a world unknown to us, but we will find you. Those with you will end in the same fate as the ones here and now. Wait for me, and fear for the day when I take your life! Know that there is no hope for your kind! I am coming."

A clashing sound, like two planets colliding, echoed in his mind, and the inky form had him. A mental force he could not resist encased his presence, searching for a way to tear him from the neither-here-nor-there. The shrieking laughter rose in pitch, the pulsing dark tendrils seeking a way to tear his life force from his distant body. He was trapped. Pain stabbed in his mind, and he thought it was his end.

Gasping for breath, his eyes snapped open as he choked for air that seemed to never come. It felt as though someone had been holding him under water past the point where there was no choice but to fill his lungs with burning liquid. His eyes filled with tears, and he finally wheezed and coughed uncontrollably. The room around him spun, and he had to fight to regain his senses. It was far worse than anything he had experienced, and when his mind cleared, he realized how close he had been to death. Tears ran down his face, both from the pain of nearly suffocating and the hurt he felt after witnessing the brutal extermination of so much life on those distant worlds.

As his vision cleared, he saw that his holographic screen was already active. On it, a warning flashed in the module that tracked his vital signs whenever he slept. He saw that he had flatlined for nearly ten seconds before returning to consciousness. The room's AI had administered a shot of adrenaline that had saved his life. It took him a moment to come to terms with it, the fact that he had technically just died, it frightened him, and he laughed, happy to be alive.

He reached with shaky hands for his tablet, forcing himself to start the process of sketching out images and notes of everything he could remember. He shook but fought it, detailing the star system, the timing, the numbers, the meditating forms, and then the contact with evil, and as he recalled the dream, the words came back to him: "The one who got away." What did that mean? *Who else could the Dark One be referring to other than me?* Questions flooded his mind as he scribbled on the digital pad, entering every word, image, and sensation into the database. He had heard those words specifically: "The one who was lost. The one who got away." There was no mistaking it. This creature of the darkness thought it knew him. The souls he saw meditating in his dream—*They must know who I am as well*, he thought, recalling how they had tried to protect him. *Did they?* He switched a section of the display over to the developer's workbench. There was no sense sitting idle when there was something so incredibly impossible happening, and he dove right into it.

He needed a new app that would compile the planetary sketches and model them in real space and try matching them up with existing systems in the galactic database. The workbench flashed as he plugged various modules into what would be the foundation of the new software's architecture. His fingers danced, writing a few commands here and there before transitioning to just pulling building blocks of code together. The node-based developer's tools Jimmy and Stas put together made writing new task processors superfast and he was done before he knew it.

Next, he created a subroutine in the main AI's objective list. A new kind of surveyor drone was born: the galaxy spore. The spore drones were a ten thousand cubic kilometer miner flotilla mother ship. Their sole purpose: to process large bodies of space rock and use it to print out complete mining, storage, and printing flotillas at the galaxy level in an ever-expanding sphere of discovery. He recalled the time he unknowingly set into motion the survey that scanned over one-third of the Milky Way. This time, though, he was initiating the new survey with the purpose of finding the source of his dreams.

Each new spore ship was sent to corners of galaxies farther and farther out, into the local major galactic group and then beyond. They were designed to lay seeds that would expand the United Earth Fleet's capabilities, while using resources from mineral-rich lifeless regions to print more and more surveyor drones. Tens of billions of volleyball-sized surveyor drones and trillions of newly designed marble-sized scanning bots came online every day, executing their tasks quickly and efficiently, ever adding to the highly detailed point clouds of the universal map.

He hoped there would be some sign or encounter with the destroyers from his dreams, but at the same time, he was not sure the U.E. Fleet would stand a chance against such a force. The swarming hordes that devoured entire planets in his dreams were on a scale he hardly believed possible. "Would it be better to never find them?" he questioned, but something inside him scorned the idea. He knew in his heart that they must, at all costs, save those who were left and save all others who would fall if the darkness was not stopped.

After this near-death experience, over a week went by, and there was nothing—no dreams, no contact—and a part of him was relieved but another part of him was afraid, afraid he would miss the chance to learn of a deciding clue. He began waking up with a slight sense of disappointment and falling asleep with the anxious hope that this time he would discover a way of finding them.

Daniel closed his eyes and fell into a deep sleep, and everything shifted.

He drifted through a landscape of stars, racing across the universe. It was peace, it was safety, and then there was a blinding flash. For a moment white light engulfed his mind. As his vision came back, he found himself standing in an enormous chamber, a cavernous white hall with glittering gold trim sparkling under the brilliant light from high above. Below him there was a blanket of white mist, and he looked out in search of clues to his location, seeing only distant pillars rising into the sky. Slowly the mists dissipated, revealing millions of people, all of them sitting in the familiar lotus pose. The hall was immense, so large that its ends were beyond the distant horizons of the planet itself, and the floor was packed full.

From where he stood he scanned the uncountable numbers of people all gathered around the elevated platform. In awe, he slowly turned, taking in the spectacle, and when he came full circle, he wondered what, if anything, was to happen next. As the question entered his mind, they answered in a smooth, single voice.

"The one, the one who escaped, felt by all, the memory of a day long past, you, our hope, from the first days of the Sethree, the first days when the Gods of Death came to destroy us; we are your people." He heard them, yet not a sound was made. They spoke with a power born of those at peace, their ideas entered his mind as thoughts, and he understood them naturally—without effort.

They told of the destruction their galaxy had suffered since the Dark One's arrival and that only he had demonstrated a will strong enough to escape. "How can I find you? Where is your galaxy? We will rescue you!" He thought in the hope they would understand.

Their reply was not what he expected. "We cannot be helped; our fates are what they are. Promise you will create a new Olomnri in the people you have found." They felt him in a form none of them knew, and a new hope emerged, one that would carry on their people's legacy, far from where the only future was death. They told of how they had protected him as much as they could, guiding his presence to those whose pain somehow called him. He had appeared in their minds when he walked among their dying worlds, his presence enabling them to see what he saw. While he dream-walked among them, so close to the Dark One, they shielded his presence as much as they could, and for a time, he had been safe. Now their enemy's strength was far greater, and there was no longer any way they could protect him.

"We have brought you here to these sanctuary worlds in your spiritual form. In this system, one of the farthest from the swarms of creatures who devour everything they find, we wait for them to arrive. We have searched the universe for the hope, the one felt so many cycles ago, and today we have finally summoned you to know our story and your past."

He cut them off, forming thoughts of his own. *"I will find you. I will save you from this evil. This I know is my purpose. How can I find you?"* he mentally shouted.

It happened with a sudden, thundering crash. Audible, mind-splitting laughter filled their consciousness, laughter he recognized with a fearful chill the moment it broke the chamber's silence. The shrieking, insane laughter of the Dark One pierced the connection, slicing through the meditative calm held by the billions gathered around him, and he felt them sway. The Dark One had found him! The distance the Dark One traveled to disturb their meeting, though, was too far from its physical form for it to have any real power over them, but there was still strength enough.

"You have been protecting him from me! The one who escaped has come to witness the destruction of your worlds these past cycles. What is your purpose in this when you know there is no hope for any of you?" the demon asked, followed by more laughter, a power that slammed down on them and piercing their ears while filling their minds with chaos and fear.

"I am Draykon, and to the one who watches, the hope, safe in the distance beyond our awareness, know that we will one day find you and all who exist among you," the Dark One shrieked, and the pounding throb crept into Daniel's mind. The dark tendrils lashed out for him just as they had done before. This time, though, those who had summoned him gathered their strength, and before he was clutched by the darkness, he was gone. As a group, the Olomnri resisted the Draykon's mind and sent Daniel back, before casting the demon out.

He awoke in a violent spasm, his eyes snapping open, and with relief he found air in his lungs. He turned to look at the motion sensor charts, readouts showing he had hardly moved for over three hours, right up until those last few seconds, when the Dark One arrived. He wrote down verbatim what the Olomnri had shown him and then what the Dark One had said. They had been protecting him? Well, maybe that was best. The dreams had been taking their toll, but how was he to save them without knowing how to find them?

The massive survey continued, expanding in normal space-time as the *Frontiersman* made brief time-dilation jumps. Daniel's main purpose for the short jumps was to allow the spores to expand and seed more and more galaxies. But it seemed to be hopeless; even after billions of new galaxies had been scanned, there was still no sign.

John questioned Daniel after the third week of short dilation jumps, asking him if he was okay and wondering if maybe it would be best for Daniel to just let it go. It had not gone well; John had not expected to be told that if he didn't trust his son he could take the next opportunity when they entered normal space-time to board a viewer ship and transmit to the colony, where he could live out the rest of his life in peace.

As Daniel brought them in and out of time dilation, eighty years passed in Earth space-time. As they entered normal time once more and downloaded the huge new databases collected while they moved ahead in time, the AI alerted Daniel of a significant find, one that attracted his full attention. He dragged the packet of information onto the huge display, and when it came up, he saw a small dwarf galaxy over a billion light-years from their own Milky Way. It looked strangely darkened and shattered, and his interest was piqued even more. He queried "unique features," and ruins of a long-dead civilization appeared on his display. His mouth slowly opened in shock. There were systems with half-dead stars, where planets appeared shattered and left adrift. It was eerily like the destruction he'd seen in his dreams. Yet why it was only half destroyed?

After seeing all he needed, he knew they must look into this in person. He triggered his command chair and was on the control deck a moment later. He transmitted right to where Dillon and his father were looking at tropical worlds in faraway galaxies, and when he arrived, they turned. He saw their tired expressions; these past weeks were a little hard for everyone on the ship as they shifted from normal space and dilation speeds frequently. They all paused, waiting, and just before Daniel began telling them what was found, they both started expressing their minds at the same time.

"We need a vacation, Dan. We have been out here for almost four months, constantly in and out of time dilation, and we just need to change the pace a little, you know?"

Dan smiled. "I have just the thing. How about an ancient civilization that was just discovered? Ancient ruins in a dwarf galaxy as old as the universe and appearing to have been scorched, shattered, and destroyed, except for a few planets with strange inscriptions carved into their landscapes. I think we need to go see it."

Daniel ordered the AI to send waves of microsensors into the dwarf galaxy to fill in gaps the initial surveyor drones had yet to scan. Husks of huge cocoons were found, and he realized he might not want to wake up anything still lurking in the darkest regions of this galaxy. And in a panic, sent instruction to the AI to keep the survey to within ten light-years of the ruins.

They transitioned to time-dilation speed for just ten minutes so that three weeks in real space time would elapse to allow for the survey of a larger portion of the dwarf galaxy to take place. Over a million light-years away, they reentered normal space-time and checked the new surveys. Ten light-years of information in every direction out from the ruins of a world with huge carvings and symbols etched into its surface flashed on, filling the holodeck aboard the *Frontiersman* with a glittering point cloud of information.

Daniel was there a moment later as the point cloud appeared and felt a crazy rush as his eyes brought it all into focus. He checked his display to find his friends and in an instant, he was floating next to where Dillon, John, Stas, and two of their most trusted friends in the United Earth Fleet admiralty—Clair and Abhijit—sat, floating in their own control chairs. Together they observed the three-dimensional footage of a galaxy in utter ruin.

As the hologram showing the dwarf galaxy zoomed past their field of view, they saw shattered worlds drifting in the cold emptiness of space.

Daniel triggered the huge holographic chamber and centered on the planet they now orbited. The symbols etched into the landscape made them all pause as they viewed the planet from outside its atmosphere. It was one of the only systems with an intact world and a shard of a star; somehow it had survived whatever passed through this place long before now. Huge canyon-like scars and craters pitted the planet's surface, along with shattered remnants of what must have been great cities; all of it painting a picture of an unstoppable horror.

Daniel's closest friends were the only ones who knew about his nightmares, and they made the connection to his dreams without needing to ask. Dillon looked to Daniel with an expression of knowing fear, and as Daniel caught his eye, he returned a silent nod that said, *"This is it."* Clair looked to her friend and comrade Abhijit with a cold expression, and they shared the private feeling that this could lead to very bad things.

MATTHEW J. BALDWIN

The AI indicated a location on the other side of the planet with a unique energy signature, and the hologram rotated toward it. As the anomaly came into view, they saw an area that somehow escaped the devastation inflicted on the rest of this world.

From their perspective, they saw a ring of standing pillars and in its center a pedestal with a strange florescent glow. Zooming in closer they all saw it at the same time—a blue crystal shard, no bigger than a golf ball, hovered above the flat top of an intricately carved pedestal. The AI brought up wavelengths of an energy signature that showed a frequency unfamiliar to even the AI's vast databases. There was nothing left to wait for, the group of them along with Samantha who joined in the last minute boarded a Viewer One craft and Dillon transmitted it down to the new discovery.

Abhijit blurted out, "What do you guys think it is?"

Daniel replied without thinking. "There's only one way to find out. Let's get closer."

"What if it's dangerous? What if it's a trap?" The intensity in Samantha's voice was something Daniel was not used to hearing. He wondered what had gotten into her. "Please, Dan, let's send more drones down there to check it out before we get too close. Please," she begged.

"Don't worry, Sam. We'll be protected. I'll put the automated self-preservation settings on Viewer One up to the highest level; it'll jump us back at the first sign of danger. Besides, haven't you noticed that the drones are shielded from passing the outer ring of pillars? I need to go down there and see for myself what is happening," Daniel insisted.

"Okay, in that case we are putting on protective spacesuits before going anywhere near this thing. That way, if Viewer One is compromised, at least we'll get back in one piece."

He knew there was no arguing with her. Why should he? It would be good to include her, and maybe there was something down there requiring her expertise.

They suited up and strapped into their seats before Dillon dialed in the coordinates and transmitted Viewer One to within three hundred meters of the outer ring of stone pillars. Viewer One hovered as they observed the intricate stone rings around the central pedestal, and Dillon, at the controls of the ship, slowly inched them forward. He intended to land just inside the central rings, but when they got to within ten meters of the outer stones, an

286

invisible and undetectable field stopped them with a sudden shuddering impact. The sensors detected nothing, but there was no moving forward, and they all looked at each other, puzzled and somewhat amused.

"Well that is strange, I am getting nothing on the sensors." Daniel commented. "I wonder ..." he whispered as he covertly tapped the control panel on his forearm. Then, before any of them could react, he was gone, transmitting himself to the surface just below where their ship hovered. They were left guessing for a moment before they saw him come out from under *Viewer One*'s lower blind spot. He was walking confidently toward the pillars and the invisible wall. They watched as he walked through the undetectable field that prevented their ship's access, and to their amazement, he walked right past the inner rings of pillars as well, directly toward the central pedestal.

Dillon pressed the coms tab with his thumb. "Dan, what the heck are you doing?" But there was no reply. "Copy, Daniel. Do you copy?" Still Daniel made no reply. The field preventing the ship from entering had to be preventing all transmissions from passing through as well. Dillon looked to John, who sat on the other side of the central control chair. "If something happens, the suit won't be able to transmit him to safety! Damn that boy!"

When Daniel was within five meters of the central platform, he stopped and turned to look back to where his friends hovered in the ship. He waved to them. "There's atmosphere, and the temperature is a stable thirty-five degrees," he said into his mic. There was no response, and he realized what Dillon had understood only a few moments earlier. He shrugged and popped the seal on his helmet before pulling it off and tucking it under his arm. He waved again and gave a sharp thumbs-up while inhaling the crisp, clean air.

He was surprised at how fresh it was, considering how long this air had been isolated on this lifeless planet. He paused, calculating just how it could be possible, as his friends watched from the safety of *Viewer One*. Sam, John, and Dillon finally snapped into action, transmitting down to the surface and following his steps. Soon they all stood in a line with their helmets at their sides, all except Dillon, who kept his helmet on, considering that if something did go wrong, he would need to save the boy by carrying him to safety.

"It is incredible, isn't it? I have no idea what it is or what we should do, but I'm glad we came to see it firsthand—whatever it is," Daniel exclaimed.

As if triggered by his voice, a hologram shimmered to life, revealing an ancient-looking figure wearing gold, red, and white robes, like that of a

Catholic priest at mass. His skin was gray and aged beyond time, and as he raised his hands, they all noticed that there were only three fingers on each. The figure's eyes were solid white with a faint emerald green around the edges. As they watched, the figure stood silently for a time before spreading his arms to acknowledge them.

"Greetings, humans. For eons, we the Alkayins have moved on from this place. Those of my kind who survived the days of destruction, the days when darkness fed on the minerals of our worlds and our people's lives, they have gone beyond the boundaries of this universe. Our bodies expired long ago as our galaxy turned dark. The Draykon and its swarm of creatures caused more damage than even we could reverse. Our heart stones were destroyed, and nearly all of our people were taken by the Lord of Death. But before we lost everything, we found a way to repel them, winning a battle we had thought impossible; we stopped the Draykon—we killed it. When it happened, the swarms of creatures lost their feverish drive to consume our worlds. We pushed them back and tried rebuilding our once interplanetary civilization. But alas, all hope was lost. Without stars and atmospheres around our planets, no life could survive, and so as a species, we passed on to a new plane of existence. We found transcendence to the realm of all that is light."

The figure hung its head, silent for a time, until Daniel asked the question. "How did you defeat them? How can you kill a darkness that has power over creatures who consume entire worlds?"

Looking up, the figure smiled at them. "The only way possible, my friends. To defeat death, you must overwhelm it with life, a light to chase away the darkness. This crystal is that weapon, and has the power to trap the Draykon's dark life force, locking it away for eternity. We left it here, hidden and guarded. We created the field to protect it; only beings with good hearts may enter its sanctuary. We did not know if ever it would be needed, but we believed that if ever there was a need, those who required its power would find their way here and take it. Please take it, protect it, and use it to defeat the ones who feed on life. You will have to lure the Draykon, and when it is within sight, reveal the crystal. Raise it up and defeat the demon. This crystal you see here is the very same that stopped the Draykon in the days before the last of our kind fought for survival."

The figure began stepping back, its voice trailing off to a whisper. "Take the crystal and use it to free this universe from the Draykon. Even though we, the forefathers of time, are gone, you can still protect those who will otherwise perish under the hand of evil. Good luck to you, and may your light chase away the darkness." The figure vanished, and they were left considering the words.

They stayed silent, their eyes locked on what they now knew was their only hope, while at the same time realizing with complete certainty that Daniel's dreams were, in fact, leading them to face off against what could be the greatest evil in the universe. Dillon silently stepped up to the pedestal and gently took the crystal in his hands. He carried it to where his friends stood, and they all just stared in disbelief.

"Well, there's no doubt your dreams have a real connection to something, somewhere, Dan. The question is, where is this threat, and is it a good idea that we get involved?" John stated.

Daniel's eyes lingered on his father and then glanced to Dillon, who stood in a strong, solemn pose. Dillon looked down at the glowing crystal in his gloved hand. "If we don't do something now, the evil will only grow stronger. It will sweep away entire civilizations unchallenged. What about those we could still save? It will destroy everything it encounters until the day it finds and makes us its victims. No, we seek out this evil, and end it before it's too late!"

Sam's eyes hadn't left Daniel. *What a strange look*, he thought, and as she turned away, his eyes lingered on the features of her lips and jawline. He shook his head, looked around, and forced himself to focus on the challenge ahead. They lifted their helmets back over their heads and walked back toward the outer ring of pillars, where they transmitted back into *Viewer One*.

It was time to return to the colonies, and on the voyage, they engaged the dilation drives so that nearly one hundred years passed for those in normal space-time. When they arrived back, they saw that the E.U. population had ballooned to over 120 billion, all of them living in newly constructed facilities and freshly terra-formed worlds in over fifty solar systems throughout the Milky Way. The newly rescued people abducted from Earth, thousands of years ago had taken to the educational requirements with enthusiastic vigor. They were strong and athletic, many of them joining the fleet in homage to those who had saved them and others finding enjoyment in the games. The fleet had grown; forty billion were now full-time members and in the colonies, the new favorite sport, Gravity Ball, was truly amazing to watch.

There were no limits to what could be created as the resource stock piles appeared near limitless from the mining operations continuedly spreading out into billions of other galaxies. The stockpiles were beyond anything Daniel had ever envisioned, and mankind's ingenuity showed in the cities they were building, games they were playing and creativity they were displaying. Particle assemblers and vast 3-D printers continued to provide people with what they needed.

Statues of Daniel and his friends were not uncommon throughout the new installations, not for worship but in honor of the achievements and impossible advancements that made all of this possible.

When they returned to Earth's solar system, many of the admirals and council members still looked nearly as young as when they'd last seen them. They greeted Daniel and his friends with admiration. The advancements in health through stem-cell regeneration were astounding, allowing people to live and stay youthful long past when they would have otherwise succumbed to old age.

When they arrived above Mars One, where the most accomplished and largest contributors to humankind's developments still lived, an invitation was sent out to a select group for a meeting. Dillon, Daniel, top council members, and the admirals of the fleet gathered on the garden patio of one of the towers in a newly constructed wing of Mars One. They discussed what had been going on in the time that Daniel and his group were away. A number of detention centers had been constructed to handle crimes and misconduct, impressing them with the efficiency of the offenders' rehabilitations.

Even more impressive was how peaceful things were. Intellectual competitiveness was held as one of the highest moral standards, and the athletics and sports enabled by antigravity made for exciting entertainment.

When the niceties were over, Daniel cloaked the garden-top patio and presented their discovery of the ruins in the dwarf galaxy. They all watched the recording, footage showing the holographic figure describing the tragic end of their people. When it ended, they considered the weight of these revelations. Finally, Admiral Brad Fitzgerald spoke in a calm and respectful tone.

"Have we made contact with these destroyers? These Draykon—do we know where they are, or if they know of us?"

Daniel replied, "I don't know if there are more than one. I have been having dreams where I find myself watching entire worlds destroyed, as well as the souls of dying beings like us taken by an dark spiritual form." He broke eye contact with the seemingly hardened older man. "I know it's hard to believe, but a dark cloud of inky smoke in the form of a woman's figure pulls souls from the dying bodies and feeds on their life energy. Entire stars are consumed, along with everything and everyone in every system the swarm of creatures comes to. They are a plague with an insatiable hunger and no remorse for those they destroy."

Tanya Argot, a decorated officer from the war against the Alaigeer, entered the conversation. "Should we stop all exploration and hope they never find us? What if, in finding them and engaging them, we discover that we are no match, and they destroy us, as they have done to so many others?"

Daniel shook his head at the idea, but before he could speak Admiral James Robins cut in.

"The rabbit who hides in his hole in fear starves until the day he must venture out, forced by necessity to forage. Because of those long days of fear and hiding, he is weak and is caught easily by the predators that have grown fat and strong on those like him. The pack of wolves that goes after the herd, even though the herd has the power to trample them, they survive the long winters. What I am saying is, if we do nothing, they will grow stronger and one day find us. Should we live in fear until the day we face the enemy? Your dreams, Daniel—is there anything more to them?"

"I think ..." Daniel paused, unsure if he should continue. "I think it's happening right now. I think there is a galaxy out in the ocean of galaxies being consumed at this very moment! Hundreds of billions of peaceful, highly intelligent beings are having their lives taken, having their souls taken." He paused again, a tear running down his face, the anguish of it plainly visible to all those at the table. Even his closest friends had not known exactly what Daniel was going through until now as they saw the true burden he had born, the emotion, so heavy on his heart. He held fast, composed himself and continued, his tears drying on his face as he unashamedly looked them all in the eyes. "I think these people, this galaxy, is my home. They are my people. The Olomnri."

"In my dreams it feels as though I know them. I think I may have been one of them in my previous life, a life that I think ended as my home planet was taken. If what my dreams have shown me are true, I am the only one who managed to escape being taken like all the billions of others. I feel that we need to do all we can to save them and stop the evil that, if not halted, will only grow stronger and one day, inevitably, threaten all we have built—and all we dream to build."

There was no dissent from the group at the table. They nodded thoughtfully. Was it worth the risk? What if confronting this enemy brought on the end of mankind? The loss of life could be unthinkable, but the cause was just and necessary. They concluded their meeting with the understanding that they might never find the dark swarm and never have to engage them, but if they did, they would not hide from doing what was necessary.

For the next three weeks, Daniel pored over star maps, spending most of his time in the galactic charts dome, a five-kilometer-wide holographic viewing chamber floating in Earth's solar system. This was the largest holo display of the filament viewport, the dimension that enabled mankind to jump across space to any location in the universe, while at the same time providing real-time communication over unlimited distances.

Floating in his control chair, he randomly picked regions of the universe, gazing at them in the hope that he would stumble across the one speck of light in a sea of endless refractions.

Slowly, he lost hope but diligently he searched and painstakingly reviewed the notes from his dreams. Dreams that had stopped completely. He wondered if all had been lost, but still he searched, unwilling to give up hope that there might be some left to save. After nearly three weeks of staring dumbly at the glittering points in the holo-deck, each of them an entire galaxy with billions of stars, something occurred to him—something so simple he could not believe he had not thought of it sooner.

How had he been so blind? He cursed, pulling up the developer suite and writing a quick algorithm to filter galaxies with irregular star configurations. Hundreds of trillions came up in a list that seemed to perpetually grow. He sat defeated for a moment. *There had to be a way. It was the only way!* "I won't give up!" He cursed and tried another filter, calling for galaxies with disproportionate mass and unique formations, where stars had once been. Hundreds of millions appeared in the room, which, at that very moment, felt far too small. He tried another string, creating a filter for galaxies where stars had disappeared in the last three hundred years and were replaced by objects with irregular movements.

One galaxy appeared in the room. His heart jumped, and he felt like panicking. He knew he had found it as he registered the shattered remnant in front of him—and for a few minutes he just stared in disbelief—afraid to make the call. Parts of it were drifting off in all directions, with entire arms of it gone completely dark. His eyes focused and saw that only a small corner was left where bright stars still burned.

When he came out of the trance, he sent Dillon a message that said everything he needed to know in only three words: "I found it." Minutes later, five admirals of the fleet, who had been in the meeting weeks before, arrived, and within ten minutes, every one of the twenty people to whom he had sent the notification hovered in a group, all of them looking at the filament reflection of a galaxy torn to shreds and darkened by evil they could not fathom.

"For all that is just! Look at it all," Dillon exclaimed, a sentiment felt by everyone in the holo-chamber. Black strings of thick matter coiled through areas where there had once been bright stars systems. There was nothing left to do but stop all exploration programs and divert all resources to saving the last surviving systems.

Chapter 26

Last Hope

The United Earth Fleet mobilized. Hundreds of millions urgently moved with purpose while billions of others returned to active duty. Three-hundred-trillion survey drones were reassigned and given priority-one orders directing them to the distant galaxy. Knowing the threat, the entirety of the survey drone armada materialized at what fleet command thought would be a safe distance.

The drones stationed in a grid, holding positions at fifty light-years from the outer edges of the doomed galaxy. From there, they started collecting long-range imagery. After holding the position for a day, they established a detailed long-range bassline. 99% of the drones jumped to new positions; one light-year from the outskirts. Point cloud information streamed in real time to holo-domes everywhere. What they saw looked like nests, huge cocoons growing through space like dark, porous roots.

After another twenty-four hours, hundreds of millions of drones were given reconnaissance assignments, sending them into the nests to capture up to the minute intelligence.

Everyone saw what the drones recorded, all on a shockingly massive scale. Monsters that looked like deep-sea creatures the size of moons and small planets, all of them glowed from faint translucent sections along rough outer shells. Energy pulsed within them and lightning flashed across long scale- and thorn-covered tentacles. Flashing shards of energy lashed across space, arching like webs into the far reaches and distant networks of nests. For a time, the U.E. drones went unnoticed. The United Earth Fleet's motto was "Pride, Accountability, and Courage," and they took the call to arms with an unmistakable confidence.

In the infested galaxy, where darkness was overtaking the light, only a few hundred systems were left, refuge to those awaiting a dark and unjust fate.

As more detailed scans came online, humanity saw dark honeycombed strands spanning and twisting through space. There was no doubt what they were: hives, where the creatures Daniel described as planet-destroyers spawned more and more of their kind. Some of the hives even spanned between long-dead solar systems, stretching tens of light-years in all directions.

The drones moved in fast, never staying in one area for more than a few seconds where their sensors picked up trillions of data points before jumping to the next location. Central Command processed the data with incredible efficiency; teams of fleet personal in command chairs hovered in the domes, analyzing and cataloging. Others, with layers upon layers of holographic screens in front of them, plotted strategic locations for future fleet positions and strike points. Commanders and admiralty designed decisive offensive strategies and they approached readiness to engage the enemy.

The drones did not stay undetected. Dark creatures came to life, their spots and stripes glowing hot as they sprang into action. They moved in fluid tangles of claws, tentacles, and thorns, their forms leaping off the dark cocoons and in flashes of impossible speeds they destroyed the typically hard-to-kill drones

millions of drones transmitted to the last living solar systems on the opposite side of the galaxy and scanned everything. As the point clouds formed in the holodecks of fleet command, mankind saw who they would be fighting for. There were planets filled with majestic architecture and giant temples with billions of what looked like people, deep in meditation. The Olomnri seemed calm, at peace, and seemingly unaware of the drones flying overhead. As the data formed in the holo-domes, everyone in the fleet saw who they would be fighting for and felt their call, hardening them to the task ahead.

As more and more drones entered Sethree space, fleet command saw some of the largest, monstrous, planet-destroying creatures. Their massive forms appeared out of nowhere and attacked with ruthless cunning. They fired walls of electromagnetic radiation, balls of plasma, strings of super-heated magma, and an acidic gas that went right through force fields, melting the carbon shells of the drones.

Massive centipede-like creatures emerged from the honeycombed hives, their insides glowing with red energy and showing through gaps in their hard-black shells. They slid through space, moving at speeds far faster than anyone would have thought possible, and their effectiveness was devastating. Thousand-kilometer-long tentacles whipped out, and from them, bolts of energy arched into space, destroying hundreds of thousands of drones at a time. Behind them came swarms of smaller creatures that swooped in to consume the meager wreckage left behind.

Those in the command domes went eerily silent as they watched, frozen in terror by the enemy's cataclysmic force. The silence went on for longer than it should have. As fear invaded command's resolve, a doubt crept into their minds. It did not last. Out of the silence a voice rang out—a hard voice, one of endless confidence and ability. He barked at them over every channel in the U.E. Fleet, and they listened.

"What are you people made of? This is our job. We have trained for this. Evil is taking innocent lives out there, and we are going to save them! Now swallow your fear and remember who you are! Believe that we will prevail in the face of any odds, and know that we must succeed, no matter the sacrifice!"

It was what they needed. They were experts in their crafts, and the efficient engine at the heart of the fleet pushed forward once more. A new attack drone was designed with offensive lasers, mini-rail guns loaded with incendiary rounds, and three-hundred-megaton payloads that would activate when the drone was damaged and in proximity to the enemy creatures. Over a hundred billion of them were printed and transmitted into the regions farthest from the surviving star systems. They hoped that it would draw the enemy away from those they wanted to save.

The centipede-like creatures flooded out from the hive structures and jumped across empty space with impossible speed. They sent out waves of electromagnetic energy, along with clouds of acidic vapor that cleared entire regions of the militarized drones as quickly as they appeared.

On the outskirts of the darkened galaxy, in the farthest regions from where the Olomnri still lived, groups of fleet ships assembled. They were learning by watching the creatures destroy their drones. They watched and analyzed the deep-space monsters' capabilities and noted definite patterns.

Cannon ships, newly designed to fire thousand-ton steel slugs at nearly half the speed of light, initiated the attack. They opened fire, transmitting the heavy shot along trajectories to within a few thousand meters of their targets, where the slugs rematerialized, impacting the creatures and the massive hive structures with incredible force. World-sized monsters were hit with hundreds of thousands of shells that were far more effective than the drones had been. The heavy shot ripped into them, punching through their miles of protective armor and even crippling some. Cheers rose on the ships of the fleet as billions watched the enemy buckle under their fire power.

The cheer was short lived, though, and just as suddenly as it started, a hushed silence took hold as they witnessed what came next. Like hornets swarming from a disrupted nest, uncountable numbers of young squid-like beetles and millions of full-sized, planet-destroying creatures emerged in search of the threat. The smaller ones writhed, twisting and turning as they rushed forward, while the largest of them appeared to jump ahead faster than the speed of light.

In less than an hour, not a single drone was left in the region, their nuclear payloads clearing clusters of the five-hundred-kilometer-long, half-squid/half-beetle-like deep-space creatures. But they were far too many.

Ten million fleet destroyers and battleships, backed by the standard contingents of cruisers, gunships, and attack craft, were ready for action. Admiral James Turchal jumped them into range of the ever-expanding swarm and tightened his abdomen in preparation to giving the order. These larger ships, equipped with power cells that output enough energy to supply entire space cities, showed their ability immediately. The acidic mists rolled off their more powerful deflector shields and, after learning their foes' patterns, they cleverly punished these creatures.

A massive swarm of the moon-sized planet-eaters and their spawn appeared out of a ripple in space and rushed Turchal's armada. Millions of enemy creatures leaped across vast distances as fast as Daniel's filament teleportation technology allowed. Yet they did not seem to be able to jump unlimited distances and were not as accurate as United Earth's teleportation technology. Still, it enabled them to move beyond the restrictions of the distances of space, and that made them even more dangerous.

"Dear Lord, look at them all," Turchal muttered, just loud enough for Commander Sonia Jordan to catch it.

They were both veterans of the Alaigeer conflict, where they had fought alongside each other on a smaller version of the destroyer-class flagship they now commanded.

"Don't worry, sir. We aren't going to die … at least our names in history won't," she said. His wink just caught her eyes as she sent orders out to hundreds of other commanders controlling vast contingents of the fleet's ships.

They faced an enemy that outnumbered them by uncountable odds, but they were calm and hoped the rest of the fleet's command felt as cool and collected as they did.

The creatures came on fast, leaping forward through space in micro-jumps. Jordan filled her lungs. "Fire! Let's show these creatures who we are!" Plasma cannons, spear shot, rail guns, and cluster bombs fired along the fleet's formation.

At Central Command, when the fleet opened fire; a ripple passed through the viewport map. Every single beast in the galaxy turned. The moon-sized beasts stopped, paused and in a rush, they raced toward where this new threat was attacking them. Central Command watched as entire portions of space appeared to come alive. Dark clouds sprang off the web-like nests and moved toward the fleet. Everyone who witnessed it, they could not help their reaction, their hearts dropped at the magnitude of it all. They had awoken pure evil, and all hell was headed toward their ships.

Covert drones, no larger than a hockey puck, tracked the onrushing creatures and, when given the opportunity, latched onto their metallic shells, providing exact coordinates for the fleet to lock on with long-range ballistics. Ten million ships on the galaxy's outer edges transmitted heavy fire into the paths of the onrushing creatures, yet they powered through.

Cannon-ships fired as fast as they could, their slugs transmitting across space into the paths of the giants and their impacts landed with greater effect. The artillery crippled some, while others seemed to barely slow, but it was all they could do, these creatures with their massive scale, they were going to be hard to kill.

The strategy was to damage them as much as possible, before close-range fighting began. Planet-sized creatures rushed on with what seemed a single mind. Destroy at all cost.

Billions of creatures hurled themselves at fleet positions. Shots of plasma, molten steel, and forks of energy fired from the bellies of the moon-sized creatures. Their attacks broke down the fleet's shields, and hundreds of thousands of ships were lost. Fortunately, fleet engineering had learned from their conflict with the Alaigeer and modified the AI to transmit crews back to safety whenever their ships were critically damaged. It saved so many. But even with these safety precautions, two million fleet personnel were lost in the first weeks of this battle.

With the swarms distracted, rescue teams went into action. Transmission gates materialized around the temples on the remaining home worlds, and the exodus of billions began.

Daniel feared the demon would see and snuff out every one of the remaining worlds with quick, hard strikes, but as the first few days passed, it seemed every eye of this evil swarm was turned to the threat spanning a full third of their nests on the dark side of the galaxy.

Another two hundred million ships jumped into regions on either side of the raging battle, attracting even more of the enemy's attention as warhead drones shot deep into the nests, and long-range cannon fire shattered huge walls of the hive structures. Many of the attacking ships in these contingents drove five- and ten-drone gunships. They came in fast, flying as close as they could get, and hit the monsters hard, disabling and crippling many of them.

Battle groups of ten thousand ships followed waves of long-range slugs fired from the cannons standing light-years off the front lines. The huge moon-sized creatures hit hard by the leading heavy shot were then pulverized by the close-in fleet ships, but the enemy creatures were very hard to kill. Their thick skins withstood more punishment than anything the fleet could deal, and their sheer size and speed allowed them to smash ships with long, whipping tentacles, horned hooks and waves of energy beyond what the shields could withstand.

The fleet got complacent, the creatures learned to trace the trajectories of the heavy shot constantly crashing into them, and it showed they were not simple-minded. Their first move was indirect, fooling the United Earth Fleet, before jumping across space and surprising the undefended cannons, where they decimated whole contingents of the long-range and incredibly valuable weapons.

With the heavy guns disabled, fleet ships were caught without the supporting fire. It was devastating. Some ships were skewered by massive spikes fired from the creatures' tentacles, while cables of plasma smashed others. Casualties skyrocketed, and a momentary pause swept Command as they witnessed the huge losses, but they were always learning and changed tactics. The cannons would only fire from one location for no fewer than one hundred shots before transmitting to new locations.

They found that it was just enough for the creatures to lock in on the cannon fire source and knew a swarm of them would soon jump to attack that position. Knowing this, they sent battle groups and drones poised to ambush the oncoming creatures. Their revenge was tenfold. They left carcasses of their enemies floating in space, and a new confidence among the fleet was born by a cycle of lure and ambush that enabled them to fight the monstrous creatures and win.

For three weeks, the enemy's attention was drawn to the fleet's attacks far on the other side of the darkened galaxy. The Olomnri were escaping, continuously moving through the transmitter gates Daniel and fleet Command sent to every population center. Daniel kept sending more and more gates to all sides of the largest gatherings, but these Olomnri were not moving quickly enough.

Draykon

She sat in her chamber, eyeing the dark crystal walls where souls of the strongest-willed waited, locked in time and space until she chose to feed on them. They were like the fine wine of life energy—strong, ambitious, spiritually aware leaders of their kind, and as she thought of them, she pushed her hordes against these new combatants ever harder.

Her mind's eye watched through billions of her creatures' awareness; she watched the human ships fight, and she relished in the battle. They were no match for her and the swarms she commanded. She considered unleashing her most powerful juggernauts, and the thought sent a thrill coursing through her. *Wait until the humans show their full strength.* She considered and let out a shrill cry of joy that echoed throughout her lair; she was enjoying the humans' efforts, letting them succeed against small groups of her swarms before sending twice their number, always destroying ships as the humans pushed deeper and deeper into her nests. She gave the hordes of creature's purpose, driving them to rampage against the human ships, causing carnage on an immeasurable scale. The joy of war consumed her, and she lost herself to it, but then, out of nowhere, something made her look back to the remaining worlds where she knew so much life was waiting in fear of her coming. A sliver of her consciousness went to them, sweeping over them with an expectation that she would see hundreds of billions. What she saw instead made her see the deception, and in a heartbeat, she changed her entire focus.

In the holo-domes of the U.E. command centers, they all saw it at the same time. The dark mass, entire portions of the galaxy turning again, and heading back to where the evacuations were underway. Every creature not engaged with human ships turned at top speed toward the remaining Olomnri worlds.

In response, the fleet moved decisively, transmitting more than three-quarters of the armada into positions between the oncoming Sethree creatures and those they wanted to save.

Her fury exploded in a shattering crescendo. *How is this possible?* She thought, and called to her planet-destroying creatures, along with billions of smaller planet-eating swarms. A cold rage raced through her, an insatiable hunger for life, and she pushed her own powers to move the horde across the galaxy so quickly.

In the space between the dark Sethree region and the bright living zone of the Olomnri, the diamond ship appeared, followed by a mass of writhing planet-eating, deep-space creatures. It took fewer than three days for them to form up in front of the half billion fleet ships, all positioning themselves to guard the last of the surviving systems. The creatures' numbers ever increased as they jumped the gaps of space toward the fleet ships, and then it began. Vast webs of plasma and carbon shards shot out toward the fleet, and the human ships scattered in practiced evasive maneuvers.

Creatures materialized at high speed amid contingents of battleships in fast surprise attacks. Every fleet ship was ready, anxious to show their mettle in the fight, and they moved with cunning, avoiding massive tentacles, claws, and streams of plasma in practiced countermeasures.

From the tentacles of attacking creatures, arcs of lightning lanced out, crackling against ships' shields, as attack groups strafed the enormous creatures. They were forced to fall back, courageously fighting to hold the swarms at bay, but they were losing ground all the same.

The fleet's long-range artillery returned to full strength, and they fired nonstop from always-shifting strategic locations light-years away from the battle. Humankind fought for all remaining life in this galaxy, and for a time, the fleet, with its cunning commanders and reinforced cannons, they held the massive creatures and incessant swarms, but as their hopes returned, the Dark One shifted the tide of battle with her will alone.

With a new surge, the immense beasts smashed into the United Earth Fleet lines. They came in flashes of speed, tearing into the formations of ships where they sacrificed themselves to break through to the escaping life on the other side of the blockades.

Where the diamond crystal ship waded into battle, there was complete devastation. Yet the fleet fought on. Brave and committed, they persisted in the effort to overcome all odds. They were prepared to die, and as the battles intensified, every ship's crew thought only one thing: "Hold your ground."

Creatures three times larger than anything they had faced yet appeared in the front lines of the oncoming hordes. They fired streams of plasma with far more power than before, blanketing battle groups and paralyzing their transmission systems.

Central Command watched the destruction of their forces in utter dismay. They thought they had figured out these creatures' tactics, but now they saw how wrong they were. Within an hour, millions of living, fighting, thinking people were dead and gone; they were on the retreat and looking at defeat.

The massive swarm pushed incessantly forward, and over half the fleet's ships were destroyed. Many people were lost, but in nearly every case, the AI saved some. Those with injuries would not return, but every able hand saved from ships lost in the heat of battle eagerly rejoined others on newly printed, larger, and more capable destroyers.

The foundries throughout the Milky Way's local galaxy group worked nonstop. As each new ship was printed, crews on standby boarded them and joined up with newly assembled battle groups to reenter the fray.

The evacuation of the refugees did not happen quickly enough. Even with reinforcements arriving along the blockade, the creatures began breaking through. Five of the nearest systems, where the Olomnri were still pouring through the matter transmission gates, they found themselves engulfed in flames as skies over their worlds filled with massive creatures that came down through their atmospheres.

As the monsters crashed down like burning mountains falling from the sky, they poured lightning and plasma into the surfaces of these worlds. Huge horned claws tore deep into the crust of every planet they hit, reaching deep and easily into the mantle and feeding on the lava now pouring up and out of freshly opened fissures. The landscapes turned to ash and the air to flame, as whole systems were consumed in a ravenous frenzy.

The fleet did its best, destroying the single-minded beasts now paying no attention to the lethal Earth vessels that peppered them as they crashed into the home worlds of their victims. The fleet ships killed quickly, but for each one they managed to destroy, five more took its place.

She fed on the first systems in a rush of rage-filled power; there was nothing they could do, she thought, and turned a portion of her consciousness to direct a new group of creatures to hunt the human ships.

Huge monstrous beasts with thorn-covered, thousand-kilometer-long tentacles crackling with energy jumped into the United Earth Fleet ranks. They tore ships apart, forcing the fleet to scatter and counterattack. She enjoyed the destruction and picked off the tiny souls left behind, as tens of millions—and then billions—of the human ships were destroyed.

Leaving a portion of her mind to feed on the humans, she directed the rest of her focus to where the richer life forces of the Olomnri still gathered around strange gateways that sent them away.

Newly formed battle groups jumped across space, taking up positions to defend the last of the planets, while upgraded cannon ships went to work, firing even larger slugs packed with warheads powerful enough to crack open the heavily armored creatures. The fleet attacked and destroyed as many as possible, pounding the huge planet-eaters with barrage after punishing barrage, but the swarm inexorably pushed forward.

Days of pitched battles continued as the United Earth Fleet defended the last of the Olomnri. They lost more and more ground, as over half of the region fell to the dark creatures. As the days passed, a greater number of the home worlds were fully evacuated, and the fleet managed to stall the horde with valiant bravery and sacrifice—but it would not last.

Daniel spent all his time hovering and watching in the Central Command holo-dome back in the Ort Cloud of Earth's solar system. He hardly slept, as day after day the cost of human life grew heavily on his heart. But whenever he looked at the numbers of those being saved, he knew the sacrifice was worth the cost. From time to time, Samantha came to him, locating his more-often-than-not cloaked figure and innocently attempted to comfort him, but Daniel was distant, and it was hard to get through to him.

Over fifty billion were rescued, but there were still nearly ten billion left on the last of the safe worlds, and their time was up. The horde would not be stopped and concentrated its forces. They broke through to the last of the Olomnri.

Everyone at Command monitoring the closest living planets to the swarm saw it at the same time. She arrived as a cloud of black inky smoke ahead of the creatures on a world where billions were waiting to pass through the gates. In the physical plane, she swept across the landscapes, and from the smoky tendrils, crackling lightning struck out at every Olomnri. Inky black tendrils lashed at the air around the falling, lifeless bodies, and a rainbow of flashes winked in momentarily glowing traces, as the souls she was feeding on were taken. In the next moment, she was gone, appearing on the other side of the world where still more were not yet through the gates.

Daniel cursed, dreading what he must do; he knew it must be him. Somehow, the ego and pride of this demon would be its weakness. "It is time," he whispered to himself and reached behind him into the concealed pocket to feel that it was there—the crystal from those who had found a way to kill one of these demons—and then he was gone.

He closed his eyes and transmitted across the massive distance of space, and a moment later opened them to see crowds of the Olomnri gathered around a massive transmission gate way off in the distance. He stood waiting for what would come and cut his communication lines, just as Dillon began questioning what he was doing. Next, he deactivated the emergency transmission protocols on his suit, making sure no technical safety measure would transmit him away and restricted anyone from transmitting to his location, lastly, he put full power to his personal deflector field and then just stood there, in silence, listening to the wind and watching the horizon. He was alone with his thoughts, and then it hit him, fear entered his mind.

"Come to me you demon, come to meet the one who will destroy you!" Daniel called out in his mind, a part of him knowing he must face this evil, while another part of him internally screamed in fear. He was filled with adrenaline, his body shaking from an unstoppable anxiety rising within, but he focused and set his mind to the task. "Draykon! I am here! Take me!" he shouted out in his mind.

The sky went dark, and the air seemed to blacken. He knew the time was near. The darkness enveloped the land, and a nauseous feeling filled every sense. The presence of the Dark One drifted over the distant crowds, hundreds of millions of forks of lightning smashed down from the dark, inky smoke in the sky; the thunder rolled across the landscape and his heart broke seeing so many die in front of him. The black smoky strands he had seen in his dreams lashed out. It nearly took him to his knees. He felt them, the souls of so many, consumed by the coldest malevolence in the universe.

What if he was wrong? What if the demon just took him like all the others? Would the suit's protective force field stop the inky strands or the lightning strikes? A new kind of fear flooded him and turned to panic. His eyes looked to his forearm holo-display. He needed to reactivate the self-preservation protocols, but his mind was befuddled, and his hand forgot the motions. He didn't know it, but the fear he had allowed into his mind had replaced his strength and purpose and attracted the Dark One right to him. It was like blood in the water, and then a cold feeling washed over him, she was there.

"It is you," she shrilled, the inky smoke forming to represent her physical form. "You have come alone? Where is your army?" She cackled in a glorious cacophony of triumph as black ethereal strands of smoke formed a half sphere behind her figure. "Do you plan on fighting me, little man?" Her voice rose in pitch as her power crackled across the sky in an all-powerful lightning storm. Her voice was deep and imperial, with richly beautiful velvety tones of nobility but laced with that of a demon's rasp. "Have you come to lead me back to your people?" she bellowed, and pebbles lifted up off the ground.

Daniel felt her; his suit's protective field was at full power, yet her tones reached his bones, and it gave him a chill. He could hardly imagine the frequencies ripping the air around him and knew that the protective energy field was the only thing keeping his flesh from being torn off his body.

"Draykon!" he screamed, fighting to take measured steps toward the inky black figure. "Remember me, demon? See me. Do you remember the one who got away?"

Lightning flashed off his protective field, strike after strike lashing at him, and Daniel staggered. The impacts on his personal force field were so powerful every impact felt like a hard punch to his body. Blood dripped from his nose, and he gripped his ribs, raised his eyes, and looked hard at the dark figure.

The laughter began once more, louder than ever, a shrieking hysteria that broke his resolve. Its power penetrated deep into his consciousness, and the insidious voice stole away all his inner strength. His vision blurred, and his legs shook, forcing him to drop to a knee. More arcs of energy lashed like lightning at his deflector shield, there strikes knocking the air out of him with such force that for a moment he dreaded he might never take another breath. His head sagged as his body folded under the heavy blows, and his hands went to the ground. She broke into his mind, nearly pulling his life force right from his living body. Daniel felt it, the feeling that all would be lost, and was beaten to within inches of giving in. But, something inside him switched on, with an effort born of a distant memory, he lifted his head and locked his eyes on her form once more.

She was amused with his effort and impressed by his strength. She let him stand, let him believe in himself, and relished in the knowledge that she held all the power. He was what she wanted! His soul would be worth allowing the remaining survivors to escape; they would live until she and her creatures inevitably found them. She enjoyed his defiant look and refined her appearance so that he could see her human form in all of its beauty.

She raised her arms, and all around them the dark smoke crackled with power. It rose in frequency, charging to strike with enough strength to vaporize this entire world. Her red lips formed a cruel smile, basking in the moment she believed would be his last.

"You should not have come, Last Hope. What will your people do, now that they have lost what hope they had?" Her laughter saturated his mind, breaking him down once more, stripping him of the strength she had just allowed him to reclaim.

"You will not have me, Draykon!" he shouted, summoning every ounce of his strength to surge forward with shear desperation. He reached behind into his hidden back pocket and grasped the crystal he found on the inscribed planet in the dead dwarf galaxy. He felt a power rise from the crystal and thought of the tale—of how this crystal killed a Draykon long ago. He hoped this would work. Her laughter rose even higher and he watched her eyes lock on his grin, and he smiled more intensely and saw her confusion.

He knew it would have to be fast, and with abandon, Daniel thrust the crystal high above his head.

She struck with the force of a supernova, yet everything seemed to slow down. The crystal saved him. It folded time and space, pulling the massive surge of power that would have vaporized everything in this solar system into its heart. As the energy shifted and swirled, dancing between dimensions, it painted a tapestry of arching colorful weaves, reflections of power trapped beyond this dimension.

As the energy flashed away and his eyes cleared, he saw her horror. Daniel stood, his feet wide apart, the crystal held high above his head. And he noticed how the confident shrill tone of the Draykon changed, he heard fear enter her. He laughed with joy at the realization that his foolish plan was going to work and watched as the inky smoke slid across the dimensional plane into the heart of the crystal.

"Can you feel it? Can you feel the same hopelessness that you have caused countless others to feel? The fear of knowing your existence is about to end, Draykon? You shall be no more!" Daniel screamed, tears running down his face from the sheer effort and emotion coursing through his body.

A thunderous clap of energy hit the landscape all around them—a blast that rippled past in a huge wave, heading straight down into the planet's core. The ground under Daniel's feet heaved, shifting upward, while fleet command watching from every angle reeled back in shock as the opposite side of the planet blew out into space.

Glowing white light came in from every direction. At the center, Daniel held the crystal firmly, the forces causing his skin to shake. He felt a strength unfamiliar to him as the heart of the stone shared its power in the effort to destroy this darkness.

Her confidence was gone, replaced by the booming echoes of one who knows their own doom. He watched, locked in place and in awe, as this evil that had reigned with impunity writhed in its final death throes. It lasted for what seemed like hours, yet it was only a few short moments. The last of the Dark One was finally pulled into the stone. As the air cleared, the ground he was standing on slowly came to a stop, after rising over seven hundred meters in the cataclysmic impact the heart stone released while capturing the life energy of this being of pure evil.

He looked around, hardly believing what had happened, and came to grips with the fact that it was over, and he was not dead, not yet. In a rush, the adrenaline that had kept him on his feet was gone. He collapsed to the ground and closed his eyes, unaware that this planet was now adrift and slowly fracturing beneath him.

The instant he went unconscious, the AI unlocked Daniel's overrides and sent notifications to his closest circle of friends.

"I hope you will all understand there was no other way," Daniel said in a short video linked to the notification that told them transmissions to him were fully restored. Fearing Daniel had given his life to stop the Dark One, John, Sam, Dillon, and Stas transmitted to his position. Sam wasted no time in running to him. She dropped to her knees and injected a nanoparticle concoction used to rejuvenate cellular damage directly into his neck.

After securing him, they transmitted to the *Frontiersman*, where Daniel was put into intensive care, still unconscious. When they were sure his vitals were stable, they left him, all except Sam, who watched him like she might still lose him forever. He slept for over three entire days, and Samantha slept on the couch in the room, not wanting to ever leave his side.

The moment he sat up, she felt it and opened her eyes. Their eyes locked, and for a moment they just smiled.

"Hi," she said shyly, as though they were meeting for the first time. "You're safe. It's over."

"What happened?" he asked.

"After you and that crystal confronted the Draykon, the creatures bolted in every direction! They just went into a panicked frenzy. Some of them even turned on each other as our ships fired into them. It's over," she whispered again, her hand finding his as their eyes stayed locked.

A tear trickled down his cheek. "Thank God. The refugees? The last few worlds—did they make it?" he asked.

"They are safe. There are so many! As you know, new installations are being assembled and brought online, along with a series of blue planets now with atmospheres calibrated to meet the new demand for habitable real estate. These Olomnri—they are different but the same; they are beautiful. It seems humanity is taking them in with open arms and doing its best to make them feel at home. The AI is referencing architecture from the Olomnri worlds it scanned while the evacuations were taking place and has used it as template reference for the designs of the new facilities."

Delegates from the Olomnri came to him, wishing to thank him for saving their people. In every case they looked at him with deep eyes, and he felt their minds reaching for his. They searched for the consciousness of the one who had found a way to escape so long ago, the one who had visited them unconsciously over these many years to witness their people's destruction, and the one who had discovered a way to find and save them.

After a few weeks his strength returned, and he and his friends traveled the colonies, they found and experienced diverse cultures that had formed in the newly forged enlightened civilization in space, a civilization where mankind and the Olomnri would continue expanding into the stars, spreading life, technology, and their species.

For now, they are safe.

About the Author

Matthew J. Baldwin created a ballad of hope for humanity, a dream of limitless technological possibility, a knock on the corruption of our world, and a look at what transcendent spiritual enlightenment might be. He writes of pursuing knowledge, enlightenment, and even immorality on his journey through life. Baldwin believes the trick is simply to start in order to eventually get somewhere. *Earth's Emergence: Transcendence* is his first book